OUT OF SIGHT

PROGENITOR SERIES BOOK 1

MATTHEW S. COX

DIVISION ZERO PRESS

Out of Sight
Book 1 of the Progenitor Series
© 2018 Matthew S. Cox
All Rights Reserved

Cover Art by Jackson Tjota (Tjota.deviantart.com)

Interior art by Ricky Gunawan (http://goweliang.deviantart.com)

Cover layout by Alexandria Thompson (www.gothic-fate.com)

ISBN: 978-1-949174-04-5 (ebook)

ISBN: 978-1-949174-05-2 (print)

CONTENTS

1

TOO OLD

Unimportant words fell from a passing drone, an endless rain of government drivel that meant nothing to people who didn't matter, people like Sima Nuvari. The digitized voice rambled on about a shift in the wind bringing increased pollution, an update to curfew times, and resumed reminding everyone not to do any of the thousand or so things that would violate the law on their way to work.

Clouds of mist belched from the noodle counter across the street, breaking against the river of Citizens hurrying back and forth along the narrow sidewalks. A wash of salty shrimp-scented air, thick with humidity and the reek of people, brushed at her face. No one hurrying by so much as looked at her, not even when she tried to catch their eye.

The baleful whirr of fans drew near. Sleek, yet battered, the dagger-shaped drone, one of thousands, carried the 'official' truth to the ears of the masses. Red lights blinked from the tips of six tiny fins at the back end. The silver camera ball in the middle of its belly swept back and forth, constantly scanning.

She tugged her hood down to shield her face from the ever-watchful flying eyes of the Earth Government Security Force. Her tunic had once been pale pink, but wearing it for years had left it brown in places and made holes in others. Hard plastic bits at the end of the sleeves still lit up showing their electronics connected to Dreamland, the global information network. She lacked the implants necessary to overlay graphics on her eyes, but had little envy for the suffocating amount of data that danced in most peoples' vision. The holographic display floating over her arm let her consume Dreamland in bite-sized pieces manageable enough not to be overwhelming.

Outcasts, civilization's unwanted, inhabited a razor line between the society they rejected and an underworld ready to consume them. Some bucked the social order for ideological reasons while others had more personal motives for running away. Few Outcasts bothered to draw attention to themselves by combating injustice or challenging politicians. Even seeking to improve the lives of the poor caused problems better off avoided. Care too much, the EGSF would make you disappear. Care too little, suicide, starvation, drugs, or worse lurked behind every corner.

Apathy and Rebellion strolled hand-in-hand with Death, and the second she made friends with either, he'd come calling.

Once the drone glided far enough away that its camera wouldn't spot her, Sima tugged her hood down and fluffed at her tunic in an effort to hide her breasts. Baggy, black pants concealed the true position of her legs and allowed her to squat ever so slightly to make herself seem shorter. A girl who looked closer to twelve had a lot better chances at scoring a handful of glint from someone with a scrap of conscience than a girl of sixteen. No matter the age she appeared to be, her olive skin didn't help. The fair kids—especially blondes—always scored twice her haul without even trying. She understood no one asked to be born with a particular complexion, but couldn't help but resent them for it. *Society* considered them 'cuter' than her, so she held that against them.

Not that her enmity took any form harsher than dirty looks or sulking off to find another spot. Younger kids remained *children*, and she couldn't hate them personally for being born a few years after her or with lighter skin. None of them asked to be who they were. But that didn't mean she had to *like* the little ones, or even tolerate being anywhere near them.

Sima tended to work alone whenever possible to avoid the younger kids soaking up all the charity of a given area. Citizens likely to part with a handful of glint would always gravitate to the smallest kid with the widest eyes. Having little ones nearby always left her standing there holding out empty hands. Today alone, she'd already had to relocate to six different intersections due to infestations of children. She scowled at the three nearest alley openings.

I swear, if another damn kid shows up, they're going into an ORC... headfirst.

She shifted her gaze to a waist-high red-and-silver bin a short distance to her left by an alley. A person could put anything in one of the Omni Recycling Corporation bins, and it would eventually be carted off for processing. Everything from food waste to trash to old appliances, even a hot-cell from a gee-vee (radiation and all). As far as she knew, no one had yet tried stuffing street urchins in the bin for recycling. Or maybe they had, and the little buggers weren't cooperative enough to stay there until pickup.

A pale-skinned man in a dark blue-grey suit, two rows of white buttons down his chest, caught her eye. He walked with the crowd of pedestrians, but had the far-off look of someone with their attention fixated on Dreamland. No doubt, a dazzling display of photons bombarded his retinas from corneal implants. He didn't appear wealthy enough to have the deep-brain model that bypassed the eyes entirely.

Sima stepped away from the grime-stained wall she'd been leaning on, enough that he'd walk right into her.

Unlike most people, the man stopped short before plowing her over and muttered, "Sorry."

Hope bloomed. That he hadn't called her some horrible name meant good odds.

"Please, sir," said Sima, trying to sound younger. "Can you maybe spare a kid some chips so I could eat?"

Irritation shone clear in his eyes, but his cheeks radiated guilt. "Uhh..." He fidgeted and looked around as if searching for an escape route, but gave in with a heavy sigh and fished in his tunic. "Yeah, sure, kid. Just don't pick my pocket, okay?"

She bit her lip, widening her eyes. "I'd never. I'm not a thief, sir. I'd rather not eat for two days than get caught stealing. Only thing I'm more scared of than the Blanks, is the EGSF."

At the mention of Blanks, the man shivered and withdrew a cluster of shimmery, chromatic plastic chips from his side pocket, each a half-inch in diameter. "Here, kid."

"Thank you!" She cupped her hands together and bounced with happiness as he dropped the money into her grip.

He nodded once, then rushed off with the crowd, which parted as a lumbering gee-vee forced its way down the street. She hurriedly stuffed her haul into the front pocket of her tunic and flattened herself against the wall as the six-wheeled passenger vehicle rolled by. Another advantage of the narrower streets: fewer drivers tried to navigate them. The woman inside it slept peacefully. Sima knew better than to attempt begging from anyone driving around. Most either slept or busied themselves in Dreamland, leaving the navigation to computers.

And the computers didn't have any sense of compassion. Ahmed, a boy a few years her junior, had his foot flattened by a tire soon after Sima hit the street for the first time at twelve. Fortunately, gee-vees couldn't go fast enough to do real damage in the back streets, and no one bothered begging at major roads.

She pressed herself against the wall, a mismatched assortment of ill-fitting metal panels coated in a thick layer of grease and road dust. Silver streaks marked the sky overhead wherever aircars cruised. Long before she'd been born, anyone with money migrated to the skies. The market for wheeled cars dried up almost a century before she drew her first breath. Ground vehicles, or gee-vees as people called them, no longer came in an assortment of brands, only sizes. As far as she knew, the government made them, selling to the upper end of poor people. Of course, some things—like cargo trucks—remained on the ground. Heavy loads cost too much to lift.

Upon spotting a tall, thick-bodied woman with large gold earrings and uncommonly dark skin, Sima stepped away from the wall. "Excuse me, miss. Could—"

The woman shoulder-bumped her with enough force to knock her on her rear end.

Sima, plenty used to that, caught herself in a fairly graceful landing, and sighed.

"Watch where you're—" The woman's shout stopped at a bewildered stare. "Oh, honey, I'm sorry. I didn't see you."

"No one does," said Sima in a despondent tone, before picking herself up to stand. "It's all right. Can you maybe spare a little glint?" She knew better than to use that term with the well-to-do looking man, since it sounded too 'street.' But this woman's outfit said lower-middle-class. She might find the Outcast term for money endearing.

"Well, if I thought you'd actually use it to eat, I might." The woman shook her head. "You look clean enough, but I think you're maybe going to get high."

"I don't do drugs," said Sima.

"Mmm hmm." The woman folded her arms. "And I'm Empress Maharani."

A few nearby Citizens turned at the mention of the planetary ruler.

Sima bit her lip, staring at a potential score inches from walking away. Out of desperation, she gestured at the noodle counter across the street. "It would be so very kind of you to buy me a bowl instead of giving me money. Watch me eat it if you like."

The woman glanced back and forth between her and the vendor, a fortyish man wearing a red fez and yellow tunic. "All right. You do kinda look like you haven't eaten in a week."

"It's only been three days." Sima somewhat remembered downing the contents of a nutri-pack either last night or the night before last, but adding a day for extra sympathy couldn't hurt.

"Come on." With a sigh, the woman walked with her over to the counter, eyed the holographic menu floating above the vendor, and pointed. "Let me get a number six for the kid here, and a number four to go."

"Right away," said the vendor, tapping his fingers in midair as if pushing invisible buttons, no doubt using a Dreamland interface only he could see.

A small device on the counter chirped and projected a hologram of a green mesh around a hand shape. The woman reached into it and a small, red dot glowed under her skin near the base of her thumb in time with a *chirp* from the machine.

Sima sat on one of the stools, folded her hands in her lap, and waited. The man behind the counter tossed ingredients together and set a covered bowl in front of the woman. A moment later, he placed an uncovered bowl of seaweed ramen in front of Sima.

"Thank you," said Sima to the vendor before looking at the woman. "And thank you so much!"

Her benefactor waited until she started to eat, still suspicious. However, the genuine hunger causing her to attack the too-hot-to-touch ramen convinced her. With a half-hearted, "You should get off the street while you still can," the woman wandered off with her take-out.

"This is really good, Amin," said Sima.

The vendor sighed at her. Though he always found an excuse not to give away free food to Outcasts, whenever she had the spare glint to buy a bowl, he'd throw in an extra hunk of meat or two. She had no idea what kind of meat he used, but chances were high that it came from soy protein, not anything that ever walked around. Still, it tasted awesome compared to sucking the vaguely nutty-flavored sludge out of a nutri-pack.

Without the pressure of someone watching her to ensure she ate, she slowed down enough to taste the food and not scald her mouth. She had every intention of finishing it, but preferred to do so without pain. That woman buying her dinner meant the glint she'd scored from the other guy would last a little longer.

She huddled over her food, hating having to sit with her back to the people walking by. After being chased away from multiple corners, ever farther away from where she slept, she'd gone into a somewhat nicer part of the city. At least here, she ran less chance of being attacked by the Blanks, E6ers, Pluggers, Zap-fiends, Scathers or any of the other numerous street gangs or opportunists. Begging alone did come with risks, after all. In a group, even with little ones, they had much less chance of some skeever targeting them. Even Scathers knew a pack of ten-year-olds with knives could be dangerous. But in a group, especially being the oldest, she also stood almost no chance of scoring glint. Most Outcasts her age or older gave up begging for crime, prostitution, or scavenging a demolition zone for stuff worth selling. All three of those options terrified her.

Damn kids.

"'Sup Girl," chimed Callie. "Look who got lucky."

Sima leaned down over her bowl to protect it, eyeing the young woman sashaying over. The older girl swooped past her, tracing fingers across Sima's back, and plopped herself down in the next stool. The girl's pale skin had given her a noticeable advantage back when she begged, though she had to be nineteen or twenty by now, too old to really coast on charity anymore. It'd been a couple weeks since Sima had seen her, so the neon blue dye job in her over-styled hair came as a shock. Skin-tight black leggings bore numerous strategic slices to show off skin, and the girl's top amounted to little more than a shredded rag over her breasts. Black fingerless gloves with metal knuckles completed her outfit. One even had dried blood on the studs.

"Not talkative, honey?" asked Callie. "Oh well."

She plunked a pair of Universal Monetary Unit chips down on the counter, the chromatic plastic discs gleaming in the light. "Hey Amin. Lemme get a shrimp bowl, huh?"

"No Dreamdot?" asked Amin, taking the chips.

Cassie shook her head. "Are you kidding? That's how *they* own people. I ain't gettin' one of those damn things stuck in *my* butt."

"They go in the hand," muttered Sima, between bites.

Amin laughed while putting together the shrimp bowl.

"So she *does* talk." Cassie spun on her stool to face Sima. "How goes?"

"Okay."

"Not lookin' too okay. You're even skinnier."

Sima smirked at her. "I'm alive."

"Alive and okay aren't the same." Cassie waved her hand dismissively. "Won't be long before you give up and join the Blanks or something."

"Screw that," muttered Sima, shivering. Those cultists gave her the creeps. "No way am I goin' near those freaks. I like my parts right where they are."

Cassie laughed. "You believe those stories?"

"Why not?" Sima shrugged.

Word on the street claimed the Blanks sometimes dragged an Outcast no one would miss into an alley and stole their vital organs. Some wealthy Citizens supposedly paid big money for transplants. Of course, the Blanks creeped her out enough even without those rumors.

New members painted their faces white, full members wore shiny white masks, all the same expressionless, androgynous person. They eschewed material wealth as well as individuality, and had had declared war on commercialism. Other rumors claimed they did something to their own people, making them emotionless, mindless servants to some sort of hive mind. Some people even went so far as to claim once a Blank wore the white mask, their brain had been mostly replaced with electronics. If given a choice between death or having her sense of self taken away, she'd jump in front of a gee-vee.

"You shouldn't believe it because they're stories. Probably the EGSF trying to freak people out." Cassie looked over as Amin put her food in front of her. "Thanks."

Sima kept eating, faster since the soup had cooled enough to taste.

"Not havin' much luck, huh?" asked Cassie.

"Doing all right."

"Yeah, sure." Cassie play-punched her in the shoulder. "You should try heading over to Block 92. There's a nest of little ones there. Poor little buggers are afraid to go begging. They'd probably work with an older kid for protection."

Sima grumbled. "Yeah, and they'll get all the glint."

"Work something out." Cassie jabbed her chopsticks into the bowl and lifted a huge bundle of noodles. "You're not thinking the angles out properly. Charge them protection."

"Yeah right. *Me* protect little kids?" She shook her head. "I don't wanna be a Keeper. They don't *protect* the kids; they *use* them."

Older Outcasts sometimes gathered children around them, forming a personal army of beggars, thieves, and spies. Those who did that, Keepers, varied in benevolence. Enough stories about the worst ones painted all of them in a bad light. People who got a reputation for being Keepers stayed deep underground for good reason, and sent their little minions out into the world to beg, steal, and sometimes do worse.

"Ain't saying you go Keep. Still a kid yourself. Look, I know you're jealous, but what do you want more? Pride, or food?"

Sima grumbled. "I don't want the responsibility. And kids are annoying as hell."

"You gotta do somethin', girl. Ain't got much begging left in you."

"I can still beg." She held up the bowl as if to show it off as evidence of her continued ability to obtain charity, then slurped up the last bits of broth, chasing flecks of noodle, garlic or seaweed into her mouth with the plastic chopsticks.

Cassie shook her head. "You're about at the end of that particular O-Tube. Won't be long before you're gonna have to steal, whore, have a kid, or try to get in wit' the Underground."

"Ack, no!" rasped Sima. "No way am I gonna do that. Don't even say that word out loud!" She lowered her voice to a whisper. "You're crazy even talking about them. I don't give a crap about the government. Bad enough how the EGSF treats us when we *don't* break the law, I'm not gonna declare war on them."

"Yeah, well..." Cassie shoved another wad of noodles in her mouth and chewed for a while. "If you saw how I lived now, you'd change your mind."

Sima's eyes bulged. "You're *not* with the Under-you-know-what..."

"No. Wow, you're clueless. I work for Magdalena."

Ugh. Sima pressed her knees together at the mere mention of that name. The woman, who must've had half her body replaced by plastic and metal at this point, gathered Outcasts to staff her brothel. Usually girls, but she'd take boys too if she thought they'd sell. Go figure, the one person in the area who *didn't* discriminate only wanted to use people. Honestly, she only hired young, pretty Outcasts. Perhaps that counted as discrimination, even if she didn't care about age, gender, or skin tone.

"Oh, don't look at me like that." Cassie rolled her eyes, then whispered, "I get to keep like forty cows a day."

Sima gave her the side-eye. Only the middle-class Citizens (and the upper end of the poor) referred to physical money as 'cows,' a degeneration of Universal Monetary Unit shortened to MU or *moo*, which then, due to the small plastic discs, became cow chips— shortened to cows. Who had this girl she used to beg with become? On Sima's best day, back when she'd been twelve (and looked like ten), she'd made about thirty-two glint. That would feed her for three or four days, so she'd been stupid and only begged when she ran out. Had she approached it like a job, she might've saved some and wouldn't need to go a couple days at a shot without eating now.

Still. She refused to turn to whoring. If she'd been willing to have sex in exchange for safety, she'd never have run away from home in the first place four years ago.

Cassie patted her shoulder; without conscious thought, Sima moved her right arm down to protect the pocket at the front of her tunic. The older girl ignored the gesture, continuing to smile.

"You could probably get maybe another year outta begging, but you'd make a lot more at Mag's place. Especially if you do that face you're giving me now."

"What face?" asked Sima.

"The one that makes you look like you're thirteen."

She shuddered, wanting *nothing* to do with the sort of men who'd be drawn to that. "Umm. I'll think about it."

"Forty cows." Cassie pushed her empty bowl back toward Amin. "Per day. Anyway, gotta go. Later, *kid*."

After another playful shoulder punch, the nineteen-year-old slid off her stool and walked away with the crowd. Sima looked away from her almost-friend, staring down at the little bit of brown liquid at the bottom of her bowl. It made no logical sense to prefer begging or potentially starving in the street to letting men pay to use her body like that. Especially for so much glint, not to mention food and a place to sleep. Perhaps a girl like Cassie lacked whatever Sima had inside that recoiled at the mere notion of it. For that girl, sex had become a mundane task, a simple way off the street.

But no...

Sima was not that girl. *If* she ever trusted someone enough to become intimate, it would be for love—if such a thing even existed anymore.

2

A USE FOR URCHINS

Her belly full of warm soup, Sima returned to her spot across the street and again adjusted her clothes to hide her true age. She sighed at her sad excuse for shoes: sandals made from the scavenged soles of a man's boots tied to her feet with old power cables. The sneakers she'd run away in had long since ceased to fit.

She decided against taking Cassie's suggestion to find that nest of little kids who'd become too scared to beg on their own. Children weren't her problem. She had herself to watch out for. Just being around kids made her angry, mostly out of jealousy. They needed to eat too, so she didn't begrudge them what they could beg for, but that didn't mean she had to play nanny.

People should have to take a test or something to be allowed to have kids. She scowled, thinking of her real father. She didn't even remember his name, only that he belonged to either the upper middle class or the lower end of upper class. How her mother met him, she couldn't explain. Though her mother was a Citizen, she occupied the lower end of that social stratum. Sima existed for one reason—a ploy to guilt the man into marriage. Surely, had her father not been well off, Sima's life would've ended after only a few weeks in the womb. Unfortunately, her mother had overestimated the man's humanity and underestimated his contempt for the poor. When the man left her, somehow that became Sima's fault. Mom resented Sima for her failure to be a successful trap. Though her mother had never been physically abusive, she'd offered her daughter about as much affection as she did her desk lamp. As soon as Sima could fix food for herself, their relationship had devolved into basically roommates, without the affection of even distant relatives.

Once, she'd had the idealistic dreams of a little girl that she'd find her father and he'd welcome her with open arms into a wonderful world of comfort. Alas, she'd tried to contact him on numerous occasions years ago, but he'd never replied. She didn't even know what Block he lived in, or if he even remained in this district.

Probably married. Maybe he has 'real' kids and doesn't want me.

One hour slid into the next as she observed the crowd. Occasionally, someone mumbled in another language she couldn't follow, but most spoke GANSEC, the official language of the Earth Government. When she'd been in school, her language teacher went over the history, explaining how it had come about as part of the treaty process outlining the End of Nations. At the time, the Earth Government required all people, Citizen or not, to become at least capable of simple conversations in the new language, derived from Chinese, Spanish, English, German, Arabic, and Norwegian. Though, that had happened long ago, almost two centuries. Sima'd never known any other tongue. Her mother had sometimes spoken Arabic with Sima's grandparents, but never bothered teaching her any. Hell, the woman barely wanted to provide food.

Whenever anyone in the crowd made eye contact, Sima would approach, slinging one of her well-rehearsed lines. One or two parted with a little glint, but most ignored her. Every so often, she'd have to duck someone taking a swing at her or trying to shove her to the ground. In three hours, only two people parted with chips. Cassie's taunting words kept circling her thoughts, like buzzards waiting for the last breath. Perhaps she *had* reached the point in her life where she could no longer rely on 'being cute,' and would need to do something else.

Eyes closed, Sima leaned back against the grungy wall, trying her best to ignore the stink of the city—a brine of chemicals that settled on her tongue with the flavor of dirty metal and swamp. A nest of black, flexible hoses hanging like dreadlocks from some giant, boxy machine at her left undulated with whatever fluid coursed through them.

She pondered potential futures.

Option one: find a job—but she had no skills and only a sixth-grade education.

Option two: work for Magdalena—but she'd prefer starvation to selling her body.

Option three: crime, specifically thievery—but she'd have to steal from people only slightly better off than her, and that didn't seem fair. Not to mention, the security forces were unduly harsh on Outcasts caught committing crimes.

Option four: she could try falling in with one of the gangs—but they'd surely *take* her body and she'd wind up on drugs.

Option five: join the Underground (or Separatists as Citizens called them)—but that may as well be suicide, plus she didn't care about politics. The Earth Government was so corrupt it had embraced duplicity as a form of procedure. No amount of 'change from within' would fix that. The Underground knew this, so their solution had become 'burn the cancer out.' But a couple thousand Separatists against the EGSF... yeah. She'd rather leap in front of a speeding gee-vee.

Option six: (which wasn't really an option at all) Go into the demolition zones and try to find abandoned tech that someone might buy. She didn't care if the rumors of danger had been made up or not. Despite scavving representing the most legal of her options, she'd sooner work for Magdalena. Even if it cost her all sense of self-respect, she'd still be alive.

A sick feeling spread across her stomach, churning the essence of hours-ago ramen into her throat. Of those options, the only one that even approached plausibility kept circling back to Magdalena. Her hang-up there came from a deep, inner revulsion, not some practical matter such as fear of death or incarceration/torture. Could she set aside her dignity to continue to exist? After a week or a month working for that woman, would she even *want* to continue to exist? She shuddered at the memory of her mother's new man sliding his hand up her dress and touching her butt while she'd been fixing her dinner one night. He'd come out of nowhere, sidling up behind her while she worked at the kitchen counter, his body trapping her with no way to escape the fingers sliding over her skin.

Sima hated him at first sight. Even at twelve, she understood the meaning behind the way he looked at her whenever Mom wasn't around, and the way he often touched her arms or back at every opportunity. Or how he 'really needed' to use the bathroom while she showered. And *that* moment, the two of them alone in the apartment with his hand up her dress, had been her breaking point.

Terrified and stunned, she'd remained still as a statue while he squeezed her bottom and whispered awful things at her ear, awful things he wanted her to do with him. Fortunately, he left her at the kitchen counter without doing worse. Perhaps he'd sensed her hesitation, or maybe he simply feared her being within arm's reach of kitchen knives.

Head bowed, Sima tried to hold back tears at the thought. She'd told her mother about what he'd done, but the horrible woman had accused *her* of trying to steal her man. That night, she'd run away from home with only the clothes on her back, and of those, only her tunic remained. Her baggy pants, she'd found in the trash, same for the wretched shirt she wore under the tunic. If she sold her body for Magdalena, she could buy new clothes and real shoes, have a bed to sleep on and a roof over her head. But, would it be worth the nightmares?

The sudden, rapid patter of small footsteps snapped her back to reality. A barefoot boy in an olive drab tunic way too big for him darted out of the crowd, heading straight for Sima. He couldn't be older than six, and at first, she assumed he'd stolen the tunic since it looked new. But it soon became apparent that he fled not from an angry shopkeeper, but a trio of bigger boys who all looked at least twice his age.

He crashed into her, clinging, and yelling, "*Saeiduni min fadlik!*"

Sima smirked, palmed his head, and shoved him away. "I don't deal with kids. And I have no idea what you said. This is my spot, go find your own."

The force of her push knocked the boy to all fours. His pursuers slowed from running to walking. Between ten and twelve, none of them looked keen on getting into a fight with Sima. Fortunately, her tunic concealed her scrawniness, or even boys their age might think they could take her.

"Please, help," said the boy, switching to GANSEC. He scrambled to his feet and clung to her again, hitting her with a wide brown-eyed stare. "They're gonna hit me and take all my stuff!"

The older boys hovered a short distance away, eyeing the kid like dogs after a scrap of meat.

"So, run faster," muttered Sima.

One of the older kids smiled.

"Please!" whispered the little one. "I'll give you half my glint. Don't let them steal my stuff."

Sima glanced down at the kid's round, brown face and wild hair. *Wow, he's really scared if he's offering to pay me.* She argued with herself between the ease of making a little glint and feeling crappy for extorting a six-year-old. While she hadn't lived in paradise at that age, her crummy home life had been far better than the street, at least before that man started visiting. Still, having a child that close would virtually guarantee she'd not make another bit of glint all day.

He clung tighter, evidently sensing the disinterest in her eyes. "Please! We can help each other."

"Oh?" She folded her arms. "How can you possibly help me?"

"I'll pretend to be your kid. Tell people you gotta feed me."

Having a little boy clinging to her felt about as welcome as a smear of animal waste on her tunic, but as distasteful as she found it, being covered in child beat going to Magdalena.

"Okay, fine."

The three boys shot her sour looks and wandered off back into the crowd. They probably thought she carried a knife or something, since most Outcasts her age did. Little did they know she feared the EGSF too much to let them catch her with a weapon. They'd probably arrest her anyway if she so much as made eye contact with one, but better to be arrested without broken limbs.

"*Faqat 'akhbar alnaas bi'anani abnak,*" said the boy.

"What?" Sima blinked at him.

He stared up at her in shock. "You don't speak Arabic?"

"No." She shook her head. "I already told you that."

"Your father didn't teach you?"

She grabbed his tunic at his chest and lifted him up on tiptoe, ready to throw him into the crowd, but a mere two seconds of looking at his pitiful stare defused her rage, and she set him down. "No. I've never even seen him."

"Oh. Sorry." The boy kicked his toe at the ground. "Mine taught me a little, but he died. So did my mother."

Sima narrowed her eyes. "Is that a line or did they really die?"

He raised a hand. "Swear. I only make stories for 'Zens. My name's Sayed. What's yours?"

"Sima."

He grinned. "Okay. You gotta stop looking like a girl and be a woman."

With a sigh, she shifted her stature, standing upright. Sayed rubbed his chin, studying her unimpressive chest. After a moment, he shook his head then scampered over to the nearest ORC from which he pulled out some trash paper. He trotted back over, offering it. "Here. Make your boobies bigger."

Blushing, she took the papers, wadded them up, and tried to get them to stay put under her shirt. After some adjusting, she felt ridiculous, but did appear more adult. She couldn't do much about her youthful face though.

"No one is gonna believe I'm your mother," she muttered.

He wrapped himself around her left arm and stared pathetically at the passing crowd. "They will if you sell it. If the 'Zens don't believe, I'll be your little brother. We share glint half and half."

Sima's jaw tightened in resentment at the implication she *needed* a little kid to help her beg, but it only bothered her because she believed it. "All right."

For the rest of the daylight hours, Sayed stayed at her side hamming it up for the crowd. Whenever a gee-vee came by, he'd yell, "Mommy" and cling as if frightened of it—or when a person in nice clothes gave them dirty looks, he'd overact being terrified. Sima had trouble selling the whole 'mother' thing for a while since she couldn't help but think of *her* mother, and how much the word 'mom' had become something of a swear. Eventually, she found the acting easier— certainly putting up with a small boy holding her hand beat working in a brothel. For a while, Sayed pretended to be sick, coughing and shivering, and Sima worked the passersby with lines about how she couldn't feed him enough to keep him healthy.

By the time it became dark, they'd raked in fifty-three glint. Done for the night, they retreated into an alley to divide their earnings. She knelt by two piles of twenty-six chips, holding the stray.

"You can have it," said Sayed, "for protecting me."

She'd been thinking of taking it just because the boy couldn't do much about it, but she'd also been considering giving it to him because he was only six. As much as she resented kids for the easy time they had begging, he didn't exactly *ask* to wind up an Outcast. His telling her to keep it made her angry with herself for wanting it and angry with him for not being greedy, because that made her feel like a bitch. Sima would've kept the stray chip if not for how damned pathetic he looked. She sighed and dropped it on his pile.

"You need it more," said Sima, her voice mostly sigh.

Sayed's expression yelled 'wow really?!', but he didn't hesitate to pull his pile close and pack it handful by handful into his pocket. "Those guys woulda taken my tunic and beat me up."

She glanced at the olive-drab fabric, all the embedded electronics in its sleeves aglow. "Looks new."

"It is." He smiled.

"Did you steal it?"

He shook his head. "No. Begged."

"I don't believe you." She scoffed.

"A woman bought it for me."

Sima narrowed her eyes. "How do you beg a hundred-glint tunic?"

He shrugged. "Lucky, I guess." The boy lifted up his tunic to show off a threadbare set of tiny shorts, and ribs that hinted he hadn't eaten well in a while. "She saw me shiverin' 'cause the wind, and pulled me inside a store. I don' think it cos' a hundred glint. The man there said it was old models."

Grumbling that this boy with his giant brown eyes and innocent face could guilt a Citizen into feeling so bad for him that they bought him a tunic, Sima pulled the paper stuffing out of her shirt and threw it aside. The whirr of drone fans approaching made her pick it back up, fearful she'd been caught on camera littering. Though, a six-month stint in jail might not be a bad thing given how her life had been going —at least the EGSF would feed her. But if she got arrested, she'd have a record, and then every time the security officers saw her, they'd give her a hard time. So far, she'd stayed out of trouble. They'd look at her, but nothing came up in their computers, so they let her be.

Once the flying menace disappeared around a corner at the end of the block, she chucked the paper over her shoulder. In the secluded alley, she transferred her glint from the tunic's front pocket to a pouch she wore under it around her neck. There, it stood far less chance of falling prey to thieves or spilling out all over the ground if she tripped. She counted forty-one total after adding the day's haul.

It never lasts long enough.

"How much do you want to walk me home?" asked Sayed. "I'm kinda scared of the dark."

She tried to get mad at him for accusing her of being so mercenary, but the truth hurt. Sima swallowed the urge to ask for money and muttered, "Don't worry about it. Where do you live?"

"Coupl'a blocks south. Tunnel next to the fat man shop."

"Fat man shop?"

He held his arms up. "Got a big fat man outside with a big white hat."

"Oh." She figured he meant a donut/coffee counter with a holographic cartoon chef mascot. As best she could remember, it sat near an old access shaft down to what had once been a subway a few blocks away. No one used the tunnels for much since the overhead tubes, or O-Tube, went in. "Come on."

She stood and started walking, ignoring his attempt to take her hand.

"Aww, but *Mom*, I'm scared."

Sima scowled at the wall. As tempting as it might be to keep him around, she felt no better than her mother for it. That woman had used Sima as a device to exploit a man. Using Sayed as a tool for begging bothered her almost the same way.

Ugh.

If she never encountered another child in her life, it would be too soon.

3

FIVE GLINT FOR DEAD

S ayed waved and darted off down the stairway leading underground. Across the street, the coffee shop's life-sized holographic chef waved a donut around. Sima squinted at the brightness of his white outfit and hat, certain she'd be hearing the comically jovial voice say, "Free black coffee with three donuts" in her dreams.

She pulled her hood up, stuffed her hands in her front pocket, and hurried along back to her squat. For the past several months, home was a section of decommissioned sewer tunnel that became accessible after a patch of road caved in. All things considered, its proximity to a former sinkhole probably didn't make it the safest place in the world, but it had held up so far. Dozens of other kids around her age and younger made a home of the underground chamber as well. Fortunately, trouble had been sparse. Only two deaths and six assaults in three months.

She walked a few blocks before hooking a right turn onto a wider street that could handle gee-vees passing each other going in opposite directions, though at the late hour, only two whirred by.

Head down, Sima hurried along for a few minutes before two hulking forms, a pair of EGSF officers in armor, wandered out of a side street on the left. Tiny spotlights mounted to their shoulders flicked on and bathed her in the pale glow of intense LEDs. She kept her gaze on the ground, trying to project innocence.

"What are you doing outside at this hour?" called a thick-voiced woman. "You're an inch from breaking curfew."

Sima stopped, her heart pounding. An Outcast had about a forty percent chance of death in any encounter with the EGSF. Girls had somewhat better odds. "I'm sorry! I had to hide from some Scathers! I'm going home right now."

"Pull your hands out slow," said a man, his voice crackly with electronics.

She extracted her hands from the front pocket on her tunic and raised them.

The female EGSF officer crossed the street and walked up to her. "Do you have any contraband?"

"No, ma'am." Sima kept her head down.

"What's in that bag around your neck?" asked the male officer as he walked up from behind and grasped her left wrist, studying her hand. "No Dreamdot?"

"No, sir. I was too young for one when I lost my home." She knew the officer could see her pouch courtesy of scanners, and probably also the UMU chips in it. He asked only to test her. "Just a little money."

"You steal it?" asked the man.

"No sir," she said to the sidewalk. "I've been begging."

The female officer looked her over once more, then stepped aside. "All right. Don't let us catch you up to anything. And get off the street. You've got four minutes before you're in violation of curfew."

"I won't, ma'am. Thank you, ma'am."

Sima scurried onward, lightheaded from anxiety. She hoped that one boy with the red hair and permanent glazed eyes had been right about karma. Every time she resisted the temptation to break the law, she banked on that coming back to help her out if she had to deal with the EGSF. Then again, some rumors also accused the cops of using Outcasts for rifle practice when they got bored. But stories like that sounded (and often were) purely tall tales to scare kids.

A few streets later, she rounded a leftward corner into the pink-purple glow of Oman's Oasis, a cheap bar that also specialized in plugs, narcotic inserts for those with permanent cybernetic injector implants. The technology came about for those in need of medication for chronic issues, but, naturally, the unsavory element within society adopted it for vice. Since the Oasis sold the stuff, it attracted Pluggers, a street gang that got its name from their drug habit.

She crossed to the opposite side of the street to give the place some distance, since a handful of light-skinned punks leaned against the wall, their faces glowing various shades of neon from LEDs in the collars of their tunics or courtesy of phosphorescent tattoos.

"Hey, sweetie," yelled one.

"Paz, check that out." A guy with a bright raccoon mask of green light swatted the man next to him and pointed at her. "Want a little dark meat?"

Sima walked faster, regretting her choice not to carry a knife. Although, if she had a weapon, she wouldn't have needed to worry about these morons. Those two EGSF would've hauled her in for possession. Outside of a kitchen, carrying a knife without a permit would get her at least a year. Probably more for being a minor, and another year or two for being an armed Outcast.

Don't be stupid. My best weapon is running.

"Yo, beautiful," called another Plugger. "Give ya five glint for head. Right here, right now."

Sima walked even faster, not the least bit tempted. Ignoring the sheer disgustingness of his request, she had little trust they'd let her walk away alive, and even less trust they'd pay her. The End of Nations had resulted in a 'One Earth' government, but it hadn't done much for prejudice. Six pale guys one tiny notch up the social rung from a girl like her would do whatever they wanted to her without fear. A group of men had assaulted Anahita, a girl she knew a year older than her and not even as dark. When she went to the EGSF about it, they treated *her* as though she'd done something wrong. Then again, those men had been Citizens, so naturally, an Outcast girl lied about being assaulted, only trying to get money or sympathy. Why would *Citizens* want to have sex with a filthy street rat?

The Pluggers, the youngest of whom looked past twenty, pushed off the Oasis wall and started after her. With a gasp, Sima broke into a run, but didn't cry out. A frightened young woman screaming would often attract more danger than help. The rest of the Pluggers decided to chase her, the whole pack whooping and hollering—except for two dosing a chem so strong they couldn't walk.

Sima leaned into her stride. The electrical wire holding her sandals on pinched at her ankles each time her heels struck the ground. Wind in her face pulled her hood back and let her long hair fly loose. The men continued yelling at her, everything from "Hey, wait up, we won't hurt you" to threats of a severe beating if she didn't stop.

Where are those cops? She bolted around another corner but realized too late that she'd gone the opposite direction from where she'd run into the EGSF. No guarantee they would've been there anyway, so she kept on going. Only getting away from those Pluggers mattered. Much like Sayed had feared from the older boys, those gangers would likely steal everything she had that stood even the smallest chance of being sold to buy more plugs. *If* she survived, she'd probably be left semiconscious in an alley somewhere with only her sandals. Or maybe they'd drag her back to wherever they slept and keep her as a pet.

A fearful whine leaked from her nose; she ran as if Death himself chased her.

Streaks of light from small LEDs embedded in the walls smeared by on both sides. Dark doorways offered little hope of escape. No one with any sense in this lower-end residential district dared open their doors at night.

One ganger surged up to a hard sprint, gaining on her. He got a grip on the trailing end of her hair, and pulled, trying to drag her to a stop. She screamed in pain, her sandals clomping the pavement as she slowed. Before the man could get an arm around her, she abruptly spun around and drove her knee into his groin. He barked like a goose going under the tires of a gee-vee and let go of her hair. Another guy dove at her; she leapt aside, avoiding him—right into the grip of a third man.

He held a composite plastic knife at her throat, his rapid breaths pulsing at the back of her head. "Easy there, girl. This'll only hurt a lot."

The other four men circled up around them.

Sima glanced down at the forearm over her chest, staring at a square metal well grafted into his flesh two inches above the wrist. A teal green narcotic plug, about the size of a corn kernel, sat in the chamber, the electronics gradually liquefying it and feeding the drugs into his bloodstream.

The guy holding her shifted left and right, as if he couldn't decide which of his buddies to 'offer' her to. "This one'll probably bite."

"Best not use the teeth, lovely," said a guy with a snow-white strip of hair over the middle of his otherwise bald scalp. "A dead girl can still do what we need her to."

Eyes wide, Sima grunted and pushed her feet at the ground, trying to back away from him. Out of desperation, she reached up and grabbed the man's arm, mashing her finger on the implant's 'dose plus' button. The man muttered an incoherent non-word and fainted over backward, dragging her to the ground. His arm went limp, the knife flopping away from the soft skin of her throat.

Sima kicked her legs up, adding to the momentum of falling, and rolled in a backward somersault to her feet. Their reaction time dulled by their high, the Pluggers stood there for a second or two in confusion before they realized she'd gotten away.

Too terrified to scream, Sima ran to the first possible corner and raced around. A block later, she ducked down an alley to the left—which turned out to be a dead-end. She spun to go back, but the Pluggers had already entered the mouth of the alley, trapping her. Sima backed up, eyeing the wall behind her for a way to climb. Everywhere else in the city, mismatched wall panels offered plenty of places to grab or put feet to climb. She had the wonderful luck of finding the one alley in the entire city still with intact original construction—no seams. However, a narrow ventilation grille offered a tiny scrap of hope. She darted over to it, sliding to a stop on her knees.

The cover came away with a desperate pull and she leapt headfirst into a square duct only an inch or two bigger than her on all four sides. It went in about two feet before bending a corner to the left. Her hands squeaked over the bare metal as she pulled herself forward. Sima screamed at the sudden tightness of fingers clamped around her left ankle.

"Hah! Gotcha!" yelled a man.

Shrieking, she grabbed on to the corner, fighting the guy pulling her out. Near total panic gripped her as she stomped backwards in a wild, flailing frenzy. Her heel connected with something solid after a few kicks at the air; the man let out an *oof*, and lost his grip on her other leg.

Sima crawled forward as fast as she could move, scooting around the bend. Once she got past the corner, she lay there gasping for breath. Her present surroundings ranked about an eleven on a scale of one to ten for claustrophobia, but in that moment, she adored it. No way would any of them fit in there.

Much cursing and threatening continued outside, but the Pluggers lost interest after a while and got quiet. She didn't trust the silence, so made no effort to move. Shivering from fear, she wondered if Sayed had been this frightened of those older boys. A kid his age had no concept of what the Pluggers would've done to her. To him, the worst thing in the world was getting beat up and robbed down to his shorts.

How scared had he been to risk running up to her, an older Outcast and total stranger, to beg for help?

Sima wiped her eyes, sniveling. With those gang thugs chasing her, she wouldn't have hesitated dashing straight up to an EGSF officer. The worst they'd have done to her would've been a quick death, but more than likely, they would've arrested her for bothering them— certainly, a better fate than what the Pluggers had in mind for her.

In her mind's eye, she saw herself pushing Sayed away, and felt like a total bitch.

Minutes stretched into an hour. Still, she lay there in the dark vent, breathing slow so as not to make any noise. Living on the street had sounded like such a great idea four years ago. Really though, how much forethought did she have at twelve? If she knew back then what it would really be like, would she have still done it? An indifferent mother and a creep of a potential stepfather compared to running for her life three nights a week?

Maybe I should go home… if I could even remember where it is. Would Mom even let me come back? Did she even notice I'm gone?

Sima traced lines in the dust in front of her face with her finger, wondering if her old room still existed. Not that she had all that much, a simple bed and a small desk, some toys she'd gotten from a boyfriend or two her mother had when she'd been too young to attend school. Men who had little reason to pay attention to a kid had shown more affection than her own mother. They'd been different from the creep, more genuine, though none had stayed around long enough to form any sort of relationship with her. All had merely been nice to the kid of the woman they wanted to sleep with. Would her mother have left her room as is in case she decided to come home? After four years, did the woman give up on ever seeing her again?

It didn't seem likely she would care. In the twelve years she had lived with her, Mom hadn't spoken to her much more than to yell about her using too much protein gel or not cleaning up the bathroom. If they traded words, it had always been a complaint or an order. Never any 'unnecessary' conversation and most certainly no comments of affection or curiosity about her daughter's life.

No. I can't go home. I might be able to go back to where I lived, but it wasn't 'home.'

She sighed, and listened to silence for a few more minutes before crawling backward. Keeping a good grip on the corner in case the gang had been unusually determined to catch her, she shimmied back until she could peer out the opening. No sign of the men remained.

A long breath of relief slid out of her throat.

"Karma..."

This must have been the universe chiding her for trying to be mean to Sayed. Certainly, if she had gone through with her initial jealousy and refused to help him, this vent wouldn't have opened, and those Pluggers would've gotten her.

After a guilty stare at the pavement, Sima pulled herself out of the cramped space and trudged down the alley. Soon after she emerged on the street, another gee-vee, a large cargo truck, rumbled by. She flattened herself against the wall to let it pass, the high-pitched whine of its electric wheel motors vibrating in her bones. The ponderous machine trundled off into the night, leaving her in a rush of air and swirling trash.

Head down, she fast-walked to the end of the block and made her way back to the street that led to the Crash, her present home. The collapse of either sewer or old subway tunnels had opened a hole in the road with a convenient ramp of paving. She held her arms out for balance on the way down, walking past jutting pipes and wire bundles sticking out from the walls.

Her sandals slapped on wet concrete at the bottom. She ducked a low-hanging steel support beam that bowed under the weight it held up, and proceeded through a doorway created by a slab of collapsed concrete.

The room beyond held many fragmentary walls that divided it into dozens of little alcoves and chambers. Outcasts had set up their beds among them with the older, bigger teens claiming the 'better' enclosed spaces that offered more room and privacy. Sima nodded in greeting to those who noticed her as she went by, but not a word passed between them. This shelter offered as much safety as anything in an Outcast's life could. Anyone caught stealing or messing with someone else's stuff in here would face a vicious beating from everyone, then be exiled.

Sima maneuvered around broken hunks of rubble and walls, trudging down narrow passageways to her 'room,' a freestanding concrete box close to the rear corner, about half the size of the bathroom at her mother's apartment. Plastic bags and a couple blankets softened the bottom of a space she could just about lay down in straight.

She sat on her bed and untied the cables from around her calves, rubbing the sore lines the wire had left on her skin. Though they protected her feet from harm, the sandals did not cope with running well at all. Sima set them aside in the corner behind her head and curled up to sleep.

4

MURDER PIXIE

Commotion yanked Sima out of sleep.

She shot upright in bed, arms raised wielding an imaginary knife she'd long ago chickened out from carrying for real. Shouting echoed in the subterranean vault, voices both shrill and deep. Foggy, she curled into a defensive ball until her brain woke up enough to realize the other Outcasts weren't punishing a thief but screaming about a corpse.

Sima rolled onto her feet and poked her head out past the cracked wall of her 'room.' A crowd had gathered a few spaces to the left, along the innermost wall where only shallow partitions divided separate 'bedrooms' like bathroom stalls without doors. Everyone congregated around Draz. Tying her sandals on would take too long, so she padded barefoot down the short passageway to the open channel at the back, lightly pushing her way into the crowd.

When she reached him, she gasped in horror at a haze of brilliant pink dye along his upper lip, residue from fumes that leaked out his nose. His face held an unnatural grey pallor, not the rich brown it should've been; however, the two tiny lines of blue LEDs he'd had grafted in to replace his eyebrows continued to flicker. She didn't have to touch him to know he'd died in the middle of the night.

An inhaler of Pixie lay clutched in his left hand.

"Damn, Draz. Hope that last dream was worth it, man," said Oema. The maybe-thirteen-year-old huffed a strand of snow-white hair off her face.

"He's dead." Torsten, a past-twenty guy with a black buzz cut and giant muscles, gestured at the group. "Fair game."

The thirty or so Outcasts around her all shouted, "Fair game," and descended upon Draz. One boy grabbed at his sneakers. A girl Sima's age went for his jacket. Three others invaded his sleeping area, raiding plastic crates full of stuff he'd collected. Oema dove headfirst into the blankets, crawling under the dead teen to claim a small portable video game system he kept under his pillow. The instant Liz got the jacket off the body, Gordy went for the T-shirt.

Outcast rules declared 'one person, one item' when someone living in the Crash died. They viewed breaking that rule no different from stealing, so the frenetic mob scene of looting throttled back to a reasonably polite competition for stuff, followed by a few people trading. Soon, Draz lay there in only his underpants. No one wanted them, likely due to the unidentifiable stains. Not a soul touched the Pixie inhaler either.

As everyone trudged off, Sima shouted, "Wait!"

The other Outcasts paused, looking back at her.

"We should do something," said Sima. "Not just leave him here."

Murmurs of agreement swept over the crowd for a few seconds before Torrent, a seventeen-year-old boy with sky blue hair, said, "Float him."

Sima cringed. As much as she disliked the idea of leaving Draz where he lay, she also didn't want to touch a dead person. She did, however, stoop and pick up the Pixie inhaler with two fingers.

Oema gasped at her. "Yo, that stuff's death in pink. A murder sprite. What you doing?"

"And the EGSF will aerate your butt for havin' it," said Theof, scratching his shaggy brown dreads.

"I'm just getting rid of it before one of the little ones finds it." Sima held the inhaler out to arm's length as if it would bite her. "No way am I gonna huff this crap."

"Careful, yo," said Demona. The somewhat older teen sidled up next to her, dark skin hiding her facial expression in the gloom. Neon green letters spelled 'Super Fusion' across her black tank top. "That stuff'll explode like a grenade you ain't careful."

"I know."

A few people repeated, "Float him."

Older boys, men really, clustered around Draz and grabbed him by his legs and arms. They hoisted him off the ground and carried him to the right, following the rear wall of the Crash to a round passageway leading into the old sewer system. Out of some strange sense of community, Sima followed along. She stared warily at the Pixie inhaler until a sharp rock underfoot reminded her she left her sandals behind, at which point, she watched where she stepped.

The procession marched down one corridor into another, the boys carrying him grunting from the struggle to move dead weight. Twice, they put him down to better their grip. Each time Draz hit the floor, puffs of glowing pink vapor burped out of his nostrils. Everyone held their breath.

Eventually, they reached a passage where water still flowed. The boys shuffled up to the edge and started swinging Draz side to side in preparation to throw him in.

"Isn't anyone gonna say something?" asked Sima.

"Like what?" Oema tilted her head, clutching the game system to her chest.

Sima shrugged. "I dunno. Seems like someone should say something."

"Sucks to be you, man." Theof saluted Draz.

"He wanted to float." Demona sighed, shaking her head. "People who huff Pixie *wanna* check out."

"Okay, umm…" Torrent held his arms out to the side. "If no one has anything, like *epic* to say about Draz, let's just like have a minute of silence for him."

The Outcasts stood there in somber quiet for about forty seconds before the ones holding him tossed him into the brackish water. Draz landed face down with a quiet splash, and glided off in the current, surrounded by solid lumps of brown matter and bits of trash. Overcome by a combination of disgust at the dead body and claustrophobia of the crowd, Sima shoved past everyone and ran off down a side passage. She wound through a series of tunnels and stairways to a pipe big enough to serve as a corridor. Her feet splashed in a few inches of water that trickled along the bottom, following the downward slope toward a ring of daylight at the end.

She hurried to the opening and stepped out on a narrow ledge of debris, mostly drywall slabs, plastic cups, hunks of rebar-studded concrete, and scraps of insulation. Fresh air, or at least the freshest the city had to offer, lifted her hair and her spirits (somewhat). Below her, a cliff of shredded building led down about twelve stories to a landfill. Sunlight sparkled from glass bits and twisted metal shards here and there. Numerous tiny waterfalls spilled from the exposed floors beneath where her toes curled over the edge. By the time the flow reached the bottom, it formed a brackish river of trash and mud.

The height stirred a twist of fear in her stomach. She gripped the wall at the right, her hand two inches beneath a drawing of a penis, and stood there seeking comfort from the solitude. As long as she stopped looking down, the quiet calmed her.

Draz, a boy only a year older than her had died less than thirty feet away from her sometime last night. Gone, silent as a ninja in the dark. She'd spoken to him a couple times, but she tended to avoid boys her age as they often had only two things on their mind: food and getting in her pants. Draz hadn't been like most. He never once made a move on her or even said she looked pretty. She doubted he preferred boys; more likely, he'd been lost to some deep pit within his mind that ultimately led him to kissing the Pixie.

Knowing that could be her at any given day brought a shiver and sent her thoughts racing back to her mother's apartment. *How bad could it be?* Maybe she could still go home, even if that creep would be there. It might not be as bad at sixteen as it felt at twelve. Maybe he wouldn't even try since she'd gotten older. She debated if she could she bring herself to tolerate that in exchange for a safe place to sleep and maybe going to school again? If she missed anything about being home, it would be school. Not that her mother ever cared at all about her grades, but Sima enjoyed learning and did well. Her determination not to end up like Mom pushed her in school. Somehow, the idea of the creep nauseated her less than working for Magdalena. Not like the man had any blood relation to her. Better one guy than hundreds paying for it. Better still not to do either, but she'd rather trade her body than *become* a body floating down the sewer.

Or would she?

She'd missed four years of school, so they might not even let her re-enroll. No telling if her mother even still dated that man. Sima hadn't gone anywhere near her old home since she'd run off. Her mother could've moved, died, been arrested… that apartment could belong to someone else for all she knew. And even if she'd never run away, by sixteen, Mom might've kicked her out anyway, thinking her 'old enough' to be on her own.

Her stomach tightened as she peered down. Twelve stories into glass, metal, and a torrent of mud would probably be a fast way out, but she shied away from the edge. The sky had too much blue and too much sun to die today. And no one held a gun to her head forcing her into a brothel or a creepy relationship with her stepfather.

A soft *crunch* in the trash beside her announced the arrival of another person. She turned her head as a skinny tow-headed boy of about eleven crept out onto the ledge. His grey tunic fluttered in the wind, ice blue lights dancing along the soles of his black sneakers wavered back and forth in response to how much weight he placed on each foot.

"Hey," said the boy, who she vaguely remembered as named Pim.

Ugh. Why can't I seem to get away from damn kids? "You shouldn't be out here. It's dangerous."

"*You're* here." Pim crept closer to the edge.

And this is why I can't stand them. "Fine. Fall. See if I care."

"You gonna jump?"

She shook her head. "No. I just needed air."

"Cool." He leaned forward and spit over the side.

Ick. What is it with boys?

A flash of white and pink caught her eye. She glanced over at Pim as he lifted the Pixie inhaler up toward his face. *Crap! I must've dropped it when I ran off.*

"No!" she yelled, and swatted at his hand, knocking the inhaler from his grip and sending it plummeting into the landfill.

"Hey!" yelled Pim, staring at her with surprised indignation. "What'd you do that for?"

The inhaler struck the ground and exploded with a *crack* like a gunshot, creating a small, pink fireball.

After a momentary glare, Pim punched her in the shoulder. "I found it."

In a flash of rage, Sima grabbed him by the tunic, two fistfuls of fabric at his throat, and shook him while shouting, "Do you wanna end up like Draz? Floating? That crap will kill you!"

Pim's eyes widened. For a few seconds, he hesitated, but once the fear left his expression, he snapped, "What do you care? You hate kids."

She didn't try to hold on when he twisted away and stormed back into the pipe, nursing wounded pride. Soon, the echoing scuff of his sneakers faded to silence. Sima sighed at the passageway, then turned her gaze out over the landfill far below.

"I don't hate you guys," she muttered. "I'm jealous."

5

HOMELESS

Begging had kept Sima alive for four years. Sometimes, she'd approach a food counter and offer to do work in exchange for a meal, though proprietors took less pity on a sixteen-year-old than on a younger kid.

She roamed the streets looking for a good high-traffic spot to set up shop for the day. Since she hadn't eaten last night, she swung by a few breakfast carts and counters that catered to the 'on the way to work' crowd, but three out of seven asked her for a handie or going down on them in exchange for food while the rest responded with demanding she buy something or get lost.

It seemed the world had made up its mind that she would be forced into doing something disgusting before she wanted to. Not that it would be disgusting when she *wanted* to. The act itself didn't nauseate her as much as the commercialization of it. By some stroke of luck, wits, or karma, she'd managed to last four years on the street without suffering worse than gropes and squeezes, though there had been *many* close calls—like the one the other night with Pluggers.

Maybe I should find Sayed... Pretending to have a kid to take care of certainly helped her begging profits, but she doubted the boy would do that again. At the time, he'd basically been paying her for having helped him with the bullies. He didn't need an older girl pretending to be mommy for him to earn glint begging. He had everything required for that with his young age and giant, sorrowful eyes.

She stopped by another food counter and bought a scrambled egg pita for two glint. It came with a coffee she didn't feel terribly interested in, but since she had it already, she drank it. After finishing her food, she roamed onward, sipping the coffee until it cooled enough to chug. Much to her surprise, one of the better spots, a five-way intersection, only had a couple of teen boys trying to run a hustle selling flower-like weeds they'd found somewhere. No little kid beggars had set up shop anywhere she could see.

Wow. Guess karma likes me today.

Sima positioned herself at one of the points of the intersection and fluffed her tunic to conceal her breasts and make herself appear younger. Some Outcasts faked missing limbs, but getting caught doing that a couple times tended to stick out in people's minds. Not as if the crowd walking by changed much from day to day. Sure, the occasional visitor from another Block would always happen, but by and large, any given area had roughly the same men and women going to the same jobs day in and day out. A scam artist would soon run out of luck, or have to move elsewhere.

An hour later, she'd made eighteen glint with her usual sad-eyed 'Please help me' routine. After four years, she'd worked out the best targets. Older men responded to her the best, especially the 'socially aware' types who felt an innate sense of pity for someone in her position. If conversation ever lasted long enough, she'd always say her mother kicked her out after she refused to go to bed with the new boyfriend. The tale always garnered sympathy and a few extra glint, and didn't *quite* feel like a lie.

"Sima!" shouted Cassie, jogging toward her.

Ugh. She tugged her hood up, about to walk the other way, not interested in hearing yet another sales pitch for Magdalena's, but the older girl had an uncharacteristic expression of urgency, so she waited.

Cassie pushed and weaved among the pedestrians on the opposite side of the street until breaking free at the corner and running over between a pair of rumbling gee-vees. "Sima..." She stopped, out of breath, and leaned on the wall beside her.

"What?" asked Sima. "Why do you look freaked?"

"They're gone!" yelled Cassie. "All of them."

Sima tried to make eye contact with a guy in an expensive suit, both his arms shrouded in holographic displays, but he averted his gaze after one brief glance at her. *Grr. With Cassie here, he thinks we're either pickpockets or prostitutes. Gotta be alone.* She sighed at the sky. "What. Who's gone?"

"Remember yesterday when I"—Cassie gasped for air, and took a few seconds to catch her breath—"told you about that group of little ones who were scared to beg?"

"Yeah." Sima folded her arms.

"Well... I kinda felt bad for 'em, so I went there this morning to play big sis."

"Easy for you, since you got a 'job' now and don't need money."

Cassie grabbed her arm. "Hey. Easy on the cattiness, 'kay? Something happened to those kids. I found their nest and it was cleared out. Not one kid remained."

"Maybe they moved?" Sima pulled her hair off her face and held it against her chest.

"No... I ran into Ollie across the street and he told me the EGSF like *raided* them. Straight up rolled in with armored gee-vees and everything. The cops hauled them all off."

Sima gasped. "They arrested children outta their beds? For what?"

"No, that's the really tweaked up thing!" Cassie's blue eyes bulged. "They didn't like 'arrest' them at all. No restraints or anything. Walked 'em out like they was takin' 'em to school or some crap like that. Ollie said none of the kids was cryin' or looked upset."

"Whoa. That's kinda scary." Sima folded her arms and leaned on the wall. "EGSF rounding up Outcasts, especially little ones? I wonder what kinda BS story they used."

"Pff." Cassie pulled on her arm. "No idea girl, but your butt is too old for this begging stuff. Come on and talk to Magdalena."

Sima shuddered at the rumors. Depending on who she talked to, the Outcast Madam had a robotic spider for a lower body, or long metal claws, wild black hair made up of stinging cybernetic filaments... and the worst, her eyes. "I dunno. Those purple eyes creep me the hell out."

"Yeah. I hear she can see in the dark with them things. I'm sure she'll take me on."

"What?" Sima shot her a look. "Didn't you say you already worked for her makin' like thirty a day?"

Cassie waved dismissively. "I said that's about what we can expect. Was tryin' ta get you to go with me, but after seein' them kids vanish, I'm gonna do it myself if I have to."

"I'd really rather not be a whore," muttered Sima, ashamed of herself for even saying that word.

"What do you think?" asked Cassie.

Sima glanced left at a pair of pale, bare breasts wobbling in her face, Cassie having lifted her shirt to show them off. "Gah!" She looked away, mortified.

A rustle of fabric preceded Cassie laughing. "Wow, I've never seen someone blush so hard. You're kinda dark so it's weird."

"I've never had a girl wave her boobs in my face before," said Sima, a touch louder than a whisper.

"So, what do you think? Will Mags like these?"

"I dunno. I'm not into girls. They look, umm, fine. Not like I'm some kind of authority on boobs."

Cassie shrugged. "Maybe if you had some, you would be."

"I do!" Sima glowered at her.

"You spend so much time trying to hide them and pretending to be twelve that I think they got the hint and went away." Cassie stuck out her tongue.

Sima sighed, and in a rare moment of boldness, thrust her chest out. "They're *not* that little."

"Oh wow." Cassie faked a gasp. "You *do* have tits."

She squirmed, wanting to hide her face from all the Citizens walking by.

"Look," said Cassie. "All I'm saying is, somethin's goin' down, and you need to get off the street before it comes down right on top of you."

"If they're going for kids, they're not going to care about me. I'm too old to be cute anymore."

"Exactly." Cassie bumped her in the arm with the back of her hand. "Time to graduate to being a woman."

"I dunno. It would take me literally starving to be able to just, like, do it with some strange man for money."

"You ever do it before?" asked Cassie.

Sima looked away. "Of course."

"Liar." Cassie laughed. "You're such a bad liar for a girl who's trying to make a living at lyin'."

"I don't make a living at lying. It's called 'begging.'"

Cassie poked her in the boob, making her gasp. "And making those things 'disappear' is what, if it ain't lyin'?"

"Technicalities."

Cassie pulled at her. "Come on. Let's go to Mag's and get real beds, real food, and actual clothes. You're a little skinny, but you got big eyes so you're like cute. I'm sure she'll take you."

Sima couldn't help but laugh and blush at the same time. "Clothes? I've seen that place. Everyone sits around in their underwear."

"That's working hours. They have clothes when they're not on the clock. Come on. Go with me."

"You shouldn't want to do that to yourself either. You're gonna end up on drugs or dead in a couple years."

Cassie gave her a light shove. "Don't believe that stuff. Mags is like super anti-drug, treats the girls like her own daughters. I heard some dude got rough with one of 'em, and she sliced him up like nothin' right there."

"And you wanna go work for someone who can do that?" Sima leaned back. "Not unless I'm gonna die if I don't."

"I get it." Cassie edged closer and threw a companionable arm around her back. "You ran away from home 'cause of that creep, so you're like scared of sex. It's not anything like you think it is. You've got it made out to be this horrible, evil thing in your head."

"Cass... If you think it's what's right for you, go for it. I wish you wouldn't do that to yourself, but I'm not ready to go *there* yet. Find something less... skeevy and I'm in. Even if it's a bit risky, just no breaking the law. I don't wanna get killed."

"Hmm." Cassie fidgeted. "I can look around, but 'worth decent money' and legal don't go together. You're describing a 'job,' and people won't hire us. Face it, Seem, there's two options for girls our age: Magdalena's or crime."

"I can't believe that," said Sima. "There has to be something."

"Well, you could always find a sugar daddy or go Keeper."

She sighed. "No, I mean like maybe learning a skill or something and getting a job."

"Girl, you haven't seen a school since you was twelve. That don't open many doors."

Sima tried not to glare at her sorta-friend. "Give me a couple days, okay?" She thought about Draz floating away, a corpse in the sewer, and cringed. Magdalena's *did* sound better than that. Maybe Cassie had a point about her fear of sex. Then again, having a grown man touch her bum at only twelve—and her mother becoming furious with *her* over it—left a mark. "If we don't come up with anything better in a couple days, I'll go with you to Mag's."

"You mean it?" Cassie beamed, bounced on her toes, and hugged her. "Awesome!"

This girl is way too happy about giving away her soul. "Yeah, but don't skeev off on trying to find something better, okay? Magdalena is a *last* resort."

"Okay, yeah, sure." Cassie grinned. "You still at the same Crash?"

"Yeah."

"Meet you there after dark. Think I can zonk with you?"

Sima flashed a coy smile. "I don't have a lot of room. It'd be kinda intimate."

"Only if you make it that way. I thought you didn't like girls."

"I don't."

"Well, neither do I, so it won't get weird."

"Right."

Cassie winked at her and hurried off, hopefully in search of something that they could make a little money on that didn't require doing anything Sima would hate herself for.

Hours went by, back to her usual routine. With the lack of small beggars in the area and the fear of having to become a prostitute lending genuine desperation to her eyes, she wound up pulling in fifty-seven glint by the time the sun headed for the western horizon. Having zero interest in being caught outside after dark again, she hurried to an OmniMart and bought a wrap sandwich from the cooler case for only one glint. The bread, vegetables, chicken, and sauce had all probably come from the same basic organic slime, but they offered the most food for the least cost of anything around. So what if a steady diet of such fakery might give her cancer by fifty. She didn't expect to make it to that age anyway.

Sandwich clutched to her chest like a precious baby, Sima jogged the couple blocks back to the Crash, reaching the entry ramp before sundown. The single worst part of living there, other than no showers, was the bathroom. A direct tunnel to the sewer more or less wound up causing people to do their thing right off the side into one of the canals, much the same way they'd tossed Draz. Frequently, others would show up at embarrassing moments, but since everyone eventually caught everyone with their pants down, the Outcasts living there all tended to ignore it happened.

After using the 'toilet,' mercifully without anyone else showing up, she scurried back to her 'room' and curled up like a squirrel with a nut, devouring her wrap. If she closed her eyes and pretended real hard, she could almost make believe the bread, lettuce, tomato, and chicken had different flavors and she didn't chow down on one giant log of mushy food-like something.

Still, the wrap's decent heft filled her almost *too* much. By the time she finished eating, she felt a little sick and had no desire to move. She slouched against the wall, staring at the wires tied around her legs to hold her sandals on, lacking even the urge to reach down to undo them.

Cassie should be here soon. She's got no idea where my spot is, but she'll yell or something. Or ask. That girl is not shy.

Hands on her belly, Sima half-closed her eyes, basking in the satisfaction of having had a meal.

A blur of time later, the mental fog of almost-sleep broke at a commotion in the distance, sounding near the entryway. Indistinct voices shouted, but the complicated chamber with dozens of little internal walls blurred the voices into non-words. Something in the tone set her on edge, so she stood and crept toward her 'doorway,' a large crack in the concrete.

Oema stuck her head in, her fluffy white hair glowing cyan and purple from light outside. Fear made the thirteen-year-old look more like eleven. "Run! EGSF is here!"

The younger girl didn't stick around to see if Sima would listen. She darted off, still carrying the precious game system she'd scavenged from Draz. It took a few seconds for the meaning of her words to soak into Sima's brain. The shout of an adult man amplified by helmet-mounted speakers shocked her into motion.

Security force!

She leapt out from her space, yelping when Torrent ran by, nearly plowing her over. She darted after him, following a group of five or six Outcasts down the same shaft they'd gone the other day for the 'funeral.' EGSF officers shouted, "Do not run. This is not a raid. We are here to talk," repeatedly, but Sima didn't trust a word of it.

Someone grabbed a fistful of her tunic from behind, but pushed/carried her along a little faster, helping her run. She didn't bother looking back, instead concentrating on not slipping into the sewer channel or tripping over any hunks of stone in her way. Panic drove the group onward. In their fear, they split up passage by passage. For whatever reason, she didn't feel like going down any of those particular side shafts, and kept on running for a while more until randomly veering left.

The tunnel reeked of sewer and mold, though the narrow path beside the wave of foulness looked reasonably clear of biological matter. She slowed to a rapid walk, somewhat relieved that the amplified shouts of EGSF officers no longer echoed in the darkness behind her. No matter why they wanted Outcasts, she doubted they'd bother going this deep to catch them.

Stench made it difficult to think and even more difficult to breathe. Upon finding a ladder in a recessed alcove on the other side, she jumped across the channel of effluent and scrambled up the old metal rungs, rust and dirt crumbling at her touch, to a metal cover that blocked the top. She pulled her hood over her hair and pressed her back and shoulder against it, pushing upward with all four limbs. It took every bit of her strength to shove the steel disc up a few inches. Once it cleared the street, she grabbed the edge and shoved it aside. The scrape of metal on paving sounded a bit too much like a tomb being opened for comfort.

Callie's right... I'm gonna die out here.

She pulled herself up out of the sewer into an alley, fortunately empty of people. With the EGSF actively hunting Outcasts, her friend's suggestion they go work for Magdalena started to sound reasonable. Even cops patronized the place, so she doubted it would be raided any time soon. Her eroding hesitance to become a prostitute scared her to the core, and brought tears of mourning for the girl she might've been if not for *him*.

That man couldn't shoulder *all* the blame. She reserved some for her mother as well. Not to mention the father who never bothered to even meet her once. All three of them had set her up for failure from the start, her mother most of all. Plenty of Outcasts had only a mother taking care of them until death, arrest, or disease got in the way. She knew a *good* mother could've made all the difference in her world.

But she hadn't been that lucky.

Karma took a giant crap on me right when I was born. I never did anything to deserve this. Why? Where's the other side? When is something good going to happen for me?

She sniffled and fought her way to stand. Sobbing in the middle of an alley at night was a *great* way to wind up dead. Sima figured she'd head to the other Crash, the one where the little kids had been taken from. The EGSF wouldn't go back to a location they'd already raided not too long ago. That place should be safe.

She hurried along for a few cross streets, trying to get her bearings after emerging from the sewer. None of the alleys or building fronts around here looked familiar. *We must've gone for like a mile underground.* Sima rounded a corner, heading toward the sound of traffic while squeezing the white square at the end of her left sleeve. The semi-squishy rubberized module chirped and projected a static-laced holographic panel.

While walking along, she tapped at the screen, trying to get a navigation app to load. She hadn't exactly taken good care of the tunic, wearing it more or less nonstop for four years. Before long, the batteries gave out and all the lights went dark, including the holographic display.

Most people charged their tunics up at home, but since she didn't exactly have one of those, she'd have to go to a café or something... and the charging adapter sat in her pile of stuff back at the Crash. No way did she want to set foot anywhere near there until at least tomorrow.

She looked up from the fabric of her left arm, about to growl in frustration, when she spotted a large black U in a circle painted on the wall, the symbol of the Underground.

Eep!

That meant somewhere around here, anti-government Seps hung out. The EGSF usually shot anyone they even suspected of associating with the Underground on sight, no questions asked: too many anti-interrogation suicide bombs took out too may cops. The Separatists didn't use them as weapons, but if capture became unavoidable, they'd set themselves off to protect others, and escape brutal interrogation.

Suppressing the urge to yelp, Sima ran as fast as she could down the alley to get away from the Underground. At first, she thought it stupid for them to paint their symbols around like that, but Torrent mentioned that ordinary people started making the graffiti to mess with the EGSF. Only the actual Underground members knew which marks were legit and which the work of pranksters. Still, she didn't want to risk a trigger-happy cop.

A few blocks later, another crumpled-in section of road reminded her of the entrance to her Crash. Despite the drones not announcing a curfew today, going underground again at night seemed a good idea, so she made her way down the ramp. This one hadn't collapsed as neatly as the other, breaking into three distinct pieces she had to jump between. At the bottom, a broken section of concrete sewer pipe formed a round entrance to a subterranean chamber. Mostly bare blue-grey concrete, it had a few columns decorated with so much spray paint she couldn't tell where one logo ended and another started.

Low voices murmured from the tunnel ahead, one of which kinda sounded familiar. Possibly Theof or one of the older Outcasts from her Crash. Maybe they'd come here. She couldn't be *that* far away.

Sima crept up to an archway on the opposite end of the large chamber and peeked around the corner. Seven twentysomething adults lounged around on old furniture, some sleeping, one couple making out, a few huffing on inhalers. No luminous pink mist filled the air, so at least they didn't use Pixie.

Probably a gang… I should get out of here before they see me.

She took a step back, and turned—her face nearly bumping into the chest of a large man.

"Hey there," said the guy. Before she could scream, he grabbed her. "Hello, treat."

"Sorry!" whisper-yelled Sima. "I didn't realize this was your turf. I'm just lookin' for a Crash."

He held her by the arms and whistled loud. The others filed out of the room and surrounded her.

"Little young," said a woman with cherry red hair.

One guy grabbed her breast through her tunic. She whimpered but didn't struggle too much.

"Please don't. I'm only fourteen."

The woman and one guy rummaged her pockets, the guy generously squeezing her backside while doing so. By some miracle, they didn't notice the pouch of glint she had under her tunic.

"Bah, this kid ain't got nothin' worth stealin'. Even her Omnicomp's outta juice," said the guy holding her.

An older guy, maybe even in his thirties, leaned into her face. Though muscular, he didn't stand any taller than her. Despite his short stature, his stare froze her in mute fear. "You got any fanciness you, uhh, don't need?"

She shook her head. "I don't do drugs. Nothin' on me."

"Aww a good little girl," chimed a man with forest-green hair and a white goatee. "She's adorable."

Sima's lip quivered.

Short and scary pulled up the front of her tunic and shirt, exposing her stomach. He felt around her sides and upward, but didn't slide his hand far enough to make contact with her breasts, again missing her pouch of glint. "Bah. Nothin'." He nodded to the guy holding her.

"Get outta here, kid." The man released his grip and shoved her to the side.

She dashed out, not wasting a second, racing back up the broken pavement ramp to street level and racing away from the area with the Underground markings. Two blocks later, her body had enough of sprinting, and she collapsed to a gasping stagger.

Those guys just let me go... She couldn't think of any gang that would let a girl walk away without doing anything at all to her, well, not unless the girl happened to be like ten or younger. It hit her that they might've been Underground pretending to be a street gang. She whined out her nose, wanting to run again, but her body wouldn't listen. If anyone had seen her there and those people *were* Underground, her life might've gotten a countdown timer.

"Stop," said a male voice, tinged with static crackles.

Sima about soiled her pants. She froze statue still—except for the trembling—and burst into tears. Five minutes away from being in the same room with Separatists, and of course, she trips into an EGSF ambush.

Heavy boots and small searchlights ambled closer. She shifted her gaze upward at a pair of men in the blue-grey armor of the Earth Government Security Force.

"Not getting a signal," said the one on the left.

His partner pointed at her tunic. "Looks dead. No lights."

"ID?" asked Officer One.

"I'm sorry. I don't have any. I've been on the street since I was twelve." Sima looked down, unable to stop shaking, expecting at any second they'd grab her for associating with Seps.

"How old are you now?" asked Two.

"Four—sixteen. Sorry. I tell people I'm fourteen when I'm begging for money so I can eat. I don't steal or anything. Just ask for help."

"What are you so nervous about?" asked One. "What'd you do?"

Her shaking intensified. All sorts of rumors said the EGSF officers had lie detectors in their helmets, and telling a simple lie to them could turn into a year or more in prison depending on how much of a prick the officer wanted to be. Even something as harmless as her almost-fib about her age. "I didn't do anything wrong."

"Then why do you look like you're hiding something?" asked Officer Two.

Sima gulped. "I, umm, saw an Underground mark on the wall back there. I'm scared of them. I don't wanna get shot."

The officers exchanged a glance.

"Those marks are all over the place," said One. "You see anything else?"

Sima stared at her feet. "I got grabbed by a gang. They searched me for stuff to steal but didn't find anything so they let me go."

"And you think they're Underground," said One, shaking his head. "Well, I suppose I can see that reasoning."

"Why don't you come with us, kid?" asked Two.

She gasped, staring up at them like they'd offered to put a bullet between her eyes.

"Relax." One held up his hands in a placating gesture. "You're not being detained. We've got a new program going on to help out street kids. Since you're under eighteen... pending verification, you'd be eligible for it."

Sima thought back to the 'raid' on the little kids in their Crash. That didn't sound voluntary. "Umm. Can I think about it?"

Officer Two leaned close, the small, rectangular spotlights on his shoulder pads nearly blinding her. "You look like you really could use a decent meal and real bed, plus some vaccines. There isn't much out here for you, kid."

"I know..." She shivered. "But it kinda sounds, like, you know... too good to be true. I don't wanna get sold to a hospital and used for tests."

Both officers chuckled.

"Nothing like that, I promise," said One. "But, it's not mandatory." He held his forearm up, presumably taking her picture with electronics in his armor. "You go on and think about it. Find any EGSF officer and ask about the Progenitor program. You'll have a soft bed, hot food, clothes, and a shower faster than you'd believe."

"That kinda sounds like prison," muttered Sima.

Officer Two chuckled. "Well, yeah, now that you say that, it kinda does. But it's not. We probably should work on our sales pitch. There's also school and adoption assistance."

She eyed the two of them. Having EGSF officers talk to her, an Outcast, like a human being was too weird to comprehend. Something did not feel right about it, not at all. Though, why they wanted to *convince* her to do something instead of simply dragging her off in handcuffs, she had no idea. They could quite literally shoot her in the face for no reason at all and not get in any trouble for it.

"That sounds nice," said Sima. "I'd still like to think about it if you don't mind."

"All right." Officer One pulled a small clear plastic fob from a storage compartment on his belt. "If you change your mind, use that."

Sima accepted the holocom. If she squeezed it, the city-wide holo-net would connect her to this guy. "Okay. Thank you."

"I hate watchin' you walk off homeless, kid. But, you're free to go." Officer Two stepped aside and gestured at the sidewalk.

"Thank you." She put the holocom in her tunic's pocket. As bizarre as the experience of meeting *friendly* cops was, and as unbelievable as their offer sounded, part of her felt tempted, more so than becoming a whore. "I want to talk to a friend of mine, but she's nineteen. Is she eligible for the program too?"

Officer One scratched at his helmet. "Umm. Possibly. It would depend on a couple factors, but we can try to get her in."

"Okay. I'll holo you tomorrow or the day after, I promise. Even if I'm too scared to do it, I'll let you know."

They nodded at her.

Sima fast-walked off down the street, beyond confused at why cops had been *nice* to her. The sky could've turned fuchsia, and that would've made more sense.

6

DESPERATE FORTUNE

Sima's world shuddered, knocking her out of a restless sleep into darkness. The earthquake caused a pile of trash bags to collapse on top of her as gravity upended itself. Overcome by panic, she screamed.

The shaking ceased.

A sliver of sun overhead broke the night. She squinted past the plastic bag mushed into her face at a narrow line of day on either side of a shiny, chrome head with two glowing blue eyes.

"Human," said a robotic male voice. "Why have you placed yourself in an Omni Recycling Corporation collection unit?"

She glanced around at assorted junk and the steel walls of a chamber larger than her room at the Crash, though not by much. A vague memory of crawling into the giant ORC bin to sleep free from prying eyes came back to her. "Uhh, to sleep."

"Human. I am unable to complete processing of recyclable collection while it may cause harm to a living being. Please effect self-removal of non-recyclable material."

Sima rubbed her right eye with the heel of her hand, trying to avoid yawning in a mouthful of stink. "Yeah, sure. Gimme a sec to wake up."

The robot stared at her. "One second has elapsed. Please effect self-removal of non-recyclable material."

She sighed and fought her way out from under the trash bags to grasp the top edge, the bin wobbling with her effort to move. Once she peered out the top, she realized the container hung from lifting spars jutting out from the side of a massive gee-vee with an open-top. The tilted angle made the container's front wall more of a ramp than a vertical barrier. Sima pulled herself to the edge, threw a leg over, and dropped down to stand on her feet. She took two steps before the robot emitted a warning buzz.

"Human, Your self-removal has created four potential misdemeanor infractions for littering. If you proceed to leave the area, this crime will be considered intentional."

"Seriously?" She leaned her head back to sigh at the overcast sky. "Great. It's going to rain…"

Feeling like a scolded child, she turned around and collected a few scraps of paper and plastic she'd knocked out of the ORC bin. The instant the fourth piece went back in, a loud mechanical whining noise from the huge gee-vee startled a yelp out of her. Spindly metal arms hoisted the container up and dumped it into the top of the collection vehicle.

"Have a nice day," said the robot, before walking past her and climbing in to the cab.

Sima hurried off, cringing at the *boom* of the empty ORC bin landing once again on the paving. Fortunately, she'd picked a relatively tame one, and the trashy smell clinging to her clothing didn't reek *too* much.

Still in a part of town she didn't recognize, she walked around for a while, one hand to her growling stomach. Eventually, she spotted a public access point, and trotted over to the little metal box mounted to the corner of a building. At her touch, a large holographic screen appeared in front of her, tinting the whole world yellowish-green. She swiped her fingers into the tingling panel, selecting the city map. The 'you are here' dot told her she'd gone two-point-four miles outside her usual territory, but getting back to familiar ground would be easy.

"Two intersections that way, turn left, then just keep going straight." She shot 'finger guns' at the panel and walked away.

No longer sensing a person near it, the display shut down.

A few minutes of walking later, the wonderful aroma of seafood ramen pulled her toward a noodle bar three times the size of the one she usually went to, and fancier. It occupied the ground floor of a twenty-story tower of gleaming silver windows, wrapped around the corner. Forty stools, twenty per side, held a handful of people munching away. Those on the left feasted on sushi or maki rolls while the nearer ones had bowls of noodle soup. Two men worked behind the counter, each attending to one side of the building.

Sima approached the older, friendlier-looking cook, squeezing up to the counter between two empty stools. "Excuse me, sir. Could you maybe spare some plain broth and noodles? I haven't had any food in over a day."

The man waved at her like he swatted a fly in the air. "Get lost or pay like everyone else."

One rule she followed: never pull out glint and buy food from a place she failed to beg from. They'd remember her as a manipulator. Head hung, she trudged off. She only made it three steps before a hand reached out and caught her right arm at the bicep.

"Hang on, kid," said a man. His grip didn't hurt, more intended to get her attention than hold her.

Sima glanced at a hand wrapped in black cloth strips approximating a fingerless glove. From there, her gaze climbed a roughed-up grey sleeve. Scraps of tech embedded in the fabric blinked and flashed. She looked along the arm to the shoulder, where more small metal boxes adorned his tunic, bedecked with wires and a mixture of displays both physical and holographic. The tiny hard-screens all showed strings of numbers, some changing every few seconds while the holographic ones showed small face pictures, like from IDs. She shifted her attention to a brownish beard, then up to the face of a man in his thirties with hazel eyes and thick brows. His brush cut hinted he might've been former EGSF, but his clothing called him an Outcast. Dusty black BDU pants and beat-to-hell combat boots confirmed it.

"What?" asked Sima.

He let go of her arm and patted the stool next to him. "Have a seat. Let's talk. I'd like to buy you a meal and pay you for a little errand."

Sima looked him over again. His gaze didn't strike her as *too* predatory, at least not in the sense he intended to hurt or take advantage of her in a sexual way. No, he seemed like one desperate person looking for an even more desperate person to do something dangerous or illegal. After a moment of standing there weighing the idea, another growl from her stomach convinced her to slide onto the indicated stool.

"Excellent," said the man, offering a hand. Dirt smudged at the sides of his eyes parted to reveal thin webs of clean skin in wrinkles as he smiled. "Nalas Corvin."

Sima tentatively accepted the handshake. "Sima Nuvari. What kind of errand?"

"Nothing terribly difficult. I need a package delivered to a woman who goes by the name Magdalena."

She stiffened. "Umm."

Nalas shook his head. "Relax, girl. This isn't some trick to get you kidnapped and forced into prostitution. Magdalena does not do that. I'm a simple coordinator of goods and shipments. People need things done or things moved from one place to another, and I arrange it."

"Oh." She looked down at her lap, brushing her hands over her black pants. They, too, might have been BDUs at one point, before she repaired them into something else. "So you just want me to carry a package there?"

"That's right."

She shifted her eyes toward him. "It's drugs, isn't it?" Her stomach growled, loud and long.

Nalas didn't flinch, continuing to stare at her with the same placid smile. "Do you really care?"

"How much are you paying?" asked Sima.

"Hundred glint."

Whoa! screamed Sima in her mind. Unfortunately, being only sixteen, she couldn't quite keep her shock from showing on her face. Nalas chuckled and gestured at the man working that side of the counter.

"One order of whatever she wants." Nalas nodded toward Sima.

Still numb from the offer of so much glint, Sima gazed up at the holographic menu and zeroed in on the seafood ramen that brought her here in the first place. "Number six please."

The cook nodded and set to the task of assembling the ingredients in a bowl. Nalas took out three UMU chips and placed them on the counter. The chromatic plastic caught the sunlight, casting tiny rainbows over the fake marble surface.

"Okay. I'll do it," said Sima. *A hundred glint! I could get real clothes! And food! Maybe even like an apartment or something if there's more work.*

"Your eyes already said that." He patted her shoulder.

"So you like, do stuff?" asked Sima. "What about other errands?"

"Oh, there's always things needing to be done." Nalas glanced at the cook. "Refill on the tea when you get a chance?"

The man nodded.

Her head swam with possibilities. Carrying a package to Magdalena's place might take an hour at most. Making a hundred glint in one hour for simply walking somewhere sounded far too good to be true. But also too good to walk away from. Sure, she'd probably agreed to transport drugs, or something that would likely get her arrested. That only meant she needed to be extra careful to avoid the EGSF on the way there. She *could* do that, if she kept herself from letting her thoughts wander over random worries on the way. The cops only snuck up on her when her head left the real world behind.

I can do it. She shivered with dread at breaking the law, but it seemed like the EGSF had already decided to round up Outcasts. Whatever that 'Progenitor' thing was, it didn't sound friendly. Creepy more like. The EGSF had treated people like her so poorly for so long, a sudden switch to wanting to be nice and take care of them rang false.

Nalas didn't talk much while they waited for her food to come out, but a few other people, mostly older teenage boys, came by and chatted with him. Sometimes, a small package exchanged hands, sometimes glint. One boy a year or two older than her with white hair and dark brown skin said a few words in a bizarre code. Nalas reacted to the meaningless phrases about dancing frogs or spinning turkeys as though they held great significance, and handed the boy twenty glint for whatever he'd said.

The chef set her food in front of her, and Sima pushed everything else out of her mind but enjoying her free meal. Bits of fish, shrimp, squid, and scallops mixed with noodles and ramen broth occupied her for almost twenty minutes of sheer joy.

"Looks like you were hungry," said Nalas with a smile.

"Yes. Thank you." Sima took a few breaths to mitigate her feeling of fullness. "So, how does this errand work? I carry the thing to Magdalena, and she pays me?"

"Not exactly. You'll come back to me here for your fee."

Sima nodded. "Okay."

"One moment." Nalas reached over and tugged her hood down, then brushed her hair off her shoulders so it fell behind her back.

"You said I wouldn't get made to prostitute. Why are you checking me out?"

"No." He shook his head. "You will most certainly not have to do that." Nalas held up a thin metal ring, but before she could get much of a look at it, he closed the choker around her neck with a soft, but sharp *click*.

Her hand flew to the front of her throat where the narrow band touched her skin. It didn't feel heavy or thick enough to be any sort of restraint device, more a piece of jewelry. "What's this for? Those boys didn't have them. Is it like proof I'm working for you or something?"

"Those associates of mine don't have them because they've been in my employ for a long time and I trust them. Call it a bit of insurance." Nalas pulled a metal box out from under his tunic, about the size of a brick, and set it in Sima's lap. "Here's the delivery."

"Insurance?" She fiddled with the choker, not liking the sound of that word at all.

"It is nothing to worry about provided you do not screw me over, in which case, it will blow up." Nalas continued smiling that same pleasant smile. "Disappear with the shipment, you lose your head. Take too long to return to me, you lose your head. Bring that box to the EGSF, you lose your head."

Sima gasped. Instant regret at agreeing to this job crashed into her meal, sending a bit of undigested food into the back of her mouth. She grabbed her throat and forced herself to swallow it again.

"Calm down, Sima." Nalas grasped her shoulders, patting one side. "I wouldn't have hired you if I didn't have every confidence you would do the job as requested. Forgive my distrust, but some of the more innocent looking Outcasts are often the most shady."

There's a bomb around my neck. She shivered. "I-is it gonna go off if it gets wet or I fall or something?"

"Well, I wouldn't pull at it. It's steel, but not terribly thick. If you did manage to break it off, it would detonate. Water's not a problem. I don't buy cheap." He winked. "Look, kid. Run the package and don't take any stupid shortcuts. I'm not an unreasonable man. All I want is to ensure my client's interests are satisfied."

Sima closed her eyes. *A hundred glint. A hundred glint.* Still shivering, she looked at him again, and nodded. "Okay. I swear I won't screw you over. Please don't hit the button."

"Take a moment and relax." Nalas tugged her hood back up. "If you run around looking that frightened, you'll attract attention."

She fidgeted at her pants where the fabric bunched up around her knees. "If you want me to calm down, you could forget about the bomb."

"We won't need that little bit of insurance once you prove yourself reliable enough." He held up a steaming cup of green tea in toast. "Just act natural. Oh, and try not to lose your head."

The ramen in her stomach did a backflip.

7

HOT POTATO

S ima hurried down the street, walking at a pace a hair shy of jogging. The thin metal band around her neck seemed to tighten with every step. She'd teased death numerous times in her life: narrowly avoiding gangs, being crushed under the wheels of a gee-vee, flirting with suicide at the landfill cliff… but walking around with a detonator strapped to her throat beat them all for sheer terror. Worse, the EGSF would probably arrest her for possession of an explosive device—assuming she survived meeting them.

Nalas' package sat in her tunic's front pocket, bumping against her stomach in time with her stride. She kept her hands stuffed in there as well, holding it. Mostly so she didn't surrender to the panic making her want to grab the choker and pull at it. The click it made going on sounded an awful lot like a lock. Despite knowing it wouldn't come off, the urge to try grew distracting.

She stopped walking and leaned against the wall, eyes closed and breathing hard. *Stop thinking about it. I gotta focus.* Worrying too much about what might happen would only keep her from noticing EGSF officers before she stumbled right into them. Every time she roamed around while her thoughts drifted off to daydreams or fears, cops came out of nowhere. She had to stay sharp as her life rather literally depended on it.

Go to Magdalena's. Give her the package. Leave. Easy. I can do this. I'm not breaking the law. Nalas never told me what's in this box. I'm not knowingly breaking the law. She bit her lip. Of course, the EGSF would say that she should've suspected illegality when he needed a bomb collar to keep her obedient. Even the very nature of the arrangement reeked of illicit endeavors. Though she'd only made it partially through sixth grade, Sima wasn't stupid. When she had actually gone to school, she did quite well. They'd look at her profile and know this, and they wouldn't believe her saying she had no idea what she did.

Grr. I'm making it worse! And I'm taking too long!

Eyes open, she pushed away from the wall and resumed heading toward Magdalena's. Thoughts of what she could do with a hundred glint helped take the edge off her fear of exploding or being arrested.

Unfortunately, Magdalena's brothel sat at the edge of a demolition zone two Blocks to the west, about three miles away. Much of Earth had been covered in city. In history class, she'd learned that cities used to have lots of open space between them back before the End of Nations. Now, without 'countries' to name places, the government divided the city into districts roughly 300 miles square, and each district had thousands of blocks.

Various places in the city had been demolished, either due to deliberate demolition for construction or as lingering aftereffects of the war that brought about the End of Nations. The purposeful ones tended to be tamer, as the others had been left to fester for centuries. Those held the treasures that scavengers could make a good living on —if they survived. Like layers of paint, some areas of the city had grown upward over the centuries. Scavvers could also explore the depths, occasionally finding antiques left behind. However, one misstep could send them plunging down a shaft they'd never escape.

Before Sima had been born, a swath of three or four Blocks near Mag's had been razed to the ground in preparation for rebuilding that still hadn't started. All manner of rumors circulated about the dangerous thugs living out among the rubbled high-rises and collapsed buildings. Though, Magdalena's palace occupied the very edge of it, closest to the city, and she had mercenaries working for her. Only an utter fool would venture past it and go out into the demolition zone. A fool, or an escaped prisoner who needed to flee a death sentence. The EGSF didn't go in there. Probable death beat definite death.

Side street after side street passed. Sima tried to act as casual as possible, hiding her face with her raised hood, avoiding eye contact with people, and keeping her attention focused on her surroundings. Any sign of blue and grey armor would be a major problem. Finding Magdalena's didn't take much effort. She had only to head west until she reached the border of the destruction, then figure out if she needed to go north or south along the edge. No Citizen dared go there, but someone like her wouldn't have much trouble. At least, not unless a pack of men decided to take interest in a lone young woman.

Blue in the crowd ahead caught her eye. A trio of EGSF officers emerged from a coffee shop about two blocks away. She calmly continued to the next cross street, the officers only one block distant, and crossed to the other side, continuing in that direction like she meant to go that way all along. A furtive glance to the right allowed her to relax: the officers hadn't mystically sensed her criminal activity and come running.

Heart pounding, she continued to the corner and hooked a right past an office building. Two slender black cameras on the wall panned to follow her. Sima shrank in on herself, unsure how loaf-shaped electronics could convey such disdain, as if the cameras themselves didn't trust 'someone like her' near the building. She hurried onward, once again heading west. Sweat coated her palms, her hands overly warm inside the pocket. She left them there, as she knew she'd not be able to resist fidgeting at the death locked around her neck.

People from Citizens to Outcasts milled back and forth on the street around her. She occasionally bumped shoulders, but no one paid her much notice. Eventually, she managed to scrape up a reasonable amount of confidence that she didn't look as terrified as she felt.

Just a girl with somewhere to be.

About a half-mile later, another set of EGSF officers came around the corner. Sima stopped short, the crowd continuing to flow around her. She stared at them for a second or two and did an about face, heading back the way she came.

She peered over her shoulder out of the corner of her eye, and her breath stalled at the sight of them looking right at her. *Crap! Stupid!*

Could I have been any more obvious? The instant both officers started walking toward her, she nearly hurled the ramen she'd eaten all over the street. Struggling to keep her jaw clamped shut, she rushed across the street and headed for the nearest alley.

The officers picked up their stride, clearly interested in checking her out.

Dammit! What was I supposed to do? If I walked too close to them, they'd have picked up the explosive… or the drugs. Panic set in and she broke into a sprint. The officers followed suit, likely convinced she'd done something wrong since only the guilty ran away.

Tears streaming from the corners of her eyes, Sima barreled around the corner into the alley. She jumped a series of vagrants asleep out in the open and grabbed the edge of an ORC bin to avoid wiping out on a hard left turn. Clomping EGSF boots echoed off the walls, drawing closer and closer.

The third alley she swerved into had a whole line of broken windows on the right side, barely a foot above ground level. Taking cover and hiding sounded like better odds than running, so she leapt through the first window and landed on an ancient floor of faux wood boards.

Tattered decorative paper hung from the walls. Little remained of any furniture, but the room held decades of windblown trash and dirt. The huge chamber must've been some sort of lobby or restaurant seating area. Frantic, she looked around for anywhere to hide. Only a decrepit counter and a hallway at the far end offered any sort of concealment, and the counter stood at an angle that would let anyone at the window still see her.

With the plastic clatter of EGSF armor rushing up to the alley outside, she sprinted across the room, straining to make it to the dark hallway before the cops got close. Going inside had been a gamble. This building would either offer a hiding place or be a trap.

Her sandals sent puffs of silt and dirt into the air as she dashed across the room. Seconds away from the opposite side, the old boards under her feet gave out when her foot plunged through a weak spot.

Sima fell in a flailing mass of limbs and broken bits of synthetic wood. The back of an old couch hit her in the gut, knocking the wind out of her and reducing vision to blank whiteness. She lay draped over the rotting furniture, unable to breathe in or out. Existing terror at the EGSF chasing her piled on top of her fears about the bomb. Sheer panic at her lungs no longer working pushed her over the edge.

The next thing she knew, she stared down at the floor, her body still draped over the couch. She could breathe again, though her stomach throbbed in pain. Realizing she must've blacked out, she scrambled back to her feet and looked up at the hole. At *not* seeing EGSF officers staring down at her, she almost fainted a second time from relief. When she swallowed saliva, the snug metal ring around her neck reminded her she had a time limit.

Tears ran down her cheeks. *I'm such an idiot! Why did I do this?* Shaking, she gathered her tunic over her mouth to shield herself from the heavy cloud of dust hanging in the air, and took in deep, slow breaths. Freaking out wouldn't keep her alive. She had to think.

I can do this. I'll be okay. Never again. I won't let it kill me!

The concrete-walled chamber she'd fallen into appeared to be a storage room for furniture. Dozens of decades-old sofas, loveseats, divans, end tables, and other things stood around in clusters. *This must've been a hotel or something. Guess I'm close to the demolition zone.* Only one opening offered a way out, unless she tried to build a ladder out of old chairs. Considering the floor had already given out under her, she didn't trust it. At least, not when she had a doorway to check first. With any luck, she could find the basement stairs and get out that way.

After a quick self-exam for splinters and wounds, which found only a bruise on her stomach, she limped toward the exit into a corridor of cinder blocks and mildew. Squiggles of black graffiti covered everything, including the ceiling. Plastic narcotic inhalers and needles crunched under her sandals. That a gang likely made its home in this place added another level of anxiety she didn't need. Her heart raced so much she became light-headed.

Karma… What am I doing breaking the law?

Naturally, everything possible would go wrong to punish her for flouting the promise she'd made to herself about the law. *Life lessons and stuff. Okay. I swear I'll never do anything like this again. I'd ditch the box and run if I didn't have a damn bomb on me. I don't have a choice. Please don't kill me.*

Sima crept forward, holding her breath as she entered a patch of awfulness that reeked like a sewer, though heavier on the acridness of urine. Holes in the ceiling let scraps of daylight in, enough to make out the general shapes of things but not give much detail. The darkness comforted her, since it helped hide her. She approached one room after another, peering around the doorjamb with one eye in search of stairs while expecting to find a gang. The first space had boilers, the next appeared to be a storage room full of boxes with no way out. She advanced with a slow creeping gait, trying to avoid stepping on crunching plastic that would give her away.

Distant voices murmured somewhere ahead, but echoes made it difficult to tell which direction she did *not* want to go. A group of mostly men laughed and howled, though a handful of women cheered or whooped along with them. She caught a random snippet about Newstar, a drug that put the user in a trancelike state for several hours. For all she knew, she might be carrying a whole box of that stuff.

Crack.

With a gasp, she whirled behind her toward the noise.

A man with lime green hair in a spiky sphere stood only a few paces behind her, frozen, having evidently been attempting to sneak up on her. Knife scars decorated his face, shoulders, and arms. Black mesh covered his chest, leaving little of his sinewy pectorals to the imagination. Below the waist, he wore a black skirt decorated with random metal fragments over dark blue pants. Both tall boots held giant blades in sheaths on the outside.

"Tasty," said the man.

She ran like hell.

Heedless of noise, she stomped across the inches-deep trash, crushing inhalers and take out cartons.

"Scathers!" roared the man. "We got rats!"

Sima knew screaming wouldn't help, but couldn't stop herself. She feared the Scathers more than any other gang—with the possible exception of the Blanks—due to murder games being their primary form of amusement. The man chased her from one corridor to the next until she wound up skidding around a corner into a dead end. With nowhere else to go, she sprinted through a double-door-sized opening on the right.

And ran straight into a pack of Scathers.

Men and women grabbed her, cheering and screaming as they pushed and tossed her back and forth. Sima clutched the box to her stomach with her left hand while feebly throwing punches. A never-ending sea of hands pulled and squeezed. Ugly faces, many covered in glowing colors from phosphorescent cosmetics or electronic tattoos, leered at her. Many chanted "Fresh meat."

She shrieked when her feet left the ground, the crowd drawing her up over their heads. Flailing and kicking, she flowed like a log upon a river of humanity, helpless to fight the current carrying her along. The chaotic swirl of bodies ended with a few seconds of freefall.

Her scream barely started before she landed flat on her back upon a damp mattress, ending her cry with a noise like a kicked chicken. Sima lay stunned, gazing up at the walls of a concrete pit about fifteen feet square. More spray paint writing surrounded her. 'Despair,' 'Fresh meat,' 'death,' 'Scathers rule,' and other heartwarming phrases weaved among crude renditions of skulls, Grim Reapers, and stick figure sex.

She lifted her head to peer past her feet at blurry lumps that focused into shapes she did not want to see. Gasping in disgust, she cringed away from mutilated hunks of dead bodies—or possibly bloody blankets. On the chance she might be sharing a pit with corpses, she refused to look.

Somehow, the Scathers had been so overjoyed at finding a victim for whatever depravity they intended to inflict upon her that they didn't search her. Nalas' precious cargo remained in her tunic pocket. She stared in horror at the top edge of the pit easily ten feet over her head or more. Perhaps they didn't search her yet because they'd have all the time in the world to pick over her corpse.

She raised a trembling hand to the front of her neck and clasped the detonator choker.

How long before I'm 'late,' and he kills me?

Stuck in a pit with no way out, surrounded by murderous Scathers, *and* with certain death locked around her neck, Sima curled up in a ball, shaking and crying.

Mommy! Help!

8

THE PIT OF DESPAIR

S cathers overhead continued to party… or do whatever it was they'd been doing before she arrived. Shouts of elation, screams of anger, and wild howls of abandon echoed off the grey concrete over hard music with shrieking vocals. She couldn't tell if someone *played* a guitar or fed it into a grinder.

Sima didn't dare yell out for her mother. Her instincts kicked in, specifically the need *not* to draw any attention to her existence. Quiet meant life. In a few minutes, she distanced herself from total panic and felt foolish. Her mother wouldn't lift a finger to help her, even out of this situation. In fact, the woman likely preferred that she had run away, as it spared her the financial burden of supporting a child.

A minute or two passed of incessant noise. Sima stood and looked around at her prison. The left wall had a bunch of broken-off pipes. To the right, what may have once been a narrow stairwell had been covered up with cinder blocks, converting the sunken hole into a true pit. Large pipe openings in the wall at the ground level hinted that this room once did something with water or other liquid, but she couldn't imagine what. Unfortunately, those pipes would be a tight squeeze even for a little boy as scrawny as Sayed. Sima had no chance of fitting, even if they would go somewhere useful and not be simple dead ends.

Three mattresses lay about, though she did her best not to look toward the wall behind her. Again and again, she told herself she'd seen only bloody blankets. Whether or not the stuff back there really was filthy cloth or actual dead bodies, she didn't care. As far as she allowed herself to think, she shared this hole with stained fabric and nothing worse.

I have got to get out of here. She peered up at the edge again. No telling how long the Scathers would keep her down here. Maybe she'd languish until they captured more people for whatever sick 'murder game' they would play. Of course, she wouldn't last too long thanks to the bomb.

Fear and desperation ganged up on her timidity. Having a few options with most of them ending in death made for a great source of artificial courage. Sima grabbed the mattress she landed on and dragged it up on edge. Since the Scathers decided to ignore her, she'd risk trying to escape. Doing nothing translated to death in at least two ways, so she had no reason to simply sit there and accept whatever fate had in store for her.

She didn't bother holding back grunts as she hauled the mattress to the side with the small pipe fragments. No one would hear her over the continuous shouting and awful music blaring overhead. After upending the mattress, she pushed it against the wall and grabbed the upper edge. Her sandals slipped over the padding as she tried to climb it. By sheer arm power alone, she pulled herself up enough to get a foot on one of the pipes. Fortunately, she didn't weigh enough that the mattress slid out from under her.

Using pipe handholds, Sima climbed until she stood upon the narrow end of the mattress. She stretched up to get her hands on the rim, set her foot on a six-inch pipe, and pulled herself up over the edge. The instant her chest passed the level of the floor, a man roared and grabbed two fistfuls of her hair.

Sima pounded her fist into his groin. He bellowed a wheeze, abandoning his grip on her hair as he doubled over cradling his crotch. She reached up, seized a fistful of beard, and wrenched downward, pulling him over the edge. The Scather screamed as he fell into the pit, landing with a meaty *smack* on bare concrete where a mattress used to be.

A woman with wild pink hair and a metal bikini top sprang at her, grasping her by the tunic and inadvertently *helping* her climb up out of the pit. The second Sima had her feet on the floor, she rammed her forehead into the woman's nose, setting off a waterfall of blood. The Scather staggered backward. Sima gave her a shove into the others coming toward her, which knocked them all back a step.

Surrendered to desperate panic, Sima lost all hesitation. She ducked another hand coming for her and sprinted three steps before driving a field goal kick into another man's crotch. He went down to his knees as a second woman grabbed her from behind. Thrashing and kicking, Sima flailed at her abductor. The woman lifted her off the ground, allowing Sima to mule-kick another man in the face with both feet, knocking him tumbling into the pit.

The woman tried to squeeze the air out of her lungs. Gurgling, Sima grabbed at the ganger's body until she got her hand on a knife. She tore the blade from the sheath and jabbed it backward. A scream of pain blasted the stink of cheap alcohol over her hair. The powerful grip around her chest released.

Sima stumbled forward, vaguely aware of the woman falling sideways, clutching her thigh. She swiped the twelve-inch blade at another man coming in to grab her, but he leapt back, avoiding her strike. Still, his hesitation gave her enough of an opening to dart past him to the door.

A gunshot rang out behind her and a spray of concrete dust showered her face from the left. Sima ducked and ran into the corridor. The gun went off three more times, but she had no idea where the shots went. Thirty or so Scathers piled into the hall behind her, delayed by so many attempting to squeeze into a single doorway at once.

She rushed past room after room, peering in at useless dead ends. Another shot rang out a half-second after she rounded a rightward corner at the end of the hallway. Sima flinched, crying out in shock at the *ping-ping-thunk* of a ricochet too close for comfort. Red steel doors at the end teased her with hope.

Leaning into her stride, Sima turned her left shoulder forward, not caring how much the approaching impact hurt as long as the door opened. She had only seconds before the armed Scather came around the corner behind her and had a clear shot, and she doubted he'd miss. Diving into an opening on the side might protect her from the immediate bullet, but a dead end room would mean certain death.

Sima crashed into the red door, bashing it open to reveal a stairwell. Wasting no time on happiness, she leapt ahead, taking the steps two at a time. She gripped the railing at the top, hurling herself around the switchback right as the onrushing mass of Scathers came into view out in the hall. At the top of the second landing, she flung herself at the door, but it wouldn't budge. After ramming it twice to no success, she kept going up.

The second story door also refused to budge.

"No!" she yelled, and kicked the push bar, the hollow *clank* echoing in the stairwell. "Damn!"

Angry shouts continued in the stairs, drawing nearer.

She darted around two more switchbacks to the third floor, which had no door at all. Most of the walls on that level had disintegrated, leaving it a giant open area full of columns. Her heart sank at the total lack of cover. An instant before she decided to keep going up, a glimmer of metal caught her eye from a fire escape outside. Deciding in that split second to go for it, she bolted into the room.

Fragments of wall, hunks of drop ceiling foam, and empty bottles scattered away from her feet as Sima sprinted across the vast openness of a destroyed hotel. She jumped past a curtain of tattered plastic tarps out the window onto a suspended deck that likely hadn't been touched in decades. Metal creaked and groaned under her, but held her weight despite all the bouncing. The big Scather appeared out in the room and leveled his handgun off at her. With a yelp, she dove flat on her chest upon the steel gridding fast enough that he didn't bother taking the shot.

Gangers roared and cheered—chasing a 'murder ball' is exactly what they'd wanted of her, though she'd started the game early. The rapid clomping of many boots drew nearer upon the debris-strewn floor.

Sima crawled to the end of the fire escape and slithered onto the steps down. She got her feet under her about halfway to the next landing and ran, shrieking as bullets glanced off the steel around her, setting off sprays of sparks. Metal objects whistled by, thrown knives or other pointy things she didn't dare look at.

At the second story, she decided to leap straight off the end of the fire escape, aiming for the top of an ORC bin. The plastic lid absorbed her impact and bounced her a little back into the air. She landed on the pavement, arms flailing, but kept her balance and dashed out into the street.

Four cross-streets later, she threw the knife aside so she wouldn't be arrested for having it. Her legs quit on her not long after, but she refused to stop. Though she couldn't run anymore, she managed a wobbly walking pace, terrified she might have only seconds left before her head exploded. Nalas hadn't given her any indication of *what* her time limit was, only that she had one. Blacking out for who knows how long, plus being thrown in a pit had both been unnecessary and potentially fatal diversions.

Sick to her stomach, Sima wanted only to curl up somewhere and cry for a parent she never really had, but that wouldn't accomplish a damn thing except make her miserable for the last few moments of her life—until the choker went off.

Another turn brought her back to a street with pedestrian traffic. She forced herself to fall in with the people around her at an unassuming stride. Her forehead ached from where she'd mashed that Scather's nose in. A few wipes with her hand cleared some blood away. Sima huddled forward and pulled her hood up, trying to hide any blood or bruises that might attract unwanted attention.

Soon, she entered a familiar area packed with the poor, as well as criminals and lowlifes. She only had a little way to go before reaching Magdalena's. Still, the poor had actual social standing, being Citizens rather than Outcasts. They mostly made an honest living at legal employment. Almost no one would hire Outcasts for legit jobs, except trash cleanup or handling dangerous materials, or doing tasks no Citizen would dare touch.

While the next few streets she needed to traverse would likely not hold the sort of gang punks who'd spontaneously attack her, they had other dangers: thieves, dealers, and pimps mostly. Well, perhaps not pimps. Not this close to Magdalena's. Rumor had it that she arranged for pimps to disappear if they worked too close to her front door. Other rumors said she did more than 'arrange' their deaths, having a more hands (or claws) on approach.

Sima clutched the precious box tight in her tunic pocket. The holocom the EGSF officer gave her brushed her knuckle. That 'Progenitor' thing couldn't be as terrifying as winding up in a Scather's pit. Still, she didn't quite trust it. Maybe she'd talk to Magdalena about becoming a prostitute. Even that didn't scare her as much as a murderous gang or a bomb locked around her throat.

With all her heart, she wished she'd never talked to Nalas and wound up in this predicament. But wishes were for children, and at sixteen, she'd left childhood way behind.

Sima smirked, thinking about cooking for herself, doing her own laundry, making sure she got to school on time, and living with a mother who barely even looked at her.

I left childhood behind at like seven.

People in tunics and ponchos eyed her warily as she navigated dirt streets packed with merchant stalls, traders, and shifty-eyed men. Poor Citizens kept their eyes down and hurried along. Anyone who made eye contact with her either wanted to sell something or had darker intentions. She did her best to keep her gaze on the ground like any other innocent person, though did peer up every so often to check for EGSF. She'd gotten past the worst part, the 'nicer' areas where she usually begged. EGSF didn't come out this close to the demolition zone often, at least not unless a specific event attracted them.

Her stomach twisted up in mixed emotions when she came within sight of Magdalena's. The brothel occupied the lowest four floors of a bombed-out looking high-rise. Little of the front wall remained for at least ten stories, allowing wind and prying eyes easy access to the interior. Gaudy folding barricades of red and gold blocked off much of the second, third, and fourth floors. Higher than that, the place looked deserted.

An open courtyard in front of the building held a ring of sofas against the crumbling walls, as well as a bar counter selling alcoholic drinks to anyone willing to overpay. The décor clashed in a bizarre mixture of modern day and an aesthetic she'd heard described as 'Old West.' She couldn't understand why a society that routinely explored space, having created settlements on the moon and Mars, would bother with the styles of centuries ago.

Ignoring the stares of men lounging about and drinking, Sima hurried across the courtyard toward the gaping maw of the ground-level rooms. Lacy red bras and women's underthings dangled from rebar struts jutting from the broken edge overhead. Above it, a holographic sign displayed the words 'Magdalena's Parlor.' She leaned around the undergarments and stepped into the shade of the hanging concrete slab that comprised the second story floor.

The interior lobby had fancier divans and sofas. Women, girls, and two boys about her age sat around waiting for clients. Most dressed in little beyond their decorative underthings and a handful even bared their breasts. One blonde girl stretched out on a pink divan wore a lacy lavender bra that clearly held nothing but air, frilly panties, and thigh-high lavender stockings. A ring of purple silk roses adorned her left ankle. Sima gawked in horror at the small prostitute, who couldn't have been older than thirteen. The child waved a dark red folding fan at her face, tossing her hair about while smiling at Sima as if inviting her closer for a good time.

Another girl to the right appeared a little older, but still younger than Sima. The rest ranged in age from late teens to their early forties. A few she even recognized, having seen them begging a while back, but none so familiar she knew their names.

"Can I help you, sugar?" asked a woman with red curls and an overly elaborate dress, standing behind a counter at the back of the room.

Sima pulled her gaze off the too-young blonde, a bizarre sense of rage welling up inside her. She fumed at a society that could allow such a thing, at the sort of men who'd hire a prostitute that young, and the people running this place who'd take advantage of her. Her ambivalence toward Magdalena melted into a quiet hatred. Again, she glanced over at the blonde, barely covered in small, frilly underthings. The girl's look of ease at her situation suggested she'd been here long enough to have no trace of innocence left.

A hollow emptiness weighed Sima's heart, as though she stared at a dead girl who continued to move around.

"Sugar?" asked the redhead. "Are you okay?"

No. Sima swallowed, again becoming acutely aware of the metal around her neck. She snapped out of her guilty fugue and approached the counter. The woman's dress had flickering lights arranged around its Old West stylings. Eye rings holding the cord cinching her black lace corset all lit up purple. Glowing gems along the decorative sleeves likely served the same function as the white square at the end of her tunic, controls for a built-in Omnicomputer. Her puffy shoulders and tiered skirt had a deep red color, like rose petals, the fabric glowing in the castoff light from a holo-terminal on the desk that displayed a list of rooms, timers, and girls' names.

"You here to forget stuff for a while? I can set you up with Flora if you like. Noticed you looking at her," said the woman. "She's never worked with a girl before, but she's a fast learner. Of course, she's a premium fare: only 300 glint per hour."

The too-young blonde winked at Sima.

She cringed inside, and shook her head. "No, thanks. I need to see Magdalena."

"Oh, Mag doesn't work directly with clients anymore. If you can't afford Flora, what about Dawn?" The redhead gestured at a woman in her later twenties with pale skin and black hair. She can take care of you for fifty. Or do you fancy a boy?"

Sima grabbed the counter and leaned up on tiptoe. "I'm not here for *that*. I need to see Magdalena." She lifted her head and tapped the choker. "It's urgent. I'm delivering."

"Oh!" The redhead's green eyes widened. "I'm sorry. I misunderstood." She moved to the far right side of the counter and gestured at a hallway lined with fading wallpaper, white with gold fleur-de-lis. "Go down there to the last door."

Sima did her best not to cry as she rounded the corner and headed into the dim hallway. At least two (probably four) of those prostitutes had no business being there. *How* could the EGSF allow girls that young to do *this*? How could any reasonable adult stand idly by and not do something about that? Leaving young Outcasts to fend for themselves in the streets was bad enough, but *prostitution?* Every breath of air she drew in this place tasted like the death of innocence.

The corridor went past six doors on either side before hitting a right turn. The second section ended at a pair of ornate double doors with four men standing two per side, one pale, two Middle Eastern, one African. Three pulled tunics aside to reveal handguns on their belts, while the larger of the Middle Eastern guys pointed a submachine gun somewhat in her direction.

Sima stopped short, raising her hands.

"Private area. Get lost," said the guy with weapon trained on her.

"I've got a delivery for Magdalena." Again, she tapped the choker.

The African man stepped forward, waving at the others to calm down. When he got close enough, he put a finger under her chin, lifting her head. Despite his being huge, armed, and likely willing to kill anyone who pissed him off, Sima felt paradoxically safer in his presence after her run in with the Scathers. She entertained a momentary daydream of him machine-gunning down that pack of thugs who had been chasing her. Fear must've continued leaking from her eyes, as the guy gave her a sympathetic sigh.

"Looks fine," said the guy. He put a hand to her back and guided her over to the door.

"Let's see the package," said Submachine Gun Man.

Sima withdrew the brick-sized box from her pocket, but didn't let go of it.

"Give it a little shake," said the man.

She did, and it rattled like a tin full of tiny beads.

"All right." He lowered the submachine gun and opened the door for her. "Don't do anything you'll regret."

"I won't. Trust me, I wanna get out of here as fast as I can." She managed a weak smile and stepped past the door.

Magdalena's office looked like something lifted out of many centuries ago. Faux oil lamps, paintings on the dark wooden walls, the style of chairs and tables, even the curtains around a huge four-poster bed in the back. A tall, ghostly-pale woman with fluffy black hair sat behind a huge desk littered with holocoms, small computer components, and a terminal display. She wore an elaborate shoulder-baring old-timey dress of dark violet, accented here and there with black fabric roses. The cord cinching her ebony corset glowed pale lavender.

The breath caught in Sima's chest when the woman lifted her head and made eye contact. Striking violet eyes with glowing irises fixated on her. Other than the outlandish color (and luminosity) they looked more human than Sima had expected. The woman's arms, however, were metal. Dark, burnished steel approximated the contours of delicate femininity, but ended in razor-sharp claws so thin they appeared as likely to snap as leave horrible wounds. A few subtle lines in the woman's face and down the side of her neck suggested the skin might be artificial, or at least heavily infused with augmentation. The desk blocked any view of the woman below the waist, so Sima couldn't tell if the rumor about her eight-legged metal spider body had any truth.

At the corner, a huge, square bottle held a few inches of dark brown liquid, probably booze.

"Hello, girl," said Magdalena, in a voice far more normal than fit her appearance. "You must have something for me if you're standing here."

"Yes." She crept up to the desk, holding out the box. "This is from Nalas."

"Ahh, yes. Thank you." Magdalena's fingers shrank from nine-inch tapered points to human-length with a faintly audible whirr, and *clicked* against the metal box as she clasped it. "I hope you didn't have too much trouble with this. What has frightened you so?"

Sima gulped.

"Oh, girl." Magdalena set the box down on the desk. "I can see your heart racing, all the blood rushing to your face, and how fast you're breathing. Something happened. Do you want to talk about it?"

Hands clasped in front of her, Sima looked down. "Well… I'm a little nervous about having a bomb locked around my throat. And the Scathers almost killed me."

Magdalena's expression darkened. "I've told that man how I felt about those things…" She pointed at the choker. "Excuse me a moment." She got a far-off look in her glowing eyes.

Patient, Sima stood there in silence.

"Hello, Nalas," said Magdalena to thin air. "Your courier has arrived. I couldn't help but notice you gave her one of those necklaces." She paused a moment. "I'm aware of your concerns, but you know how I feel about that."

Sima figured the woman had some kind of communicator in her head. Normally, when someone placed a holocom call, a digital 'ghost' of the other person would appear to facilitate a face-to-face conversation. Given the state of the surrounding building, it seemed unlikely any functional trace of the holo-net remained nearby. She wanted to back away as Magdalena launched into a tirade about how angry it made her watching young ladies be put at needless risk. The idea that an explosive choker around her neck pushed this woman to such a state of rage, the same woman who employed too-young prostitutes, left her speechless. Though she entertained the idea of saying something like if she wanted to protect young people, she shouldn't force them to have sex with strangers for money, Sima decided against ticking off a woman who could possibly turn her into thinly sliced Outcast with a single swipe of her hand.

The rant ended with Magdalena's clipped, "See that you do." Her gaze once more focused on Sima. "Do not fear the detonator. I've assured him the product is intact. Your life is no longer at risk, though I suggest you return to him soon to be rid of it and collect your fee."

"Thank you." Sima took a step back.

"You have such soulful eyes," said Magdalena. "I sense you've experienced much pain in your short life. It'd take a little scrubbing, but I could certainly make room for you here if you're tired of being on the street. Alas, I also get the feeling you've got a few misconceptions about what we do here."

Sima couldn't get the image of Flora out of her head. That girl remained a child young enough to cause feelings of jealousy in regard to begging. She couldn't process how someone that age would willingly subject herself to what went on here. Doubt crept in that perhaps she placed too much significance on sex, trying to wait for the boy she'd want to be with for the rest of her life. Perhaps the rest of the world had an entirely different view. Magdalena had become angry at Nalas for risking Sima's life with a bomb, yet paying a child to entertain grown men somehow didn't bother this woman. The contradiction short-circuited her brain.

"Well, it looks like you've got a lot to think about." Magdalena rose from her chair without a sound and glided around her desk. The elaborate purple gown with black underpinnings concealed her legs, but her motion and appearance looked completely human. She had two legs, though whether metal or flesh Sima couldn't tell. "I will let

Clare know she can send you back to see me if you change your mind."

Sima could only blurt, "Thanks," her mind too burdened with contradictions, fear, and the need to get away from the damn bomb. Even if Nalas promised not to set it off, she wanted it *gone*.

"Now, you should probably run and get that nasty little thing off your neck." Magdalena tapped the choker with a loud metal *click-click-click* that made the hairs on the back of Sima's neck stand on end. "It would anger me greatly if he were to accidentally harm such a pretty young thing."

The nauseating thought that this partially-human woman radiated more of a sense of motherly protection toward Sima than her actual mother ever did bubbled in the back of her throat. Could she ever be *that* desperate for protection that she'd cling to a figure like Magdalena for shelter?

After her run-in with the Scathers, she horrified herself with the answer.

Yes.

With a tentative nod, Sima muttered, "Thank you," and scurried out of the room.

9

MOMENT OF OPPORTUNITY

Her near miss with the Scathers caused Sima to stick to more populated streets on her walk back to meet Nalas.

True, the EGSF might detect the explosive device. True, despite it being *locked* around her neck, a chance existed they would charge her for possessing it. Hood up, hands in her front pocket, she kept her gaze on the ground, hoping they didn't notice her and finding it difficult to care that much if they did.

Magdalena somewhat offered a potential mother figure, but what mother would ask a girl as young as Flora to sell herself to men? She doubted 'Flora' was the girl's real name, but maybe using a false name helped her not think about what she had to do. The kid could be playing a role like an actress, thinking 'Flora' did all the nasty things, but her 'real self' remained innocent. Perhaps she could do that as well, stuff all the horrible sights and feelings away into some made up name. She pretended to be thirteen or fourteen all the time to beg; she could play a role, too.

"Ugh." Sima shivered.

As tempting as it would be not to have to worry about gang punks using her as a murderball in some twisted sport, she couldn't quite get past that woman's creepiness. With each step farther away from the brothel, the more *inhuman* Magdalena seemed. Not a woman, not a mother, merely some creature pretending at both. In some way, she or it may care about the physical health of her charges, but perhaps only because a dead (or mutilated) teen couldn't work for her.

She fidgeted at the holocom between her hands. The small hunk of plastic would trigger a call to the nice EGSF officer. Even thinking 'nice' in the same mindspace as EGSF barely computed. Sure, the few times she'd encountered them as a young child before she became an Outcast, they had been reasonably civil. Her mother hadn't been rich, quite far from it, but she had been a Citizen.

As a minor, she would legally fall under her mother's social class until eighteen. At least, unless the woman had disowned her. If the woman died before she reached eighteen, Sima would've reverted to her biological father's level. However, since the man wanted nothing to do with her, he'd certainly reject her. She'd wind up as an Outcast legally, at least until eighteen when she could apply for citizenship. Normal kids with normal parents became Citizens automatically upon completion of advanced school at eighteen, provided they entered university or trade training. Considering she hadn't touched schoolwork since twelve, she'd never pass any citizenship exam.

Her three choices wound up being:

Die (brutally) on the street.

Die (inside) at Magdalena's.

Die (painfully) at whatever sick science project the EGSF wanted her for.

The only reasons she could think of for the officers to be nice to her all painted vivid, nightmarish scenes in her mind involving medical experimentation. However, a little nibble of doubt remained. If they meant to hurt the young Outcasts, why *ask* her to go? Wouldn't they have simply arrested her and forced her into that 'Progenitor' thing?

Did they get Cassie at the Crash? Sima lifted her head and scanned the crowd. A few people made for prime begging targets, but she lacked the motivation to bother. She *still* hadn't stopped shaking from her scare with the Scathers, and thoughts of becoming either a prostitute or a guinea pig left her mood dragging along the ground behind her. Plus, the only somewhat-friend she had, Cassie, might be in jail or worse.

Her tunic remained dead, so she couldn't try to call her.

She sighed, and kept on walking.

Twenty minutes or so later, she sidled up to the corner noodle bar. Nalas sat on the same stool, only with his back to the counter, observing people walking by.

"Hey, Sima." He raised an arm in greeting.

She tried not to scowl at him for putting a bomb around her neck. "Hey."

He tapped one of the numerous bits of electronic hardware sewn into his tunic, and a holographic panel opened beside his shoulder. After two finger pokes, the display collapsed and a beep came from the choker. The back end popped open with a sharp *snap*. Sima grabbed it at the front of her neck and yanked it away, tossing it to him.

"So..." She fidgeted, nauseous at the smell of ramen.

"Nice work, kid. Much faster than I expected."

Sima rubbed her neck. "I thought I was running out of time."

"Nah. I almost never actually hit the bad button over a courier taking too long. Unless they go where they really shouldn't."

"Tracker," muttered Sima.

Nalas grinned. "Hah. You're pretty smart for an Outcast. How'd you figure it out?"

"Huh?"

He held up the thin choker. "This thing's only a tracker, kid. I ain't stupid enough to carry explosives around the city. That'll get me forty years. Besides, the last thing I wanna do is blow some little girl's head off."

Sima doubled over, almost ready to puke. As soon as she no longer feared vomiting if she opened her mouth, she sprang upright and yelled, "You lied to me! Do you have any idea how terrified I was?"

He leaned back with a rogue's grin. "I can estimate with a reasonable degree of accuracy."

Ooh! She balled her hands in fists, ready to punch him straight in his lying face—but he still owed her a hundred glint. "That was... mean!"

Nalas chuckled and took a plastic case about the size of a soap bar out of his left pocket, offering it with a well-practiced smile. "As promised."

She took it and gingerly lifted the lid, gasping at the sight of five neat rows of UMU chips in foam. Never before had she possessed so much glint at a time. A hundred was almost a large enough sum for a middle-class Citizen to have to debate spending.

"I could use an honest runner," said Nalas. "It's not a glorious life, but you'd do much better than begging."

Her head started shaking before she even thought about it. "I dunno." The shaking migrated until her entire body trembled. "I don't think I wanna do that again."

Nalas tilted his head, a look of concern in his hazel eyes. "What happened?"

"Well, uhh, thinking I'm gonna die at any second from a bomb. Getting chased—"

"The bomb was just a story to make sure you came back and didn't steal." He took a sip of hot tea.

Sima glared at him. "Still! You let me think I was gonna die! And explosives! The EGSF would've arrested me for having explosives even though it was locked around my throat!"

He nodded. "Yeah, they probably would... *if* you'd had actual explosives on you."

"I almost got killed by a gang..." She ranted at him about the pit, and feeling trapped between the bomb and Scathers, so terrified she *attacked* people.

"Whoa. Damn, girl. Hey, look. You passed the test, okay? If you work for me again, I promise, no jewelry will be involved."

But he'd still ask me to carry stuff that'll put me in jail. Couriering drugs, whoring, or trusting the EGSF. That ledge over the landfill started to sound like the least painful option, since all roads appeared to lead to death. "I got a lot in my head right now. Need to think, okay? Maybe I will, but I don't know."

"Understandable. I'm here three days a week, so if you decide you'd rather sneak around alleys than sell yourself for Mag, come right on back. Ain't all about moving special boxes either. Sometimes, you'd only carry messages or try to slip in somewhere and listen in on stuff."

She nodded. It sounded both interesting and dangerous as hell, the sort of thing she'd love to read about in a story, but not actually *live*. Maybe Cassie had a point after all. Sima tried too hard to be the 'good girl,' despite what life had done to her. Deep down inside, she remained the frightened twelve-year-old who ran out her mother's door. The way she continued clinging to begging—like a child—only proved that point. She'd been sixteen for a whole month already, time to grow up. The good girl act would only get her killed.

"I got a couple things I might do. Just trying to figure out what I want, yanno? If you mean it about no more, umm, jewelry, maybe I'll work for you."

"Sure, sure." Nalas gave her a confident nod, as if he knew already she'd be back. "Take a couple days, enjoy that glint. Go get yourself a nice meal and spend the night in a mod bed."

She hadn't even thought of that. Near the district center, hotels offered cheap beds in chambers a little bigger than coffins. It had been a *long* time since she slept on something nicer than ripped up plastic bags. Frivolous as that sounded, she couldn't help but be tempted.

"'Kay."

He smiled again as she wandered off, not really sure where to go. Around and around, her brain spun, weighing Magdalena, the EGSF, and Nalas. Flashes of screaming Scathers flickered by, along with the horrible, heart-melting sadness lurking in Flora's eyes. It hadn't struck her at the time, but she felt certain the girl had been staring at her asking for help. Or maybe Sima simply refused to believe a girl that age could be capable of existing in that situation without being broken. A fantasy stirred in her mind of sneaking in to 'rescue' Flora, but she couldn't exactly offer that girl much of a better life.

What's wrong with me? She wiped a tear she hadn't noticed until it tickled her cheek. *I hate being around kids.*

She wandered for a while, numb in the head. When it started to get dark, she ducked into a small restaurant named H355. The last time she'd gone into one, she tried begging, but the manager kicked her out. Unlike the outdoor food counters that charged between one to four glint a meal, these places charged ten or more per plate—though they claimed the food came from grow tanks rather than printed by fabricators from protein slime.

A woman behind the order counter in a white tunic with bright cyan hair shot her a dirty look. She had vaguely Chinese features but snowy skin, and unnatural eyes the same shade of blue as her hair.

Sima approached. "I can pay."

"What perfume is that?" asked the woman with a catty tone. "Smells familiar."

Ignoring the comment about how she still reeked of trash, Sima read over the menu. "Can I get the chicken parmesan please?"

The woman folded her arms.

"How much?"

"Ten."

Sima pulled out the case Nalas gave her, took ten UMU chips out, and held them up.

"At least sit in the corner over by the window," said the woman while taking the money.

"Yeah, sure."

The woman tapped at the holographic screen. "Please have a seat. Your food will be out in a few minutes."

"Okay. Thanks." Sima headed over to the corner table by the front window and sat with her back to the wall.

A little while later, a man entered with two preteen boys following. All three wore neat, black tunics with blue electronics and white pants. The boys glanced her way out of curiosity, but neither spoke. They hovered at the counter murmuring with the woman for a little while before moving off to a booth on the other side. Sima couldn't help but notice the man hadn't handed over any money.

Minutes later, a robotic cart rolled out from a back door and brought plates over to the guy and his sons. Sima sighed. She waited a little while more before getting annoyed enough to complain, but as soon as she started to stand up, the robo-cart emerged from the back and headed toward her.

She relaxed, waiting as the machine set a plate of food and cup of water in front of her then glided off to its door again. It had been years since she had an actual meal while sitting at a real table. The sight brought her back to being a kid at home, even if she had to cook for herself. Her mother never ate at the same time, since Sima couldn't use the fabricator and stove while Mom did, but naturally, she wound up responsible for doing *all* the dishes.

Sima took her time with the chicken parmesan over pasta, savoring every mouthful. She could've eaten five meals for what this one cost, so she damn sure wanted to enjoy it. The man and his sons finished eating. He approached the counter again, this time to pay, but she refused to let that woman's treatment of her ruin the meal.

Even if she had to prepay for it, the food tasted amazing.

The man and his boys left. Sima finished her meal and remained sitting at the table, leaning against the corner wall.

"Are you planning to sleep there?" asked the woman behind the counter. "We're not open all night, you know."

"Sorry."

Lacking the energy for an argument, or the desire to have the EGSF called on her, she stood and walked out. Two blocks later, she felt like an idiot for spending so much on one meal. Cassie always said as soon as a street kid got real money, they blew it all on nothing. One decent meal couldn't be superfluous, but it still felt like a waste. Not as if she'd bought drugs or fancy clothing—though she still might drop twenty or so glint on real shoes, having become tired of power cables digging into her ankles.

She trudged aimlessly for about an hour before realizing she'd auto-piloted back to her Crash. The place appeared deserted, so she went down the ramp of collapsed street into the multi-chambered hollow she'd used as a home for the past few months. With all the trash lying around, she couldn't tell if much appeared out of place, but her personal space looked the same as she remembered it.

The charger for the tunic remained in her little pile of possessions. She fished it out and stuffed it in her pocket before flopping upon her mattress of trash bags. After taking her sandals off, she curled up and closed her eyes. Despite having the most terrifying day of her life, she'd become so exhausted, she passed out in only a few minutes.

SIMA AWOKE IN A FOG.

Before she could even sit up, her brain launched into the circular worry storm that had plagued her for the last half of the previous day. Magdalena. Nalas. EGSF. The three options went back and forth, rearranging themselves in order from least appealing to blah. She felt as though the universe mandated the end of her life and offered her a choice between gun, knife, or poison.

Nalas, at least, left her survival more in her control. Working for him wouldn't require she sell her body, and the chances of her being killed roughly equivocated to her degree of caution, skill, or luck. He offered decent money, but working for him could kill her or land her in prison.

Magdalena on the other hand would require she abandon the deepest parts of her dignity to total strangers. She tried to understand why she felt *selling* sex somehow wound up being worse than her mother's boyfriend wanting to take it. *I'd be surrendering instead of being attacked.* She hugged her knees to her chest, shivering at the memory of him touching her in the kitchen. *That wasn't my fault. I don't care what you said, Mom. That wasn't my fault. It was his.* Working for Magdalena felt hypocritical. She'd run away from home to *avoid* that. Throwing herself into the life of a prostitute would make her mother laugh at her.

No. Magdalena was out.

The EGSF confused her. What they offered—insertion back into a 'normal' life somehow—sounded far too good to be true. But she still had no explanation for their *asking* instead of merely dragging her off against her will. Could she ask them more questions without being stuck?

Sima decided she needed more information about that to make a decision. She'd either wind up working for Nalas or trusting the EGSF, which, based on past experience and rumor, would probably be a bad choice. Though, she couldn't stop thinking about the oddity of them being friendly. It gnawed on her brain and made her distrust the situation even more.

After tying her sandals back on, she climbed out of her 'room' and went down into the sewer tunnel to relieve herself. With the Crash abandoned, she enjoyed a sense of security she'd almost forgotten. Despite being in a wide-open hallway, she had privacy. Instead of the embarrassment of other Outcasts seeing her, she only had to worry about not falling into the effluent flow while balancing on the side of the walkway next to it.

Upon returning to the surface, she pulled her hood up to protect against a light drizzle and walked out of the alley, turning right onto the street before falling in step with pedestrian traffic. A few minutes passed before she realized she'd lapsed back into her old routine, automatically going toward the area where she'd spent the past few months begging. She had to be carrying about 140 or so glint, though she hadn't counted the contents of the pouch around her neck. She *could* last a week or two without having to do anything at all before money got tight and reality forced her to make a decision. The EGSF probably wouldn't raid her Crash again, but being the only one there had been eerie.

Sima stuck her hands in her front pocket and made a smaller decision: she'd buy real shoes, and then use the holocom to talk to the EGSF officer and see what he had to say about her suspicions. With a plan came a smile, and a slight increase in her stride. Now, she had only to find a store that both sold shoes in her price range and wouldn't kick her out for smelling like an ORC bin. If she would wind up dead working for Nalas or dead in some lab, at least she'd have good shoes.

Screams rose out of the crowd behind her, rushing closer.

She whipped around, staring at a pair of green gee-vees racing down the street, neck and neck. The one on the left swerved toward the opposite side, clipping a few pedestrians and throwing them into the wall. One guy disappeared under its six wheels. Three EGSF gee-vees covered in flashing lights pursued them; armored figures hanging out the sides fired their rifles at the fleeing cars.

Sima shrieked and dove to the ground two seconds before a man less than fifteen feet away from her took a bullet in the leg and hit the sidewalk howling. All five vehicles rumbled by, kicking up a wind that whipped her tunic and hair about. Moans of pain emanated from those hit by the cars or shot by accident.

Tires squealed in the distance, and a tremendous *crash* shook the earth. Seconds later, a great moan of stressed metal like the final wail of a dying giant rang out. A second heavy *crash* rumbled, much stronger than the first. Sima pushed herself up to stand. Four blocks away, a huge cargo transport lay on its side, the nose end smashed into a building. The box portion at the back had ruptured, spilling thousands of small, silver packets all over the road.

EGSF officers leapt from their vehicles and opened fire on one of the gee-vees that lay in the street near the truck, its nose end crumpled from an impact. The two men and one woman inside never even got the doors open before the hail of bullets shredded them. Another pair of women and two men scrambled out of the second gee-vee, which had rolled upside down. They all had guns, but none made a move to return fire at the cops, instead ducking and shouting while disappearing into an alley.

The EGSF officers gave chase, ignoring the bleeding man struggling to crawl out of the flipped over cargo transport.

Normally, a scene like that would send any rational Outcast looking for the nearest place to get below ground, lest they got caught up in the fallout. However, the temptation of thousands of nutri-packs laying out in the open proved too strong to resist. Sima headed toward the crash, against the flow of fleeing pedestrians. She weaved around people for about a block and a half before the crowd thinned enough to let her up to a full run.

A few other Outcasts came running from nearby side streets and dove into the sea of free food, scrambling to stuff their pockets with as much as they could get their hands on. Sima joined the fray with the eager abandon of a small girl encountering a vast field of candy. She skidded to a stop on her knees in the glorious bounty, scooping up handful after handful of the squishy Mylar pouches, and stuffing them in her front pocket. When that filled, she pulled the front of her tunic up to form a bowl, and kept on grabbing.

The driver from the cargo transport shouted at them, calling them thieves and rats.

She ignored him, scrambling to gather up as many packets as she could.

"Seps!" yelled the driver. "Stealing my cargo!"

No! Sima lunged to her feet, clinging to an armload of nutri-packets. Even the mere accusation of being a rebel could be fatal. A few pouches slipped from her grasp as she pivoted toward an alley, but before she could take two steps, EGSF officers came running out of the side street where the gunfire had been raging seconds before.

"We're not Separatists!" screamed Sima. "He's lying!"

"Don't move!" called a male officer, pointing his rifle at her.

Sima couldn't have run if she wanted to; every muscle in her body locked.

The other Outcasts, some dozen or so, panicked. A man and a boy about her age reacted as she did, with paralysis. Other teens and some twentysomethings took off running in random directions, a few dropping their collected nutri-packs.

Three officers opened fire on the fleeing Outcasts, but the one pointing his weapon at Sima didn't shoot. Voices cried out in agony from seeming everywhere. The terrible thunder nearly made her bladder let go.

Sima stared down the barrel of a rifle for two seconds before shrieking, "Please don't kill me! I'm just a kid!"

"On the ground. Do it slow," shouted the man aiming at her.

She let the packets fall around her feet and raised her hands out high and to the side. Gradually, she lowered herself to kneel and then lay flat on her stomach, gazing sideways over a sea of shimmery silver plastic at two inert bodies and three teens writhing in pain.

Boots tromped up, inches from the top of her head. She couldn't see, but *felt* the rifle still pointed at her. Seconds passed. A woman shouted, "Clear." Hands wrapped in armored gloves patted her down. Upon finding no weapons, the officer pulled her arms behind her back and locked metal restraints around her wrists.

She gasped at the painful tightness, unable to suppress a whine of, "Ow."

He grabbed her by one arm and dragged her upright. "So you're not a rebel, huh?"

"No, sir," she mewled.

"Name, age, registration."

"Sima Nuvari. I'm sixteen. CR23910822-dash-B0642F12."

She'd memorized that number in first grade. Her identity. Citizen Record, birthdate August 22, 2391. The twelfth female child born that day in Block 642.

"What are you doing here if you're not part of a rebel attack on this food truck?"

"I swear I was just begging down the street, but when I saw all this food, I couldn't help it. I'm sorry. I haven't eaten much in a couple days."

The officer lightly gripped her chin and lifted her so she made eye contact with his blank silver visor. Silence stretched over a minute. Wounded Outcasts nearby howled in pain, causing her to flinch. She figured he probably scanned her, or sent a picture of her face back to the system. If her mother had any care at all, there might be a missing report, but she doubted it. At least she didn't have a criminal record yet, so he might go easy on her. He pulled all the packets out of the front pocket of her tunic, tossing them on the road before he held up the holocom. The clear plastic bar glinted in the sunlight.

"I got that from another officer. I was gonna holo him but then the crash… I promise. They wanted to help me."

He lifted the front of her tunic and examined her grimy grey shirt. Between its holes and her scrawny figure, it had to be obvious she didn't hide any drugs or weapons. He emitted a grunt of either annoyance or disdain and let the tunic drop back in place before gripping her shoulder and guiding her over to a large, blue-and-grey gee-vee with EGSF markings.

No! Please don't arrest me. Tears brimmed in her eyes.

Too frightened to resist, Sima walked as he pushed her, stepping over a boy her age, shot multiple times, but still alive. Blood bubbled out between his teeth with each breath. Only his eyes moved, tracking her.

"Shouldn't have run," said the female officer tending to him with some manner of medical kit.

Sima trembled like a frightened child as the man packed her in the cage-like rear seat and slammed the door. Automatic straps crisscrossed over her chest and snugged her against the padded seat.

Trembling out of control, she almost cried for Mommy, but even if the woman somehow heard her, Sima knew she wouldn't care.

10

CHOICES

Minutes passed in blurry sobbing.

The opposite door opened and the officer shoved an Outcast man in his younger twenties into the other rear seat. Sweat dripped from his face, still red from screaming. Blood spattered all over the left leg of his pants, though he no longer appeared to be bleeding. However, he did look as if the officers gave him an enormous dose of a narcotic. Barely conscious, he lolled sideways as the automatic seatbelt grabbed him.

Sima looked down at the X of strap across her chest. Between it and the handcuffs, she'd never felt so helpless in her life. Still, if the EGSF hadn't killed her already, she hoped they wouldn't hurt her. For the past few days, she'd been trying to make up her mind what to do, and it seemed that the universe hated indecision. Fate chose for her.

He kept the holocom. She burst into tears again.

When the same officer climbed in up front and shut the door, she tried to lean up to the metal grating, but the straps kept her immobile. "Please, can I have the holocom back?"

He pushed a few buttons on the console and gripped the control sticks. The vehicle lurched forward, a faint whirr vibrating the entire frame. She chickened out of asking again, and sat meekly as he drove down street after street. Fortunately, the windows appeared black from the outside, so none of the vendors who'd recognize her from long hours begging could see her shame.

Eventually, the car turned left and passed through a three-stage security gate into an EGSF facility. A short driveway past fake grass and a gleaming silvery sign reading, 'Earth Government Security Force' led to a ramp that took the car below ground. At the bottom, he steered right, going past several rows of similar gee-vees, then parked in a small space. He pushed a button on the console, which activated a rolling, barred door behind them, turning the parking spot into a large cell.

When two female EGSF officers and another man emerged from a doorway in front, Sima's trembles started all over again. The women came around the right side of the car and opened her door. She looked up at them with the most pathetic stare she could summon, not an ounce of it an act.

"Out," said the tall woman.

Sima looked down at the straps. "I can't move. I'm tied in."

"Oh, my fault," said the guy behind the wheel.

A *beep* came from the front, and the automatic harness released her.

While the man who arrested her and the other guy dragged the unconscious male Outcast away, Sima wobbled to her feet in front of the two women. The shorter one, an Asian with the name Cheng, L according to her uniform, shook her head. Her partner, a much taller dark-skinned woman with short dreads, sighed, almost radiating pity. Sima glanced at her nametag, Hunt, A.

Each grabbed one of her arms in a firm-but-not-painful hold, and walked her across the little garage cell to the door. She kept her head bowed, sniffling, barely managing not to throw up from nerves, as they led her down a corridor, past a doorway, and around another curving hallway to a door.

The room they stopped in had a small metal table and two chairs on the left. Straight in front of her, a showerhead stuck out of the wall over a drain, but it had no privacy curtain or barrier of any kind. Storage cubbies, all with code locks covered the right wall.

While Officer Cheng moved to shut the door they entered from, the other woman removed Sima's handcuffs.

"Now, listen up, kid," said Officer Hunt. "Don't do anything stupid, okay? You know you'll only make it worse for yourself."

"Yes, ma'am," muttered Sima.

Hunt pointed to the table. "Place all your possessions on the table, including your clothes."

"Do I have to take my clothes off?" whispered Sima.

"This will go better for you if you obey commands without question," said Cheng.

Blood rushed to Sima's cheeks, but she walked the three steps over to the table and stared at it.

A minute later, Hunt sighed. "Look, kid. This isn't fun for us either. Just procedure, okay? Do it and get it over with, and we can all get on with the rest of our day."

Sima sniffled as she pulled her tunic off over her head. The faded pink garment had been one of the last things her mother ever—begrudgingly—bought her. She made a halfhearted attempt at folding it and set it on the shiny steel table. One by one, she untied the power cables around her calves and stepped out of her crummy sandals. The ice cold steel floor made her gasp.

She next untied the string holding her pants up, and let them drop, stepped out of them, and put them on the table. Standing there in a ratty grey T-shirt and panties, she turned toward Officer Hunt and clutched the pouch hung around her neck. "What about this? It's all the money I have."

"Everything goes in a box," said Cheng. "You'll receive it all back when you get out."

"How long am I going to be here?" asked Sima.

Officer Hunt shrugged. "Not our call. We don't even know what you're here for, other than being a NV."

"NV?" asked Sima.

"Nonviolent offender. That's why you're taking your own stuff off and we're having a nice little pleasant moment," said Hunt, smiling. "Move it along a bit, huh? You smell like an ORC. I'm sure you're tired of bein' covered in stink, right?"

Sima took the pouch off and set it on the tunic before peeling her T-shirt off. That it stuck to her back made her cringe. She couldn't bring herself to face the women with no top on, and stood there shivering in shame for a moment before working up the courage to remove her underpants. Those, she'd had for a little over a year. One of the few non-food items she'd spent money on.

"You know," said Sima, half-laughing out of sheer embarrassment. "I don't remember the last time I was naked."

"Yeah, you smell like it's been a long time since you had a chat with a shower unit," said Cheng. "Grab the edge of the table and bend forward."

"What?" gasped Sima, wide-eyed.

"Take it easy, kid," said Hunt. "No contact. Just a routine scan to make sure you don't have any contraband hidden on you."

"I'm naked!" She grasped the table as instructed. "Where would I hide contraband?"

"Wow. You're either innocent as hell or a really good actress." Cheng removed a small electronic device from her belt and walked up behind her.

Sima braced for awfulness, mentally feeling her mother's boyfriend grab her butt. Fear pushed her up on tiptoe, and her legs almost gave out.

"Easy, kid. Relax," said Cheng, way too close behind her. "It's over already. Scan's clear."

"I told you." Sima stood upright and covered herself with her hands. "Where could I possibly hide stuff with no clothes on?"

Cheng pointed at the shower. "Clean yourself up."

"You're gonna watch?" She gawked.

"Have to," said Hunt. "For your own protection, in case you might try to hurt yourself or others."

Sima bowed her head and padded over to the showerhead. It had been quite a while, but it's not as if she forgot how to use one. She tapped the control screen, and soon, warm water blasted her in the face, purging the freezing chill of the room from her bones. A tiny shelf nearby held a bottle of generic blue soap gel. She squirted some into her hand and washed herself, every so often peering back at the two officers who kept a reasonable distance, chatting with each other. Neither one stared at her, though they did keep tabs on what she did.

After lathering up her hair, she smeared the cleansing gel all over her body. For a little while, the relief of finally escaping the stink of the ORC bin tamped down her anxiety over being arrested.

"Come on, kid. This isn't the Hotel Excelsior. Wrap it up," said Cheng.

Sima rinsed herself off, hit the button to kill the water, and stood there dripping.

"Walk over there." Hunt pointed at a spot near the wall, a few steps to the right from the shower.

She obeyed.

"Face me," said Cheng.

Sima, blushing as hard as ever, did.

"No visible tattoos or markings," said Hunt. "Turn left ninety degrees."

Sima did.

"Turn left ninety degrees again and lift your hair off your back."

Sima obeyed.

"No visible tattoos or markings," said Hunt. "Turn left ninety degrees again."

The woman examined Sima's left side for a few seconds, then pointed toward the cubbies, at a red X on the floor. "Stand on that."

Sima, head down and trying to cover herself as much as possible with her hands, obeyed.

Officer Hunt punched a code into one of the panels. She opened the door, rooted around inside, and threw a sports bra and set of white underpants generally at the vicinity of Sima's chest.

She didn't wait for the order to put them on, and scrambled into them as fast as she could. When she looked up, a blindingly pink jumpsuit hit her in the face with the force of a cloud.

"Put that on," said Cheng.

No kidding. Thanks for telling me that. She stepped into the garment, which wound up a little short in the leg, pulled it up over her shoulders, and secured the Velcro at the front from groin to neck. The fabric smelled new, an unusual sensation. Despite it being a hot pink jumpsuit with *Juvenile* printed in large black letters on the left sleeve and *Inmate* on the right sleeve, she didn't mind it so much.

Officer Hunt dropped a set of thin shoes on the floor, a cross between a plastic bag and slippers. Sima put them on, grateful to have something between her skin and the chilly floor.

"Hands," said Cheng, while holding up a pair of rigid cuffs without a chain, merely two lockable rings connected by a hinge.

Sima considered pleading with them not to, but couldn't force a voice past the lump of terror in her throat. Mutely, she held her hands out and said nothing as they shackled her wrists. The officers added a thick nylon belt to which they locked the cuffs, then Hunt took a knee to lock a set of ankle chains on her.

Tears spilled down her cheek at the harsh steel reminder of her status as a prisoner. She fidgeted at her hands, unable to lift them away from her waist. If anyone took a swing at her, she wouldn't be able to protect her face. With the shackles on her legs, she couldn't run from danger. Being in restraints mortified her more than having to shower with an audience.

Cheng punched in a code on a panel by the room's door, which opened it. "Follow me."

Sima shuffled out, able to walk at an almost-normal stride, though she kept stepping on the chain and stumbling. The other woman followed close behind her, but didn't grab or push. They led her down the hall past several similar rooms where other women and one girl of maybe fourteen stood in various stages of showering, putting on jumpsuits, or being shackled the same way she had, each one under the watch of a pair of female EGSF officers. Realizing that anyone going by in the hall would've seen her showering earlier, she instinctively tried to grab her face to hold in the vomit, but her hands jerked to a halt an inch away from her waist.

The officers guided her down several stark white hallways before entering one with dozens of small, plain doors. They stopped at the sixth one on the right and pulled it open to reveal a tiny chamber with white walls and a single slab of foam for a bed on the left.

"Have a seat, kid," said Hunt. "An investigator will be with you soon."

She stepped in, her plastic shoes crinkling, and turned to look back at them. When the woman began to push the door shut, Sima blurted, "Do I have to stay handcuffed?"

"Until you get sorted out. You won't be in here long enough to be worth the time to take them off and put them back on," said Cheng, before sliding the door shut.

Sima stood in silence for a few seconds until a sharp *click* from the lock made her jump. The door had no windows, only a small hatch at the middle about a foot wide and three inches tall. She looked down at herself, squinting at the glare of the jumpsuit. Stark white walls, the intense pink, and powerful overhead lights hurt her eyes. Metal rings around her ankles pinched, less comfortable than the old power cables that once held her sandals on.

She paced around for a few minutes, absentmindedly fidgeting at her handcuffs. It all seemed so overkill to restrain a twig-thin girl her age so severely she couldn't even wipe her nose. Were the EGSF officers *that* afraid of her? After a while of no one coming to retrieve her, she sat on the bed and pulled her heels up. She wanted to wrap her arms around her legs, but couldn't. She wanted to wipe the tears streaming down her cheeks, but couldn't. Oh, sure, she smelled like soap and none of this new clothing stuck to her anywhere. None of it had rips or stains, and even the flimsy prison shoes were more comfortable than her old sandals (if nowhere near as tough). She couldn't even remember the last time her hair didn't stink like mold or garbage. The stretchy bra compressed her chest with an unfamiliar tightness. She'd gone a few years without one, making do with only a thin cloth shirt. Then again, she didn't have the biggest bosom in the world, so it hadn't exactly been necessary.

That, of course, made her think of Sayed suggesting she stuff her shirt. That made her angry at him all over again out of jealousy. *The cops wouldn't have chained him up like this.* She scowled. *Damn kids. Everyone's so nice to them no matter what they do. I'm still a kid, too!* Jealous and furious, she struggled at the chains for a moment before her emotions plummeted to despondence and fear.

Terrified at what would happen to her, she curled up on her side and bawled, trying to stay as quiet as she could.

Eventually, she cried herself out and lay there feeling sorry for herself. The foam her face mushed into reminded her of the bed she had at home before she ran away. Her old room had been much bigger than this cell, but compared to what she'd been sleeping on for the past four years, this place *did* rank as an improvement. Granted, being locked in was a *huge* downside.

How long are they going to leave me in here alone?

Sima rolled on her back and stared at the blank white ceiling and its cluster of six small, round lights. She felt like a sandwich put in a display case at a food counter to keep it warm. Soon, her nose itched. Trying to ignore it made it worse. Thinking about how her hands remained locked to a belt around her waist made it itch even more.

With a grunt, she rolled over and wiped her face back and forth on the white sponge slab.

After, she lay there staring at the door. *This is cruel. Why are they treating me like this?* She huffed, blowing hair off her face. *Because I'm an Outcast. I don't matter. They can do whatever they want to me and they won't get in any trouble. I should be grateful they didn't beat me.* Trembles took her again. The only chance she had to survive at this point would be to play as meek as possible and do whatever they told her to. Maybe she could beg for the holocom back and talk to that one nice officer—but would he still be nice after her arrest?

"Mom," whispered Sima. "I know we didn't really get along and stuff, but if you're like still out there, and if, maybe, you have a teeny tiny little feeling of still being a mother... please help me."

Time passed in agonizing slowness. She swished her feet side to side, tried to lace her fingers together, and stared at the ceiling.

Eventually, the door swung open. A different pair of female officers, both with medium brown skin and straight, short, black hair gestured at her to follow. Sima sat up and scooted to the edge of the bed, having to rock back and forth a few times to get enough momentum to stand without using her arms.

The women led her back out of the holding cells toward the shower rooms, but took a right turn before going that far. A short corridor ended at an elevator, which they rode up four stories. The chain between her ankles clattered at the floor as she walked, hurrying to go as fast as the women holding her arms tried to make her move. These two didn't say a word, and didn't look at all happy to have to deal with her. The way they glared at her made her feel like they thought her some horrible criminal who'd be better off executed. She wondered if the little kids she used to glare at feared her the same way.

She kept her head down and struggled not to fall flat on her face.

They led her into a narrow passage with a clear wall on the right and evenly spaced doors on the left, all with windows tinted dark. Beyond the barrier to her right, a farm of cubes, each containing a workstation and worker filed an enormous room.

A hard tug on her left arm jerked her to a stop by a door marked *Investigator Ral Marr*. The yank gouged steel into her wrists and triggered an involuntary whimper.

One officer knocked twice and barged in, dragging her sideways into a small office. The man behind the desk looked to be in his later thirties, with a somewhat messy head of thick, brown hair and a few days of beard. A single coffee stain marked his otherwise immaculate white shirt, and he wore an underarm holster with a fat handgun. So much clutter covered the desk it didn't appear possible for a fly to land on it without knocking something to the floor. As soon as he locked eyes with her, he sighed.

"Sir, you requested the detainee from cell 33B?" asked the woman who'd pulled her into the room.

Sima cringed, unable to escape the painful grip on her biceps or the even more painful shackles.

"Fuentes," said the man behind the desk, "can you explain to me why you've got a minor in high security posture?"

"Umm. It's standard procedure to secure intake detainees in transport restraints, sir," said the woman. "This inmate is still in processing and hasn't been remanded to a custody facility yet. And detention was initiated in close proximity to rebel activity."

The man leaned back in his chair, rubbing the bridge of his nose. "Did you two even bother looking at her file? I don't know what kind of operation you think we're running here, but I'll not have a damn kid shackled like a serial bomber, especially a NV." He lowered his arm and stared Sima in the eye. "You *do* know how to behave yourself, don't you?"

"Yes, sir," muttered Sima at the floor.

"Get that crap off her. She's only a kid," barked the investigator.

The women holding her by the arms squeezed a little tighter before letting go. As the slightly shorter one stooped to unlock the shackles from her ankles, the other woman removed the cuffs at her wrists, then pulled the restraint belt off.

Sima stood there as limp as possible without collapsing to the floor, letting them control her body until they'd finished removing all the hardware.

"Thank you. Dismissed," said the investigator.

The two officers backed out of the room, but hesitated in the hall.

"I think I can handle an unarmed hundred-pound sixteen-year-old, thank you very much," muttered the investigator. "Or are you lingering to watch *me* so I don't do anything inappropriate with her?"

The door shut behind her, a little too hard.

He sighed and gestured at a white-and-silver chair facing the desk. "Have a seat, kid."

Sima sidestepped and sank into the chair, rubbing her wrists. "Thank you for asking them to take the cuffs off. I swear I'm not gonna do anything wrong."

Investigator Marr gestured at his desk terminal, the light from the screen casting a faint glare on his face where it overpowered the ceiling lights. "So… you conspired with members of the Underground rebellion to strategically cause a ground vehicle accident which resulted in the spill of nutri-packs for your personal gain."

Sima shivered, speechless.

"Yeah, right." He scoffed.

Was that a joke? Her eyes opened wide. "Umm. What?"

"Someone's trying to fill a quota. This is total BS. You're out of the system since twelve. Got a report here from one of the instructors at your old school, a Mrs. Noriega. Says she spoke to your mother when you missed a week of school, and learned you'd run away. There's nothing here from your parents at all."

"Yeah, well…" She fidgeted at the jumpsuit in her lap, staring at her hands. Her skin appeared darker than normal next to the painfully bright pink fabric. "No surprise there. She didn't want me. Probably happy I ran away."

"What made you do that? Didn't get along with the old lady? No mention of your father here."

She sighed. Anger at her mother snuck up behind her fear of this place and held it down, stalling her trembles. "My mother only had me because she was seeing this Citizen with money. Instead of marrying her, a baby made him leave. Mom blamed me for it. When I was eleven, she started seeing this other guy. He always looked at me creepy. Sometimes, he'd walk into the bathroom when I was in the shower. He lied and said he couldn't wait, or something lame like 'hey, we're family now, right?' but I know he just wanted to see me naked."

Investigator Marr leaned forward, a distinctly angry look in his eye. "Did the man touch you?"

"The day before I ran away, I was in the kitchen making myself dinner. Mom wouldn't cook for me once I got tall enough to reach the fabricator. He came up behind me and put his hand up my dress, touched my butt. Said a bunch of sick things, but that's all he did. I told my mother the next day, and she got pissed at *me*. She accused me of trying to 'steal her man.' I ran out right in the middle of that argument and never went back."

"Sorry," muttered the investigator. "Wish I could get my hands on that guy. Look. I don't for a minute think you've got any connection to the Seps, or had anything to do with 'planning' to tip over that cargo transport. You made it to sixteen without a single blip on your file. That doesn't fit any sort of pattern that would lead me to believe you were up to something."

She shook her head hard. "No, sir. I swear. I was just begging and saw all that food and… just did something really stupid."

"There's a fine line between desperation and stupidity, Sima. The officer who decided to detain you made some comments on the incident report that makes me think he actually brought you in for your own protection, and the 'stealing food' charge is like the stick in the other hand opposite the candy bar. There's additional comments from some officers who spoke with you a few days before that about getting you off the street. Since you ran off, I'm pretty much of the opinion that these charges you're facing are a bunch of BS so they can stick you on the *Progenitor*."

"Yeah." She lifted her head enough to peer through her still-damp hair at him. "They said something about a progenitor."

"Right. The comments from the officers you spoke with a few days ago indicated you were apprehensive, and might not be in a good state of mind to make decisions."

Sima bit her lip. "I'm kinda stuck... Not really making much glint begging anymore, and my friend wants to go work for Magdalena, but I can't do that." She blinked. "Hey, there's this kid there who's like twelve or thirteen. I think her name's Flora. Can you get her out of there?"

Investigator Marr tapped at his keyboard for a few seconds. "Can't make any promises due to some... arrangements, but if there's a working girl there *that* young, I'll see what I can do."

She leaned forward in her chair, almost wanting to trust the guy. He'd gotten angry when she told him about being groped, and that same flicker of rage reappeared at the mention of Flora. "And there's this guy who I ran an errand for, but I don't wanna do that either. I didn't trust him." She rambled about the bomb, omitting that it had been a tracker the whole time, and told the investigator about the Scathers almost getting her. "I dunno. I'm scared of everything. That progenitor thing sounded like they'd put me in a lab and cut me open."

He let out a sad chuckle, shaking his head. "Damn, kid. You've had a really rough life. Look, I won't lie to you. Our patrol officers can be little heavy handed with Outcasts, and even the poor Citizens. Not everyone behind a badge has a true sense of civic duty. Some of them just do it for the paycheck. Others think the badge makes them better than everyone. I totally get why you didn't trust us, and I wish you'd have given Gröen and Herling more time to explain."

Sima glanced over her shoulder at the door, both female officers still waiting outside. "Looks like I have time now. Will you explain it?"

"I'd be happy to." He smiled. "The *Progenitor* is a third generation colony starship. A crew of like eight thousand people is set to leave Earth for some other planet the eggheads found that's pretty much an exact copy, only without all the pollution and overpopulation. I'm sure you know we're running out of room on this rock."

"A ship?" She gawked. "Seriously?"

"The *Progenitor* is going to establish humanity's foothold on that other planet, and over the next few years, more and more ships will be sent out there, provided the colony flourishes."

She gulped.

"Hey, relax. They wouldn't be sending the ship in the first place if they weren't ninety-nine percent sure it *will* flourish."

"Umm." She hugged herself and tried to stop shaking. "I'm not really cool with the idea of going into space. That's like really, really scary. Can you like just let me go, since you like think the charges are made up?"

Investigator Marr tapped a finger at his chin for a moment. "There's only so much I can do without risking my job. I'm sure the charges are inflated, but I'm stuck here. We can either charge you with theft and you go to juvie, which will probably turn into you being dragged onto the ship anyway... or you can go willingly and we dismiss the charges so you avoid a criminal record."

She covered her mouth and nose in both hands, breathing hard. "But..."

"Be honest with yourself. What exactly do you have here that's worth sticking around for? Becoming a prostitute? Running drugs for some street fixer? Starving in an alley somewhere, maybe catching a stray bullet the next time those Underground whack jobs pop up out of their rat holes?"

"Umm."

"Do you *want* to die?"

She looked down. "No."

"We've been taking in young Outcasts such as yourself and trying to give you all a new lease on life. The colony trip includes guaranteed adoption. When you arrive, you'll get parents who actually give a damn about you, a home, a real bed, food... schooling and training. I saw your education record, Sima. Your grades were amazing. You deserve better than being in the street. This is a shot at a real life for you."

She stared into his eyes for a long few minutes. In the four years that she'd been on her own, she'd had a *lot* of people lie to her. Either this cop told the truth, or someone had fooled him and he believed it. "They're not going to send me to a lab and like use me for drug testing or cut me open?"

"No way, kid." He smiled. "I give you my word. This is totally above board. You know how frightened you are of leaving Earth?"

She nodded.

"Well, that's why they're sweetening the deal with adoption, school, and everything. Most of the volunteers are engineers, scientists, doctors, builders... established adults with the necessary professional skills to get a colony up and running. Few of them made time for families, so there aren't a lot of children involved. Someone got the bright idea for young Outcasts to go up there and bolster the population. Do you want to spend the rest of your life, all three years you'll probably have of it, stuck down here in this hellhole on the streets? Wouldn't you prefer a chance at a real existence, in a place where there's no such thing as Outcasts or Citizens?"

"That does sound good." Sima rubbed her hands up and down her sleeves. "Too good."

"Leaving Earth is a big deal, kid. That's why it's not *too* good."

Sima looked down at her plastic shoes. The man had a point. What did she really have here to miss? She missed her old ratty tunic more than her mother. Her father had never even spoken a single word to her. She didn't really have any friends. Even Cassie only kinda counted as a friend. More like two young people who bumped into each other more than twice. And the girl had been trying to talk her into becoming a whore. A friend would not do that. For the past few days, she'd been staring at death coming from three angles and no real way to avoid it. On Earth, she'd die running drugs, starve in the street, succumb to gang violence, or wind up at Magdalena's and die inside.

Really, she had nothing to lose.

"Okay," whispered Sima. "I'll do it. You're serious about dropping the charges?"

"Great, and absolutely. Give me a second to update the system."

"Am I still under arrest?"

Investigator Marr typed without looking at the keyboard or screen, smiling at her. "Insofar as a technicality goes, yes... until the ship leaves with you on board. However, since you have *volunteered* for the Progenitor program, you'll be treated like you are in protective custody rather than inmate detention. The charges will be vacated once you're off the planet."

She glanced at the word *inmate* down her right arm. "Do I need a new jumpsuit?"

He chuckled. "That won't be necessary. They all have that on them. Just be glad you're not in an orange or red one."

"Some of the women back there had orange ones. What's that mean?"

"Adult." He winked. "The red ones are for violent offenders."

"Why does it have to be pink?" asked Sima.

Marr tapped at the holographic screen a few times, swiping pages to the left. "Probably because it's so damn bright it can be seen from outer space."

She laughed.

"Okay." Investigator Marr faced her. "Now for the boring part."

"Boring part?"

"You'll be staying here until the ship leaves in a week or so. Unfortunately, I have no way around that policy. However, the accommodations will be better than what you've been used to."

She folded her hands in her lap and trembled a little. "A prison cell?"

He nodded. "It's not that bad. Think of it like a private room. No one will hurt you, and it's only a week. Then you're on a whole new planet with clear skies, open fields, and whatever else is up there that Earth no longer has. As a PCD, you'll have access to Dreamland, so it won't be *too* boring."

"PCD?"

Investigator Marr smiled. "Protective Custody Detainee."

"All right." She shrugged. "Not really much choice, right?"

"Well, we always have choices. Some are *much* better than others. You made the right one."

The door opened and the same two women walked in.

"Officers Ahmadi and Mahmoudieh will escort you to medical for a check-up, then to your room," said Investigator Marr.

Sima stood. "Okay. Thank you."

He got up as well, walking out from behind his desk to put a hand on her shoulder. "This is a great chance for you to start over. You didn't deserve what your mother did to you, and nothing that happened, except maybe running in to grab food packets"—he winked—"was your fault. Go up there and *live*. Forget this mess."

"I'll try."

Officer Mahmoudieh, the slightly taller one, pulled handcuffs off her belt.

Sima glanced back at her and whimpered before shooting a pleading stare at Marr.

"Hey," he muttered. "I've seen a *lot* of Outcasts in your position. A lot of young women. You're only like the third one who considered Magdalena as bad as death. You've got a good soul in there. I know you'll be okay."

Sima's eyes accused him of betraying her as the woman cuffed her hands behind her back.

"Since you're still technically detained for a bunch of charges, bogus as they may be, it's policy when moving you around the building." Marr hardened his gaze at the two officers. "She's volunteered for the Progenitor project, so treat her like a kid in protective custody, huh? I hear she wound up in high security posture again, it'll be someone's butt."

The women nodded.

"Best of luck, kid." Marr sat back in his chair. "And I'll pay Mag a visit tonight and check up on that Flora you mentioned."

"Thanks." Sima looked down as the women escorted her out.

A few hallways later, they brought her into a medical room with two other women in white smocks plus an old man in a lab coat. As soon as the door closed and locked behind them, Officer Ahmadi removed the handcuffs and nudged her over to the exam table.

The doctor, the older of the two women, ran a bunch of tests on her while the senior tech (the old man) kept giving her injections with an air-hypo. Sima spent an uncomfortably long amount of time in only her underwear getting poked, prodded, and scanned. By the time they let her put the jumpsuit back on, she had a headache, runny nose, and her bones ached.

"Umm," said Sima.

The doctor looked at her. "Yes, child?"

"I feel horrible."

"That's the vaccines hitting you a little hard." The doctor patted her on the shoulder. "You'll feel a bit rough for a few hours, but it'll all clear up soon." She looked at the officers. "Let her skip lunch if she doesn't want to eat, but she should have dinner."

They nodded.

"All set then."

Sima slid off the exam table, but her legs collapsed. The doctor caught her before she crashed to the floor. Draped in the woman's arms, she muttered, "I can't feel my legs."

"We gave you a standard detox shot, to take care of a few of the common issues Outcasts tend to pick up. It's a potent antiviral, antifungal, antimicrobial agent, though it does have a relatively strong muscle relaxant effect." The doctor handed her off to the cops. "No need to restrain her for at least an hour."

"Right," said Mahmoudieh. "She's a bag of jelly."

The officers each took her by one arm, but after a frown of disapproval from the doctor, Mahmoudieh picked her up and cradled her sideways like a child.

I thought doctors are supposed to help people get better... not make *them* *sick.* "Ugh."

She blearily stared up at the ceiling passing by as the woman carried her. An elevator replaced the plain white tiles for a few minutes, then more hallway. Finally, they deposited her in a cell that looked much like the last one, only about twice as wide. This room had a cloth mattress with a thin blanket, and even better—a toilet. Officer Mahmoudieh set her down reasonably gently.

Sima passed out before the door shut.

11

THE WHITE ROOM

S ima sat on the bed, back against the wall, a foam pillow wedged between her head and the concrete. This cell at least had a basic terminal that allowed her access to a library of fiction novels via holographic display, and limited connectivity to Dreamland. She couldn't send messages or call anyone, merely view educational archives or movies. Unfortunately, the damn system knew her age and wouldn't let her access any really interesting sounding media.

She'd taken the flimsy plastic shoes off after the first few hours, and three days later, hadn't left the room once. No one had even opened the door. Only the small hatch had moved, someone outside passing her pre-packaged meals in big clear plastic cartons. No one had ever asked for the empties back, and the room had no ORC bin, so they wound up sitting on the floor by the wall.

Being kept in solitary confinement would've been maddening if not for the ability to read or watch movies. However, as twisted as the thought sounded, this locked room with a soft bed, working toilet, and reasonably decent food three times a day made her old Crash feel like prison. *This* almost amounted to a decent existence.

For seventy-two hours and change, her world had been a white cell, retina-burning pink jumpsuit, and the floating electronic display.

She'd had fried chicken, shawarma, mystery meat with peas, green beans, Salisbury steak, hummus, mac and cheese, salmon, turkey in gravy, French fries… a whole bunch of other foods she hadn't touched since she'd been little. And some (like the salmon) that she'd never had before at all.

The idea of leaving Earth terrified her, but whenever the quiet isolation of her cell got under her skin, she'd think about her narrow escape from the Scathers. She'd *much* rather be locked in here than be anywhere near them again.

A double knock at her cell door startled her into yelping.

"Nuvari," said a husky sounding woman.

"Yes?" she asked.

"You're to be transported to the *Progenitor* in a few hours. I'm sure you can't wait to get out of that little room."

Sima glanced around at the walls. "It's not *so* bad, but yeah."

"Do you want a shower before you leave?" asked the woman.

"Are you going to watch?"

The guard chuckled. "Are you going to hurt yourself?"

"No."

"I'll say I believe you, so no… you can have a partition."

Sima shut off the e-reader and stood before pulling on the plastic shoes. "Okay. I'd like a shower." Not like wearing the same clothing for three days straight bothered her, but an opportunity to get out of the little room couldn't be wasted.

A loud *clank* came from the cell door, followed by a hiss as it slid open to the side, revealing a stocky woman no taller than her. The officer's dark blue EGSF jumpsuit had sergeant stripes and the name: Bäumler, E.

Sima approached the door and turned her back, putting her hands behind herself.

"Ach, we don't need to do that. Yer a shippie, aren't ya?" asked Officer Bäumler.

"Yes." Sima turned to face her, eyes wide the same way they got whenever someone gave her glint. "Oh, thank you!"

The stocky woman nodded. "C'mon."

Sima walked with her down to the end of the corridor, around a corner, and to the fourth door on the left. The room looked similar to the first one she'd been searched in, only the shower here had a privacy barrier around it. A large plastic can stood by the table, upon which sat a sky blue jumpsuit and a new sports bra/panty set so white it hurt to look at.

"Take everything off and chuck it in the can." Officer Bäumler pointed at the blue jumpsuit and clean underwear. "That's for you, after you're cleaned up."

Her cheeks warmed with blush, but not quite as bad as before. At least this room didn't have windows to the hallway. Sima stripped, tossing everything into the can before hurrying around behind the privacy barrier. She showered, neither rushing nor taking excessively long. This stall had a hot air dryer, so once she finished washing, she basked in the downblast of hot air until her hair had no trace of dampness.

Timidly, she crept out from behind the barrier. Officer Bäumler sat at the chair behind the table. She glanced over enough to notice Sima peering around, nodded once, and turned her full attention to a handheld electronic device.

Sima streaked across the room and rushed into the new underthings before grabbing the blue jumpsuit, exposing a pair of foam sandals underneath. Her new jumpsuit lacked words on the sleeves, but also had too-short legs, leaving about half her shins exposed. She picked up the foam shoes, dropped them on the floor, and stepped into them.

"All right." Officer Bäumler put her device back in a belt holder and stood, smiling. "I do have one small bit of bad news for you."

Dread turned Sima's eyes into platters. "What?"

"You won't be able to eat before going to the ship. Like everyone else on board, you'll be spending the voyage asleep, and they can't have any food in you for that."

"Asleep?" She blinked. "Seriously? How?"

Officer Bäumler shrugged. "I've no idea how that stuff works. You'd need to ask one of the techies on the ship. All I know is that the trip will feel like only a couple of minutes to you."

"Oh." She shrugged. "I guess that's cool, right? Won't get boring."

The officer escorted her back to her cell and locked her in with a, "See you in a little bit."

Sima sat on the bed, her head filling with random memories of her time on the street. She savored a few happy moments, but most frightened or saddened her. "Well... at least I won't wind up being floated." She closed her eyes. "Sorry Draz."

After a few minutes of silence, she became restless and paced. The foam slippers made soft *pops* as they snapped up against her heels. Her stomach growled, loud enough to echo off the walls. She hadn't been too hungry before, but being told she *couldn't* eat made it worse.

Perhaps a half hour later, the cell door opened. Officer Bäumler motioned for her to walk out. A taller, muscular female officer with short dreadlocks and dark skin offered a pleasant nod of greeting. Her nameplate read Eke, C.

"Hi," said Sima, with a halfhearted wave.

"Well, this is your big moment." Bäumler smiled. "Finally free of this rat's nest."

"If it's so good, why aren't you going?" asked Sima, trying not to sound sarcastic.

"Too old." The thick-bodied woman shrugged. "They wouldn't let me. I don't have any skills that'd be useful up there."

"Neither do I," muttered Sima as she followed them down the hall.

"You're young," said Officer Eke in a surprisingly feminine voice compared to her powerful stature. "There's plenty of time for you to learn skills."

Sima wasn't quite sure if she should feel like a kid being taken care of or a prisoner under escort. She stared down at her feet for a few seconds. "They're not gonna like force me to have kids with some random guy, are they?"

"You've got quite the imagination there," said Officer Bäumler. "No, dear. Nothing of the sort. It might not be Earth, but there is still society."

They took her to the elevator, downstairs, and to an underground garage where a blue-and-grey EGSF gee-vee waited for her. Unfortunately, she had to ride in the cage part, but they didn't restrain her.

Officer Bäumler drove. Sima stared out the window at the grimy walls of the city. Every now and then, she spotted a storefront or vendor that made her remember various people kicking her out of their places, cursing her for being poor. Sometimes she'd find a nice one. She'd coasted along on a fair bit of charity at first, being twelve, but the older she became, the more people regarded her with dark glares that wondered what she would steal instead of radiating pity.

A simultaneous sense of loss and revulsion filled in her stomach, killing her hunger.

In some way, she'd miss this place—or at least the familiarity of it. But she also hated it for everything it tried to do to her. Everything from her mother to the gangs to the everpresent threat of landing in the employ of Magdalena.

That would never happen now. No matter what the future held for her, she clung to the relief and joy of that single idea. And what if Investigator Marr's promise of adoption had been true? She'd get to lower her guard, be a kid again, have someone taking care of her. Not to mention, she wouldn't have to worry about damned little kids soaking up all the pity. On whatever planet the *Progenitor* would take her to, she wouldn't have to care at all about tiny brats. If they existed or didn't, it would make no difference to her. Someone, whoever they assigned to be her parents, would care about her.

She bit her lip, not having any guarantee new parents would be *nice*. But the odds went in her favor that they'd be better than her mother. Even if her adoptive father turned out to be super strict, she'd call that better than her real dad who couldn't even be bothered to say a single word to her.

Sima had never even seen him. Not so much as a single photograph.

The gee-vee coming to a hard stop snapped her out of her mental wandering. A few minutes of city had slipped by unnoticed while she'd been lost to her thoughts. She momentarily felt cheated of those final memories of her old home, but decided it not worth the effort to ask them to drive around a little longer.

Officer Bäumler opened the side door, allowing a brisk wind to billow into the vehicle. Sima squinted at the brightness of shining chrome outside and scooted to the edge of the seat to get her feet on the ground. The wind nearly stole one of her foam shoes, but she stomped on it before it got away, and scooted her toes back around the thong. Brilliant sunlight gleamed from a massive tower of metal that reached at least sixty stories into the sky. It took her a few seconds to realize that she stood in shadow despite the glare from the building.

Sima looked up.

A great expanse of metal stretched in both directions overhead, studded with thousands of winking lights and hazed by puffs of fog and cloud. To the right, the ship thickened, ending at four giant cylinders sprouting an array of long, pointy rods, but it stretched much farther to the left, narrowing to a flat-sided rectangular profile like the world's largest box of chocolates stood up on the narrow edge. More pointy bits jutted out here and there. From below, the hull appeared dull blue, and had to be miles long nose to end.

"Whoa," gasped Sima, almost falling over backward from staring at it, but Officer Eke braced a hand at her back.

"Come on, we're on a schedule." Officer Bäumler patted her on the shoulder.

Sima clenched her toes to avoid losing her foam slippers to the powerful gale as they crossed the shiny metal courtyard in front of the tower. A few other EGSF gee-vees parked around, likely having brought other young Outcasts here.

"Umm, what about my stuff?" asked Sima.

"Rags?" asked Officer Eke. "That's all trash. You've got real clothing now."

"I had some money…"

"Umm." Officer Bäumler held up her left arm and poked a glowing bit at the end of her sleeve. A holographic panel stretched open. She pored over it for a few seconds before lowering her arm. "Your money has been transferred electronically to an account within the *Progenitor's* system."

"Oh." *Wow. I thought they were gonna steal it.* She blinked. *Wait! I have electronic money? Only Citizens get e-MU.* She grinned, hopeful that she might not only escape Earth, but escape being an Outcast.

The women led her into a small lobby, devoid of people, and over to an elevator.

A long ride within a plain silver capsule ended in a large room with hundreds of seats lined up in a manner similar to the waiting area of an airport. Only one old man remained, staring morosely into the distance as though someone he'd loved dearly had died. Cups, plates, and some trash items littered the floor, like the room had recently held a big crowd, but they'd all gone away.

That's kinda eerie.

She followed Officer Bäumler down a wide, but short hallway that had bathrooms on either side as well as a row of snack-selling vending machines before it rounded a leftward corner to another room with a large observation deck. Floor-to-ceiling windows spanned the far wall, offering a clear view of the ship from about thirty feet away. Blue-grey metal bore the word *Progenitor* in black lettering taller than some houses. One doorway at the center of the windowed wall connected to a swaying tunnel of transparent plastic that spanned the 200 or so feet between the tower and the ship.

"Umm." She stared at the fluttering, swaying tube. Her stomach bottomed out, sliding deeper into her gut. "Uhh…"

"Almost there," said Officer Bäumler with a big smile. "This is your new life."

Sima crept up to the end of the boarding tunnel. The elevator behind them squeaked. She hesitated at the edge, watching the tunnel bounce in the wind outside, which sixty feet off the ground, roared like a tornado. Worse, much of the tube consisted of transparent panels, giving her a horrible view of exactly how high off the ground she was.

"Umm, I dunno about this," muttered Sima. Earth, its grimy streets, high likelihood of death, and gangs, seemed like a not-so-bad option all of a sudden. "Heights aren't really my thing."

A pair of male officers entered the observation deck with a group of six preteen children, four boys and two girls, all in similar blue jumpsuits like Sima's. The smallest, a barefoot little blonde girl of five or six, clung to the man carrying her, wheezing and coughing. If they'd given her foam slippers, they'd fallen off somewhere outside. She looked barely awake, but couldn't stop smiling. With Sima standing there in petrified fear of the swaying hallway, the other group went around her and into the boarding ramp.

The smaller kids didn't have an issue with the tunnel, running into it whooping and cheering.

"Go on, girl," said Officer Eke. "If those little ones aren't afraid, you shouldn't be."

Sima whimpered, but managed to step into the first segment. As soon as it bounced under her feet, she jumped back. "I can't. I'm sorry. I can't do this. Can I change my mind and stay on Earth?"

Officer Bäumler put an arm around her back and spoke in a gentle, motherly tone. "Going forward, you're a Citizen with a family, an education, and a good life. Going back, you're a street kid doing ten-to-twenty for theft."

"Umm…" Sima closed her eyes, swallowed hard, and stepped into the boarding tunnel.

Five steps later, it bounced up and down hard enough to lift her off her heels for a second. In a panic, she twisted around and bolted, but barely took a full step before both officers caught her by the arms. Eke held her down while Bäumler secured her wrists and ankles with handcuffs. Sima thrashed and struggled, screaming, crying, and begging them to let her go as the women carried her down the boarding tube. She flew into a panic, convinced that any second, it would break apart and send her plummeting to her doom.

When they reached the airlock door at the ship's hull, she calmed enough to stop screaming, but continued trembling and whimpering. This close, the ship appeared more like the side of a mountain than anything people made. Peering out the clear tube at the massive vessel made her feel like a flea on the side of a dog. She didn't get much chance to gawk at the ship as the EGSF officers carried her inside and down a hallway with rounded walls, flat only on the bottom. Hanging by her arms in the women's grip, Sima stared past her dangling feet at black floor tiles gliding by. Light rings embedded in the tube-like passageway passed every twenty feet.

"I'm okay," muttered Sima between gasps for breath. "I'm just terrified of heights. Forget what I said about not wanting to go."

They carried her toward a bulkhead. Many voices emanated from the other side ranging from the deep timbre of men to the high-pitched giggles of small children.

She squirmed, pulling at the restraints. "Please let me outta these cuffs. It's really embarrassing. I'm good now that we're inside. I promise."

The officers carried her past the bulkhead into a huge chamber with white walls. EGSF officers in dark blue uniforms and a handful of kids stood around some of the pods along with men and women in white jumpsuits holding electronic pads. Some kids sat on the edges of pod beds in their underwear while others took their jumpsuits off as officers stood watch. A few peered over at Sima being dragged in like a criminal. None laughed or made fun of her, but they all stared.

She looked away, and wound up mesmerized by a row of coffin-like pods going by on her right. Each had a clamshell type lid, transparent except for where metal spars divided it into four panels. Teens and children inside some of them had already gone to sleep, eerily still as if they stopped even breathing.

"Please let me out of these," whispered Sima, sniveling quietly. "I'm okay now. I swear I'm fine."

Officer Bäumler sighed and stopped walking.

"Really," whined Sima. "It's the heights. I hate heights. I thought that tube was going to break."

A few seconds passed listening to the constant mechanical thrum of the starship around her.

Officer Eke removed the restraints, but kept a grip on her arm.

Sima shot her a 'gee I guess I'm still a prisoner' look.

"There's nothing here for you anymore, child," said Eke. "We want you to have a better life."

Head bowed, Sima walked with them to a set of pods all the way near the back by the wall. A grey-haired man in a white jumpsuit stood by the foot end, holding an electronic pad and smiling. She managed a feeble wave of hello, grateful to be out of cuffs. Even if she remained a detainee, at least she didn't *feel* like one.

"Hello, Miss Nuvari," said the man in white. "Please remove your footwear and jumpsuit, then hop in."

She eyed the pod, gazing at the row of rectangular loaf-shaped cushions forming the bed, and a squarish 'pillow' at the head end. Black letters marked 0137B-C1 on the side. "Umm. Do I have to get undressed?"

"Cryonic suspension may inflict injury if the temperature over your skin is not properly regulated. Ideally, subjects should not have any fabric at all, though the risk factors for the minimal interference from undergarments does not outweigh passenger discomfort at a complete lack of clothing. Feel free to remove everything if you are concerned about your health."

"Umm." Sima leaned away from the pod, which had started to feel a whole lot like the coffin it resembled.

Officer Bäumler leaned close and whispered, "There's nothing to be afraid of dear. However, I must tell you that I would *much* prefer not having to use a neural stunner on you. This is for your own good. I can't in good conscience bring you back to face made up charges."

Sima got lightheaded from fear. She'd wind up in the pod willingly or stunned. *No turning back. I can't get out of here…*

Tears leaked from her eyes as she opened the front of the jumpsuit with shaking hands, gasping at the rush of frigid air leaking in. At least they didn't force her to take her underwear off. The foam shoes made sense now, since the officers must've known she'd only wear them for a little while. A teenage boy shouted obscenities from a good distance away. Two large EGSF officers hauled a dark-haired kid about her age along the row of pods. He kicked and thrashed, fighting the same full restraints the cops had initially put on her.

"No way! I said I don't wanna leave the goddamn planet! Get off me!" shouted the teen.

Transfixed, she stood aghast and staring as the men dragged him to an open stasis pod.

Officer Eke collected the jumpsuit from Sima's hands and bundled it up.

She looked up at the cop. "Umm. What am I supposed to wear when we land?"

Bäumler pointed at a cluster of storage compartments on the wall opposite the foot end of the pod. "All in there. You'll have everything you need. You don't want a prisoner jumpsuit."

"Please, have a seat and try to relax," said the older man in white.

Six pods to her left, a woman in a white jumpsuit tried to coax a girl of maybe nine into climbing in by calling it a 'special bed' that would give her wonderful dreams. On the other side of the room, a dozen or so pods away, a female officer stuffed a shrieking little boy into a pod. It took two cops and two people in white jumpsuits to hold him down.

Sima approached the pod and gingerly lowered herself to sit on the surprisingly soft cushion. As soon as her butt touched fabric, the inexplicable sense that this thing would kill her came out of nowhere. "Is it gonna hurt?"

"Not at all, dear." The man held a small silver device up to her face, shining a light in her eye. It chirped and beeped. "All right, looks good." He attached a few sticky, white pads to her forehead and chest. Each had little blinking lights. "Now, just need to give her the stabilizers." The tech hummed to himself for a few seconds, while administering three injections. Each one made a loud *pfft*, but she didn't feel a thing. "There. Those shots will keep you nice and safe. No one likes ice crystals in their blood, right? A little grogginess is normal when you wake, so don't be alarmed if you're a little loopy right after the ship arrives. You're all set. Just lie down and relax. You'll get tired in a moment, and the next thing you know, you'll be home."

"New family, new life," said Officer Eke with a big smile.

Shivering from the frigid air as well as nervousness, Sima scooted her butt back, rotated, and lay flat on the cushion. A heavy, mechanical whirring shook the whole pod as the lid closed down on her. Sudden claustrophobia made her scream and raise her arms. She kicked at the lid. "Let me out of here! Wait! No! Don't lock me in!" Sima burst into tears, wailing like a child. Leaving Earth had been such an abstract thing, she couldn't fully process it until people tried to trap her in a coffin with a glass top. Again and again, she kicked at the closing lid until she no longer had the room. Screaming and pounding on the glass, she continued begging to be let out, lost to her panic.

"Oh, I almost forgot." The tech hit another button, which caused the lid to open again.

Sima tried to dive free as soon as she had the room to get out, but Officer Eke pounced on her and held her down.

"Might as well sedate her," said Bäumler.

The man in white nodded. "Mmm. All right."

Sima struggled to get away from the two women, but they overpowered her easily. Within a few seconds of a sharp prick at her shoulder and a faint hiss, everything got blurry. She wanted to keep fighting, but her arms and legs stopped listening to her brain. Dizzy from the injection, she could only look wherever her head pointed. The boy who'd been in restraints stripped down to his briefs with a neural stunner aimed at him. They shoved him in the pod. As soon as the lid closed, he, too, lost it and had a panic attack. Wails of distant terrified children mixed with giggles of others who seemed not to know what these people wanted to do to them.

She struggled to turn her head, but couldn't move the rest of her body, couldn't get away from the *killing machine* they wanted to put her in.

"There, there," said the man, his voice seeming to come from everywhere at once. "You're perfectly safe." Something emitted a faint chirp. "Assignment mode. Sima, Nuvari. Female. Passenger Record E9207."

Another chirp followed.

Something cold touched her left wrist.

"Dream happy things," said Officer Eke. The woman's deep brown face and broad smile filled Sima's vision. "You're no longer a street kid. Welcome to real life, hon."

Sima couldn't figure out how her body worked. Unable to get her limbs to move, she lay there like a loaf while the muscular woman lifted her legs back onto the bed, tucked her arms at her sides, and gently brushed her hair off her face.

"Oh, I'm jealous," muttered Officer Bäumler. "Good on her getting off this landfill of a planet."

The tech laughed. "We still have a few bunks left."

"Heh. Not *that* jealous," said Officer Bäumler's echoey voice.

Mechanical thrumming vibrated Sima's bones as the pod lid came down over her. The chamber sealed with a faint hiss, and a shockingly cold wind blasted out from behind her head.

Sima opened her mouth, but her attempt to cry out for Mommy never left her brain.

12

OMNICOMPUTER

Discarded plastic boxes lifted from the floor of Sima's featureless cell. Her hands and bare feet stood out as dark against the perfect white walls, white cushioned bed, and white ceiling. The stink of the street clung to her dense black hair while her new outfit—a bright pink jumpsuit with the word *Juvenile* down her left arm in black block letters, *Inmate* on the other—reeked of detergent.

Nine eight-inch clear cartons ascended from the floor like helium balloons trapped in syrup, gliding past her bunk toward the ceiling. The glint of the overhead light on the rising plastic transfixed her, as did shadows from the crumbs of former meals stretching over the walls.

Boxes shouldn't fly.

She squeezed her fingers into the firm foam cushion as the empty meal cartons neared the top of her holding cell. Surreal fear pressed heavy on her chest, making her heart race from the inexplicable dread something bad would happen if they touched the ceiling. At the instant of contact, she cringed, expecting pain, loud noises, or destruction.

Nothing happened.

The cartons gathered at the ceiling for a short while before sinking toward the floor at different speeds. Locked in her cell, she couldn't escape the increasing sense of terror radiating from the *wrongness* of watching plastic boxes rising and falling. She tilted her head back to stare at the featureless white door that trapped her, not even a knob on this side, and sucked in a breath to shout for the guard.

Boxes don't fly. Air hissed out between her teeth. *I'm dreaming. That means…*

Sima sat up fast, cracking her head on plastic. She fell flat upon soft padding, bright spots dancing across her vision. Whimpering, she rolled to her right, grabbed her face, and curled up. Once the blinding pain faded, she opened her eyes to a close-up view of her forearms. A glimmering band of silver as thick as her finger, rounded on the outside but flat against her skin, encircled her left wrist, while a hint of bruise adorned her right. She no longer wore the garish detainee jumpsuit, only a basic sports bra and panties.

Her breathing fogged on the clear barrier two inches in front of her nose, echoing loud inside the coffin-sized compartment. Pale grey metal formed a cross overhead, dividing the transparent cover into four equal quadrants. She stretched out on her back, gazing up past the lid of a stasis pod. The room had been too bright to look at when she arrived, but now, a foreboding arrangement of indistinct boxy shapes and shadows surrounded her, too dark to perceive much detail against the strong light inside her capsule. Panels in the ceiling hung askew, with the occasional dark wire dangling from gaps where tiles had buckled downward. *The roof was taller when the cops dragged me in here.* A continuous stream of cold air fell over her from vent ports behind her head, causing her teeth to chatter and her body to tremble.

She sat up as much as she could, twisting half onto her side and propping her weight on her elbow. A tug at her skin made her look down at a pair of white pads; she plucked two sticky sensors from above her heart and two more from her forehead. She didn't remember anyone putting those on her, but that man had given her an injection that made time feel funny. Fluttering lights on the foam discs announced whatever wireless connection they used still transmitted. Her muscles had become stiff and difficult to move. As her eyes adjusted, her heart thudded with fear. She curled up, trying to breathe warmth into her fingers to fight off creeping numbness, and strained to make out the room around her capsule.

A plain white wall stood two feet to her right, where there had been a long row of stasis pods before. She looked past her toes and yelped at a six-foot slab of metal jutting through the ceiling like the sword of a giant, piercing the floor between her pod and a wall of storage cabinets. Sima twisted around and crawled to the foot end, rolling onto her back to get a good look up at the damage. A hint of sunlight filtered from the gash, fluttering with the motion of branches bearing blue leaves. Wisps of fog curled around the hole, like a cloud trying to squeeze inside. She gulped, fearing the gory sight possibly waiting behind her. Eventually, she forced herself to glance over her left shoulder at the only other pod that still existed, which sat mercifully empty.

Sima closed her eyes, shivering at the haunting memory of her surroundings as they had been: a room hundreds of feet long filled with blaring light, the antiseptic smell of a hospital, and the voices of children, some happy, others terrified. She'd caught sight of one or two, all quite a few years younger than her. Most of them didn't fear the 'special beds.' There'd been only one other teen she could remember; like her, he'd been locked in binders up until they'd made him strip to his skivvies next to his pod. *The little ones didn't know enough to be terrified.* She curled up again, teeth sounding off a staccato rhythm from the air conditioning. Before she had slept, the chamber outside had been cavernous, glaring, and full of people. The tiny room beyond the transparent shell over her head looked dark, scary—and freezing. Sima blushed, thinking back to the pathetic, terrified version of herself who had wailed like a five-year-old, begging not to be shut inside.

"What happened? This isn't right. Why's it so dark?"

A beep came from her left wrist. She uncurled enough to look at the thin silver bracelet snug to her skin. Three points of blue light flashed from within the mirrored surface at the underside of her arm.

When did they put that on me?

"For 'protective custody,' this sure feels like I'm in jail." Sima grunted as she grabbed the metal band, twisting and pulling in an effort to slide her hand out. When she gave up, the bracelet projected a five by seven inch holographic screen along the underside of her forearm. "Whoa."

Her answer came in the form of text, typing out with a faint fluttering noise: ‹Stasis pod 0137B deployed in lifeboat mode. 1/1 passenger survived. Pod 0137A empty.›

Sima looked around, imagining the ceiling coming down and the walls moving in as the giant hold full of stasis pods sectioned itself off into escape capsules. "Lifeboats? Oh, no... Why isn't this thing opening? If I'm awake, that means we're here. How long was I sleeping?"

The bracelet's text changed. ‹02Y 08M 11D 14H 27M›

She fidgeted with the metal, but couldn't find any clasp or button to open it. "Okay, so you can hear me, whatever you are. Are you some kinda restraint?"

‹No.›

"Then why can't I take this thing off?" Her breath fogged. She scooted as far as she could to the foot end to get away from the air conditioning.

More text scrolled across the small screen. ‹Tracking and monitoring device mandatory for all minors aged twelve to seventeen. Sima Nuvari, DOB 08/22/2391. Omnicomputer bracelet security will disengage in 01Y 11M 20D 09H 13M›

Sima scowled. "Hey I was asleep for two years! I'm at least eighteen now."

The screen blanked for a second. ‹Nice try. All biological function paused in stasis. Sima Nuvari remains as status 'minor' legal age: 016 years.›

Her exasperated sigh broke into stutters as she shivered. "Hey, open this thing." She slapped her hand on the clear barrier overhead.

Digital tapping noises made her look at more text appearing on the insubstantial screen.

‹Stasis pod 0137C-1 should be open.›

"Well, it isn't. I'm stuck in here." She moved to all fours, pushing her back against the icy lid, which wobbled, but refused to open. Frigid air from the vent above the headrest washed over her backside and thighs.

‹That is abnormal.›

Sima glared at the floating hologram along her forearm. "Yeah, thanks. If I don't suffocate in this thing, I'm going to freeze." She rolled onto her back and kicked at the clear plastic, screaming. "Help! Is anyone there? Someone let me out!"

Her shouting in the confined space rang in her ears over the thumps and thuds of her feet on the thick transparent plastic. A similar tantrum when the technicians sealed her in hadn't accomplished anything either. She attacked the barrier until her body refused to move. Shivers took her as she lay coated in a layer of sweat that made the air conditioning ten times colder. Huddled with her hands over her mouth, she tried to warm her fingers with her breath.

I'm locked in a coffin. The escape pod jettisoned me on who-knows-what planet. Tears streamed hot out of the corners of her eyes, slid down the sides of her head, and collected in her ears. She sniveled like a child. Standing in the street surrounded by nutri-packs watching police shoot other Outcasts back home hadn't been half as frightening as being locked in a transparent death trap.

Sima sobbed, banging her hands on the clear panel to her right while yelling, "Please, someone help me... I don't wanna die. I didn't even do anything wrong." She scowled up at the lid, fogged opaque except where foot and handprints from her futile battle remained.

The bracelet shocked her.

"Ow!" The brief jolt of pain halted her tears. "What was that for?"

‹You couldn't hear me beeping.›

Sima glared at the text. "Why were you beeping?"

‹I am reading a malfunction in the pod.›

"No crap. Really? Thanks." She growled. "Go to hell."

Text deleted and retyped. ‹Pull the pillow up.›

After a glance back and forth between the patch of blue light above her arm and a crummy box-shaped pillow that looked more like a pad from a baseball diamond, Sima forced herself to crawl into the stream of frigid air. Hair fluttering in the blast of icy air, she grabbed the cloth-covered foam tile with shaking hands, and pulled. With a Velcro rip, the 'pillow' peeled up from the cushion around it, revealing a small control panel. Next to status monitors for the cryonic system, vital sign readouts, and power levels, sat a two-inch button labeled 'Emergency Open.'

Sima didn't wait for the bracelet to type anything else. She pounded her fist on the red button. A labored, mechanical whine from somewhere below her vibrated the entire pod. The lid separated from the base with a soft sucking noise, opening upward on powered struts. She clambered out of the pod before the door stopped. Frigid floor on bare feet brought a squeal of surprise from her lips as she ducked around the jagged flange of metal impaling the room, and headed for the storage lockers.

When she pulled the first locker open, she found empty space. Thin plastic film still adhered to the interior walls, like brand new electronics. "Empty?" She blinked and opened the next one. It, too, held nothing. "This is an escape pod right?" The third storage bin contained only air as well. "Where's the supplies? Where's my damn clothes? Bäumler said there'd be stuff in here! Crap! I'll take a jail suit over being naked." Shivering and grumbling, she pulled open number four, and found it held only more empty space as well.

The bracelet buzzed.

She glared at her arm, her impatient foot making a soft rhythmic clapping on the icy floor.

‹You are technically not naked. That would imply a complete lack of clothing. Lifeboat storage compartments should be stocked with survival gear. They should not be empty.›

Sima grabbed her left wrist as if to smash the bracelet into the wall, yelling, "Stop telling me obvious things. What happened to the stuff?"

‹I can only theorize.› After a pause, text continued to appear. ‹The fabrication company responsible for outfitting the EDS Progenitor likely decided to save money by omitting certain 'optional accessories.'›

"Optional?" She stomped. "How can survival gear be optional?"

‹These pods were not officially occupied according to the flight roster. You were part of a special relocation project rushed in at the last moment.›

She folded her arms over her chest, unable to stop shivering, but took care to keep the underside of her left arm facing up so she could see the screen. "Yeah... send the street kids to a colony world. No one wants to deal with 'em." She sank into a squat, forcing herself not to cry again. "They should've just shot me in an alley like they do with Seps."

‹You would be dead then,› typed the bracelet. ‹Separatists who are shot to death are no longer alive.›

"Oh, being stuck on some alien planet in my underwear with no food and no supplies is *sooo* much better." She sniveled.

‹You are not stuck in your underwear.›

She blinked. "There's some clothes?"

The bracelet hesitated a few seconds. ‹You could remove them, hence they are not 'stuck.'›

"Off!" She smacked her arm onto one of the cabinet doors. "Get off my arm you literal piece of crap. I hate you."

‹That is unwise.›

Sima glared through tears at the three taunting words. *I can't feel my toes anymore.* She shrank in on herself, shivering.

‹You should exit this pod before your body temperature drops to dangerous levels. I am detecting another malfunction in the cryonic unit. It is warm outside and the air is breathable. And please don't hate me. :(›

She crept to the only visible door in the corner to the right of her pod. Parts of the roof had been compressed by external forces, bent down to the point her hair brushed the ceiling as she walked. "Are there any other survivors? Did the ship crash?"

‹No signals received. Status of the *EDS Progenitor* is unknown.›

Sima leaned up on her toes to reach the four-inch window in the white door. After wiping a layer of crystallized fog from the glass, she peered out at a world lush with traces of emerald, azure, and violet in the foliage.

"Whoa. That's not Earth."

‹Correct. You have landed on Mirage.›

"Huh?" She squinted at the words above her arm. "Mirage? Is this like some head game? Am I still locked up and plugged into a computer?"

‹I am sorry, Sima Nuvari. Your present situation is not virtual reality. This world received the designation of Mirage when astronomers found it to be a close match for Earth-like conditions. It was so similar they did not believe their eyes.›

"So I'm not gonna wake up?" She bounced in an effort to warm herself up.

The bracelet chirped. ‹You are awake. Shall I shock you again to prove it?›

"No." She grabbed the bracelet. "Please don't."

As soon as she whimpered, she hated herself for sounding so vulnerable. She wanted to fume at it, be as angry with it as she had been with her absentee dad and all his money she hadn't been good enough for. How could she fight an unbreakable Omnicomputer locked around her wrist for the next two years? It could shock her whenever it wanted to, and she couldn't do a damn thing about it. At least cops responded to wide eyes and pouting lips. This thing scared her more than a tiny white cell.

Sima grabbed the rubber-coated handle on the exit door and leaned down on it with all her weight. For a few seconds, her feet left the ground, until she gave up with a gasp.

Beep.

"What?" she screamed, whipping her arm up to glare at the display.

‹Lift.›

She wanted to smash something, but decided against slamming her unprotected toes into metal. The lever moved with little effort when she pulled it up, and the heavy slab of duralloy came free from the hull with a rush of air. She grunted and shoved the door into a blast of hot, humid air. When it opened enough for the wind to stop howling in the gap, the noise receded to a faint whispering over a canopy of azure foliage.

Sima gawked at a verdant forest, the only time in her life she'd ever seen plants for real… but the colors and shapes looked nothing like what she remembered from pictures.

Clusters of brown roots formed dome-shaped chambers at the bases of massive plants with the general shape of trees. The smallest looked large enough to allow one person to crawl into, while others could hold small houses. Blue leaves, some at least twenty feet in length, drifted like ribbons in the breeze.

The ground in front of the pod appeared soft, covered in strands of wavering blue-green that looked more like fur than wild grass. Nowhere did any sign of a trail exist, other than the forty-meter trench her lifeboat had gouged when it landed. The world appeared somewhat close to Earth: brown dirt and tree stalks, the sky blue with white clouds. Wet air carried the smell of moss and vegetation, tinted with the occasional hint of floral. Patches of pink in the highest leaves flickered back and forth amid smears of fluorescent blue flowers and long, hanging vines that fluttered like ghostly hair. A standing cloud formed in the doorway around her as the humid heat of this world butted heads with the over-pumped air conditioning of the escape capsule behind her.

Awe made Sima forget all about being outside in her underwear. She squatted, grabbed the rim of the pod, and slid down the six-foot mound between the lifeboat and the ground. Hot air wrapped her body like a blanket, the warm dirt underfoot like cozy socks. She didn't know where she'd wound up, but outside offered a world of paradise better than freezing to death.

She stood in the trench the lifeboat gouged into the ground, deep enough by the pod that the grass at the top wound up over her head. The escape capsule's crashing slide had come to a halt when it met the edge of a forest. Sima crept up to the side of the trench, intending to climb, but hesitated. The powder-blue grass appeared delicate and harmless, but it might be sharp or painful. After a few tentative pokes with one finger, she caressed the strange plant matter with her whole hand. It resembled grass but felt like a fluffy rabbit. The blades reminded her of feathers, composed of hundreds of thin filaments projecting outward from a central shaft. After petting the meadow like a cat for a moment without anything stinging her, she gathered the courage to trust it and grabbed the top of the crash scar. She changed her mind, opting for an easier climb a moderate distance away from the pod where the sides only reached up to her waist. There, she pulled herself up out of the sunken channel into an embrace of fluffy plant matter.

With no frame of reference to go by, she picked the direction that looked prettiest and decided to follow a meandering clearing between two banks of trees, where the grass flowed like a shifting blue-grey river into the strange forest.

13

RABBIT HOLE

Warm wind rushed down the open path between sections of forest, chasing the last of the chill from Sima's bones and lofting her long, dark hair like a flag behind her.

She walked around in circles, giggling at the grass tickling her legs. Her gaze flicked from one wonder to the next. Here and there between trees, three-foot spiked pods with ruddy crimson shells and long yellow spikes dangled from the ends of sky-blue tendrils like gargantuan thistles. Potato-sized lumps of brick red adhered to the pods between thorns as large as her arms. All her life, she'd only ever seen city: buildings, cars, the wealthy, and the poor crammed together so densely that humanity choked off the world. The splendor of this place took her breath away, and she found herself staring for a while.

A croaking bird-like cry drew her attention to an almost twenty-foot-tall creature striding overhead. Dark emerald feathers covered a rounded body atop blue stilt legs. Tucked wings fluttered. The creature moved with long, graceful strides despite having the overall appearance of a giant flamingo. Sima stared straight up as it passed over her; the breath caught in her throat when its bright orange beak peeked around its breast, an upside-down head staring at her. The creature emitted an undulating warble, studying her with two volleyball-sized eyes at the ends of stalks as big as her legs.

The bird's flexible neck craned, moving its head closer to her. The beak approached within a foot of her face, and appeared large enough to engulf her entire torso. Sima stopped short, blinked, and raised a tentative hand to wave.

"Hi. Please don't be a carnivore." She glanced to her side at wrinkled blue skin on a leg at least a foot in diameter. An uneasy whimper slipped from her clenched jaw.

The great bird squawked again, bathing her in a blast of stink—rotting vegetation. Sima gagged and swooned backward as the creature swung its neck up and strode away into the trees. When she could no longer see it moving amid the shifting forest, she resumed walking.

For several hours, she followed the grass 'river' until spotting a dark grey stone the size of a gee-vee embedded in the ground. It seemed like a good a place as any to rest. Two and change years in stasis had blunted the endurance she'd built up living on her own for four. Coarse, hot rock greeted her skin when she sat against the edge. She ran her hands over the curved surface, accepting it for stone and not some dead creature's messed up skull. The chill of the lifeboat had long departed. Between the humid air and hours of walking, trails of sweat raced over her back. She glanced down and scratched at her bare stomach.

"This place would suck if I had any clothes on." She blushed out of reflex. "Not like there's anyone else here."

Reclining over the top of the stone felt too much like being a steak on a heating element. She tolerated it for less than two minutes before sliding down to sit on the ground. There, she rested for about half an hour until a pronounced *thump* in the nearby tree line made her jump to her feet. Minutes passed in silence as she swept her gaze over the forest, searching for what moved. A light *pop* preceded another *thump* in the underbrush. Slow, tentative steps brought her closer to the spot. The sound reminded her of a rock being dropped in dirt, and didn't seem scary enough to dampen her curiosity.

A few feet in from the edge of the clearing, a cluster of dull, crimson lumps the size of huge potatoes collected on the ground beneath one of the horned pods. She prodded one with her toe, finding it firm.

"Hey, bracelet." She raised her arm. "What are these?"

‹Out of range.›

Sima squatted and held her wrist closer to the nearest lump. A pyramid of bright blue laser lines projected from the metal band, sweeping back and forth over the object. She froze in place, waiting. Forty seconds later, the pretty dancing lights ceased, and more text scrolled across the holographic screen.

‹Plant matter. Initial analysis suggests high chance of edibility.›

"Space cucumbers. Great."

The bracelet emitted the soft pattering sound of typing. ‹Specimen is closer to fruit. Sugar content detected.›

"So this won't kill me to eat?" Her stomach growled; she shivered. "Damn, there's no food in those storage compartments. I gotta find something to eat."

‹I calculate death an unlikely result of consuming this specimen.›

"Can you give me a definite answer?" She glared at the bracelet. "Wait. Don't even say it. You're going to say eat it and if I die, you'll know."

‹Humor detected.›

I hate this thing.

‹Pierce the skin and re-scan interior. My role is to safeguard you while you remain a minor. I am incapable of suggesting an action that would cause you harm... even if it would be funny.›

"I'm not a kid." She sighed, squatted, and sliced a fingernail along the rubbery rind. "I haven't been a kid since I was like nine."

‹Your medical report shows no signs of forced—›

"Stop." She licked her finger without thinking. A flavor like raspberry hit her strong before it faded to a pungent rhubarb aftertaste that made her wince. "I didn't mean *that*. I meant I had to look out for myself."

The lasers swept over the rip in the fruit for a few seconds. ‹Safe.›

She picked her prospective meal up in both hands. The dull red, pointy-ended, tubular fruit studded with little black 'thorns' of soft material was far from appetizing to look at. Bright purplish-pink in the hole she'd made tempted her to sniff. Finding it sweet, she bit it and got an explosion of bitter.

"Bleh!" She spat out the rubbery rind. "That's nasty."

After peeling it, she nibbled only the inner flesh, struggling with the overwhelmingly powerful flavor of raspberry. It soon melted into an unpleasant rhubarb aftertaste. She shivered, but if she ate fast enough, a new bite of 'raspberry' muted the rhubarb-like slap and made it tolerable. After devouring three of them, she rolled over on her back, too full to move, and spent an hour reclining in the grass, listening to her stomach make odd noises while watching airplane-sized creatures cruise overhead.

They reminded her of ocean mantas. Each had a long fluorescent tail in either orange or blue. The blue ones tended to be longer and narrower, and she noticed after a while that the ones with orange tails had a different shape to their 'wings,' broader and longer.

"Males and females." She swished her feet back and forth. "I wonder which is which?"

‹Out of range.›

Eventually, Sima bored of lying still and got up to wander. The river of grass wound among the trees, though the density of the foliage kept her from venturing too deep from the open. Lime green runners crisscrossed the forest floor, brimming with red thorns. A sense of imagined fire flared in her feet at the mere sight of them, and she spent the next fifteen minutes walking while looking down, despite remaining in the grass. Even those cheap foam shoes would have been awesome to have.

If I get hurt, I'm going to die. There's no doctors here.

Distant roaring filled her mind with images of a waterfall and tempted her away from the safety of open grass. Careful to watch where she placed her feet, she crept into the trees and startled a handful of cat-sized pastel blue furballs, which scampered away making porcine snorts and squeals. At the sudden eruption of activity, she cringed and froze until the rustling underbrush faded to silence.

Leaves both slender and wide brushed over her skin as she advanced toward the echo of bubbling water. One of the broad ones left a painful slice on her arm, its edge like that of a knife. She yelped, cradling a wound no worse than a cat scratch and whimpering at the plant. She remained wary of those leaves, navigating around them while also trying not to step on anything bright red or pointed.

Eventually, she found a creek with perfectly clear water burbling over rounded rocks in various bright colors. She stepped up to the edge, her feet sinking into cool, wet sand along the banks, and crouched to put the bracelet close to the surface. "Is this safe?"

The laser light appeared for a few seconds and vanished. ‹Water. Variances in trace elements are within acceptable range for human consumption.›

"Wow. What are the odds of finding a planet so close to Earth?"

A massive number appeared.

She sighed while fanning her face. "I wasn't expecting an answer. It's hot as hell here. I'm gonna swim a bit so you might wanna pop off."

‹Nice try. This Omnicomputer is waterproof.›

Sima grumbled and grabbed her bra. Swimming in her underwear felt weird, but doing so with nothing at all felt even weirder. Since sweat had already dampened the fabric—and oppressive humidity kept them damp—she left them on and waded to the center where the water came up to her ribs. Eager to escape the heat, she let herself sink into the weak current, drifting like a piece of scrap wood while enjoying the cold seeping over her scalp. She drank and paddled around for the better part of the next hour.

Once shivering started, she swam to the edge, climbed out of the water, and sat in the grass to dry off.

I'm the only person on this planet. She stared past fluttering cyan leaves at darkening indigo overhead. A pair of moons, one pink and one orange, dominated the sky to the right. If the scene were an illustration, the moons would be an inch apart. She tried to guess if the orange moon being a quarter the size meant it was farther away or smaller.

So what am I going to do? Grow old alone and die? I'll probably go insane. That's what happens to people when they have no one to interact with. Sima closed her eyes, thinking back to the madness of living on the streets in the city. The toxic regions outside the walls were even deadlier than the demolition zones, though the Earth Government put on such a show of being all nice and shiny in the residential areas.

I wish they'd have just shot me. She sniffled as tears fell down her cheeks. *This is a cruel way to kill someone. New life and family my ass. I'm sixteen. Who adopts kids that old? They sent me up here to be someone's wife. They probably don't care the whole ship exploded.* Fifteen minutes later, an intense wave of loneliness made marrying a total stranger seem like not too bad an option, provided he didn't hit her. *I wonder who Mom's doing now. Does she even realize I'm no longer on the planet?* "She doesn't care. I'm not little and cute anymore."

Her bracelet chirped.

"What?" She held her arm up over her face.

‹Your appearance does qualify as 'cute' to a large segment of the population.›

This piece of metal is trying to make me feel better. She twirled it around her bony wrist. "Am I going to die?"

‹Yes… eventually.›

She rolled her eyes. "You know what I mean."

The screen blanked and retyped. ‹Probability of thriving here is approximately 84%.›

Sima let her arm flop at her side and traced her fingers around her stomach, wondering if it would be more painful to eat nothing but those fruits or let herself starve. Her mood dipped and swayed. *I'm millions of miles away from any humans. Would I even want to survive? I'll go mad like one of those men they found wandering the Northern Contamination Field.*

Tones like whalesong emanated from the sky as the sun weakened. More mantas glided overhead, some pairing off while others seemed in no hurry to be anywhere. Rippling flutters ran along the edges of their ray-wings from nose to tail. She listened to them call to each other, daydreaming about the home she ran away from and the mother who hadn't even noticed.

Suicide by not giving a crap is going to hurt like hell. She sat up, crossed her legs, and played with the grass by her ankles. *Okay. I could fight for survival, but why?*

After a few minutes of staring at her still-soaked excuse for clothes, she got up and searched for leaves, grass, or vines suitable for making some manner of skirt. Violet broad leaves she found turned out to be sticky and unpleasant to touch, due to tiny pointed hairs like needles. Worse, the hairs pricked her skin, drawing blood. Narrower blue ones had sharp edges with serration, and splintered into fibers when she tried to blunt them. The broad ones that she cut herself on before were hard as wooden plates, useless for any form of clothing. While the grass felt gossamer soft, it proved too brittle to work with and fell apart when she tried to weave it.

"What's the point?" She grumbled at her exposed body, feeling like one of the girls from Magdalena's sitting around in their underthings all day. At least the EGSF had given her plain ones nowhere near as skimpy or decorative, so they didn't embarrass her quite as much. "I'll wear these 'til they fall off. Not like there's anyone else here to see me."

After an hour more of aimless wandering, the sun had gone down and taken the oppressive heat with it. The air remained warm enough not to pose a risk to health, but stuck in her damp underwear, she found the breeze chilly.

It's dark. Primitive humans took shelter at night.

"Bracelet, can you find any shelter?"

Sima clicked her tongue for four minutes and eighteen seconds of 'please wait' before a magenta triangle, a directional arrow, appeared on the holographic screen. Below it, the number 247.

"Meters?"

The bracelet emitted a happy sounding chirp.

Two hundred and thirty meters later, she stumbled out of the underbrush into a circular clearing, unnatural in its perfection. At the far side, a trapezoidal stone doorway protruded from a dirt wall covered in vines. The opening widened toward the base, but had no sign of a door or way to close it.

"Umm, whoa. That's not a natural cave." She shoved branches out of her way and jogged up to the entrance, awestruck. Beyond it, a corridor the same size and shape as the door afforded her a good deal of clearance overhead. "Civilization here? This can't be human. We were supposed to be the first."

She wandered in, arms out to the sides, fingertips an inch or so shy of touching both walls. A short distance in from the door, the ground became a ramp, leading to a rounded chamber carved of pale grey rock. Thousands of grooves formed an intricate pattern of squared spirals and sections that resembled a printed circuit board. Every inch of the lines glowed with cobalt blue light. She ran her finger along one of the grooves, finding no heat, liquid, or apparent explanation for the luminosity.

A whistle slid past her teeth. "Some kind of aliens definitely built this. Well... I guess I'm the alien here."

Electronic patter emanated from the bracelet. ‹Eight years of reconnaissance probes to this planet found no evidence of civilized life.›

"Guess they went extinct. You think whatever made them die out will get me too?"

‹Insufficient data.›

She lowered her arm and wandered around the edge. The chamber's floor consisted of dirt, except for a seven-foot metal disc in the center covered with symbols that appeared laser-etched into the metal. She circled it once and settled down to sit on the ground, eyeing the platform with suspicion.

"That looks like where the aliens would sacrifice me." Despite having 'slept' for over two years, she yawned. "Wow, being the only human on a planet is tiring. Guess I overslept, huh?"

Text pattered along on the display. ‹Stasis is not the same as sleep. All brain functions are suspended.›

"So stasis makes people into politicians?"

Sima curled up on her side, using one arm as a pillow, and promised herself she wouldn't cry. Three minutes later, the thought of never seeing Earth again made her break it. She missed Cassie, despite the girl trying to talk her into whoring. She missed the Crash, despite the danger. She even missed Oema, and that little smile the girl flashed after pushing Draz's dead body aside to loot his video game unit. But most of all, she missed familiar surroundings, no matter how unpleasant they'd been.

I hate my mother; why do I want her?

STAGNANT AIR inside the cave dragged a reluctant Sima from sleep. A night spent on the ground left her already stasis-weary body aching and stiff. Never had she imagined she'd miss sleeping on moldy, thirty-year-old sofa at the end of an alley, garbage, vomit stains, and all, or her nest of shredded trash bags in a cistern underground.

At least on Earth, she could beg for food.

Sima shifted to sit cross-legged and wiped the crumbs from her eyes before dragging her hands over her head in a rough effort to comb her hair. "Ugh. I feel like crap." She sucked in a breath through her nose and leaned back to stretch, frowning at her thigh as she attempted to massage some feeling back into her muscles. "I didn't freeze well."

‹Good morning. The current local time is 10:11 a.m.›

She gasped, staring at the display above her arm. "Oh, no! I'm late for"—her voice fell to an unimpressed grumble—"roaming around alone and going crazy." She sat like a yogi, tapping her fingers on her knees. "Might as well get started."

It only took two minutes for Sima to give up trying to think calm, centering thoughts. Outside, the sun filtered through the jungle canopy, tinting the world in vivid shades of sapphire and green. She raised an arm to reduce the glare; the heat made her feel overdressed.

"Damn, I guess I'm starting to go native."

A gentle breeze caused her hair to tickle the small of her back, an inch or so above the waistband of her underpants. She absently scratched at the spot, enjoying the brief respite from the heat. After finding a secluded place in the woods to relieve herself, she wandered back to the river, shrugged off her undergarments, and went for a swim.

The initial nervous thrill of skinny-dipping faded with the realization no one *could* catch her. Embarrassment lessened with each passing minute. A dip in this stream bothered her much less than having to shower in front of two cops. Between the relaxing warmth of the sun and the soft current, she lost herself in the wonder of an environment devoid of metal sidewalks and grime-smeared buildings.

Sima soaked for a while, swam back and forth for a while more, and spent quite a few minutes diving to examine a spread of pearlescent lavender stones on the riverbed. Her third time under, she reached out to pick one of the plum-sized rocks up, but it sprouted legs and scurried away. Her shriek filled a bubble as she kicked up from the bottom, startled. As soon as her head broke the surface, she gasped for air, laughing while choking on water.

An hour and fourteen minutes later according to the bracelet, she crawled out of the water and found a few of the fruits she recognized. Sima sat on the grass next to her still-dry clothes and ate while listening to the hiss of wind in the trees and the languid calls of sky-mantas, flying unseen beyond the thick canopy of blue leaves.

I'm sitting naked on the bank of a river on an alien world. This has got to be some messed up dream. Maybe the EGSF is using me as a guinea pig for some kinda new drug. She shivered at the thought. *I'm dead either way. Mirage... yeah right. I'm strapped to a table somewhere dreaming, with a wire plugged into my skull.*

She leaned forward, chin on her knees, long hair falling in a cascade around her feet. *Dammit, Mom. Why'd you have to be like that? Why did I run away? Oh yeah... him.* Her gaze fell, burdened by the fear she would wind up a crazed wild thing far removed from humanity. She stared into a shifting reflection upon the water's surface, counting tree stalks.

"Bracelet, how long does it take someone to go nuts from being alone?"

‹Insufficient data. Too many variables.›

Sima sighed, folded her arms across her knees, and bowed her head. The doldrums passed after a few minutes and she looked up toward the sky again, mere flecks of light leaking between leaves. A nearby *thump* made her gasp and cover herself with her arms. She glared at the spot for a moment before realizing the noise had come from a fruit falling, not a person sneaking up on her.

A long sigh slid out her nose. "There's no one else here."

Thinking about the other kids she'd seen in the stasis pods before they left Earth made her curl up and cry. *It's not fair. They didn't deserve to die.* Had all the 'good karma' she'd banked on Earth, not breaking the law for four years, been the reason she lived? In her mind, some abstract catastrophe caused the *Progenitor* to explode near this planet or during reentry. Something horrible must've happened for the ship to section the stasis chamber up into individual escape modules and jettison them. Could any others have made it? Her stasis pod had been in the deepest corner, perhaps all the way at the back of the ship. If the front end exploded first, she would've had the best chance.

Maybe there are other pods? Her hope didn't last long. *No... they would've landed near mine. I didn't see any more. And something almost smashed mine.* She shuddered at the thought of the huge metal flange speared into the floor near her pod. Had whatever struck her lifeboat hit it a few feet over, she never would've woken up.

Perhaps karma *hadn't* been kind to her after all. Better to have gone silently to oblivion without ever opening her eyes again. Being stranded alone on an unknown planet promised a far worse end.

"Blah." She lay back in the grass and let the air lift the water from her skin.

She eventually stood and put her 'clothes' back on. Despite being the only human anywhere within a two-year-long flight, it still felt improper to traipse about naked. However, if she couldn't find any usable plant material to make garments from, going full tribal would happen eventually whether she wanted it to or not. Her garments wouldn't last forever. At least they'd been new when she got them, so she had time yet. Then again, she may very well die before they wore out.

After a while of sitting there moping, curiosity pulled her into the woods. She wandered with no destination in mind, still astounded by being able to see and touch actual plant life. Loud creaking, like two giant slabs of rock scraping against each other came from somewhere off to the left.

One of those strange birds strode along at a lazy pace, its head perched atop a long neck at the level of the treetops. It sniffed at fruit pods dangling from the branches far out of her reach. Unlike the ones near the ground, these had a dark blue color with round, fluorescent green 'melons' embedded in them. Rather than pluck the fruits off the pod, the bird ate the entire thing whole, some twenty or so fruits in one go. She followed along, watching it eat pod after pod.

She thought about a movie she'd seen years ago, back when her 'bed' consisted of a ratty couch at the back of a dead end alley. Given her age at the time—about thirteen—she probably shouldn't have been allowed to watch it. Despite the graphic portrayal of the sort of thing that went on inside Magdalena's happening quite a few times, it also featured a Star Soldier stranded in the woods of an unknown world. That woman had made temporary shelter from trees. Although, the trees on that 'alien planet' looked much more Earthlike than the forest around Sima here.

Besides, the soldier also had a huge knife. Sima couldn't exactly cut down thin trees or hack all the branches off with her bare hands. Searching around for already-fallen sticks didn't get her anywhere, and a few exploratory tugs at branches close in diameter to her arms proved she had no chance whatsoever of breaking them.

"Okay, I guess I'm not building a hut. Hey bracelet, do you have a laser?"

‹Yes.›

"Can you cut down trees with it?" asked Sima, her eyebrows up.

‹No. It is only a scanning device. You have already seen it.›

"Oh." Grumbling, she turned in place, studying the jungle. A bug the size of a man's fist sailed by, emitting a deep, droning buzz. "Eep!"

Sima ran, despite the insect having no apparent interest in her, and didn't stop until her legs threatened to dump her to the ground. She stumbled to a halt, looked around at the jungle, and took a seat on an enormous root as high off the ground as an ordinary chair. Gasping for breath, she held her head in both hands, staring down at the dirt between her feet.

"What the heck was that thing?"

‹Out of range.›

"Thanks," she deadpanned. "That giant bug is going to *stay* out of range. What should I do?"

‹Locate a source of shelter. Second priority is to locate a source of water. Once you have located shelter and a ready supply of water, food should be the third priority. Technically, fire would normally be number three, but you are in no danger of hypothermia on this planet.›

She leaned back and gazed around at the unbelievable amount of living stuff. In all her sixteen years, the most vegetation she'd ever seen had been two potted plants, one of which had turned out to be plastic. 'Vegetables' in food didn't count, since most of what she ate came from slime. On the rare occasion she'd gotten 'real' vegetables, they'd been produced at hydroponics farms where they grew massive, mutant versions of what those plants had once been. Her science teacher claimed carrots had once been long and thin, not discs the size of dinner plates, but she didn't believe him. Torrent even told her that the Earth Government had to build machines to clean the air since too many plants had died off or been replaced with city.

Thinking about Torrent made her blush again at the idea of him wandering out of the jungle and finding her lounging around in her underwear. Though it had none of the decorative frilliness of the stuff worn by Magdalena's girls, she kinda felt like one of them, sitting brazenly out in the open with so little on. She clung to the notion that, unlike them, she didn't *want* to. Sima wasn't *showing off* her body, she had no choice.

And really, what difference did it make? It's not as if anyone existed here to see her, and even if they did, she knew nothing about survival in the woods, so she'd probably be dead soon. She could take care of herself on the streets just fine, but this place went way beyond her skills. At soft digital pattering, she sat forward and held her left arm up to read the screen.

‹Do not give up.›

"You can read my mind?"

‹No, but your slowing heart rate and posture indicate an increased negative emotional state.›

"Just thinking I'm going to be dead soon is all. Not that I wanna die. I'm a city kid. I don't know anything about living in the stupid woods."

‹Shelter: That cave. Food: those fruit pods. Water: you've been swimming. Collect some of those pods and move them to the cave. Use it as your base of exploration.›

"Okay." Sima stood, dusted flaky bits and soil from her rear end, and walked four steps before stopping to gaze around at alien trees that looked the same in every direction. "Umm. I have no idea where the cave is."

‹I have it marked as a waypoint. Follow the yellow arrow.›

Sima looked down at her forearm. The holographic display had become like a compass, with a bright yellow triangle floating by her wrist. She turned in place until it pointed straight ahead, then made her way into the woods. Her mind compared the cave to the Crash, and she laughed.

‹What is funny?›

A grin curled her lip. "I've spent a lot of time underground, but I didn't join the Underground."

‹I do not understand.›

Laughing, Sima walked around trees and ducked low-hanging fruit pods while explaining to a computer bracelet about the Separatists and the street gang loyal to their cause.

I'm talking to a piece of jewelry that I can't take off. She shook her head, rolling her eyes. *At least this one won't blow up.*

14

LAST BREATH

Her Omnicomputer bantered with her as she walked, chatting via the constant patter of text appearing on a holographic screen at the underside of her arm. She thought of it like she used a super primitive interface to have a conversation with a human being, as if she'd made electronic contact with someone from three hundred years ago before holographic displays and virtual reality had gone mainstream.

Heh. I used to call text primitive, but guess who's running around the jungle.

All of a sudden, the yellow triangle floating over her left forearm glided counterclockwise until it pointed diagonally off to the left. *Hmm. That's odd.* She peered in that direction, wondering if the bracelet had been leading her in a not-straight line to avoid an obstruction, or if something went wrong with its navigation ability.

About a hundred yards off, a patch of light-colored wood caught her eye where a tree had cracked in half. More damage to leaf-tendrils and branches spread from either side, suggesting something large had crashed through the trees. *Another lifeboat came down there!* Her gaze snapped from one torn up leaf to another. *That's definitely a crash path!* She gasped. *I'm not alone!*

Sima ran as fast as the foliage would allow, grimacing whenever a thin vine whipped across her shins or stomach. Desperation mounted in her heart with each delay caused by thick growth, mud, or fallen trees. Perhaps the bracelet had picked up a signal from the capsule and pointed her at it? The yellow arrow continued to guide her in the same direction the damage path had ripped in the foliage.

A few minutes of desperate scrambling later, she stopped short at the edge of a stream sunken four feet down in a channel flanked by dangling tube-shaped strands of luminous, purple plants. Both edges curved down, overgrown with the light-emitting plant. A fall would guarantee having to follow the current until the gully became shallow enough for her to escape. She tested the edge with her toes, finding the glowing plants fragile and slippery when broken.

No way I'm climbing this if I fall in.

She stood tall and peered into the trees on the other side. An edge of gleaming white metal caught the sun not too far ahead. An outline of human technology—another lifeboat—stood out unmistakable from the flora. The stream went too far in either direction for her patience. A fall would take too long to recover from. Something told her she had to get to the other lifeboat *now*.

It's a shorter gap than the jump between the Harmony Towers.

Her body trembled. How could leaping a tiny drop scare her more than a forty-story fall? After a few steps back, she sprinted and jumped across, landing with the grace of the forest sylph she had become. She kept her momentum and continued at a light run until she emerged from the woods into a large, oval-shaped clearing with trees on all sides.

The second lifeboat sat at the end of a shorter impact trench, suggesting it had fallen at a much steeper trajectory than her lifeboat. Twisted, mangled metal at the far left corner had no traces of dirt or vegetation clinging to the damage. *Whatever smashed it happened before it landed. The ship hit something... or something hit the ship.* Her thrill faded to terror, expecting the occupants would be dead. *I... gotta know.*

Sima crept up to the door and crouched. Her escape capsule had landed with a rearward tilt, which elevated the exit. This one came to rest in the opposite manner, forcing her to spend a few minutes digging out the door with her bare hands. As soon as she exposed the entire bottom of the hatch, she stood and grabbed the handle. It didn't budge, so she added a second hand, gritting her teeth and grunting as she pulled. With a grind of metal, it broke loose and opened. She braced her foot on the wall and pushed the door inward. The expected blast of ice-cold never came.

Warm, muggy air greeted her, hotter inside than out. A crimped beam pressed down in the middle of the ceiling, along with a 'waterfall' of mangled metal that divided the chamber like a wall. Of the two stasis pods in the lifeboat, the farther one vanished under the enormous pile of ceiling bits, wires, and scrap metal. The closer pod looked intact, though the windows had fogged to the point of opacity, except for one small hand pressed against the transparent plastic from inside. The occupant couldn't have been older than nine or so.

"Oh, no." Sima gathered her hands to her mouth and cried. Morbid curiosity pulled her closer. Paradoxically to the heat inside the escape capsule, the stasis pod windows had a coating that resembled frost. She set her hand against the dusty crystals, which didn't feel cold, and brushed away a clear swath.

Two small children inside curled up facing each other. The girl looked about six, scrawny, pale, and blonde. The boy had rich brown skin and appeared a little older than the girl. His hand pressed against the transparent cover as if he'd been trying to open their coffin before he gave out. Both of them had been stuffed in the stasis pod in their underpants, as the Earth Government Security Force had done with Sima, though the girl had no top.

A lack of blood or visible injury did little to make the sight of two tiny bodies less horrible.

Sima stared at the girl, overcome by a memory of being petrified at the entrance of the boarding tunnel. She'd seen the little girl before, barely conscious over the shoulder of an EGSF officer carrying her. The child hadn't appeared at all frightened, even smiled like she couldn't wait to get on the ship. Little had she known how the trip would end. Sima draped herself over the pod window, and wept.

What were their last thoughts? As terrified as she had been about leaving Earth, she couldn't imagine what the experience must've been like for little kids. Not long ago, she'd have looked at these kids with a scowl, hating them for being tiny and adorable, muscling in on her begging territory. But the sight of them dead broke something inside her heart. Despair exploded into rage.

Sima shrieked curses at the smashed ceiling. "Who gave you the right to do this? What did we ever do to your perfect society? You lied! It's not a project! You rounded us all up and shot us into space like trash!" She pounded on the pod's window. "They're just kids!"

A faint knock startled her. The boy's eyes had opened and he stared at her through the foggy glass as if he'd seen a ghost.

She gawked in stunned silence for a few seconds before yelling, "You're alive!"

The boy sat up, slapping the lid. "Help! We can't get out."

Sima pointed at the head end. "Rip up the pillow. Hit the red button."

He crawled around, jostling the girl, who also sat up.

"I told you someone would find us." The girl flashed a dazed smile, her eyes fluttering as if she teetered on the verge of losing consciousness again.

"I'm going to get you out." Sima patted the lid near the girl. "Stay awake."

Velcro ripping preceded the sound of a small fist banging on plastic.

"It's broke," yelled the boy. "The button ain't doin' nothin'."

Sima stood on tiptoe to see over his shoulder. Sure enough, he slapped at the red mushroom-shaped button that had released her. *They've been trapped in there for two days.* She ran to the foot end, finding the console dark. Bent ceiling panels, exposed wires, and random bits of metal dangled from overhead. Dark gaps in the junk flickered with the occasional spark. *No power.*

Reason fled. She grabbed the motorized lift arm and attempted to force it open by hand. The task felt as though she tried to wrestle a stone statue. The boy sat still, watching Sima punch, kick, and strain against the machinery for a few minutes.

"We are gonna run out of air." He put an arm around the girl. "She's been sick."

"No." Sima growled, clasping her hands together and bashing at the transparent panel. The crack of plastic echoed over and over. *I can't let them die. No way. I can't bear to watch that.* She backed off, rubbing her sore hands. *I can't leave them either.*

"Break the glass!" shouted the girl before lapsing into a coughing fit.

Sima spun around, nearly slipping on the condensation-covered floor. She ran to the storage cabinets and ripped open one door after the next. As with her lifeboat, the 'emergency supply' cabinets were all empty.

"Cheap bastards!" she screamed.

She looked up, eyeing the damaged ceiling near the middle of the pod where the metal crimped down. Maybe a strut or hunk of debris would be heavy enough to crack the plastic windows. Before she could take a step, a splash of bright red caught her eye on the left. A box on the wall bore the word 'fire' in plain lettering. Sima rushed across the room and tore it open, finding a fire suppression cylinder and a beautiful, shiny all-metal single-bladed axe with a rubberized handle.

As if claiming the Holy Grail, she plucked the weapon from its clips and beheld it. The composite blade weighed like heavy plastic, lighter than it appeared for its size, with most of the mass concentrated at the head end. She smiled back at the kids, but her elation died when the girl slumped over. The boy blinked, swaying side to side.

"You tried," he mumbled.

"No!" yelled Sima.

She scrambled to run to the pod, but slipped and landed on her butt before sliding, skin squeaking, into the side of their stasis chamber with her legs in the air. Ignoring the pain, she clambered to her feet, waving the axe at him. "Get to the pillow end."

The boy dragged the limp rag-doll of a girl with him to the top, and curled an arm over her protectively.

No. No. No. Sima raised the axe and brought it down with all the strength she could muster. The blade glanced off the plastic each time with a sharp *click*. Again and again, she chopped, leaving scratches and scuff marks in the thick material. "Please, no. Come on." She bashed it six more times, aiming for the same spot, but succeeding only in making a bigger white starburst as the curved blade skipped away. Another three swings left her winded. She glanced at the kids inside the pod while pausing to catch her breath.

The boy had collapsed over the girl, neither one moving.

15

THE OTHER SIDE

Defeated, Sima slid to her knees, sobbing.

The axe clattered to the floor in front of her knees. Tears streaming from her eyes, she stared at the useless thing. For all the sharpness of its edge, it kept bouncing off the window. *I hate this place. This is too cruel.* A few breaths later, her focus settled on the opposite side of the head—a four-inch spike shaped like an elongated pyramid.

She let off a primal roar and sprang to her feet, seizing the axe in both hands. *They're not gonna die. Not in front of me.* Her weary arms trembled as she raised the weapon over her head. Desperation flowed along every fiber of her muscles. With a banshee shriek, she drove the point into the same spot she'd been striking with the curved blade. It caught rather than glanced, sticking into the plastic. She rocked it back and forth to free it, staggering when it came loose. A quick peek at the two little figures slumped inside the pod triggered a surge of adrenaline. Again, she brought the axe down with a deep *thud*, three inches of spike punching a hole in the pod window.

I'm gonna get them out. I have to get them out. I can't stop.

She pushed the axe like the tiller of a boat, side to side, cracking the plastic. *Yes! Come on. Come on.* Sima jerked it loose and swung again at a spot nearby, then another one, creating the outline of a larger circle.

After three more swings, a chunk of plastic fell in, creating an opening large enough for her arm.

"Hey! Come on. Wake up. Breathe!" She yelled into the hole.

Neither child moved.

Eyes blurred with tears, Sima launched into a fury, swinging over and over at the general vicinity of the damned window. With a hole to aim for, she used the blade side, which easily sliced into the vulnerable edge. Clattering strikes of titanium on plastic rang off the walls of the lifeboat. When she stopped moving, she gawked at the ruin of the entire right lower panel, fragments of the half-inch thick resin glimmered like ice crystals on the white padding.

She dropped the axe and leaned in, stretching to reach the kids. Up on tiptoe, she managed to get her hand on a tiny foot. Patting and squeezing the girl, she yelled, "Wake up! Please... wake up."

"Mmm," moaned the little girl.

The boy stirred. He blinked dazedly at her and coughed.

Sima slumped limp on the cushions, overwhelmed with relief.

"Hey, you're inside," muttered the boy.

"Come on, get out of there," said Sima.

He crawled over and grabbed her arm. She gripped the girl's ankle and dragged her close, slipping her other arm under the child and easing her out of the pod. Within a second of her standing upright with the girl in her arms, the boy clamped onto her. His weight pulled her to her knees. She fell sideways and wound up seated on the floor with her back against the pod, two little kids holding on for dear life.

Her arms throbbed. Soreness spread around from the base of her neck into her ribs and down to her hands. She could only sit limp while the children clung to her. The boy trembled in terror, but his face appeared calm. The girl coughed and shivered, seeming too weak to cry. A resonant wheeze in her chest, like someone crushing bubble packing, accompanied every breath.

"You really broke it." The boy's rich brown eyes grew wide and wet. "I thought we were gonna die. I was going to sleep."

"No, you're not. I got you." Sima found a little strength and wrapped her arms around them. "You need water... as soon as I can move."

"We're not supposed to trust grown-ups," whispered the girl. "But you saved us."

Sima sniffled. "I'm not a grown-up. I'm sixteen."

"That's old," said the girl.

Both kids jumped at the sudden start of a laboring mechanical whine. A groan of protesting metal followed two seconds later. The entire wall of twisted metal dividing the room in half shuddered and rattled, a few small scraps of metal clattering to the floor. After a few seconds, the whirring halted.

Sima looked up at the ceiling. Debris around where the large girder pierced the white tiles wobbled as though something had moved it.

"Help!" yelled a muted child's voice from the pile of rubble.

Oh, no. Another one? Sima struggled to stand, but the kids held her down like ten-ton weights. "Hey, I need you two to let me up. There's more kids in here."

"Just one." The boy slid away from her and sat on the floor. "They stuck me and Lissa together 'cause we're small. He's bigger."

Lissa tightened her grip, shivering. "Don't go."

Sima grasped the child by the wrists and eased her grip open. "I'm not going away. I have to help the other boy."

The gaunt little girl sniffled, but complied. She slid down to her feet and took a step back. New, white underpants the EGSF gave her almost slipped off her insubstantial frame. She looked like many of the unwanted Outcast kids roaming the streets. Despite the inside of the lifeboat being hot and humid, the little one shivered. Her breathing picked up speed, accompanied by a faint crackle of mucous. Sima plucked sticky sensor pads from the girl's forehead and chest and tossed them aside.

"You need food," said Sima.

"Hey, I can't get out," yelled the other kid, likely a boy. "It opened a inch, but it's jammed."

Sima crawled around the empty stasis pod with Lissa hovering close. The way the roof crimped in allowed a small passage between the two sections of the room, but getting through would require sliding on her belly under a mass of mangled metal.

"Lissa, stay with…" Sima pointed at the boy.

"Juan," he said.

Lissa pouted.

"Please, sweetie." Sima hugged her. "I'll be right back. I promise."

Once the child trudged back to Juan, Sima flattened out on the smooth floor and pulled herself under the debris fall. Grit scratched at her sweaty skin, which otherwise slid with ease over the metal tiles. Jutting scraps poked her in the shoulders, butt, and leg, making her feel as though she crawled under a mass of deadly knives. She twisted to peer uneasily up at the twisted remains of the lifeboat's roof and the machinery responsible for pumping air into the stasis pods.

If this thing shifts, I'm going to be trapped… or shredded. Ugh, don't think that. Go forward.

Inch by inch, she crawled. Something pointy scraped along her back and threatened to pull her underpants off, though it didn't hurt, so she hoped it hadn't cut her. She exhaled to make herself smaller, freed her snagged waistband, and grabbed at the floor to drag herself forward. Once clear of the debris fall, she got to her feet. The avalanche of warped metal divided what had been one single room into two, the rear chamber somewhat smaller than the outer one. Several large metal beams pressed down on top of the second stasis pod, pinning the lid closed. Sparks spat from openings in the rear wall where metal panels had fallen away, revealing the mechanical workings that had split the once enormous stasis pod bay into individual lifeboats. Head-sized holes in the hull at the back wall offered a view of the grass outside.

Sima rubbed a scratch on her left thigh and hurried over to the pod.

A frightened boy a few years older than Juan huddled inside, curled up by emergency open button, his teeth chattering. Fog leaked from a crack in the upper window at the point where a thick girder had cracked it, as well as the opening where the clamshell lid had gone up a few inches.

She stepped closer into the fog, cold enough to make her gasp. The fear on his face gave way to hope when she brushed at the ice crystals on the outside of the lid. He fell on his side, reaching an arm out the few-inch gap between the stasis pod lid and the bed. She took his hand in both of hers, alarmed at the coldness of his skin. This pod's cooling system appeared to be working still, leaving the inside like a freezer. Huge brown eyes set in a round face brimmed with tears. He seemed to be fighting to look brave, but couldn't stop sniffling. Numerous small scars marked his shins and forearms, trophies from jumping among buildings and ruins—another Outcast street rat in brand-new EG-provided briefs.

Sima rubbed and patted his hand. Gratitude at finding him alive stole any words from her tongue. He didn't have to beg for his life, the expression on his face did all the work.

No wonder he looks healthier than the other two. He's a master at that look.

For an instant, old jealousy welled up inside her. This boy could make four or five times what she could at begging—but that didn't matter anymore. She sighed out her nose, feeling like an awful person for being envious of a kid stuck in a broken stasis pod. The most well practiced pleading stare in the world couldn't convince death to leave him alone.

Sima frowned at the girder pinning the lid down. The boy must've overheard her tell Juan to check under the pillow, and the mechanical whine came from the pod attempting to open. She didn't trust her arms to be able to withstand another smashing session... that she had broken the first window defied belief. *I'm not strong enough to do that again... and I think I hurt myself.* Minutes passed as she studied the way the duralloy beam draped over the stasis pod and stuck into the floor like a javelin.

An idea dawned.

"Be right back." She let go of his arm and scooted to the gap she'd crawled through. "Juan?"

"Yes?" asked a small voice from the other side of the tunnel.

"Slide the axe to me please."

Lissa coughed.

A moment later, Juan crawled in from the mangled tunnel, stood, and held up the axe. She patted him on the head and pointed back. "Stay with Lissa. She's scared."

"So am I." He stared down at his toes.

Lissa crawled in behind him and grabbed Sima around the thigh, peering up at her with soulful blue eyes.

"Okay, fine. Stay on this side, but wait here. I'm going to try and move that beam, and I don't want it falling on you."

The kids huddled against the wall of useless storage compartments.

Sima knelt by where the metal girder pierced the floor and wedged the axe head under it, using it like a pry bar to lever the duralloy shaft out of the divot it made. It gave a few centimeters, but she couldn't get it to pop over the lip of the gouge.

"Hit the button again," yelled Sima, while pulling on the axe handle.

Whirring came from the pod as its motors protested the weight bearing down on the upper half. She clenched her jaw and growled, straining already-spent arms. The struggling pod lid shifted the girder forward. Something exploded with a sharp *bang* in the wall, and a shower of sparks rained down over the pod's lid. Sima reared up on her knees, and pushed downward on the handle with all her weight.

The beam popped free of the hole. Tension released, the axe sprang loose and went flying into the wall with a ringing series of clangs as Sima fell flat on her face. A spine-wrenching screech of metal flooded the room from the girder scraping over the floor, bending from the force of the lid rising. Juan and Lissa clamped their hands over their ears.

Another blast of sparks accompanied a sizzling noise and the light inside the second pod going out. At that instant, the lid jammed, only a few inches wider than it had been. The boy crawled to the foot end, stretched his arms out the gap, and slithered forward. His hips became stuck, leaving his fingertips inches from reaching the floor.

Sima scrambled to her feet, grabbed his arms, and pulled. He grunted, bracing a foot on the inside wall and pushing. After much groaning and squirming, he popped free with a sudden lurch, knocking her off balance. She landed flat on her back with him sprawled on top of her, as cold as a hunk of chicken taken out of a fridge. Sima stared at the mangled ceiling, not quite sure how to process having a boy lying on top of her, both of them in their underwear.

If he was two years older, this would be awkward.

"That was awesome!" He hugged her before crawling off and kneeling beside her. "Wow, you're pretty."

She sat up, covering herself with her arms, blushing, and staring at him. At his lighter skin tone, she figured him for culturally mixed, though something about his face suggested a strong Middle Eastern influence, probably one Caucasian parent. Juan picked his nose. Lissa stared at her, grinding her toes into the floor. After a few seconds, she ran over and clamped on.

Sima tugged the girl's drooping underpants up. "We need to get some food in you."

The older of the two boys glared at the storage cabinets. "They're empty. They stole my Wondercube. I had like a million games."

"Yeah. The cabinets in my escape pod were empty too." Sima looked at his arms. "Where's your bracelet computer?"

"You're a juvie, aren't you? Only the criminals got them, so they can't run away."

Sima blushed. "I'm... I was picking up food packets after a transport flipped. I'm not a criminal."

"Doesn't matter." The older boy folded his arms. "You got arrested and you're guilty of whatever they made up."

At the delicate pattering of electronic typing, she raised her arm. The bracelet's holographic screen appeared, text already in the midst of typing itself out.

‹The boy is not yet old enough for an Omnicomputer as he has not reached twelve years. Children are not expected to leave the colony safe zones. Adolescents such as yourself are to be tasked with jobs, which may present risk. I assure you, I am not a restraint device or a mark of criminality.›

"I'd believe that more if I could take you off," she muttered and carried Lissa over to the wall, where she picked among the swaying cabinet doors, confirming them all empty.

"Bastards skimped. They stuck us on this colony ship off the record." The older boy did a little bouncing dance, his legs pinned together. "Be right back. I gotta piss."

"How do you know that?" Sima followed him to the tunnel out. "I mean that they skimped."

He got down onto his belly and shimmied under the mangled metal. "The EGSF guys that rounded us up were talking about it."

"That's horrible. Why would they do that?" asked Sima.

"We're not worth anything to them," yelled the boy from the other side of the tunnel.

Sima set Lissa down and ushered her into the opening. "Stay low so you don't cut yourself."

The little one flattened herself out and crawled without a word. Juan followed, and Sima dragged herself through last.

Bouncing on his toes, the older boy paused at the door. "They gave us food and a bed. Even had a game room while we stayed there. It wasn't like we were arrested. 'Course, we had no choice 'bout bein' shot into space. They promised us families who'd like want us."

Lissa sniffled. "They were gonna fix my breaths even more here."

Juan mutely wrapped his arms around Sima.

The eldest boy exited the lifeboat. "Whoa…"

Sima held the smaller kids' hands and ducked the top of the hatch to step outside. The older boy had stopped three steps out of the dirt pit, staring dumbstruck at the alien forest. Lissa smiled at the sky. Juan looked confused.

"What's that?" Juan pointed.

Sima squinted. "I think it's a tree. You've never seen trees before? Not even in school?"

All three children shook their heads. The older boy looked around for a moment before selecting a bush to water. Sima sighed in her head. Like her, all these kids had ever seen of the world were rancid alleys full of desperate, cramped people. *It's a miracle they lived long enough to be sent to die here.* She closed her eyes, trying to stop herself from crying. Lissa giggled from a short distance away. *It's not fair.* She opened her eyes to find the girl chasing a butterfly-like creature with a long trailing phosphorescent blue tail. Juan explored in short steps, squirming from the sensation of grass and tall plants touching him.

The older boy returned and stood next to Sima.

She glanced at him. "So, what's your name?"

"You first."

"Sima."

"I'm Austin."

After a few minutes exploring their new environment, the children clustered around her, staring up with expectation on their faces. *Why are they looking at me like that? What am I supposed to do? I'm still a kid, too.* Hatred for the Earth Government Security Force burbled along with bile in the back of her throat. On the streets, she couldn't *stand* little kids. Either they whined, made too much noise, or got more charity because they were cuter than an older girl. Lissa's huge blue eyes hit her with a heavy crash of guilt. No words had to be exchanged. All three asked her for help.

Whatever. Not like there's an ORC bin around I can throw them into get them out of my hair.

The weight of this new responsibility made her sick to her stomach, or perhaps the discomfort in her belly came from the near miss of almost watching two children suffocate. She swallowed hard and gathered the kids close. Lissa adored the embrace, though Juan grew restless after a few seconds.

"Okay, you three need water and food. I found some fruits we can eat. Stay here and I'll get some."

"No," whispered Lissa. "Don't leave us."

"Wait!" Juan scrambled back inside the escape pod, and returned a moment later with an empty plastic jug. "For water."

"I won't be long." Sima smiled down at the girl while brushing strands of blonde away from her face. "Bracelet, set a waypoint here."

A beep emanated from her right wrist.

"That's cool." Austin grabbed her arm, ogling the bracelet. "What else does it do?"

The holo panel appeared. ‹Scanning, location tracking, time display, Dreamland access (no connection), wireless communication (no signal detected), navigation, encyclopedia functions, bio monitoring, companionship, and sarcasm.›

Sima handed Austin the axe and took the empty bottle. "Watch the little ones. I'll be back in ten minutes."

He saluted and stood like a soldier.

Lissa accused Sima of abandoning them with a glance and broke into sniffles. Juan shivered in fear, but nodded.

"I promise I will be *right* back." Sima gave her a kiss atop the head and trotted off.

The plastic jug had a plain white label with black lettering identifying the contents as 'protein base fluid C'. A thin residue of beige goop clung to the inside, the top evidently sheared off in the crash. Likely, some part of that tangled mess in the lifeboat had impaled it.

Sima headed toward the nearest water source as indicated by a handy little map display courtesy of the bracelet. She squatted at the bank of a bubbling stream and drank a few handfuls. After rinsing the bottle and filling it as much as it could hold with water, she headed back toward the lifeboat, taking a slight detour upon spotting one of the spiked pods a short distance away.

She couldn't reach any of the fruits since the pod hovered about twice her height off the ground. The thinness of the stem gave her the idea it might be easy to bend. She set the water bottle on the ground, grabbed the tall plant, and pulled. Perhaps helped along by the weight of the massive fruit-bearing structure at the top, the stalk bent with relative ease, bringing the spiky pod within reach. After gathering an armload of the crimson fruits, she let go, allowing the plant to bob back into the air. Sima retrieved the water and walked, careful to watch for thorns and not drop any of her bundle, following the yellow triangle floating above her arm.

Whoever said you grow up to be like your parents needs to burn in hell. Mom always screamed I'd have kids by sixteen, but I don't think this counts.

Soon, she emerged from the trees into the clearing the crash made around the lifeboat.

"Sima!" Lissa squealed and sprinted over, almost losing her underpants in the process.

The child's impact knocked the fruits everywhere and nearly took Sima off her feet. She yelled in alarm, focusing on keeping the water from spilling. Austin ran over and took the jug before she dropped it, and downed several long gulps. Juan, not strong enough to lift the nearly full jug, scooped handfuls of water out of it and drank. Sima decided to sit in place, and Lissa climbed into her lap, wrapping her arms and legs around her like a trembling koala. Sima's heart sank. *This kid is so convinced I'm going to abandon her.*

"Hey," whispered Sima, rubbing the girl's back. "It's okay. I'm not gonna leave you guys. I mean it. Here, you need to drink. You've been two days without any water."

When Sima eased her around toward the bottle, now on the ground, Lissa released her grip enough to stick her face in the top and suck down water in rapid gulps. Juan and Austin gathered up the fruits, making a pile nearby before sitting as if in a campfire circle.

Sima fixed Lissa's pants back in place, then used the axe to chop one of the fruits in half for her.

She held the end to the girl's mouth. "Here, you can eat this. It tastes sweet at first, but it has a bitter flavor after. Don't eat the peel."

Lissa nibbled and made a sour face, turning away. A few seconds later, she nibbled again, her expression confused.

"It tastes better if you eat it fast." Sima prodded her in the lips with the fruit until she took a bigger bite.

The boys dug in, both cringing at the initial overbearing sweetness, then grimacing at the sharp aftertaste. Soon, hunger and the raspberry flavor overpowered their initial revulsion, and the kids stuffed themselves. Lissa lost interest in food after half a fruit, but Sima kept at her until she finished a whole one. Juan drank more, and threw a little water on his face.

Sima sat cross-legged and ate two fruits, rushing the process so the nasty rhubarb-like aftertaste never quite overpowered the initial blast of sweet berry. Lissa stuck her finger in one of the abandoned rinds and painted purple lines on her pale chest.

"Wow, it's so hot here," said Austin, squinting into a light breeze that didn't do much to alleviate the oppressive humidity.

"It's nice," whispered Lissa.

Juan shrugged.

"How hot is it?" asked Austin.

Pattering came from the bracelet. ‹99.4 degrees.›

There had been a few days hotter than that back home, but there, humidity never amounted to much. Usually, those days, Sima would stay underground somewhere until it cooled off at night. She gazed up at the sky, which didn't look *too* much different from home—giant mantas notwithstanding. Though, the blue color, so rich and endless, might've been what Earth had looked like centuries ago, not the drab bluish-grey she got to see on 'clear' days.

"The sky is pretty. Look how blue it is," said Sima.

All three kids looked up.

"Ooo," said Lissa. "It *is* pretty."

"Wow." Austin gazed left and right. "What are those white spots?"

"Umm, I think they're stars," said Sima. "Saw them in school."

"You went to school?" asked Juan, awe in his eyes.

Sima nodded. "Yeah, until grade six."

"I was in fifth," said Austin. "They didn't show us anything about stars."

"A teacher I had said the EG doesn't like people to know that," said Sima. "About pollution, because it makes people want the government to clean it, and they won't."

"I never did school." Juan shook his head. "I'm only eight."

Lissa looked up at the sky until she fell over backward in the grass. "I was first grade." She counted from one to six. "I'm six years ol—" She broke up into a coughing fit, her face reddening.

Sima held her, patting her back until the choking subsided. The girl turned her head and spat a glop of faintly-pink-hued mucous into the grass.

"Eww," muttered Austin.

Lissa snuggled against Sima, having lost her talkative mood. Silent tears of pain wet her cheeks. Any of the mean things Sima may have blurted to little kids back on Earth had never caused one to make such a face. With no idea what else to do, she cradled the girl and rocked her softly.

"Aren't we supposed to start a fire or something?" asked Austin.

"There's no wood." Juan shook his head. "And it's already hot."

"What happened to the ship? Did they kick us out?" Austin glanced at the lifeboat. "Or did it blow up?"

Sima brushed Lissa's hair with her fingers, overcome by the girl's far-away stare. "I'm not really sure, but I think it blew up. I don't believe the EGSF wanted to kill us… just kick us off the Earth. The ship was supposed to land and turn into a city or something."

"Cool," said Juan. "Like *Mechopolis*."

"Nuh uh." Austin smirked. "That's a cartoon robot. The ship's not gonna turn into a robot. It just lands and opens up like a noodle bar awning. Then people build onto it. But it's not gonna. Lifeboats launch automatically. Something bad happened."

"There's no city?" whispered Lissa.

"I don't know." Sima kept brushing at the girl's hair.

"It exploded," muttered Austin. "Or there'd be people looking for us. It's been a couple days and no one's come. The lifeboats have distress signals. If anyone was alive, they would've found us already."

"Sima did," said Juan.

"Yeah, but she's another kid like us." Austin tilted his head at Sima. "Did you find any other lifeboats?"

"No. I haven't seen even one other. Just yours and mine."

Austin gestured with his hands, trying to draw a sketch in midair. "If the ship blew up in space, the escape pods would've come down all over the planet. If it was lower, maybe some are closer."

"It's going to be dark soon," said Sima. "We can look around a bit in the morning, but now, it's time for bed."

"We don't have anywhere to sleep." Austin eyed the wreckage. "Except back in there."

"No," wailed Lissa, triggering another brief coughing fit. "I don't like it in there. Can't breathe."

They almost suffocated in that pod. "It's okay. We don't have to go back into the lifeboat. It's warm. My first night as an Outcast, I slept on this old sofa outside in an alley. I was crying so much, and so scared I couldn't sleep. But, I never had the sky over me at night before. And it was kinda pretty, even if only a couple of the really bright stars came out. We can sleep right here."

Lissa calmed and waved her hand back and forth at the grass. "This is soft. It's like tickly hugs."

"It's grass," said Sima. "A plant."

"It's not grass," said Austin. "This isn't plastic."

Sima chuckled. "There used to be live grass on Earth too, but not blue like this. Shorter, and green."

The bracelet screen activated as it typed, ‹There still is grass located in some places, though several districts away from where you lived.›

Austin reclined on the ground, his skinny frame almost vanishing in the blue fluff. "Heh. She's right, it does tickle."

"Wait here a moment," said Sima, while setting Lissa down to sit beside her. "I need to pee."

Though the girl gave her a pitiful look for walking off, she didn't follow. Sima went far enough into the jungle to find cover, but not so far she couldn't hear the kids in case something strange happened. Instead of another Outcast walking by, a couple of fuzzy pig-like puffballs trotted into view and stared at her. Somehow, animals staring at her had the same halting effect as people. She waved her hand and whisper-shouted, "Shoo," which sent them scurrying off.

Once she finished, she hurried back and sprawled on the ground. Lissa cuddled up beside her. Juan flopped nearby. Sima stared up at the vast swath of blue-indigo overhead, flecked with millions of stars, everything from faint pinpoints to huge, glowing ones. As the last traces of sunlight faded from the world, bands of pale blue and orange gas became visible, making the sky distinctly alien.

It had been a long time since she'd spent her first night on a sofa that reeked of wet dog, staring into the sky. The dread of being on an entirely different planet without a scrap of civilization made the fear she'd felt at being on the street at twelve seem trivial. At least there, she had people to beg from and the idea, however unlikely, that she could still go home.

Yet, despite the acute danger and terrifyingly real chance that they could die at any moment, the awesome celestial beauty took her thoughts far away from reality.

16

AURAK

S ima awoke to find all three kids piled on top of her.
Huh? Guess it got chilly at night.

She yawned and took stock of her surroundings. Juan lay face down on top of her, a small puddle of drool on her shoulder. Lissa curled up against her right side, Austin at her left. The long, tonal calls of sky mantas passed overhead, clicks and notes like whalesong mixed with shorter bird trills. Steady wheezing came from Lissa, though she slept with a faint smile.

The weight of three kids on top of her added to laziness, and she didn't bother trying to move right away. Austin awoke next, a little while later. He rolled away onto his back and yawned hard. A few minutes went by before he sat up, yawned again, and wandered off into the jungle. Sima eased Juan to the side and extricated herself from Lissa's grasp on her right arm. She, too, found a spot to relieve herself in private.

When she returned to their 'campsite,' she found Austin pouring the last of their water down his throat. When it ran out, he held the bottle over his mouth and shook it to chase out a few more drops. Watching him do that made her thirsty as hell.

She crouched by the two smaller kids and tickled their bellies until they woke up laughing. "It's morning, you two."

They sat up and wiped their eyes. Within seconds, Juan curled up and cried.

"What's wrong?" asked Sima, scooping him up into a hug.

"It's not a nightmare. We really crashed," whimpered the boy.

Lissa, sitting in the grass nearby, observed his meltdown with a dispassionate expression, tapping her big toes together.

"We did." Sima stared at him for a few seconds, not quite sure what to do with a sobbing small human. She eventually decided to rock him while patting his back. "We crashed, but we're okay. We have water to drink and there's so many of those fruits, we'll never run out."

"We're 'live," said Lissa, her voice breathy. "We didn't died."

Juan gradually stopped crying, but made no effort to squirm out of her embrace.

"What are we gonna do?" asked Austin.

"Oh, we'll figure a way." Sima glanced around at the jungle. "Maybe we'll wind up building a house or something. Or there's this cave I found. That might work to live in."

"I meant today, not like in general." Austin scratched his head. "There's nothing to do here. No video games. No people to beg from. Nothing to scavenge and sell."

"No school!" said Lissa, giggling into a cough.

"That's not a good thing." Austin kicked his toes at the grass. "Now we're gonna grow up to be stupid."

Lissa scrunched up her nose at him. "You *liked* school?"

"I didn't wanna stop going. It was okay."

"You didn't like it?" asked Juan. "My father really wanted me to go. Told me how great it was, but I couldn't go."

"Why not?" asked Sima. "Little kid school doesn't cost anything."

"We lived in *La Propagación*," said Juan. "Going to school could'a shot me."

Austin looked at Lissa. "Why didn't you like it?"

She pulled her feet in to sit cross-legged and leaned forward, fussing at the grass. "It wasn't happy there. Other kids made fun of me, but I guess the food was nice."

Sima raised an eyebrow. "Why would other kids make fun of you? You're totally adorable."

Lissa stuck out her tongue. "'Cause my parents didn't have 'nuff money. I had to wear the same dress all the time, and I had the yellow packets."

Austin cringed, though Juan didn't react. Sima bit her lip. While Sima's mother hadn't been the warmest of parents, she had, at least, made a decent enough living not to need the yellow packets. Any family with kids under twelve could qualify for government-subsidized nutri-packets, but the free food came in glaring yellow pouches (as opposed to the standard silver). Rumors said they were everything from toxic to radioactive to made from rejected soybeans, and many children teased people who had to eat the lower-class food.

"No one's gonna care about that here," said Austin. "There aren't even yellow packets on this *planet*."

"Yeah," said Juan, looking utterly confused.

Lissa smiled. "Stupid packets."

"We're out of water." Sima stood and picked up the bottle. "Let's go fix that."

She walked into the jungle with the kids following in a single file line. Austin started off right behind her, with Juan behind him and Lissa bringing up the tail end. Lissa began coughing less than a minute into the hike, so Austin faded back to walk behind her. Sima slowed her pace, not used to people with tiny legs needing to keep up with her.

What's wrong with that kid? She gets tired so easy. Ugh. I hope I don't catch whatever she's got.

She raised a hand to stop low hanging vines from smacking her in the face. Every so often, one of the kids drifted off to either side, drawn by curiosity of a bright flower or mushroom. Sima fidgeted at her sports bra, feeling conspicuously underdressed to be around other people. Of course, some ads she'd seen back home showed women with *much* bigger bosoms in 'bathing suits' that covered less than her underwear did. Those women didn't seem to have any problem being out in public in such garments.

Her debate about why a bikini didn't embarrass people but underwear did came to a sudden stop at a high-pitched scream from Lissa, which broke into choking after two seconds.

Sima whirled.

The little blonde girl leapt backward from a wrinkled-up powder-blue pod about the size of her head. Near it, large puffy spheres the same shade of blue tugged at their stems like some cross between helium balloons and mushrooms.

Austin caught Lissa from behind when her rapid backward scramble made her trip on a thick ground-running vine.

"What happened?" yelled Sima, rushing over.

Still coughing, Lissa pointed at the shriveled thing.

"She touched it and it made this noise and popped," said Austin.

Sima patted Lissa on the back a few times.

"Sorry," wheezed the girl. "I just touched it like this." She traced her fingertips on Sima's leg, pressure barely noticeable. "Like that."

Sima grasped her by the wrist and turned her arm over to look at her hand. Nothing appeared out of the ordinary, no damage on her fingertips, no blood, no stains. "Did it hurt?"

"No." She coughed and spat to the side. "It scared me."

With a faint puffing sound, the crumpled mass of vegetation re-inflated itself back to a head-sized bubble. Sima approached, studying the bizarre plant. Thin transparent hairs covered the outside of the bulbous gas-filled sac.

"It's probably some kinda reaction to being touched," said Austin.

"Stinks," muttered Juan. "It smelled like a fart."

Austin laughed.

Lissa giggled between coughs.

"Well, don't touch them, okay? Anything that smells bad is probably dangerous," said Sima.

She ushered them back in motion, following the map projected by her bracelet. Soon, they arrived at the edge of the stream where she'd filled the bottle before. All three kids rushed to the edge and spent as much time gawking at free-running water as drinking. Sima knelt by the bank and scooped water to her mouth in double handfuls as well.

"Can we swim?" asked Lissa.

"I dunno. Can you swim?" Sima smiled.

"Kinda. It's not deep." Lissa pointed at the water. "Behind where I lived, we had a big truck box and it had water. I swimmed in it."

"Okay." Sima reclined in the grass, staring at the clouds.

Juan cracked up into giggles.

Austin sat next to Sima. "Uhh, she just took her pants off... and so did Juan."

Sima sat up.

Both of the smaller kids had already made it to the middle of the creek, standing chest-deep in the water and splashing each other. Two pairs of bright white EGSF-issue underpants sat on the grass by the bank.

She opened her mouth to scold them for it, but decided not to bother. The other day, she'd gone skinny dipping as well, not wanting to get her only clothing wet. And both were too young to care about being embarrassed. Given the overbearing humidity, if they got their clothes wet, the fabric would stay damp all day and into the night, and be damn cold. Perhaps unhealthy even. Sima sighed.

Whatever.

"Are you gonna yell at them?" asked Austin.

Sima shrugged. "We could get sick if our clothes are wet at night."

He raised one eyebrow. "This isn't 'clothes.' It's underpants." He pointed at her chest. "And whatever that thing's called."

"I'd adore having something else to wear, but they didn't put anything in the storage bins."

He frowned. "Yeah. I'd even take a pink jumpsuit."

Juan and Lissa kept flinging water at each other and laughing. She made a squeal and dove under, swimming around behind him. The boy, evidently not having been in water before, lost track of her and refused to let his head go under. She sprang up and splashed him.

Sima glanced sideways at Austin. "Pink jumpsuit, huh. So you got detained?"

"No!" He blushed. "I mean... I saw kids in pink jumpsuits. I mean I'd even, umm, take one of them right now." Austin held up his arm. "And if I got arrested, I'd have a handcuff mark, like you do." He held up his wrists to show off a total lack of bruises or lines.

Sima rubbed a finger at her right wrist. "Not if you didn't struggle."

Austin's cheeks got redder.

She smiled to herself, but didn't want to make him talk about it since it clearly bothered him. "Are you going to swim?"

He shrugged. "I dunno. Are you?"

"Not yet. I don't really trust this place." She looked around, eyeing the plants for anything that looked potentially useful for making garments. It felt too weird to strip around kids, even if she technically remained one herself.

"You think there's dangerous stuff?" asked Austin.

"I don't know yet. Just trying to be safe."

He poked her in the side. "Or you're chicken."

"So are you." She raised an eyebrow at him. "You're not in the water either."

"Yeah." He shrugged. "But what the hell. We're tribal now."

Austin stood and walked to the bank. It took him a few minutes to work up the nerve before sliding his briefs off and entering the water. Both Juan and Lissa set upon him with splashing. Austin shrieked from the cold spray and spent a little while futilely trying to run away while hip-deep in the stream, but eventually dove under.

Sima sat on the bank with her legs in up to the knees, wondering how in the hell she went from doing everything possible to avoid being around children to winding up responsible for three small lives. Dividing her attention between the kids and the jungle around them, she found herself unable to relax. Her only knowledge of any sort of wilderness came from a few science classes as well as plenty of movies. Living creatures existed on this planet, but so far, nothing she'd seen with the possible exception of that giant bug appeared threatening. Nature most likely didn't work *too* differently on this planet, so she suspected there had to be something out there with the potential to be dangerous.

At every snap or rustle in the foliage, she tensed, staring in that direction for several minutes, but nothing ever showed itself.

"Lissa," shouted Austin.

Sima tore her gaze from the distant trees. Austin dove under the surface chasing a drifting cloud of blonde, leaving only Juan in sight. The smaller boy stood armpit deep, looking around with a wild-eyed, worried expression, unsure what to do with himself. Sima shoved off the bank, wading into the freezing water toward where Austin pulled Lissa's head above the surface.

"What happened?" yelled Sima while collecting the unconscious girl.

Austin looked up with terror in his eyes. "I dunno! She just like passed out."

Sima cradled the limp girl in her arms and carried her out of the stream.

"Hold her upside down or something," said Austin. "Maybe she breathed in water."

"Lissa!" Sima set her in the grass and held her ear by the child's mouth. Fortunately, the girl *did* seem to be breathing. She sat back on her heels, staring down at the frighteningly thin and pale girl, feeling helpless to do anything for her. "Uhh…" After a few seconds, she reached down and rolled Lissa on her side, patting her on the back. "Come on, Lissa. Open your eyes."

Austin knelt nearby and held a hand by her mouth. "She's still breathing."

Juan climbed out of the water and scurried over.

"Please wake up," said Sima, patting harder.

Lissa spat up a mouthful of water and lapsed into a fit of heavy coughing. Sima kept patting and rubbing her back, muttering encouragement. Once it became clear no more water would come up, she pulled the girl into a hug and held on. The child's skin had become cold, but not quite so much it worried her.

"My breaths hurt," rasped Lissa. "I got dizzy."

Austin let out a long sigh of relief.

"She gets tired fast," said Juan.

"I'm sorry," said Sima, tears in her eyes. "I should've pulled you out of the water before you got too tired to keep swimming."

Lissa shook her head. "I splashed too hard. My fault did it."

They sat in silence for a while, Sima holding Lissa in her lap. Eventually, Austin dried off enough to pull his briefs back on and began wandering along the creek bank. Juan, despite being dry, ignored his pants and followed after.

"Juan," said Sima. "Get dressed before you go wandering around."

He shrugged and came back to reclaim his shorts.

Sima picked up Lissa's briefs. The girl gave her a look of mild annoyance but offered no protest to being dressed like a toddler. She rested her cheek on Sima's shoulder and continued to breathe in raspy wheezes. Having no idea what else to do with a kid clinging to her like that, Sima pet her like a cat. She'd never had dolls growing up, and her mother never touched her beyond the likely changing of diapers that happened too long ago to remember. Granted, the occasional slap when they argued counted as 'touch.' As much dislike as Sima had for her mother, it deepened at the wonder how a grown woman could strike a child. She couldn't imagine wanting to hit the fragile-looking Lissa. Had something been wrong with her mother, or had *she* not been cute enough to trigger the same feelings within her mother that this girl drew forth from her? Sima hadn't even given birth to this tiny blonde sprite, and yet, somehow, she couldn't bear the thought of her being in pain.

"I'm sorry," whispered Lissa. "The doctor lady told me I shouldn't do too much. I'm not supposed to run and stuff. Not 'til the doctors here give me new breaths."

Sima rubbed the girl's back. *This kid needs food.* "Let's find a fruit or something. Are you hungry?"

"Not really, but I'll eat if you want me to. My parents didn't have food all the time."

"My mom made me cook for myself."

Lissa grinned. "But you're *big!*"

"Since I was like eight." Sima stood, carrying her. She walked to the left, following Austin and Juan, who'd since vanished into the trees.

"Boys?" called Sima.

"Here," yelled Austin. "You gotta see this!"

Sima shifted the girl to the side, perched on her left hip, and hurried up to a trot, worried at having the boys out of sight. A minute or so later, she ducked past a curtain of teal-colored vines and stopped short at the sight waiting for her.

One of those enormous twenty-foot tall flamingo-shaped birds sat in the creek, emitting sad cooing noises so deep they rattled Sima's bones. This one had sapphire blue feathers instead of green, and a white beak. Austin had tucked himself up under its right wing and appeared to be either scratching at or combing its feathers.

Juan ran in circles chasing blue, fuzzy creatures that ranged in size from ramen bowls up to bigger than an EGSF officer's helmet. They emitted squeals that sounded like a combination of piglets and chipmunks, avoiding him with relative ease. Whenever one got far enough away, it calmed and stopped running, turning its two pairs of oversized black eyes warily on him. The boy seemed to be trying to pet or hug one, but the critters had little interest in human contact.

The bird swung its head around toward Austin, emitting a soft slate-scraping noise while the lower flap of its beak fluttered.

Lissa gasped, pointing at the bird, then whispered, "Is it going to eat him?"

"I don't think so," whispered Sima. "Austin, what are you doing?"

"It's hurt." Austin ducked out from under the wing, holding up a handful of thin metal rods. "It's got these stuck all over its side."

Sima stepped around the darting fuzzballs and approached him.

"They're so cute!" chirped Lissa, reaching toward one of the 'pigs.' "Can we keep one?"

"They're wild, not pets." Sima gestured at Juan. "Stop chasing them. If they feel cornered, they might bite you."

"Okay." Juan stopped running around, but still walked toward the creatures.

Austin showed her a handful of narrow sticks, each about nine inches long, seemingly made of dull, silvery metal. They tapered to points on one end with small holes like hypodermic needles. The opposite end had a nugget of some rubbery translucent substance. "There's a bunch of these stuck in the bird. They look like darts. Think there's tribes here?"

A shiver of worry ran down Sima's back. She set Lissa on her feet and took the bundle. "Bracelet, what are these?"

Lissa wrapped both arms around her and clung.

As soon as Sima held her left wrist near the strange darts, the grid of blue laser light appeared.

‹Material composition corresponds to keratinous biological matter with an abnormally high mineral content. Cartilaginous deposits at the posterior end suggests a form of naturally growing quill.› An image of a porcupine appeared on the little holographic screen. ‹Based on the length and diameter of these quills, my calculations indicate there may be an animal here similar to this, though it would be quite large. I am also detecting traces of venom inside the quill.›

"Venom?" Sima's eyebrows went up. "Austin! Be careful."

"I am," said the boy, once more buried under a huge wing. "I'm not gonna stick myself with one." He plucked more quills out one by one, and dropped them.

"None of us have shoes," said Sima.

"So don't step on them." He dropped another one.

Sima looked up at the massive bird. Dark sapphire blue feathers shimmered in the sunlight, almost blending in with the forest canopy above. The creature's great spherical eyes fixated on Austin, though the bird didn't appear agitated at his proximity. In fact, its demeanor gave off a sense of gratitude. "Just be careful, okay?"

"Yeah," said Austin.

A sudden, gurgly noise interrupted Lissa's breathing. She coughed once, hard enough that her briefs fell. With a phlegmy sigh of annoyance, she stooped to pull them back up. "These are too big."

"Mine are too small," said Juan. "Wanna trade?"

Lissa shook her head. "You have boy shorts. And you're bigger than me. Those would still be too big."

Austin grunted and climbed up the bird's side. He perched on top of its body, straining to reach a few quills stuck near the base of the long, tubular neck. Sima bit her lip, not at all comfortable at having him that close to unknown wildlife. The bird didn't appear capable of bending in a way necessary to pluck the darts from its neck. She figured it probably could've reached the ones in its side, but perhaps the work had been too delicate for such a massive beak.

"It's a space chicken," said Lissa.

Juan laughed.

Sima looked at her bracelet. "Do these things have a name?"

‹Not yet.›

Lissa stared at the bird for a moment, then said, "Aurak."

"What?" Sima glanced down at her.

The girl pointed at the giant bird. "That's an Aurak."

"How do you know that?"

Juan laughed. "She made it up."

"Yeah. So?" asked Lissa. "When it did bird talking, it kinda sounded like"—she mimicked an avian screech—"*auraaaak.*"

The bird emitted a noise somewhere between *araaak* and *orek.*

Sima blinked at it. *Did that thing understand her? No way… not only was it an animal, who would possibly have taught it to understand GANSEC.*

Of all the names a six-year-old could've come up with for something, that didn't sound bad at all. "All right, that works."

‹Database updated.›

The Aurak twisted its head around and rubbed its huge beak against Austin's shoulder.

"Okay, okay," said the boy. "I'm almost done. Just a couple more."

It emitted the same *araaak* noise. Though the creature appeared to be attempting a soft whisper, its sheer size made the vocalization loud enough to be cringe inducing, and the rotting vegetation on its breath didn't help. Lissa got some color back in her face and the wheeziness in her breathing faded to almost nothing.

"Last one," said Austin, before tossing a quill into the water.

With a groaning cry of exultation, the Aurak lurched upright on its stilt-like legs, carrying Austin way up off the ground.

"Aaah!" he yelled, clamping himself around the base of its neck with both arms and legs.

"Down!" said Sima, waving her hands. "Let him down!"

Ignoring her, the Aurak strode forward, following the stream. Austin shifted side to side, peering over at the ground easily twenty feet below. High branches bent out of the way of the bird's tall neck, though its eye stalks reached past the top of the jungle canopy, free from whipping vines and leaves.

Sima pulled Lissa onto her back and grabbed Juan by the hand before rushing after it, having to run to keep up with the Aurak's casual stride. Austin went from making nervous whimpers to laughing, then cheering as he rode the huge creature through the jungle.

"This is awesome," shouted Austin.

A chest-high growth part root, part vine got in the way a few minutes later. The indigo plant looked much like the stem of a rose bush, only in place of thorns, it had soft, conical flowers in various shades of white and lavender. Sima hoisted Juan up on top of it, then Lissa scrambled off her shoulders to follow him. Both kids squatted and grabbed at her, helping her climb up and over the oily plant. Touching the side left her smeared with dark blue like ink. The kids jumped down to stand beside her. Lissa lifted her foot, giggling at her stained soles. Juan reached over and left a purple handprint on Lissa's chest. She returned the favor, but on his face.

"Damn," said Sima. "Is this dangerous?"

The bracelet projected its laser grid for a few seconds on her hand. ‹Chemical analysis suggests it would taste extremely bitter and likely induce vomiting if consumed. However, it is harmless on contact with skin.›

Lissa pressed her hands into Sima's leg, leaving two indigo prints, then grinned up at her. Before the child could roll around on the vine and turn herself blue from head to toe, Sima snagged her by the wrist and pulled her along. She didn't trust leaving that stuff all over everyone, but she had bigger issues—like a three-story tall googly-eyed flamingo walking away with Austin—to worry about.

Once more with Lissa on like a backpack, she rushed along the creek, which grew deeper and wider. Running made up ground, and as soon as she got close enough to see the Aurak, she relaxed and slowed to a jog. Austin appeared to be having a blast, clinging to the bird's neck and looking around at the landscape. The creature didn't move its right wing much at all, and its gait suggested the leg on that side had become weakened.

Those quills.

"Hey," yelled Juan. "You see any other lifeboats from up there?"

Austin twisted side to side, a hand to his forehead shielding his eyes. "No... just more trees. I can't see over them."

Other bird-like creatures cruised by above the tree canopy. The smallest ones looked about Lissa's size. Most had deep blue feathers, others dark green, and a handful yellowish-orange. Not one paid the least bit of attention to the humans who had invaded their home.

The Aurak stopped without warning and leaned down to nip at the treetops. It closed its beak around a large blue pod studded with lime green spheres, and snapped it from the tree with little effort. Rather than swallow it whole like the last bird she'd seen, it twisted its head around, holding the pod toward Austin.

He peered up at it for a few seconds, confused, until he decided to grab one of the green pods and pull it away from the blue part. The Aurak turned its head toward the bank, leaning close, dangling the pod in front of her. Sima stared up at it in awe.

This thing could eat me in one bite.

Dark indigo membranes on its eye spheres tilted upward on the inside, conveying an almost human emotional quality in the way eyebrows might say 'aww, how cute.' The bird cooed from deep within its throat, and dropped the pod to the ground beside her with a heavy *thump*. It nudged the fruit with its beak, then flapped the movable bottom part as if to say 'eat up.'

Austin stared at the sphere in his hands, almost bigger than his head. "It kinda smells like something I had before, but I don't know what to call it."

Sima set Lissa down and squatted over the huge pod. As soon as she plucked one of the spheres loose, the Aurak cooed again and lifted its head back into the trees to eat a second pod in one bite. She held the fruit close and sniffed it, getting a whiff of peach.

"Smells like peaches," said Sima, before taking a tentative nibble. It somewhat tasted like a peach as well, if a peach had been crossbred with a lemon. Though, since the flavor had more sweet than tart, she took a bigger bite.

Lissa and Juan helped themselves to a single fruit, which they shared.

After eating three entire pods, each of which had about twenty or so fruits on it, the Aurak resumed walking. Austin looked over the side down at Sima, with a hint of worry in his expression.

"Umm, bird?" asked Sima. "Can you maybe let him down?"

The Aurak trilled, but didn't slow—or put Austin on the ground.

Sima scrambled to her feet.

"Don't leave them," said Juan, pointing at the pod. "We can't reach those without the bird. I like it!"

Since the Aurak didn't give off any indication it meant harm to Austin, she allowed herself to turn back and grab the stalk. The whole pod weighed too much for her to lift, so she dragged it along while trudging after the bird. Though the creature moved with a lazy, ambling stride, its huge legs translated to a speed closer to a human sprinting. Sima resigned herself to the truth of having no chance of keeping up with the thing. At least it followed the river, which made losing track of it difficult.

Austin's cheering and hollering got farther and farther away, but the Aurak's size let Sima keep a general sense of where it went. They followed for quite some time, long enough that Lissa began wheezing again from the effort of walking. Sima looked back and forth between the ever-distancing shadow of the bird and the little girl struggling to keep up.

"Austin," shouted Sima. "Jump down into the water."

"No way!" he yelled back. "This is awesome! And, there's a lake!"

Sima stared down at her feet, covered in dirt. Indigo ink from the massive vine still smeared all over her, likely adding permanent stains to her feeble excuse for clothing. She pulled Lissa up onto her back again, and continued dragging the fruit pod along. Trudging through waist-high underbrush proved an exercise in caution and vigilance. Plants in this jungle so far appeared to come in three varieties: edible fruit, soft, gossamer things that broke with little effort, or razor-sharp nastiness. It didn't take her long to figure out which pointy-leafed dangers to avoid, and which unpleasant-looking red-yellow shrubs with fake thorns or black 'needles' were actually harmless and soft.

Eventually, she emerged from the jungle onto the shore of a giant lake. Awestruck, she stood there staring at the crystalline blue water and pale brown sand. The Aurak, having settled itself in the water, swam around like an enormous swan, no sign of its legs visible above the surface.

Sima collapsed to a seat on the bank, her toes inches away from the lapping water. Lissa curled up beside her, playing in the mud. Juan took a few more bites from the fruit he'd been carrying, set it on the ground, and walked into the water.

Some minutes later, Lissa ceased wheezing and smiled. "I like this place. It's pretty."

"Yeah." Sima whistled in awe, looking around at all the plant life surrounding the shore. She'd never seen so much water in one place before except for pictures of oceans. The lake was so wide, she figured it would take like an hour to drive across an equal distance of land in a gee-vee. "It's like something out of a movie."

Lissa nodded. "I'm not scared that we don't have a 'partment to live in. I like it here more than where I lived before."

"Where was that?" asked Sima.

"Like under a broke building. A big room with all old sofas and stuff. This man, Piro, kinda took care of us, but he collected our begs and gave us food."

Sima shot a nasty look off at the trees. Lissa had fallen into a Keeper's little troupe of kid beggars. One such woman had tried to convince Sima to join her band of orphans soon after she first hit the streets. At twelve, she'd looked more like ten, but even at that age, she knew the woman would've kept most of the money, exploiting the little ones' instinct to seek a caregiver for her own financial gain.

"I wasn't there long." Lissa shook her head. "Only a couple days before the cops found us."

Austin, evidently having his fill of riding birdback, jumped off the Aurak and swam for shore. Once on the bank, he removed his briefs long enough to wring them out, then pulled them back on.

The kids gathered around her, sitting and resting for a while. More Auraks in various colorations arrived, some rushing into the lake with such force they sent huge splashes into the air. Eventually, a total of nine huge birds swam about, gravitating together in a cluster. The one they had been following kept looking toward her. Now and then, the others appeared to respond to it and also looked at them.

Wow… almost like it's telling them about us.

Sick of being covered in oily blue gunk, Sima got to her feet and disrobed. Despite her innate embarrassment, none of the kids reacted. She gestured at the shore, and patted Lissa on the head. "Let's wash that blue stuff off you."

"Okay." The girl flung her briefs off and scrambled into the lake.

The inky substance floated on the water like grease, but came off skin with relative ease and a little hand scrubbing. *There's no soap in this place. What did people do before they invented soap?* She scrunched up her face, unable to think of where cleansing gel came from prior to the machines that produced almost anything from jars of gel. Food machines used protein-based slime, while other fabricators used non-organic goo. Though, some clothing, particularly softer fabrics, also came from bio-slime.

She didn't let Lissa stray too far away, or do much more than float and enjoy the water. Something told her to keep the child's activity level low so she didn't hurt herself. Lissa remained content to stand neck-deep beside her, watching spherical creatures the size of apples swim around near the lake bottom. The bracelet sensed no venom in anything that came close enough to scan, though Sima still cringed away from the 'fish,' not wanting to touch them.

Lissa's sudden squeal startled Sima.

"What?" She looked over at the girl.

"They're coming!" Lissa poked a hand out of the surface, pointing at the Auraks.

All—now twelve—of them, swam in a formation toward the humans, like a flotilla of boats with long necks. Juan squealed and rushed for the bank. He stopped in ankle-deep water and spun around to gawk at the birds.

The huge feathered creatures drifted closer, all peering down at Sima and Lissa while making pigeon coos deep in their throats. Despite her fear at being surrounded by such enormous animals, they gave off a bizarre sense of gratitude—especially one with pale blue feathers. A little larger than the others, it had an air of age about it, and paid particular attention to Austin, who remained on land.

After gently nuzzling Sima with its beak, the older bird glided as close as it could to the edge without standing up out of the water and stretched its neck out to Austin. Soon, Juan got the bright idea to lob one of the rhubarb-raspberry fruits, which grew in large numbers around the lakeshore, into the air. An Aurak snapped it up and emitted a happy trilling call.

The other birds swam closer to him.

Austin ran to the tree line and gathered some fruits as well, and he tossed them, one by one, up at the waiting beaks.

"I wanna feed the birds, too," said Lissa.

"Okay." Getting her out of the water sounded like a good idea anyway, so Sima held her hand and walked her to shore.

Lissa ran off to grab fruits. Sima frowned at the white EGSF-issue underpants on the ground, along with her top. Austin seemed to share her discomfort, being the only one presently wearing them. She debated pulling hers on while still wet, but reluctantly decided to air dry a bit while the kids threw fruits up to the waiting birds.

She sat in the grass to enjoy the steady, warm breeze. *This is so like some weird dream of paradise, but I don't think this is what the crew had in mind.* Daydreams of a nice, clean *modern* city made from the guts of a former starship came and went. The people who had planned this expedition had not been expecting to send anyone to live like primitives here, least of all a bunch of Outcasts thrown on board at the last minute. She rationalized that all the storage compartments by their stasis pods had been empty because the government couldn't get enough volunteers for the trip, so they packed the last hundred or so stasis pods with street kids to get rid of them, not bothering to include any supplies. Probably because it would either delay the launch, or no one wanted to spend glint on Outcasts. Heck, they didn't even cover whatever medical care Lissa needed, leaving it to the colonists to provide instead. Money seemed like the only reason they would've done that.

Get her healthy enough to survive the trip and let the doctors up here worry about the rest... except they're all dead.

The kids' laughing and giggling eventually lifted her spirits. She fiddled around with the grass, trying to weave it into something useful, but the gossamer strands kept breaking. Various leaves at the tree line *looked* promising, but she didn't want to go wandering around until she got dressed. Sitting in one place with nothing on made her blush plenty enough already. Juan ran back and forth from where Austin and Lissa threw fruit to the birds, collecting them by the handful, likely so the girl didn't have to wear herself out.

Once Sima dried enough to pull her garments back on, she stood and walked over to the tree line, checking out the various leaves. The broad ones here were soft, but broke apart like cobwebs at the slightest touch. Thinner ones looked (and acted) like knives, the edges sharp enough to cut her skin. Though they appeared to be leaves similar to palm fronds, they had enough woodenness that they'd work as tools to cut steak, assuming she could even grab one without shredding her hand.

Some of the tree branches looked about the right diameter and rigidity to be plausible for the construction of a hut frame. They had an almost rubbery quality somewhere between wood and cork.

"Can I make a shelter out of any of this?"

‹Out of range.›

She walked closer, holding her left wrist out at the various plants and branches.

‹The smaller stalks have a material composition similar to wood and appear to be good insulators. It should cut quite easily with the axe you found, though I am not reading anything here that would be usable as a cord or twine to lash stems together into a cabin-type structure. You may be able to weave them into a primitive lean-to or similar shelter. However, given the size of the planet, we've encountered an incredibly small percentage of what is possible. There may be better foliage elsewhere more suitable for construction of shelter and clothing.›

"Right."

‹Oh. You should also avoid those broad, red leaves. The sap has neurotoxic properties and may result in paralysis, which could become permanent if you overexpose to it.›

Sima gulped and backed away from the woods. "Well, I *was* going to say that maybe this planet isn't too bad after all. Still, I guess there's less stuff here that'll kill me than back home."

‹Fewer. Fewer things that will kill you.›

"What?"

‹You have missed too much school.›

"I'm stranded basically naked on an alien planet. I lost everything I ever owned. The only possessions I have to my name are one set of underwear and you. Does it *really* matter how I talk?"

‹You also possess the axe, and the adoration of three children.›

She sighed, and twisted around to watch the kids. They'd stopped feeding the birds and had become brave enough to climb up on one. "Is it safe to let them touch those creatures? Don't birds have like fleas or lice or something?"

‹Out of range.›

Grumbling, Sima trudged back to where she'd been sitting. "This sucks. All these plants are useless. It's going to rain eventually, right? And what about winter? Does it even get cold here?"

‹According to the long distance survey data I was pre-loaded with, we have landed in a near-equatorial region that should remain warm enough year-round that your current attire will not present a danger to health.›

"Great." She rolled her eyes, embarrassed all over again. Lissa and Juan certainly didn't seem to care at all about what (if anything) they wore. While she thought it fine for now, it would become severely awkward, at least for Sima, in a few years—and not only due to the lack of clothing. How would she handle it if Austin became attracted to her after he hit puberty? She hadn't been able to even kiss a boy her age back home. Every time the moment almost happened, she'd think about her mother's creepy boyfriend grabbing her, and she'd run away. On top of that, after two or three years regarding Austin as more of a little brother, or even son, any romantic feelings would be *totally* wrong. Hopefully, he'd think of her as a sister and not have those sorts of thoughts about her. But if they really were the only humans on this planet, she worried everything would get weird eventually. Would they invent gods or start worshipping fruits, dancing around fires at night?

Who am I kidding? None of us are going to live that long.

Lissa coughed a few times, and swallowed something.

Especially her. Sima glanced over at the scrawny girl, every rib showing clear on her back, her legs like noodles. At least she had no bruises or scars. *That poor kid isn't gonna last long out here without a real doctor.*

Her somber, fatalistic mood lasted for a little while until the kids' laughter chased it away. The Aurak were quite friendly, and surprisingly intelligent. She couldn't help but believe that the one bird had somehow communicated with the others that Austin had plucked the quills from its side to help it.

Sima thought back to a few little beggars she'd stuffed in ORC bins out of frustration. Guilt weighed heavy on her shoulders even though she'd caused no actual harm. "Karma, right?," she whispered to herself. "I'd been such a bitch to kids back home... now I get to watch three of them die."

Pattering drew her attention to the little holographic screen floating over the bottom of her left forearm. ‹With the exception of medical conditions beyond your control, there is little reason to suspect they will die if you undertake reasonable efforts toward survival.›

"I don't understand," muttered Sima. "I used to hate having kids around. I mean..." She sighed. "I didn't hate *them*. They just got all the money."

‹Being stranded in a potentially hostile environment without tools or equipment can easily cause one to rearrange their priorities.›

"Yeah, I guess."

‹You feel obligated to protect them.›

She jabbed her fingers at the ground, smirking. "Yeah. I mean, even on the street... older Outcasts looked out for little ones. I was just jealous."

‹Karma. Now, it matters. They need protection and guidance.›

"But what about me?" whispered Sima, holding the bracelet close to her mouth. "I'm terrified. I'm only sixteen. I never even really had a mother. I have no idea how to *be* one."

‹You have a lot of practice already at taking care of a child.›

"Hah. No I didn't."

‹You took care of you.›

She sighed at the clouds. "That's not funny."

‹I was not attempting to initiate humor.›

Lissa giggled and jumped from an Aurak into the water. Sima's heart leapt into her throat when the girl went under. She didn't breathe for almost thirty seconds until the child resurfaced and laughed. "I hate her."

‹No, you don't.›

Sima curled into a ball, hiding her face against her knees. "I hate that she's so small. So defenseless. So damn sick. I hate that she's gonna die, and I don't wanna deal with that!" A war of emotions raged inside. She wanted to metaphorically shove Lissa into an ORC bin and run away so she didn't have to cope with losing her, didn't have to bear the responsibility of having to look out for anyone but herself. But she couldn't do it. She hated herself even more for thinking about it.

"Why are you crying?" asked Lissa, right beside her.

"Oh..." Sima sat up and wiped her face. "I dunno. It's just so beautiful here."

Lissa tilted her head. "You're not a good liar. Did you step on an ouchie?"

Sima glanced over at the scrawny child staring back at her with a face of total innocence and concern. "No... I was thinking about everyone else on the ship and being sad that it's only us left."

"Yeah. That is sad." Lissa flopped down next to her.

"Put your pants on."

Lissa scrunched up her face. "I'm wet. I just got out of the lake."

One of the Auraks let off a long, modulating call. The others returned shorter chirps. One by one, they turned toward the humans, emitted the same short chirp, and swam off in a V, following the eldest bird toward the far side of the lake, which had to be several miles away.

"We're going to need to make a shelter," said Sima.

‹It would be best to use the lifeboat as it is much more durable a structure than anything you could fashion from plants.›

The suggestion appealed to the lazy inside her, so Sima nodded. "All right."

After giving everyone a chance to dry off, Sima got the kids dressed and picked Lissa up. Most of the day spent walking and swimming had tired everyone out, but she hadn't found any other lifeboats, any sign of debris, or anything really new other than the lake.

"Which way is home?" asked Sima.

The bracelet displayed a map, showing a waypoint at the lifeboat she'd found the children in. According to it, they'd gone one-point-four miles away. A bit far for any routine trips to the lake, though they had closer sources of water even if they weren't quite so vast to swim in.

Lissa snuggled in tight, her chin on Sima's shoulder.

The boys followed, both working together to drag the fruit pod, as she carried the girl back to the lifeboat, avoiding the sharp plants and keeping a wary eye out for danger. Something out there had quills that carried venom. The bracelet thought it a monstrously large porcupine, but that didn't make sense. How could one of those have managed to get quills stuck so high up on a bird that big? The base of its neck had to be twenty feet off the ground.

An Aurak would step on a porcupine, even one as big as a gee-vee. She said nothing of her fears, not wanting to alarm the kids, and made her way back to the crash site. By the time they arrived at the grassy field around the lifeboat, daylight had weakened enough that she calculated less than an hour before full dark.

They ate more of the lemony-peachy fruits and curled up on the cotton-soft grass to sleep. When it got dark enough that no one could see her face, Sima let herself cry in silence while clinging to Lissa and Juan like a pair of living dolls. She'd felt unwanted at home, but more than ever now. The entirety of human civilization had deemed her, and these kids, unworthy of even remaining on Earth.

This planet, Mirage—or whatever they called it—might've been beyond beautiful, but it still felt like a giant ORC bin they would never be able to climb out from. Her vision full of stars and wispy trails of glowing space gas, Sima gradually drifted off to sleep with a soft breeze wafting across her skin, and the breaths of small children puffing at her arms.

17

A CAVE OF WONDERS

The next morning after breakfast, Sima decided that sleeping out in the open probably wouldn't work as a long-term solution.

Her Omnicomputer's assurance that they'd landed near an equatorial region erased her worries about cold becoming a problem. Even in this planet's version of winter, the climate shouldn't get so chilly as to be harmful given their lack of clothing. Any garments she might someday make from leaves or plants wouldn't offer much in the sense of warmth, only modesty. Though winter-at-night could be uncomfortable.

Suggesting they use the lifeboat as a 'house' terrified Lissa, but that came as no surprise. Had Sima nearly suffocated inside her stasis pod, she'd probably not want to be anywhere near it again either. Lacking the skills or materials to build a reasonable shelter, she decided to try the second best option to the lifeboat: the cave.

Because the Omnicomputer had tracked her journey since she landed, the map had a marker at the location of the alien cave. Another option would be *her* lifeboat, but the cooling system had gotten stuck on overdrive. According to the bracelet, the interior temperature had been forty-two degrees, far too cold to sleep in, especially for a fragile child with some unidentified lung problem. Even a mild cold could prove fatal. Which brought up another worry. As soon as she wondered if this planet even *had* the necessary viruses on it to cause colds, she also wondered what other awful things might be here, diseases no human had ever experienced before.

That thought gnawed on her brain while they marched across the jungle, heading for the cave. She debated asking the bracelet about that, but didn't want to scare the kids. From what little science class she recalled, she wanted to say that since this planet never had humans, no viruses or germs would've evolved to prey upon them. While in all probability, diseases *did* exist here, whether they had the capability to infect people, she had no idea.

A little before noon, they reached the opening of the cave, which triggered an instant, "Whoa" from both boys. Austin darted in first and ran down the corridor to the dome-shaped chamber. He stopped short at the bottom, mouth agape, staring at the glowing grooves in the walls.

The eerie light emanating from the decorative carvings tinted Lissa's skin blue and made both boys appear darker. Though a few days of living had dimmed the pure whiteness of everyone's garments, the fabric remained clean enough that it practically glowed within the chamber.

"Wow…" Austin walked around the wall, running his fingers along the grooves. "The light's just coming right out of the rock."

"This is cool!" yelled Juan, his voice echoing.

Lissa shivered. "It's kinda cold in here."

"There's gotta be aliens on this planet," said Austin.

"Yeah." Juan nodded.

Sima opened her mouth to say something before the kids scared themselves.

"But it's us," said Juan.

"Huh?" asked Sima, her thoughts derailed.

"We're from Earth. So we're the aliens here." Juan waved his arms.

Lissa climbed up onto the metal disc at the center of the room. "It's cold…" Arms out to the sides for balance, she crept around the edge.

"Don't stand on the table," said Austin.

"It's not a table." Lissa kept going, staring down at her feet as she walked heel-to-toe around the metal disc. "It's a circle. An' there's no chairs, so it can't be a table."

"What if the aliens are like big slugs and don't have legs?" asked Austin.

"They're not aliens here," said Juan. "They'd only be aliens if they went to Earth."

Austin rolled his eyes. "Whatever."

Sima followed him around the outer wall, trying to make sense of the grooves. In some areas, the lines resembled a printed circuit board while others had spiral patterns. The more she studied it all, the more she felt an odd energy in the air. Something about this room unnerved her. Lissa marched back and forth across the platform. The soft *pap-pap-pap* of her feet clapping the smooth metal became the loudest sound in the universe for a little while.

"We could live in here," said Juan. "It's got room, and it's not gonna make us sweat."

"It was pretty warm in here before." Sima glanced at the metal slab. "I slept in here the first night and it wasn't this cold."

"Maybe you forgot to turn the air conditioning on," said Austin, a nervous tremor in his voice.

She rather did *not* like the implication that a cave either *had* air conditioning, or someone/something turned it on after she'd been here. It could've been automatic, a mechanism in the walls having reacted to her presence… but she hadn't come back here since.

"Is anything making it cold in here?" asked Sima, holding her forearm up.

‹The walls are emitting energy in a wavelength I'm not able to properly analyze. I calculate that this energy is likely responsible for the drop in temperature.›

"Could that energy be making me feel weird?" asked Sima.

"It is kinda creepy in here," said Lissa.

"Yeah." Austin poked at the wall. "I don't think it would be a good idea to live in here. At least not until we find some clothes. It's too cold."

Lissa jumped down from the metal disc and ran over to Sima, clinging. "Yeah. I'm cold."

"Who wrote on the walls?" asked Juan. He stuck his finger in one of the grooves, tracing the circuit pattern.

"The aliens, umm, I mean whatever beings lived here before we arrived," said Sima, gazing up at the decorations that extended well into the ceiling.

Click.

Juan screamed.

Sima whirled around. Where the boy had been a second ago, a hole in the wall revealed a round-walled tunnel bending downward. Juan's continuing howl of fear faded into the distance, echoing back up the shaft. She ran over to the opening. A door-sized section of the wall had retracted into the floor, exposing a tunnel of smooth purplish-red rock that angled away and down with a rightward curve. Slick with water or some other type of moisture, the coloration made it look far too much like the guts of a living being.

"Juan!" shouted Sima.

Austin rushed up beside her. "Whoa."

Lissa burst into tears.

The boy's distant screaming cut off with a splash.

"Juan!" shouted Sima. "Are you okay? Where are you?"

Sputtering echoed back up the tube for a few seconds before Juan yelled, "There's water down here. It's cold. I'm okay."

"Water?" called Sima.

"Yeah. There's tunnels and metal and stuff down here."

Sima leaned into the opening, inhaling the scent of mossy stone. "Can you get back up?"

"No. I fell outta the roof. There's a lot of other tunnels."

Austin squatted and picked at the groove where the wall section had gone down into the floor. "This is a door. Maybe they *were* like worms or something. There has to be another way out."

Sima looked back and forth from the tunnel to the other two kids. No way could she leave Juan down there alone, but if she went after him, she wouldn't be able to get back up, and these two would be on their own until she found a way out. *If* she found a way out. Going down after Juan felt like abandoning Austin and Lissa to their deaths. But not going felt like abandoning Juan to die.

"I'm sorry for pushing the button," yelled Juan.

Do something, Seem. You can't just stand here. Ugh. I can't choose between them. Kill two to save one. Abandon one to save two? She grabbed two fistfuls of her hair and groaned. *I'm over thinking. There has to be a way out. The bracelet can track where I go. Maybe it can even scan for a way out.*

"I can't get back up," said Juan, his voice shaking. "Which tunnel should I go?"

"He's only eight. I can't leave him alone," muttered Sima.

Lissa squeezed her. "I'm only six." She sniffled. "But I don't wanna leave him down there."

"Let's go." Austin nodded toward the tunnel. "It didn't hurt him. If the aliens made this like a hallway, there's gotta be a way up somewhere."

Sima put a hand on each of their shoulders. "You guys stay here and wait for us to come back."

"I don't wanna be alone," whispered Lissa.

"You're not alone," said Austin. "I'm here."

Sima lowered herself to sit at the top of the tunnel, and stuck her legs out onto wet stone. For an instant, she felt foolish at the idea of going down into what could be an inescapable pit, but Juan needed her. No matter what she did, it felt like the wrong choice. But Austin did have a point. If some alien creatures had made this place, it most likely did have another way out. "You two stay put. I'll be back as soon as I can."

Before Lissa could wail, Sima pushed off.

She shot down the curving tunnel feet first, water spraying from her heels. Glowing patches of moss raced by for several long seconds until she sailed out into the air. She barely had time to suck in a breath before plunging submerged in freezing water. It took her a second to get a sense of orientation after the spiral slide, but she righted herself and put her feet down, squishing past a few inches of gooey muck to smooth stone beneath. Suppressing the urge to scream at the disgusting feeling, she thrust her head above the surface and found herself standing chest-deep in a huge underground lake. The sensation similar to walking in raw eggs made her shudder. Barely holding back the urge to gag, she glanced down at the dense purple muck up to her ankles.

Juan swam over and grabbed on, sniffling. "You came after me."

"Yeah, kiddo." She ruffled his wet hair. "We only have each other, right?"

He smiled.

She turned in place, gazing around at a massive chamber with rainbow-striations on the walls. Natural stone columns dotted the room, some thicker than trees, others precariously narrow. Twelve different passageways led out of the room, all caves of smooth rock with strikingly similar size. The design didn't seem possible to have occurred naturally. Four silver metal obelisks jutted up from the water, standing in a square around the room's center. They gave off a faint noise at the edge of human hearing, more a sensation of energy in the air than any sound. For no particular reason, she decided that approaching them would be a bad idea.

"Bracelet, do you have any idea which way leads out?"

‹Insufficient data. However, I am tracking your motion so you will not get lost.›

"No!" shouted Austin, his voice echoing from the hole in the ceiling.

Sima gasped and looked up.

Lissa came flying at her feet first.

With a yelp, Sima ducked in time to avoid a double-kick to the face. Lissa splashed into the water nearby and went under. Before she surfaced, Austin sailed hands first out of the hole on his back, flipped over in midair, and belly flopped.

"Ooh!" Juan cringed.

Lissa stuck her head above the surface, dog paddling. "I can't reach the bottom!"

"I told you to stay up there!" Sima grabbed her and lifted her into a hug. "What are you doing?"

The sad, pleading stare the girl gave her would've caused any Citizen to empty their entire bank account. "I was scared. I wanted to be with you. Please don't be mad."

Sima couldn't get angry with her, especially not while looking at that face. "I didn't want you to get trapped down here."

"We're trapped?" Juan gasped.

Austin surfaced, floating on his back and moaning. "Ow."

"No... I don't *know* that. Only afraid of it," said Sima. *Well, at least I don't have to choose which kid lives...* Despite it being potentially foolish, she preferred having all three of them with her.

Lissa trembled from the dunk in cold water, her brittle cough echoing in the chamber.

"We should get out of here before we freeze," said Sima.

"Yeah," moaned Austin, swimming around to stand up. "Ow, damn. I totally landed on my face. Sorry. She jumped in before I could grab her. And eww. The floor is nasty!"

Sima decided on the nearest passageway and headed for it. "We'll be okay. It's better that we stay together."

Lissa smiled.

Each time she took a step, Sima grimaced at the ooze squirting between her toes. "Ugh. What are we walking in?"

"Feels like runny poo," said Juan.

Sima gagged.

The bracelet buzzed, so she held her arm up.

‹I am detecting a sediment layer that scans as a mixture of silt and single-celled plant organisms similar to algae. However, they do not possess any chlorophyll.›

"Whatever that means," muttered Sima.

‹It means they don't derive nutrients from sunlight. I lack sufficient data to determine how they survive at the bottom of an underground lake, but the substance does appear to be alive. Before you ask, since I know you're about to, I do not calculate it as being dangerous to touch. However, I would advise against consuming it.›

"Oh, that's not happening." She gagged again.

"What's not happening?" asked Austin, the chamber lending his voice a watery echo.

"The bracelet said we shouldn't eat the muck we're walking in."

He gagged.

The water became progressively shallower the closer she walked to the wall, reaching a minimum depth of knee-high, which continued into the tunnel she'd chosen at random. Slime also lined the bottom of the passage, though it formed a layer only an inch deep. Four steps into the tube, the combination of rounded floor and slick muck made Sima slip. She wound up on her butt, dropping

Lissa, who shrieked before landing flat on her back in the water. Austin started to laugh, but wiped out and went under a second later.

Shivering, Lissa swam over and clung to Sima's arm.

Juan didn't wait to fall, and lowered himself into the water before swimming on ahead. Sima kept trying to walk, but every few steps, the smooth goo-covered stone took her feet out from under her. Eventually, she followed Juan's lead and swam, walking her hands along the bottom to pull herself forward. Lissa floated beside her, teeth chattering. Austin kept trying to walk, despite wiping out over and over.

They followed the tunnel around a gentle rightward bend, passing numerous side chambers. Some contained inexplicable metal cubes or obelisks next to pads of plant matter that resembled sleeping mats placed in bowl-shaped depressions in the floor. She peered into the 'rooms' one by one, but since none of them offered a way out, kept going. Metal tools littered the floor of the seventh space. Curious, and eager for a respite from the chilly water, Sima pulled herself out of the passageway and sat on the dry stone floor.

All three kids followed, both boys bee-lining to check out the tools while Lissa kept clinging to her, shivering and coughing. Sima cradled the girl in her lap, rubbing her back and trying to share body heat. It didn't help that the air temperature down here felt even colder than the cave had been. The girl's teeth chattered, and she kept muttering, "cold."

Austin held up a device resembling a crowbar that got run over by a big gee-vee. Juan picked up another metal rod with various movable rings and sliding parts. It amused him longer than the crowbar occupied Austin, who tossed his find aside and checked out a small hammer-like tool.

"Wow..." Sima whistled. "There really *was* intelligent life here before us."

Austin dropped the hammer and approached a one-foot metal cube near the sleeping mat. "This thing's humming."

Sima pointed. "Don't touch—"

Austin put his hand on the cube and promptly collapsed over sideways onto the sleeping mat.

"No!" Sima lunged to her feet, clumsily setting Lissa on the floor. "Austin!"

She ran over and grabbed his shoulder, shaking him, but the boy didn't react. "No... no." She knelt beside him, feeling at his neck. He still had a pulse. She patted his cheeks. "Come on. Wake up. What happened?" She sniffled and gasped, tears falling free.

"Oh, wow." Austin looked up at her. "Just playing around."

Sima stared at him. "You little turd!"

He bit his lip. "Sorry. Didn't think you'd flip out like that."

She pulled him up and wrapped her arms around him. "Don't ever do anything like that again, okay? You scared the hell out of me."

Austin sat there for a second or two, stunned, before gingerly returning the embrace. "I'm sorry."

"Don't lie." Juan shook his head. "Lots of stuff we don't know here can hurt us."

"Please don't scare me like that again, okay?" Sima leaned back from the hug and held his face in both hands, staring into his eyes.

He looked down. "Sorry. I won't. I didn't wanna scare you that bad. Just thought it would be funny."

"I'm cold," whispered Lissa past clicking teeth.

"Me too." Sima touched foreheads with Austin, sighed, and got up. "Okay. Let's find a way out of here."

Her foot shot out from under her as soon as she stepped into the hallway. Scowling at the wall, she sat there until her rear end stopped hurting. Grumbling, Sima didn't bother getting back up, and paddled along. They swam past eight more side rooms before the end of the tunnel appeared, bringing them right back to the big room they first landed in.

"Ugh."

The bracelet buzzed.

"What?" yelled Sima.

‹Please go back and enter the last chamber on the left. There appears to be writing on the wall. I wish to document it.›

"What for? None of us will ever read it."

‹It seems foolish to find something like this and ignore it.›

"We need to find a way out. We're trying to survive, not explore."

‹Please? It will take less than a minute.›

She sighed. "Fine."

The chamber contained two sleeping areas, each with a nearby metal cube. Meaningless symbols in a general arrangement similar to writing covered the entire back wall. Neat rows and clustered groups of characters suggested sentences and words. She swept her wrist back and forth, letting the bracelet scan everything. As soon as it emitted a happy *chirp*, she pulled the kids with her into the main chamber. The next tunnel she went down had more of the same, a big loop around with numerous side rooms. Her bracelet insisted on scanning another two rooms with writing. As much she felt it pointless, she obliged. Maybe if more humans ever came to this planet, someone would find her skeleton and the data would still be in the bracelet.

While she held her wrist up to the wall, walking to the right to scan, the unmistakable sound of two boys adding to the water in the tunnel filled the air. Lissa, hovering at her side, twisted to peer back at the room's entrance.

"Eww! We have to walk in that!" yelled Lissa. "Sima! They're making pee in the water!"

"The water's moving," said Austin. "And it's better than going on the floor."

Sima couldn't help but smile to herself. The kid had a point. Peeing on the floor would be much worse. Eventually, she finished placating the bracelet by letting it scan all the text. She led the kids once more into the flooded tunnel, which frustratingly wound up looping around to connect to the main room. The bracelet projected a map showing the mostly-oval central chamber with two C-shaped tunnels connecting at both ends. Sima examined the positions of the other tunnels, picturing similar loops everywhere except for two openings where the spacing didn't look the same.

Hoping one of those would be an exit, she jumped into the veritable lake inside the central chamber and swam across the middle. By the time she reached the other side, Lissa's lips had turned blue. Juan appeared equally miserable and cold, though his darker complexion concealed it better.

Sima crawled to her feet inside the tunnel, which right away gave her a sense of hope. Warmer air blew over her only a few steps in.

"This might not be a bad place to live," said Austin. "We'd be safe from danger down here."

"It's creepy," said Lissa between shivering fits. "And too cold."

"This place is all flooded. We'd get sick staying in cold water, and what if those rooms get wet? We can't sleep in water."

"Oh." Austin shrugged.

The tunnel spiraled to the right, the water level falling bit by bit the farther she advanced. After a minute, she walked into a downward flow less than an inch deep, which appeared to be entering via hundreds of tiny holes along the sides. Slippery, smooth rock plus the constant current made the climb treacherous. Sima braced her hands on the dry parts of the walls and peered back at the boys.

"Be careful. If we fall in here, we're going all the way down. The floor is too slippery."

They nodded.

Sima kept a grip on the wall, but her feet continued trying to slide out from under her. The incline steepened after a few minutes, which made staying upright even more difficult. Her left foot shot out from under her, dropping her to her knees with a hollow *clonk* of bone on rock. She slid backward, scrambling to get a hold of the wall, but the tunnel may as well have been made of oiled glass.

Her effort to scramble for traction paid off in a few seconds when she got a grip on a slime-free patch and halted her backward slide. Afraid that trying to stand would cause a catastrophic wipeout, she crawled.

"Gah!" yelled Austin, an instant before a fleshy *smack* rang out.

He fell flat on his chest, instinctively grabbing Juan's ankle. That, of course, pulled Juan off balance. The younger boy lurched forward and grabbed Lissa's leg, causing the girl to shriek straight in Sima's ear. The combined weight of two boys pulling on her, plus Lissa clinging like a backpack proved too much. Sima lost traction and went sliding down, sweeping all three kids with her in a screaming, shrieking tangle of arms and legs. Long minutes of climbing took only seconds to undo, and they splashed once more into the lake. Once the panic of falling wore off, the little ones sat neck deep, staring at her with pleading faces.

She sighed.

"I'm sorry," whispered Austin. "I stepped on like snot or something."

"It's okay." Sima rolled over onto all fours. "We know this tunnel leads out. Just be careful and we'll be fine. Falling won't hurt us. It's just annoying."

I'd kill to have those stupid foam slippers. Yeah they were cheap, but they wouldn't slide.

Sima rubbed her soles clear of slimy algae and attempted the climb again, Lissa's constant, quiet coughing at her ear all the motivation she needed to stay calm and focused. Fortunately, the tunnel's width allowed her to keep her hands on both walls, which, being free of water, offered a far less slippery surface to hold on to.

After an arduous twenty-minute endeavor, she reached the end of where water oozed into the tunnel. Not long after that, the tunnel leveled off for a short distance, then bent left around a corner. Sima dashed forward, no longer gripping the walls for support. Falling here wouldn't send her careening down a waterslide. She raced around the corner and skidded to a stop at a dead end, blocked off by a stone slab with the same glowing circuit-board pattern as the dome room.

"Crap!" shouted Sima, slapping at the wall and kicking it.

Lissa gave her a sad look. "You tried."

"Wait." Juan ducked past her. "There's a button just like the other one."

The boy poked the stone slab in front of them, aiming his finger at a circular widening in the glowing grooves about two feet up from the floor.

"Weird that the doorbell's so low. Guess the aliens were short," said Austin.

"Or they're snails." Lissa giggled into a coughing fit. "Crawling around."

"Maybe the alien snails ate all that slimy stuff?" asked Austin.

Juan made a silly face. "Or it's their poop!"

"Eww!" yelled Lissa, shivering.

Sima squirmed at the thought, refusing to accept even the idea she might have been ankle-deep in alien poo.

At Juan's touch, the stone slab sank into the ground, revealing the dome room.

"Yay!" shouted Lissa, bouncing on Sima's back. "We won't die!"

The boys exchanged a glance.

Sima tromped out of the tunnel and headed directly for the short entrance corridor, hurrying into the warm daylight. For the first time in her life, near-hundred degree weather felt amazing. She set Lissa down and rolled flat on her back in the grass, arms and legs out to bask in the sun.

The kids all more or less did the same thing.

Screw that cave. We live in the lifeboat.

Once no lips remained blue and all the shivering ceased, Sima rounded everyone up and set a course for 'home,' such as it was. About an hour into the walk, Lissa swooned to her knees, clutching at her chest. She tried to cough, but only managed a feeble wheeze.

"Liss!" Sima pounced, grabbing the girl's shoulders.

Lissa lifted her head with a 'help me!' stare, her face already tinted purple.

Terrified and clueless, Sima held the bracelet up to the girl's back. "What do I do?"

‹Her airway is blocked. I am reading a large mass of phlegm that has partially hardened. Wrap your arms around her from behind, grasp your wrist and pull your hands into her gut as shown.› The mini screen displayed an animation.

Sima did as instructed, pulling so hard she lifted the girl off her feet with each squeeze. The fourth time, a hard nugget of pinkish-grey something shot out of her mouth. Lissa took a huge gulp of air, then proceeded to attempt crying, screaming, and coughing all at the same time. Sima did the only thing she could: held the girl's quivering little body as she spasmed. Eventually, Lissa spat up blood and wiped her mouth on the back of her arm.

"I think I choked too hard," rasped Lissa. "Sorry."

"No, sweetie. It's not your fault." Sima cradled her in her arms and stood, carrying her. The child made no effort to move, her arms limp on top of her.

Austin looked up at her, his expression asking if the girl would die.

Silent tears ran down Sima's cheeks at the mere suggestion. "You're gonna be okay, sweetie. Just rest, 'kay?"

"Mmm," said Lissa, closing her eyes.

Every horrible thought Sima ever had about smaller children on Earth came back to torment her as they trekked through the jungle. Faces of kids she hadn't seen in over a year, ones she hadn't even known the names of, danced across her mind's eye. She'd never wished anything *truly* bad on them, merely wanted them to go somewhere else to beg instead of stealing *her* money. Had she seen Lissa on Earth, she would've been furious with envy. Skinny, adorable, blonde, pale, tiny, *and* sick. This kid practically oozed glint. She could've made a hundred a day without even trying. Even the most heartless Citizen would feel bad for her. Hell, someone probably would've taken her home.

And that would've made Sima want to stuff her headfirst into an ORC bin.

She cradled Lissa tighter. "I'm sorry."

"For what?" whispered Lissa without opening her eyes.

"For a lot of stuff." Sima let a long sigh out her nose, and sniffled.

Austin turned away to hide crying. By the time they reached the lifeboat, Sima could barely see past a curtain of tears. She didn't expect Lissa would make it through the night. At what had become their sleeping spot, she sank to sit in the grass and cradled the weak child in her lap, rocking her side to side while trying to say comforting things between sobs.

"Why are you crying?" asked Lissa.

"I'm sad that you're not feeling well." Sima forced a smile.

Lissa opened her eyes. "I'm only tired. We did too much swimming. I'm not supposed to play so hard."

"That's right, sweetie. You're going to be okay." *She's still cold.*

Austin sat beside her and took Lissa's hand. Juan snuggled in closer. That gave Sima an idea.

"She got too cold," said Sima. "Austin, come closer. We gotta warm her up."

He scooted over without hesitation. Sima rolled the girl over so they lay chest to chest, with Austin adding body heat from one side, Juan the other, though he squealed when her feet touched his stomach. She considered suggesting everyone remove their wet clothing, but the fabric didn't cover much and probably wouldn't make a lot of difference.

Instead, she huddled as close as she could, listening to the girl's every breath. An hour became two. Neither boy protested lying still. Sima couldn't stop crying, but at least she kept silent.

This is so unfair. Why did they do this to us? This kid would've had better odds at Magdalena's!

Sima hated herself for thinking that as soon as she did, mostly for wishing that place on a six-year-old. But, if she were Lissa, Sima would choose that over death. She'd choose that over watching this little girl die.

If I could go back to Earth, I'd do whatever that woman wanted me to if it would keep Lissa alive.

"It's getting dark," said Austin in a tone as if he tried to speak at a funeral.

Sima squeezed all three of them, dreading that by morning, she'd only have two kids to watch over. Already, her brain tortured her with wondering where she ought to dig the little grave.

Juan squeaked. "Can't breathe. You're squeezing too tight."

"Sorry," whispered Sima, relaxing her grip. When she realized they lay in total silence, Sima's heart stopped.

The constant, repetitive little wheezes had ceased.

18

MONSTERS

Horrified, Sima relaxed her grip on Lissa and peered down at her.

The girl looked still and peaceful, her eyes closed, arms hanging limp.

"Liss?" whispered Sima.

"I'm hungry," said Lissa. She opened her eyes.

Sima let out an anguished scream.

Both boys jumped and sat up.

"Okay." Lissa's eyes bulged. "I won't eat."

Sima clamped on and sobbed. "I thought you… umm…"

"Sometimes, my breaths get quiet when I feel better. The doctor lady said that's how I know they helped."

Austin ran off and grabbed some fruits. Sima about liquefied into a puddle of relief. The girl had regained some color and no longer felt like she'd been stored in a freezer. Grinning, Lissa took the fruit Austin offered and tore into it. Sima continued crying, but out of happiness.

What's wrong with me? She wiped her eyes. *I really need to stop overreacting. I've known this kid for a couple days. Why am I getting so upset?* Once the shock of nearly watching Lissa take her last breath for a second time faded from mind numbing to nerve-wracking, she allowed herself to eat a pair of fruits. Whatever happened to Lissa had been a warning. She should try to keep the girl from overexerting herself or spending too much time in cold water. Maybe she didn't have to worry the girl would drop dead at any minute—as long as she remained vigilant. One little mistake would be costly.

After eating, they resumed a group snuggle and settled down for the night.

LISSA AWOKE SOON after dawn with a bad coughing fit.

Her little body convulsed and twisted, barking-goose sounds coming from her so loud Sima expected the child's lungs to fly out of her mouth at any minute. She couldn't think of anything to do other than hold her tight and clap her on the back. Grey-pink globs of phlegm eventually fell from her mouth. Lissa doubled over, shivering and red-faced. Austin grimaced at the substance and covered his mouth, holding back vomit.

After a few breaths, she burst into tears, whining, "Ow. Ow. Ow."

Sima rocked her, cradling the back of her head.

The boys wandered off to pee, returning in a few minutes. They sat and waited patiently until Lissa quieted down and stopped crying. Sima lowered the girl into her lap and checked her over, but saw no blood, bruises, or other signs of alarm.

"Bracelet, can you check her?"

The pyramid of blue laser light appeared, projecting a grid on the girl's chest.

Lissa's eyes sparkled. "Ooh. That's pretty."

‹Her lungs are producing phlegm. There's evidence of scar tissue consistent with tumor removal, though I do not detect any cancer. Her lung tissue is damaged, but I lack sufficient medical archives to interpret the scan data.›

Sima rubbed the girl's back and patted her while making sure she drank a good amount of water. "You okay?"

"Yeah." Lissa nodded.

"Okay. You three stay here, okay? I'm gonna go get some fruit and water."

Lissa pouted. "Aww."

"We did a lot of walking around yesterday. Recharge your batteries today."

The girl folded her arms. "I don't have batteries."

Juan dashed out of the weeds carrying a pair of slightly floppy branches. He tossed one to Austin, and the instinctual reaction of boys to any vaguely sword-shaped object followed: they began walloping each other.

"Hey," yelled Sima at a particularly loud *thwap*. "Easy. You can play swords, but don't hurt each other. There aren't any doctors here."

"Okay," said Austin.

They resumed their swordfight but more or less slapped their 'weapons' together instead of hitting each other.

Sima hurried off with the plastic bottle, leaving Lissa pouty but obediently sitting still. The nearest creek sat a twelve-minute walk away according to the clock showing on the bracelet's map.

"Is that Earth time?" asked Sima.

‹This planet's arrangement and resemblance to Earth are so close, the scientists did not believe their eyes. Hence, Mirage. Technically, this planet has a day length of twenty-four hours plus six minutes. The *Progenitor* team decided to ignore that six minutes, allowing for twenty-four hour days separated by a 'between' period six minutes long. I have rewritten my chrono app to this standard.›

"So it's 7:18 a.m. *here* then."

‹Yes.›

Upon reaching the small river, Sima filled the water jug and headed back without wasting time. Having the kids out of her sight made her nervous that something would happen to them. Roughly halfway back to the lifeboat, she veered deeper into the foliage to harvest a dozen fruits from a low-hanging pod.

Walking back 'home' with her arms full proved a challenge. Every few steps, a fruit would fall to the ground. She'd stop, set the jug down, and recover the fruit only to walk a little more and drop another piece.

When she crouched the sixth time to pick up a dropped fruit, her eyes focused on a terrifying mark in the ground: an animal track much like a cat's, only big enough that she could stand on top of it with her feet together and still not cover it all.

"Whoa," whispered Sima. "What is that?"

‹Insufficient information in your request. Please define 'that.'›

She squatted, let the fruits tumble to the ground at her side, and held the bracelet out to the track. "This footprint. What made it?"

Laser light flickered over the soil for a few seconds.

‹This appears to be the track of a large feline creature. Based on the paw width and print depth, I estimate the creature's weight at around 400-500 pounds. Assuming its bodily structure is at all comparable to Earth cats, its shoulder height would be about four feet off the ground. The closest species I can relate it to would be a tiger, however some tigers have reached in excess of 1,000 pounds.›

"Umm… what's a tiger?" asked Sima.

‹A large jungle cat that went extinct in 2208.› The holo-screen played a short video showing a huge orange-black-and-white feline standing in a cage and roaring.

"That's only a little scary." Sima poked a finger at one of the holes in the dirt in front of the print. "This thing has claws."

‹Paw pad shape and arrangement suggests a feline-type animal, so claws are highly likely.›

"Hope they don't like the taste of human." Sima shivered. "Damn… we've been sleeping outside at night like a buffet."

‹This track was not here yesterday.›

She gulped. "The kids are alone!"

‹This creature has not attacked them, and they have not seen it.›

"How can you know that!" she yelled.

‹We are close enough to hear their screams.›

Sima grabbed the bracelet, intending to tear it off. "How can you be so heartless? They're only kids!"

‹I am merely stating fact. Please do not panic.›

Snarling, she hastily gathered up the fruits and water jug. One fruit fell as she hurried onward, but she didn't bother going back for it. Soon, the repetitive thudding of rubbery-branch sword fighting eased her nerves. She dashed into the grassy clearing and breathed a sigh of relief at everyone unhurt.

Lissa played with a strand of flowers, attempting to weave it around her ankle, but it kept crumbling apart. Unperturbed, she gathered more and began anew.

"Food," said Sima, jogging over to sit by Lissa.

The boys came running.

"I really want a burger," said Austin.

Juan glanced at him. "You ain't got enough glint."

"Yeah I do. I had like 400 before the cops got me."

"Nuh uh!" yelled Juan. "That's not a real number."

"Sure it is," said Austin before taking a bite of fruit and cringing.

Juan looked over at Sima. "Is there a 400?"

"Yeah. That's a ton of glint." Sima raised an eyebrow. "How did you get so much?"

"Begging." Austin gave her the same huge-eyed stare he hit her with when she first saw him trapped in a stasis pod. "Women can't resist. One even wanted to take me home, but her friend wouldn't let her."

"Wow," said Lissa.

Sima squinted at him. Even a kid as adorably pathetic as Austin could make himself look would be hard-pressed to beg 400 glint in a short enough timeframe to accrue such an amount before spending it on food. And, she doubted an eleven-year-old boy would be able to resist blowing his money on fun stuff. If he wasn't simply lying about having that much, it suggested he acquired a lot of glint over a short amount of time. She suspected he'd run jobs for Nalas, or someone like him. Or maybe he'd done something to wind up sporting a fancy pink *Juvenile Inmate* jumpsuit. Having seen him dive on Lissa to save her from drowning, she doubted he would have been violent, so a thief if anything.

After they ate, the boys resumed play fighting with branches. Lissa continued trying to make jewelry out of the tiny wildflowers. Sima studied the map on the Omnicomputer, plotting out potential search routes that may lead her to other lifeboats or debris. Given how close the kids had been to suffocating, she doubted any other survivors remained alive. Then again, the lifeboat behind her had apparently suffered a direct hit from something external that damaged it. *Her* stasis pod lid worked when she hit the button, so barring damage, it sounded plausible for others to have made it. Though, she had no idea how widespread landing sites could be. The grim thought that she and the kids had been in lifeboats all the way at the back end of the ship could also mean none of the others even survived long enough to be launched. In a bad enough scenario, the best she'd find would be chunks of hull somewhere. Perhaps something useful survived the crash. *Some* part of that ship had to have supplies on it. Maybe a few boxes of clothes had made it to the surface. Hopefully, they wouldn't be on another continent.

"How far apart would other lifeboats be?"

‹That would depend on the altitude at which the *Progenitor* broke apart. Assuming that it did break apart. It may have jettisoned the lifeboats and crashed whole into the surface somewhere.›

"Do you have any way to tell how high up we were when the lifeboats launched?" asked Sima.

‹Normally, that information would have been recorded, but your lifeboat was not officially active, nor was the one behind us, so the flight recorders did not turn on.›

"Figures."

She spent the day mostly staring at maps, dividing her attention between that, the woods, and the kids. Swordplay got boring after a while, and the boys decided to explore the nearby jungle. Sima shouted at them to stay in sight. Lissa got up and tried chasing small butterfly like insects with all-white wings, but only lasted a few minutes before she resigned herself to walking around and giggling at the grass tickling her. Eventually, she collected some larger blue floral vines and once again sat beside Sima attempting to make an anklet.

The boys brought back more fruit for the evening meal. Everyone gathered to sit in a small circle around a campfire that didn't exist. Sima choked her portion down, already getting tired of eating the same raspberry-rhubarb flavored meal. She'd spent four years happy to have food at all, and didn't much care what it was. That she actually got sick of eating the same fruit over and over must mean something… but what?

Snap.

All four of them jumped and whirled, facing the jungle.

"Did you hear that?" asked Austin. "What was it?"

A giant cat. Sima stood. "Come on. Let's go inside the lifeboat."

"I don't wanna," wailed Lissa, going limp. "I don't like it in there. I can't breathe! We almost died in there."

"Shh. You don't need to get in the pod, just the lifeboat. We have to." Sima struggled with the dead weight of an unwilling six-year-old.

Another snap emanated from the trees.

"No. I'm scared!" Lissa bawled.

Sima whispered close to her ear. "It might be a monster. A monster can't get us if we're inside."

The child's face froze in a mask of terror; she fell silent and stopped struggling.

Sima ran, carrying her, to the hatch, ushered the boys inside, and pulled the door closed behind her.

"Now what?" asked Austin.

Sima let herself breathe. "Now, it's bedtime."

"What kind of monster?" asked Juan. "Maybe it's an Aurak."

I don't want to scare them, but I also don't want them to be clueless and get themselves hurt. "I saw a track today. It looked like a tiger."

"What's a tiger?" asked Lissa.

Juan shrugged.

Austin's eyes bulged. "Umm. Are you sure?"

"No. I'm not sure what it is, other than it's probably a big cat."

"I like cats." Lissa smiled.

"This is a really big cat. So big we would be like mice to it." Sima ruffled the girl's hair.

Austin looked around at the walls. "It can't get us in here. This is spaceship armor."

She reclined on her side upon the bare metal floor, and soon had Lissa and Juan clutched like teddy bears to her chest, Austin leaning against her back. Stifling heat coated everyone in sweat, but she didn't dare push them away. Holes in the ceiling and walls let some air in, but none looked anywhere near large enough for a tiger to squeeze inside. If not comfortable, at least the lifeboat offered protection.

Damn. "Be right back. I left the water outside."

None of the kids let go.

"There's still a little light out there. And it's hot in here. We're going to need water." Sima nudged the kids. "I'll be *right* back."

With no small amount of whining, they let go and sat nearby. Sima crept over to the lifeboat door and pulled it open an inch to peer out. Nothing appeared to be moving around, but she didn't quite trust it.

That the four of them had spent two nights sleeping out in the open felt as reckless as if she'd let them try the Harmony Tower jump. Of all the things she'd done back on Earth, that had to be the most foolish. But a guy in the E6 gang offered forty glint to anyone who could make the jump. Others in the gang made a lot of glint placing bets on who'd make it and who'd fall to go splat. Sima had been hungry enough to push aside her morbid fear of heights, but only had the nerve to go once.

She held her breath and made a run for the water jug. A *snap* in the nearby jungle made her look. Her foot came down on a slimy rind from their dinner and shot straight out from under her. She landed on her side and slid a short distance, facing the jungle.

There in the darkness between trees, a large feline silhouette with four glowing green eyes, the top pair set slightly wider than the bottom pair, stared at her.

Too frightened to scream, she grabbed the jug and ran like death itself nipped at her heels. Water splashed down her front as she sprinted and ducked past the partially sunken entrance. She handed the plastic bottle off to Austin and whirled to slam the hatch, shoving the locking bar down to seal it.

Once it refused to close any tighter, she allowed herself to breathe.

19

THE NIGHT SCRATCH

A little hand on the cheek shook Sima's head until she woke up.

Lissa knelt beside her, inches from her face. The tiny girl's bones seemed to quiver in her skin. Her underpants sat in a urine-soaked wad a few feet away at the center of a puddle on the lifeboat's plain white floor. The little color that had been in the girl's cheeks was gone, leaving her ghostly white. Sima sat up.

"What's wrong?"

Lissa crawled into her lap and whispered. "The monster's tryin' to get us. It looked at me 'froo the hole."

Sima gazed along a line from the child's pointing finger to a ten-inch rent in the hull near the stasis pod. Tiny feet braced against Sima's thigh, the child pressed close, trembling. The girl had wet herself, though Sima didn't even think to push her away or feel disgust. She opened her mouth to say something comforting, but hesitated when a *creak* came from above. At the scrape of claws on the roof, she gulped back the initial urge to scream. *I gotta look strong for them.* She glanced across the ceiling, following the soft groans of metal as weight shifted from one side of the lifeboat to the other. Scratching near the door conjured a mental image of a cat trying to get at mice hiding in a box.

Darkness lurked in the holes dotting the lifeboat's hull. The bracelet screen showed the time as 3:08 a.m.

Sima wrapped her arms around Lissa. "It can't get us in here."

"What can't get us?" Juan sat up, wiping his eyes.

"A monster," whispered Lissa.

Juan's eyes shot open. "There's monsters?"

"Ugh." Austin sat up, realized his hand lay in a puddle, and yelled. "Who messed?"

Lissa's guilt showed on her face as obvious as her wadded underwear on the floor.

"Stupid little kid. What's wrong with you? Eww."

Lissa burst into tears.

"Austin!" whisper-yelled Sima. "That was mean."

Juan punched Austin in the leg. "Leave her alone."

"Hey." Sima grabbed Juan's wrist. "Stop that. No hitting."

"Sorry," muttered Austin. "I woke up with my hand in pee."

The scratching at the door resumed, louder and more fervent. It ceased in a few seconds. After a *thump* outside, a pair of luminous green right eyes glimmered in the large hole. Lissa screamed a high-pitched tone that echoed painfully loud in the small compartment. The cat flinched.

Austin turned white.

The girl buried her face in Sima's shoulder to keep quiet.

Green glow vanished from the hole. A second later, the lifeboat jostled as weight landed on the roof. The creature emitted a low growl. Austin scurried behind Sima. Everyone kept silent. Squeaks and groans came from the hull as the beast explored, drifting toward the back end. The pod shifted ever so slightly. Sima glanced at the urine puddle spreading a few centimeters to one side. At the sight of claws picking at one of the holes in the roof, Austin threaded his arms around Sima's gut from behind, shaking.

"Austin…" Sima adjusted Lissa's weight to allow circulation to resume in her left leg.

"Yeah?"

"If you pee on me, I'm going to be upset with you."

He scoffed into the back of her hair. "I'm not a little kid."

Metal screeched overhead.

Austin squeezed her tighter and wailed, "Don't let it get us!"

"You yell like one," whispered Juan.

Contagious fear seeped from him into Lissa, who stifled whimpers. She appeared to have more practice being terrified in silence. Juan retrieved the axe and handed it to Sima. He sat nearby, calm as anything. Sima glanced at him, baffled until she remembered he'd lived in *La Propagación* and probably had to sleep while gunfights went by right over his head.

"It can't get in. She's right for making us go inside." Juan crawled off away from the puddle and curled up as if to sleep.

Snuffling at the hatch made Lissa whine and squirm. Sima set the girl down and grabbed the axe in a two-handed grip before creeping up to the door. Lissa backed away and cowered against the stasis pod that almost killed her, both hands clutched at her chin, staring at the door. A long, spine-tingling scrape of claws over metal made all the kids whimper.

"Stay behind me," whispered Sima.

"Don't open it!" yelled Austin.

"I'm not going to." She stopped a few feet from the entrance, axe poised. *I'm crazy. Am I really going to get in a tiger's face with a little axe?*

"So why are you at the door? You think the monster's smart enough to open it?" whispered Austin.

Sima smirked at the lift bar, feeling like an idiot. "Umm, yeah. No idea if this thing is smarter than a cat."

For several agonizing minutes, Sima shivered at the bone-jarring screech of claws raking over metal. Eventually, the creature gave up. Low, irritated snarling circled outside. She let the air out of her lungs as she lowered her axe. Thumps and snaps grew distant outside, suggesting the large cat had run back off into the jungle. Hopeful the worst had passed, she moved to sit on a clean spot of floor. The kids rushed over and clamped on, no one caring about the hot, stuffy air.

Half an hour after the scratching ceased, Sima allowed herself to attempt rest. She lay on her side with an arm over Lissa. The girl curled up against her chest, thumb in her mouth. Too much adrenaline had shocked her system to allow sleep. When Sima rolled onto her back, Lissa whined in her dream and cuddled tighter. Sima stared at the ceiling until sunlight leaked in from the holes overhead.

Did I even sleep?

She sat up and yawned, her face scrunching at a nasty smell fouling the air. The puddle Lissa made had become a tacky, amber stain on the hospital-white floor, not quite dried. She frowned at the wadded cloth. *If we weren't stuck here, those would be garbage. I can't leave her naked.* Sima grumbled. The kids would eventually outgrow their skivvies, and hers would fall apart. If she didn't find some usable leaves or other materials, they'd all be nudists soon enough.

This planet sucks. Okay. I'll wash them.

She sat up and yawned. Lissa startled awake and stared at her. Juan stretched, yawned, and farted.

Austin laughed.

Sima eyed the door. *Is that bastard waiting for us?*

"Is it gone?" asked Austin.

"It's quiet." Sima listened. "I only hear the birds and sky mantas."

"Can we go outside? Gotta pee," said Juan.

Sima pulled the kids closer. "Not yet. I don't trust it."

Juan stood and walked over to one of the smaller holes in the wall. As soon as he pushed his briefs down, Sima looked away, mildly jealous at how easily he could cope with being shut inside.

"Me too," whispered Lissa, shying away from Austin.

Austin said nothing, but made a sour face at his hand. He went over to another breach in the hull at the appropriate height. Lissa looked up at Sima.

"Gimme a minute." Sima roamed around checking panels and cabinets. She found an empty plastic canister in the guts of the stasis pod Austin had been in, likely used to contain the cryonic fluid. It served as an emergency toilet, which she left situated on the far side of the debris wall in the much smaller section of the lifeboat for a modicum of privacy.

Lissa insisted Sima stay with her while she went back there.

Since Sima still didn't trust going outside, they sat around for hours talking about Earth, mostly food places they liked to hit back home. Austin didn't know any of the vendors, so Sima figured he must've come from a different district... maybe even a different continent. Who knows how far the EGSF would've transported Outcasts for the ship. She vaguely remembered from fourth grade history class something about how different places used to be different countries before the End of Nations. However, she couldn't remember any of them, and since everyone had been speaking GANSEC for two centuries, little trace of regional accents remained.

By noon, stomachs growled and Sima's tongue felt like cotton from thirst. Finally having had enough of self-imposed confinement, she approached the door, but Lissa tried to drag her back.

"We can't sit in here forever." She ran her hand over the girl's hair. "We need food."

"You'll die," whispered Lissa. "Night Scratch is a bad kitty."

Sima grasped the lever and pulled the door in three inches. She yelled a few nonsense words and slammed it. "If it's out there, it'll come back now."

They waited in tense silence for a while.

"Maybe it's smart," said Austin.

"Or it only comes out at night," said Juan.

Sima shivered. "Okay. I'm going to get food. No one goes outside." She trudged over to Lissa's underwear, cringed at the thought of touching the pee-soaked fabric, but grabbed the sopping wad anyway.

"Eww," said Juan. "You touched it."

"I'm sorry." Lissa pouted.

"It's all right." Sima smiled at her. "If I was your age, I'd have done the same thing. Wait here and stay quiet. I'll be back as fast as I can. We need water, and I'm going to wash these." Sima grasped the door handle. *This is a bad idea.*

Lissa cried. "No. Don't get eated!"

20

AN ILL WIND

Sima ducked through the hatch and climbed out of the hole she'd dug to clear the bottom. She held the axe up and turned in a slow spin, searching for the cat, ready to drop everything and dive back into the safety of the lifeboat. Shining jungle on all sides appeared benign and harmless. More paw prints crisscrossed the dirt by the door, about the same size as the ones she found the day before.

No sign of anything dangerous lurked in the jungle. If the cat waited to ambush them, it would've had to turn invisible.

Maybe the kid's right and the thing can't stand daylight. She rolled that thought marble around her brain. *Its eyes glow. Maybe daylight hurts it?*

The door squeaked open.

"We wanna go," said Austin.

Lissa ran out and grabbed on to her, staring up with irresistible blue eyes. Sima didn't have a free hand to pry her away. Leaving the kids safe in the lifeboat made the most logical sense, but she hated the idea of being separated from them. Lissa's feeble cough clinched it.

"Okay. Stay close to me and keep quiet."

Sima led the way to the nearest water source, a river about twenty feet across, thankful not to encounter anything with sharp, nasty teeth. The far bank consisted of a steep cliff about eight feet tall, though the near bank met flush to the ground. By the time they reached the water, the pervasive fear of a tiger coming after them had lessened to strong worry. After all, they'd been running around in the daylight for several days now, and not once had they been attacked.

The boys slipped off their briefs and jumped in. Lissa knelt at Sima's side in the shallows while she crouched and washed the soiled cloth without any soap. Once she'd gotten the garment as clean as river water could manage, she wrung it out and tossed it onto the grass to dry. No longer giving a damn, Sima stripped to keep her clothes dry, then pulled Lissa into the water to rinse her off and also bathe herself.

Attempting to wash a six-year-old in chilly river water soon degenerated into a splash war—though she made sure to keep it calm and not push the girl too hard. She mostly sat chest-deep, amusing Lissa with shiny rocks or pointing out rainbow mushroom-like things growing on the bottom while the boys swam all around, diving and having fun like they hadn't spent most of the day in fear for their lives.

The boys headed off to the left and climbed out of the water by one of those huge indigo root/vines. Lissa got up and headed over, curious at what they had gotten into. Sima sighed to herself watching them, imagining some stuffy old narrator voice talking about the primitive tribes of Mirage. It almost made her laugh to think about how uncomfortable she'd been at Magdalena's around so many women showing their bodies off in lacy underthings, and now she sat on a planet with a population of four humans, and none of them had a stitch of clothing on.

Mag's was way different. This is innocent. And the EGSF stole our clothes. She wondered what kind of rags her three charges had before the cops collected them. How long had they been on the street? She'd worn the same tunic for four years and went through two pairs of pants after the dress she'd run away in had fallen apart. Though, being attacked by a pack of older girls trying to steal it while she slept hadn't helped. They'd torn the dress off her rather than let her escape with it intact. Fortunately, the tunic had been long enough to double as a dress. She gazed up at the clouds, thinking about her first criminal act before that kid told her about karma. She'd snuck into a clothing store, carried a pair of pants to the changing rooms, and walked right out wearing them. If the vendor noticed, he hadn't bothered to stop her.

Maybe there's more nice people than I thought.

Sudden unexplained laughing from children worried her.

She glanced over at the kids, and gasped. They'd smeared each other head-to-toe in purple ink, which they evidently found hilarious.

"You said that oil won't hurt them, right?" asked Sima.

‹As long as they don't eat it, they should be fine.›

Lissa declared herself a 'night faerie,' while the boys called themselves 'Falnorians,' whatever that meant. Based on what the boys proceed to say after that, she assumed they pretended to be some alien race from a movie.

Not liking how far away they'd gone, Sima got up and walked over to collect them. Copious hugs shared the blue dye, and all three attacked her with handprints and tickles. Laughing like a fool, she dragged them into the water to wash the stuff off. Soon, Lissa got tired and decided to sit neck-deep and soak while the boys resumed diving and swimming around. Sima took a seat by Lissa and listened to the girl ramble about her opinion that this jungle must have faeries.

"I think that's why no one saw them on Earth anymore," said Lissa, "because they came here."

"Could be," said Sima.

After another hour or so of playing, Austin swam up to her with a grim expression. "Sima, I smell something bad."

Lissa sniffled and pouted at him.

"Not you," he said. "I'm serious. On the far side. Something, uhh, smells… bad."

"Okay. Liss. Stay here with Austin, okay?" Sima rolled around from sitting to swimming, and glided to the other side by the cliff face. After a little paddling back and forth, she caught a whiff of distinct foulness. Carrion… *Dead things*. She'd run into a few corpses left in alleys after gang wars or where the EGSF killed an Outcast and never bothered to clean up. The breeze carried an unmistakable stink: dead body.

She swam back over to the kids and pulled them close to the edge by where they'd entered the water. Once she got them on dry land, she looked at Austin. "You know what that smell is, don't you?"

He nodded.

"Then you know why I don't want you kids to see it."

"What is it?" asked Juan.

"Bad," said Lissa.

"I'm going to go check it out in case there's maybe some supplies. I want you to stay here, stay together, and don't make any noise."

"What if the monster comes?" whispered Lissa.

"I don't think it likes the daytime." Sima cringed. "Or we'd have seen it by now."

The thought appeared to scare and comfort the kids at the same time.

She crossed the river again, entering the shadow of a rocky cliff topped with a fringe of cyan bushes. Loose dirt made for an easy climb. She felt foolish not having anything on, but dead people wouldn't care and she didn't want to be stuck wearing wet things for hours. She briefly entertained the hope it might only be a dead Aurak, but that smell... it had to be human. Sima hesitated, took a breath, and tried to steel herself for a horrible sight. She stretched up on tiptoe to peer over the top of the cliff—and gasped.

The smashed remains of a lifeboat lay strewn about a grassy clearing, ripped open and warped. It looked much bigger than the ones they'd been in, perhaps roomy enough for eight stasis pods. Remains from whoever had been in them lay scattered among the metal pieces. She gagged at the sight of a hand here, a bit of leg there, and bloody chunks mixed with shards of clear plastic. At least none of the pieces looked small enough to have come from children.

Adults? Maybe this pod had supplies. She glanced back at the kids huddled together on the riverbank. *Be quick.* Sima pulled herself up and ran among the carnage. The smell made her glad they'd not yet eaten anything. She clamped a hand over her mouth, half tempted to run back and grab her bra to use as a breathing mask. Vomit almost flew through her fingers when a glop that used to be inside a person squished under her foot, bursting like a balloon full of jam. The field of body parts surrounded her with dread. She sank to squat in the grass, and wept, her mind filled with visions of the starship exploding. It didn't seem possible that a bad landing could've done this much damage to a large lifeboat. Whatever smashed it open like that must've occurred in space.

They're all dead. We really are alone. Sima hid her face against her knees, trying to keep her outburst of sorrow quiet so the children couldn't hear. Tears threaded down her legs. *I can't let them see me*

crying. I gotta let them think we'll be okay until there's no hiding we're
screwed.

"Come on, Seem... pull it together." She leaned back, taking slow, deep breaths. "No big deal. Everyone else is dead. Just you and a couple kids. Don't give up. You can at least *act* tough."

Beep.

Faint pattering made her look at the small holographic screen.

‹Fifteen point six meters ahead and to the left. Take that box. It is a survival kit.›

Sima lowered her arm and followed the bracelet's instructions. A metal case about the size of a big piece of luggage lay on its side amid a gnarled fragment of escape pod hull. Large, black letters on the top read 'Survival Unit.' She hefted it by the handle, hauling it with her to the only section of the lifeboat still in one piece. It resembled a massive child's school lunchbox that had been dropped in the street and run over by a series of gee-vees.

Using the survival kit as a step, she climbed into the wreckage. Bent bolts protruded from the outlines of missing stasis pods on the floor. Of the three that had not been flung into oblivion, gore smeared the interior of two, darkened to a thick scabrous crust around a couple of fist-sized holes in the windows. Spray patterns on the wall hinted that the occupants had liquefied. The last pod's lid appeared undamaged. It held a middle-aged woman, also in her underwear, staring into nowhere with her mouth agape.

She probably suffocated.

‹Explosive decompression.› The bracelet's text appeared with the fluttering sound she'd come to think of almost as a voice. ‹Lifeboat hull integrity damaged while in orbit. The data recorder for this lifeboat indicates hull rupture in vacuum conditions. The occupants were sucked out into space, except for that one woman in the intact stasis pod.›

Sima gagged and let herself throw up. After spitting bile, she rasped, "I didn't really need to know that."

She wiped her mouth on the back of her arm and turned toward the spot where the design suggested the supply cabinets should be, but the large lifeboat's crash landing had left them an unrecognizable jumble of metal. Judging from the scorch marks and missing doors, the pod had suffered a hull breach during or before entering the atmosphere. Sima searched every accessible opening, hoping for something to use for clothing or food. The third space she checked had five cylinders labeled 'protein base fluid.' Only one compartment had an intact door, ballooned outward due to the forces that sucked the air from behind it. After prying it off its hinges, she found an empty backpack as well as a metal briefcase with a bright red cross on the side.

"Score."

The first aid kit and the protein slime bottles went into the backpack. She spotted another axe in a compartment on the opposite wall between the gore-caked pods. Sima locked eyes with the gape-mouthed dead woman as she crept over and retrieved it. The way the corpse lay in the pod with one hand raised and pointing struck her as a warning to go back. A pang of fear for the children's safety came out of nowhere.

The cat!

She slung the backpack over her shoulder, rushed to the edge of the broken floor, and leapt to the grass. After grabbing the ponderous survival kit, she hurried in the direction of the stream. The heavy case made it awkward to run, weighing close to forty pounds, but she lugged it as fast as she could. With each step, the dread she'd return to a bloodbath grew.

Two minutes later, she skidded to a halt at the top of the ridge. The kids sat right where she'd left them, clustered on the opposite bank. Sima slouched with relief. Juan spotted her first and pointed, waving with a huge grin. Lissa bounded to her feet and moved to run into the river, but Austin held her back. Sima tossed the survival kit into the water, jumped after it, and swam, dragging her loot across. Despite its weight, the survival case floated. Sima hauled it out onto the bank a few paces from the kids, and fell to her knees.

Lissa ran into a hug. "You're alive!"

"Don't be so melodramatic… and where are your pants?"

"You're not wearing pants either," said Lissa. "Mine are wet 'cause you washed them." Lissa frowned, pointing at a lump of cloth on the ground a short distance away.

"Well, don't leave them there. Come on, it'll be dark soon. We need to get inside." Sima gave the backpack to Austin. "Please carry that."

She ran her hands over her body, squeegeeing as much water off as she could, then pulled her briefs and top back on.

"Ooh, what'd ya find?" Austin peeked into the backpack.

"Survival kit, first aid kit, another axe, and some protein base." Sima took Lissa by the hand and walked with her into the jungle, heading 'home.'

"Another lifeboat?" asked Austin in a near-whisper. He gave her 'the look.'

Sima shook her head.

"How many?" mumbled Austin.

She pulled him into a hug, whispering at his ear. "Eight adults. The lifeboat was smashed."

He looked up. "Eight? That's bigger than ours."

Lissa scurried off and retrieved her pants, waving them around.

Sima took her and Juan by the hand and led them back through the woods, stopping only long enough to collect an armload of fruits on their way 'home.' When they reached the lifeboat, she eyed the trees, clutching the axe as the kids filed past her and went inside.

Not until she secured the door, did she finally allowed herself to relax.

21

CAT FOOD

Austin shook his head at the dried stain on the floor. "It stinks in here. I can't believe you picked up her pants. That's so nasty!"

I can't either. I just did it.

Lissa pouted, but seemed too worn out from the walk to cry. She sat in a slump, her breaths taking on a persistent wheeze. Sima rubbed the girl's back, her fingers tracing over prominent ribs. *Please don't let me watch her die. She's gotta survive.* She pulled the girl into her lap, holding on while the child struggled to inhale. Lissa offered up a grateful smile and snuggled against her chest. Juan crawled over and lay on his back, using Sima's thigh as a pillow. She tickled his stomach, making him curl up and giggle.

"It still smells like pee in here," said Austin. "We should clean the floor."

"With what?" asked Juan. "There's no towels."

"Use his pants," said Austin. "He never wears them."

Juan pulled them on as fast as he could. "No. Mine."

It's going to make someone sick. Sima gazed at the sky through a hole in the ceiling. "I'll think of something."

Austin flopped down with his legs spread apart, and planted the backpack in front of him to rummage it. He ignored the canisters and first aid kit, but went wide-eyed at the axe. "Can I have it? You can't use two."

"Be careful. It's sharp." Sima tugged the survival case over, opening it one-handed while cradling Lissa.

"I will." Austin jumped up and 'walked patrol' around the lifeboat with his new weapon.

Sima blinked at the different devices packed in white foam, having not the first clue what any of them were. "Uhh, Bracelet? What is all this stuff?"

The holo-panel projected an image of the case, overlaying text above the contents. It tagged the machine in the top left corner as a portable campfire, a device capable of generating radiant heat and light, albeit blue. It labeled the next object as a water purifier. The final device, which resembled a large coffee maker in plain, brushed steel got the label 'portable fabricator.'

Sima grinned, grabbed one of the protein canisters, and attached it to the fabricator's receptacle. Her mom used to have one of those in the apartment, but this one looked intended for emergency use and lacked fancy options, instead offering chicken, beef, or fish. She set it to chicken and pressed its only button. The machine generated a slab of cold 'grilled chicken,' which exuded from the left side and fell on the floor with a wet plop. At home, the fabricator could produce raw meat or cooked meat, though in either case it came out room temperature. As a kid, she printed them cooked and tossed them in a pan to heat them. Only people who had time on their hands fabricated raw meat and cooked it for flavor.

"Mine!" yelled Juan, diving on the first slab.

Once everyone had a piece, Sima sat next to Lissa and made sure she ate the whole thing plus an entire fruit. The girl adored the attention, smiling despite the occasional cough. Sima gave her light pats on the back each time. Red stains lingered around the kids' lips, and the boys smeared juice on their cheeks like war paint, conjuring the old narrator in Sima's thoughts again doing the voice over for a documentary on the rituals of strange, primitive fruitivore tribes.

"Do you think we're gonna die?" asked Juan.

"The crash didn't kill us." Sima squeezed Lissa's shoulder. "We survived the streets. I really don't know what's going to happen, but I will do everything I can to protect you."

"Is it gonna get cold?" Juan crawled over to the backpack and took a fruit. "We don't have clothes."

"We don't need clothes," said Lissa.

"Put your pants on," muttered Sima.

"They're *still* damp," whined Lissa.

"It's hot and sweaty. Everything is damp," muttered Austin. "Everything *stays* damp here."

Lissa fidgeted. "I don't wanna."

"Will it get cold?" Juan picked up another fruit and cracked it open.

Sima blinked at him. *Wow, kid can eat for a little guy.*

"This planet might not have winter," said Austin. "It's tropical or something. We're like wilders now."

"The Night Scratch is coming," whispered Lissa. She huddled tight to Sima, trembling. "I hear it."

Everyone got quiet. Seconds later, a light snap occurred inches from the door. A pink nose streaked with black appeared in the jagged hole on the wall near the stasis pod, sniffing. Lissa gasped and pulled her knees to her chest. Austin hefted his axe. Sima scooted away from the wall, keeping her body between the creature and the kids. Dark azure fur shimmered around the muzzle of a panther-sized cat. After a brief staredown with its four glowing eyes, it slinked off.

Quiet lasted fifteen seconds.

It leapt onto the roof, startling screams from the two smallest kids. Scratching and picking noises meandered overhead as it searched for a way inside.

"It smelled the chicken," whispered Austin. "Maybe it'll leave us alone if we give it some."

"No, that's for us," said Juan. "It can go eat the fuzzy piggies."

"No!" whisper-shouted Lissa. "They're cute! Don't let it eat them!"

Sima squeezed the rubberized handle, looking toward the sound of the cat's motion outside. "If we feed it, it'll only come back looking for more."

Lissa's rapid breathing knocked something loose inside her, and she lapsed into a coughing fit, but it remained mild enough not to be scary.

"We're fine," said Sima. "It can't get in."

An hour passed with no one brave enough to risk saying a single word aloud.

Sima rocked Lissa, who hadn't stopped trembling, whispering assurances every few minutes. "You're gonna be fine. The doctors fixed you."

Sima tapped the Omnicomputer. It seemed to get the hint; the blue lasers appeared, rotating and sweeping side to side over the frail child's back. *Please be good news…* Three minutes later, the holo panel appeared, scrolling full of text.

‹Scar tissue detected in both lungs consistent with tumor removal. Lung tissue has sustained damage reducing breathing capacity and endurance. No signs of progressive disease, however scar tissue is bleeding and increased phlegm production has further reduced effective capacity. Based on subject age, I calculate approximately a forty-seven percent chance she will regain majority use of her lungs within five to seven years.›

Sima kissed the bracelet and held her arm in front of Lissa's face.

"That's pretty," whispered the girl.

"You can't read?"

Lissa shook her head.

"It says you're gonna be okay."

A long scrape passed overhead, as though the cat slid across the roof. The lifeboat rocked.

"It's trying to tip us," said Austin.

"I don't think it's strong enough." Sima glanced around at the wall, estimating the cat's position as it moved. "The floor isn't open. Even if it somehow manages to roll us over, it still won't get in. Okay, it's dark. Time for bed."

Huddled together beneath the continuous scrapes of claws on steel, they tried to sleep.

22

ISOLATION

Sima pushed herself up off the floor, groggy and dazed.

The inside of the pod had to be past a hundred degrees. Sweat squished under her skin, letting her slide easily over the metal floor. Lissa sprawled beside her, arms and legs splayed like a crime victim. Evidently, even she'd gotten too hot for clinging. Juan crouched in the corner, bouncing and catching a rubber ring he must've found in one of the machines.

Sima sighed at his lack of clothing. "Put your pants on."

"It's hot," he said.

Austin, at least, remained dressed, though he looked ready to melt into a puddle. Like Lissa, he lay spread eagled on the floor, tongue lolling out, drenched in sweat. Sima didn't bother standing and crawled to the tunnel of scrap metal, pulling herself through on her belly to the 'bathroom.' After using the jug, she poured it out a hole in the wall, then slithered back to the main area, where she knelt fanning herself.

Damn, it's hot. She frowned at her clothes. *It wouldn't have mattered if I went swimming in these yesterday because they're soaked anyway.*

She drank a few sips of water from the bottle, struggling to choke down the plastic-flavored liquid. *Ick. Drinking warm water sucks.* "I'm gonna run and get fresh water."

"No," whispered Lissa.

Sima turned to look down at her. "Why not?"

"The kitty's still out there. Juan heard it."

"It was scratching before you woke up," said the boy, still throwing and catching the rubber ring.

"Where did you find that?" asked Sima.

"In the wall by the junk."

Sima sat cross-legged on the warm floor, snagged a fruit from the pile, and ate. Soft scratching came from the back end, like a cat testing the lower rear hull.

"See?" asked Lissa. "You hear it now?"

"Yeah." She shivered and glanced at the axe. *Damn. Those things can go out in the day, too. We're in big trouble. I don't wanna have to kill an animal, but if it's going to eat my kids, I'm—My kids?* She blinked. The spontaneous thought left her at the edge of crying. After sixteen years, she finally had a taste of a true loving connection to other human beings... and they'd all probably be dead in days. *If we're gonna die anyway, I might as well fight a tiger.*

Once she finished her fruit, Sima tossed the rind out a hole in the wall and hovered there for a moment breathing outside air. Since the breeze coming in the damaged hull felt cool, she worried that they would overheat. Staying inside might be as dangerous as opening the door. The pod worked out fine at night, but with the sun beating on it, they could all suffer heatstroke.

"I gotta do something." Sima walked into the gap between the outer stasis pod and the debris fall, approaching the torn-open cabinet full of circuit boards, hoses, tubes, and machine parts. "Bracelet, is there any way to get the air conditioning back on?"

It scanned the components.

‹Try re-seating board 3a, 12, and 18.›

"What?"

Three blue laser dots appeared on circuit cards.

‹Pull those out and push them back into their sockets.›

"Okay." She did.

‹Reconnect that fiberoptic data line.› Another laser dot indicated a loose cable.

She picked it up, waited a second, and plugged it in where another dot appeared.

‹Push the red square button by the emitter.›

Sima looked around until the dot appeared. She pushed the button, but nothing happened.

‹The logic unit is broken. We don't have the parts to fix it, but you might be able to initiate the system with a bypass. Locate a scrap of wire at least sixteen inches long.›

She hunted around for a while, but no such wire existed. She did, however, find a thin metal strut narrow enough for her to bend. "What about this?"

‹You will experience a painful shock. I would rather not.›

"I'll take a shock. It beats heatstroke."

‹Fine. Touch the two ends as indicated.›

A pair of blue dots appeared, one on a metal connector, the other on a tiny square of copper on the bottom surface of a removable card. Sima bent the strut into shape and, cringing, gingerly extended it until the metal touched the ends at both places.

Nothing happened.

‹I am sorry, Sima. The capacitor is discharged. This lifeboat sustained too much damage in the crash. We cannot repair the environmental control system without parts you have no way to obtain.›

More scratching at the back made her skin crawl.

"What about scavenging parts from Austin's pod?"

‹Are you referring to the one that fried when he attempted to open the lid?›

"Oh… right." Sima grumbled.

She dragged herself out and sat by the kids again, head in her hands, elbows on her knees. Glumness spread from child to child, and eventually even Juan stopped bouncing his makeshift ball. The bracelet projected holographic butterflies on the floor.

‹This is a game. Catch the butterflies for one point each. You will need to sit still.›

"Hey… wanna play a game?" asked Sima. "Catch the bugs. Each one's worth a point."

Juan looked up, smiling.

"Yeah!" Lissa clapped.

Austin glanced at her with a 'you're only trying to distract us from our inevitable, slow death' expression, but he nodded.

The game lifted the kids' spirits. They played for a while, though none had the energy to move faster than a walk or jump for any 'butterflies' that floated too high off the ground.

Lissa drooped after maybe a half hour. "I'm too hot to breathe."

"My head hurts," said Austin.

"Okay. We can't stay inside all day. We'll get sick." Sima picked up the axe. "You three stay right here."

Lissa sniffled, too overheated to even cry properly.

Ignoring the simpering, Sima walked to the hatch and opened it. A blast of cool air filled the lifeboat, chasing away the stink of sweat and dried urine. She stepped outside, axe held at the ready, and crept around the corner toward the back end. Her back against the hull, she walked sideways, clutching the axe in both hands.

I'm totally crazy. Who in their right mind hunts tigers with an axe in their underwear?

She stopped a few feet from the rear corner. The scratching continued along the back wall. *Okay.* Sima trembled in fear. It hadn't seen her yet. She could probably make it back inside before it caught her. But she couldn't let heat or big, annoying cats hurt her children.

Before the shaking grew so bad she couldn't stay upright, Sima took a deep breath and whipped around the corner with the axe raised high over her head in both hands.

And stared at a piece of thin metal flopping in the wind.

She lowered her arms, glaring at the stupid scrap of duralloy making the scratching noise that kept them all hiding in miserable heat for hours.

"Argh!" shouted Sima.

"Did you kill it?" yelled Austin, still inside the pod.

She stomped around to the door. "It's a piece of metal. Get out here before you all drop from heatstroke."

Lissa darted outside and fell to her knees in the grass, hugging nothing. "I love the air."

"Ugh." Austin wobbled out, woozy.

Sima grabbed his shoulder to steady him as Juan rushed by.

"What do you mean a piece of metal?" asked Austin.

"Look..." She walked him around back and pointed at the fluttering scrap.

He grumbled. "Guess the cat *is* afraid of light."

"Yeah. Come on. Let's get to the water. We all need to drink."

Sima scooped Lissa up and hurried into the jungle, carrying her to the closest available water, the river where they usually went swimming. She held the kids back from jumping in right away as it felt like a bad idea to go from overheating to cold water so fast, but did encourage them to stick their faces in and drink until they couldn't swallow another gulp. She did the same, and rolled over on her back, light headed.

"Can we swim a bit? I'm still hot," said Austin.

"Wait a little more." Sima raised her arm. "Bracelet, please chirp in like an hour or when you think it's safe."

‹Understood.›

For a while, everyone rested beside the river, occasionally drinking more and enjoying a cool breeze coming in off the water. Once the *beep* went off, everyone rushed into the water. Sima didn't bother peeling her sweaty undergarments off, as they quite needed a rinse as well.

23

FULL TRIBAL

Late the next morning, after a surprisingly quiet night without giant cats, Sima collected the kids, planning to head into the jungle on a fruit-retrieval mission. They emerged from the lifeboat, neither Juan nor Lissa wearing anything.

Sima pointed at the hatch. "Put your pants on."

"They're dirty," whined Lissa.

"I washed them." Sima folded her arms, clutching the axe. "They're as clean as they can get."

"It's hot," said Juan.

"Yeah. It's hot." Lissa nodded. "And they're still wet."

Sima looked down at her feet. "I know it's hot, but those things are small. They won't make you hotter."

"I don't wanna," said Lissa. "They fall off anyway."

Juan shrugged.

"You have to," said Sima.

"Why?" asked Lissa.

"It's rude to walk around naked."

Lissa looked at the jungle, then back up at Sima. "We're alone. They threw us away like recyclables. Nothing matters anymore. Not school. Not laws. Not pants. We're gonna die here, aren't we?"

A huge lump closed off Sima's throat. *She knows she doesn't have a lot of time left. Aww, hell. It's not hurting anyone. If it makes her happy, whatever.* "Fine... whatever. Just stay close."

Lissa smiled.

Juan darted off. Lissa went after him, both giggling.

Sima shook her head, watching them run into the jungle. "We've gone full tribal."

Austin picked at the waistband of his briefs. "Not yet."

"You're not gonna go nature-boy too?" asked Sima, grinning.

He fell in step beside her, following the smaller kids. "Nah. Feels weird."

"It makes sense, kinda."

"How you figure?" asked Austin.

"I bet you had a real home for a while, right?"

He shrugged. "I guess."

"How long were you on the street?"

"Like a year." He squinted past a haze of light brown hair at her. "What about you?"

"Four, but I'm older. I was older than you are now when I ran away. We both had a normal life for a while. I think the others are more feral."

"What does that mean?" asked Austin.

"Juan lived out in a bad place, *La Propagación*... the EGSF doesn't even go there. The people who live there are even lower than Outcasts to Citizens. Wild and violent."

"He's not wild," said Austin.

"No, but he's also little. And Lissa, she's so small... for her to wind up on the streets at six? Neither one of them really know what normal is."

Austin shrugged. "Yeah, I guess.

"Found some," shouted Juan up ahead.

"Fruit!" cheered Lissa.

"Ugh. Why can't we have more chicken?" asked Austin.

"We will. Tonight for dinner. There's only so much goop. I want to make it last. If we eat nothing but chicken, we'll run out of it and wind up stuck with only fruit again that much faster."

He nodded. "Oh. Okay. That makes sense."

Lissa and Juan leapt on the stalk, their combined weight enough to drag the pod low so Sima could pick a bundle of the large, pointy fruits. Lissa carried four, Juan six, Austin eight, and Sima the water jug. After filling it at the river, she led the way back to the grassy field near the lifeboat, where everyone sat around in a circle and took fruit to eat. Sima gave Lissa a second one.

She made a sour face at it.

"You need to eat a little more, okay? Please? If you wanna get better, you need energy."

Lissa sighed, something in her chest crackling. "Okay."

"So what'd you get arrested for?" asked Austin, glancing over at Sima.

Juan rubbed his hand on a rind and pressed a bright purple-pink handprint on Lissa's face, like some kind of tribal marking. He held his cheek out and she returned the favor.

She blinked at him, taken aback by the question until she wondered if it meant she'd finally earned his trust. "I wasn't a criminal. I begged… The day I got picked up, a transport full of nutri-packs tipped over. So many of them scattered on the road it looked like an ocean of silver. I couldn't help myself. A couple of other Outcasts ran in too, so I started jamming as many packets as I could into my pocket." She squeezed Lissa at the memory of staring down the barrel of a rifle and screaming, *Please don't kill me; I'm just a kid!* "The Seps caused the accident, and the EGSF was right there. They came outta the alley and shot some of the others who tried to run, accused them of bein' Seps, but they weren't. They said I was stealing even though the packets were all over the road."

"That's bull," said Austin.

Sima stroked Lissa's hair. "The investigator wasn't a butt. He actually yelled at the EGSF officers for putting binders on me. Told them to treat me like an orphan, not a criminal." *He was nice. I wish I had someone like him for a father.* Sima rubbed her wrist, remembering the two officers escorting her into the ship. She explained how the EGSF had kept their word, not using restraints on her again until she'd panicked at the sight of the boarding tube and fought as if being led to her execution. *Maybe some part of me knew how this would turn out.* "They treated me okay, but I freaked out hard at the starship, so they cuffed me and carried me in."

"Yeah." Austin licked red stains from his fingers. "The kid in the pod next to me was crying for his mother. He was old like you... had a beard too. Sobbed like a baby."

"I think I saw him... You guys weren't too far away from my pod."

Lissa attacked her second fruit with surprising enthusiasm, making Sima smile.

"Some of the stuff that can happen to us on the street, maybe this isn't so bad," said Austin. "Guess they sent us here 'cause we're 'hard to adopt.'"

"What?" Sima blinked.

Austin gestured at her. "Well, you're too old. I'm too brown... so's Juan."

"Brown?" Sima raised an eyebrow. "Peanuts are browner than you."

"Lissa's white," said Juan. "Why she on the street?"

"All white kids aren't rich," said Sima.

"Mom an' Dad made Pixie," muttered Lissa. "Men came at night and shot them. The smelly one was gonna shoot me too, but the fat man hit him and told him not to 'cause I was too little. I hid under my bed and they left."

"She's too sick to adopt." Austin sent a guilty look at the grass between his legs. "No one wants a kid who's gonna die or cost a lot of money to keep alive."

"They fixed me," wheezed Lissa. "I breathed a lot of bad, but I'm not sick now."

Sima's heart sank. "Your parents were making Pixie in their home? With you there?"

"Yes." Lissa coughed. "The police man said they would help me better an' give me new breaths if I let them put me in space."

Juan cuddled up to Sima's side.

How did I become Mom?

"They lied." Austin made a sour face and threw a fruit rind into the weeds. "Adults always lie."

"My father took me to see the city," said Juan, staring into nowhere. "He told me to sit onna bench and wait for him, but he didn't come back."

"Aww." Sima squeezed him. "I'm sorry."

Juan reached up to grab her arm. "We're from *La Propagación*. Papa wanted me to get 'dopted by rich people in the city."

Sima held him close. "I think I'd rather be an orphan in the city than have a family in that place. He had to love you very much to be able to give you up."

"Bull," said Austin. "If his dad loved him, he wouldn't abandon him."

Juan glared, but said nothing.

Lissa shook with another coughing fit. Sima slapped her on the back a few times until the phlegm broke and she sounded as though she could breathe again. She flashed a desperate 'I don't wanna die' face. After another light cough, she took a few deep, quiet breaths, and spat up another pink-grey blob.

Sima stared at it. The unnatural hot pink made sense. *Pixie.* Her thoughts leapt back to finding Draz dead in his bunk at the Crash. *A drug so prone to accidental overdose, the first trip could be the last. Why would anyone willingly inhale that crap?* Even if a user managed the dosage meticulously, it could still kill them if taken often enough.

The girl grinned with a tear in her eye. "I'm getting better."

"Yes, you are." Sima forced a smile, trying not to think of what chemical damage might've been done to her lungs. If the finished drug turned out so deadly, how horrible would the stuff it's made from be?

"What about you?" asked Austin. "You're too pretty to be a street kid."

Sima frowned. "My dad's rich, but I don't exist to him because my mother was a mistress. Mom thought she could get money out of him or convince him to marry her by having me, but he left her as soon as she told him about me. She kinda took care of me for a few years, but when I was nine, she decided I could 'take care of myself,' so she ignored me and went off on the hunt for another sugar daddy. Didn't care where I went or what I did. I mean, she still bought food and let me cook for myself to avoid getting in legal trouble."

"She kick you out?" Austin's sour face softened.

"No. I ran away at twelve. The man she started dating hated kids. He tried to hit me, but I got away. Mom actually yelled at *me* for ducking because he hit his hand on the wall and started bleeding." *Mom's new victim was such a creep, but I'm not telling kids about what he really did.* Even the memory of the way he looked at her made her feel sick.

"The police took us all," said Juan. "Made us get on the ship."

Austin grabbed another fruit. "Yeah. No one wants us, so they sent us here."

"Out of sight," whispered Sima. "Citizens hated looking at homeless kids so they put us somewhere they wouldn't have to see us."

Lissa cried. "We're s'posed ta get 'dopted and have a home an' a mommy an' daddy here."

Sima rocked her. "Something went wrong with the ship. This wasn't supposed to happen. Maybe they didn't lie to us. The investigator sounded like he really believed it."

"Yeah right," muttered Austin.

Sima pointed off toward the river. "That other lifeboat was smashed. I think something hit the ship, like a meteor. Blew it up in orbit. If they were going to dump us, they would've ejected the lifeboats and left. Besides, if they just wanted to kill us, it would've been cheaper to shoot us on Earth."

Austin stared at her for a long moment, then shrugged. "Yeah, I guess that makes sense. Costs a lot of money to fire trash into space, right?"

"Are we gonna die?" Lissa looked her in the eye.

Sima's throat tightened. "No, sweetie. We're gonna be okay."

Austin made a face that said 'BS.'

"What about you?" Sima raised an eyebrow at him. "How'd you wind up on your own?"

"Dad was EGSF," said Austin. "Some Scather shot him in the head. Didn't kill him, but he wasn't Dad anymore after. Started hittin' me and Mom. They fought a lot. One night, he killed Mom and came after me. I got his gun and..." His voice choked off.

"C'mere." Sima tried to make room for him to join the hug pile.

"I couldn't do it." Austin's face reddened. "He killed my Mom and I couldn't shoot him. I ran like a bitch."

"You're a little boy," said Sima.

"I'm eleven." Austin glowered at the grass. His angry scowl melted to a wounded stare and a quivering lip. With a sniffle, he crawled up to her right side and sobbed.

He's been holding that in for too long. Sima cradled his head to her shoulder. It took him a few minutes to calm down, after which he blushed at the ground. Sima sat in silence for a while, Lissa in her lap, a boy on either side. Sweat ran in trails down her back, front, and arms, the unrelenting sun made worse by bodies pressed close. At motion overhead, she squinted up at a huge manta drifting over the canopy. "We'll be okay. I won't lie. It's dangerous, but so were the streets."

"There's no doctors here," said Juan.

"Or bathrooms." Lissa squirmed.

"Everywhere's a bathroom." Austin grinned. "Bigger problem is no E-toilets. I miss pushing a button to clean my butt after."

Juan laughed.

Daylight waned as they reclined in the grass, chatting about the little mundane things they missed.

"When I was little, I wanted to grow up and join the EGSF," said Austin, frowning. "I hate them now. Even if I was still on Earth, I wouldn't join up. I saw what they're really like to people who don't have anything. They didn't care my dad used to be one of them. As soon as I ran away, I didn't matter anymore."

"You matter to me," said Sima, squeezing him close.

"Yeah." Juan smiled at him. "I like having a brother."

"Me too," said Lissa. Her smile soon turned to a sniffle. "I miss my cat, Orange. She was really pretty. Her fur was black and white and orange in spots. I haven't seen her since those men broke in to our 'partment and made my parents sleep forever."

Sima hugged her.

Austin's sad glower faded back to an expression of almost contentment.

"I didn't have a cat," said Juan, "but I did have a favorite can. I found it in an alley. It didn't even have no dents or nothing. I liked the cartoon mouse on the label."

Sima kissed him atop the head, making him laugh.

Austin poked the Omnicomputer. "I guess that's not really 'cause you got charged with a made up crime. They arrested me too."

"I'm sure they came up with a big lie for such a small boy." Sima winked.

He chuckled. "Nah. I actually did stuff."

She gasped, overacting a bit as she already suspected as much after his mention of a pink jumpsuit. "What could such an adorable boy do that's illegal?"

He smirked at her. "My Dad showed me how to hack electronic locks and stuff. The EGSF has all kinds of ways around them. I used to break into apartments and run their fabricators so I could eat real food. I'd take clothes and sometimes even video games."

"Wow." Sima ruffled his hair. "You're more of a criminal than I was."

He flashed his masterful pleading face. "Yeah, but I'm adorable."

She tickled him until he squealed.

Austin stuck his tongue out at her. "What's the worst thing you did?"

"I's charged with crim'nal cuteness in the first degree," said Lissa with a completely serious face.

Sima almost melted. "What?"

"Tha's what the ee-gee man said when they 'rested me." She held her arms out, wrists together. "But he didn't put the handcuffs on."

"Aww." Sima laughed.

"So?" Austin poked Sima in the side. "What's the worst thing *you* did? You're like old and stuff. Old Outcasts do the real bad stuff. You carried a knife, right?"

"Umm. For a little while, but I got scared and tossed it. I guess really the worst thing I did was run a box of stuff for this shady guy named Nalas. I don't know what was in it, but I figure it had to be drugs or something illegal."

"That's not really that bad." Austin jabbed his fingers at the dirt. "It's not mean. You could've said you were tricked if you got arrested. You're a girl. You can get away with that stuff. They don't trust boys at all. My dad used to think all boys were criminals, and girls that actually did bad stuff, all they'd have to do was give him sad eyes and he'd let them go."

Sima sighed. "Okay. The worst thing I ever did..." She looked down. "I was too much of a chicken to break the law, so I kept begging. Tried to look younger."

"That's not bad at all." He rolled his eyes.

"I'm not finished." She poked him in the stomach. "I used to be really jealous of smaller kids, because they always got all the attention from Citizens and people ignored me. I once grabbed this little girl who kept following me and put her in an ORC bin."

All three of them gasped.

"Why was she following you?" asked Austin.

"She probably wanted help," said Lissa, making a sad face.

Juan grinned. "Sometimes I got good food in ORC bins."

"That kid kept trying to stand next to me. I told her to go away because she was taking too much of the charity. Everyone ignored me with her there. After I asked her to go somewhere else, she followed me on purpose so I wouldn't get any glint."

"Oh." Austin raked his hands at the grass. "I guess stuffing a little kid in an ORC bin is kinda mean, but she sounds like a brat."

"You wouldn't put me in an ORC bin would you?" asked Lissa.

Sima reached an arm around her and squeezed. "No way. I feel so bad about it now. I can't even find her to say I'm sorry."

"Do you still hate kids?" asked Juan.

"No." She patted him on the head. "I used to be a scared, jealous, street rat. I'm not anymore."

"Dude." Austin stared at Juan. "She ran outside to kill a tiger with an axe to protect us."

They whiled away the next few hours trading stories of their lives on the street. From the sound of it, Lissa hadn't been out there long, a week or two at most. She'd wandered away from her apartment in search of her cat after the gang left, and fallen in with a Keeper who 'managed' a group of little beggars. The EGSF picked Juan up a few months after his dad left him on the bench.

Eventually, the boys went roaming the near-jungle while Lissa resumed trying to craft anklets out of flowers. Sima pored over the bracelet's map display, trying to get it to calculate the most likely spots for falling orbital debris to land, especially other lifeboats that might have supplies.

The boys wandered back out of the jungle soon after. Lissa got up and hurried over to them, darting into grass taller than her waist. Sima gave up on the map after an hour or so and reclined in the fur-like meadow. Not long after, pats of rain landed on her.

"Ugh."

The sky darkened from bright sunny to gloomy in a matter of two minutes. Yelping at the spots of cold hitting her, Sima laughed and ran over to the kids. They frolicked in the rain for a few minutes before the boys got the idea to play tag. Rain-soaked grass turned into a slippery mess. Any attempt to move faster than walking became sliding, which itself proved fun enough to keep doing over and over again. Their failed effort at tag mutated into simply trying to get as much of a running start as they could before sliding.

Sima stopped Lissa from racing around before she overexerted herself, and carried her back to the lifeboat to get in out of the rain, lest she catch a chill. If they had blankets, she might've wrapped the girl in one. The boys once again started a branch-sword duel, which set Sima laughing hysterically as neither one of them could take a swing without falling over.

"Okay, enough. The rain's cold. Come inside now," called Sima. *Ugh. When did I turn into a mother?*

Austin and Juan hurried over and ducked into the lifeboat, dripping wet. Sima held the water jug out the door to fill it, since she figured a planet devoid of pollution would have perfectly drinkable rainwater.

Still, she had a purifier unit in the survival kit, so she decided to run the water through it.

As darkness approached, the rain tapered off to a light drizzle. Sima used the fabricator to 'print' some chicken for dinner, and even cooked it using a sheet of metal off the wall as a 'pan' over the portable campfire. They sat around inside, safe from the water, though several streams leaked in from the multiple holes in the roof. Within an hour, more than half the floor inside ran with water rushing toward the low end of the lifeboat.

"You said we couldn't stay in the cave because we'd sleep in water," said Juan. "There's water here, too."

"The pods are dry," said Austin. "And they have cushions."

"No!" shouted Lissa, a pronounced rattle in her airway.

Conversation stalled in the wake of the reminder of what almost happened.

Austin and Juan broke the silence a few minutes later with a discussion about superheroes from one of the movie series they'd both seen. Lissa arranged herself in a narrow channel of dry floor and stretched out. Sima crawled under the junk wall to the 'bathroom' and made use of the cryonic fluid bucket, after which she dumped it out a convenient hole.

"He did!" yelled Juan. A faint fleshy *smack* followed.

Austin growled.

Oh crap. Sima hurried to crawl back as fast as she could, suffering a painful but bloodless scratch on her back from a pointy metal bit.

By the time she emerged from the tight passage, Austin and Juan had gotten into a rolling fistfight that wound up with Juan on his back in a puddle where the water collected at the low end of the room. Austin knelt on top of him, fist cocked. Sima scrambled over and grabbed him around the middle, trying to pull him away, though the boys kept throwing punches at each other.

"Knock it off!" yelled Sima.

Neither boy slowed their attacks.

"Stop!" shrieked Lissa, before collapsing in a fit of hard coughing.

Both boys stared guiltily at her, and gave up fighting.

"What on Earth got into you two?" asked Sima. She rushed to Lissa's side and held her, patting her back.

"He said Dad didn't love me." Juan glared at the floor.

"If he loved you, he wouldn't have abandoned you on that bench. I didn't say it to be mean." Austin folded his arms.

Juan spun toward him. "He *did* love me. He wanted me to get outta *La Propagación* so I didn't get shot!"

"Austin," said Sima. "I think Juan's father loved him a whole lot to be able to give him up. He thought his son would have a better life, even if it meant never seeing him again."

Juan darted to the tunnel, crying, and crawled in, likely to hide in the 'bathroom.'

"Ow," muttered Lissa, still coughing, but slower. "Sorry I yelled. I'm not supposed to yell."

"It's all right." Sima kept patting her on the back.

Austin plopped down to sit on the floor. "I dunno. I guess I just thought if you had a kid, the worst thing in the world would be never seeing them again."

"A parent who doesn't love their kid is like my mother." Sima frowned.

"What did she do?" asked Austin.

Lissa peered up at her with sad eyes.

"It's more like what she *didn't* do. Never really talked to me. Never hugged me. Never smiled at me or really did anything besides let me live in her apartment. Not even a 'good morning.' The only time she ever talked to me was when she yelled about something. She only had me as bait, and my dad didn't bite. So she hated me for not helping her marry a rich Citizen."

"Sorry." Austin leaned against her. "You're a much better mom than your mom was."

That lump appeared in her throat again. She put one arm around him, the other around Lissa, and felt like crying and laughing simultaneously. Her situation had gone way beyond anything she ever imagined having to deal with. Being caught between Magdalena's, running jobs for Nalas, or trusting the EGSF with their *Progenitor* project sounded so tame by comparison. Well, before she understood what would happen.

Juan emerged and sat nearby, sorta joining the group hug.

She glanced up at the ceiling. The patter of raindrops ebbed and faded, imparting a hollow melody over the steady background of Lissa's rasp. Going to work for Magdalena didn't seem at all scary now, compared to this... but looking around at the three faces staring up at her, Sima shuddered under a crash of guilt. If she hadn't wound up going for that nutri-pack spill, all three of these kids would already have been dead.

No... I'm glad I got arrested. I'm glad I'm here for them.

24

STORY TIME

Austin mumbled another apology to Juan for saying his dad didn't love him.

The younger boy made a face like he tried to think of something nasty to say back about Austin's father going crazy, but wound up looking down and sighing. "'Kay."

Sima stretched out on her back, trying to stay inside a dry patch of floor. Raindrops continued pelting the lifeboat's roof. The storm had regained strength, creating dozens of tiny waterfalls that spilled in from the various holes in the hull and gathered in numerous rivulets rushing toward the low end of the chamber. She tried to sleep, but between the noise, her mind wandering among old memories, worries about her present situation, and even fearing that any tiny itch or bug bite could turn into a fatal issue kept her awake.

Every droplet of sweat crawling over her skin made her flinch.

When the stickiness became unbearable, she looked around at the various streams leaking in and got an idea. Sima crawled under the debris wall to check the rear area for another stream, but the ceiling there had remained intact. The lack of privacy bothered her to a point, but being sticky bugged her more.

As casual as she could make herself be, she shimmied back to the larger section of lifeboat, undressed, and stood under one of the streams like a shower. The water cascaded over her head and rolled down her body. Neither cold nor warm, it proved refreshing. For a few minutes, she simply stood and basked in it before starting to wash herself as best she could with her hands, keeping her back to the half-awake kids. Sima smirked at the jagged bit of metal sticking out of the wall upon which she'd hung her clothes, wondering at what point the idea of taking a shower (such as it was) in a room with other people had gone from *no way in hell* to no big deal.

Once she grew tired of standing under a downpour, she stood beside the stream and scrubbed her undergarments. They had soaked with sweat—which didn't strike her as the healthiest thing to keep wearing—plus with the interior of the lifeboat having turned into one big watery mess, they also felt rather pointless.

"I can't sleep," said Austin. "You too?"

"Yeah," muttered Sima.

"What'cha doing?" asked Austin.

She didn't turn to look back at him. "Taking a shower. We've all been wearing the same pants for a couple days and they're kinda rank. I just felt sticky."

"Oh." He laughed. "Well, at least two of us have. I think Juan lost his."

"No. They're in the wall," said Juan in a sleepy half-whisper.

Sima smiled. "You should wash, too."

Skin squeaked on metal as Austin clambered to his feet and yawned. "Okay."

While he stood in another waterfall to clean himself, Sima re-hung her wet clothes on a jutting scrap of metal to dry, then collected Juan's shorts from a cubby in the wall to wash. He hadn't worn them in a couple days, but still. No sense leaving them dirty, and she needed something to do as she couldn't sleep. Lissa hadn't touched her briefs since Sima washed them in the river, so those, she considered clean enough to leave alone. She did, however, save them from the low end of the lifeboat where the constant flooding runoff had created a veritable swimming pool.

"Crap," said Austin, glancing down at the knee-deep water he stood in. "We're flooding."

Sima twisted left to look.

Because the lifeboat sat at an angle with the entry hatch on the downward end, water had risen to almost halfway up the wall. The edge of the flood stopped inches from where Lissa and Juan contorted themselves to avoid the runoff streaming across the floor. Fortunately, the water level remained constant. Numerous holes in the sides at that height let it drain faster than it poured in from above. Unless the storm reached impossible proportions, their 'home' wouldn't flood any higher.

Giving up on sleep, Lissa took advantage of the 'indoor pool,' sitting and splashing for a little while before noticing Austin taking a 'shower,' at which point, she gave herself a bath. Juan dove into the deepest part of the flood to swim back and forth across the room. Sima cast a longing glance at her wet clothes hanging on the wall, but resigned herself to going without them until they dried. It still bugged her a little, but not as much as having soggy fabric clinging to her.

Eventually, fatigue got the better of the kids and they all gathered close as they usually did to sleep. Normally, the closed confines of the lifeboat didn't swelter too badly at night, but the rain had cooled the air somewhat, making it comfortable if not a little chilly. They clustered for warmth, everyone still wet. Only Lissa shivered as if cold, but she grinned.

"Tell us a story?" asked Lissa, breaking the silence.

The request stymied her. Mom provided only the most basic of needs, buying food and allowing her to have a bedroom. If she could've taught an infant to change her own diapers, she would have. The woman offered nothing in the way of attention. Sima's thoughts drifted back to a language teacher she'd had in maybe first grade who sometimes read to the class. She choked up at the memory of him, more specifically how she used to fantasize about him being her father.

"Yeah," said Juan, sitting up. "Please?"

"Umm." Sima stared at the ceiling.

Lissa's soft breaths puffed over her neck. The girl had once again curled up at her side, resting her head on Sima's shoulder. If any trace of wheezing remained, it had become too faint to hear. Sima absentmindedly combed her fingers at the girl's hair, petting her like a cat while trying to remember some of the books that teacher had shared. Multiple stories crashed together with movies in her head.

"Well. Umm. Let me think." Sima muddled her way through a story about a little girl in a red cape who stole porridge from three bears. The girl ran away from the angry bears and jumped into a mirror where she met a talking caterpillar. Some fat woman in red wanted to cut her head off, so she jumped back out from the mirror. Lost in the forest, she stumbled across a cottage made out of cookies. The witch that lived there tried to eat her, but the girl tricked her into a large fabricator before finding a secret passage in the closet that took her to a galaxy far, far away. There, she joined some rebels and helped overthrow an evil empire.

By the time the girl threw the dark emperor's removed helmet into the fires of Mount Death, all three kids had fallen asleep. Still, Sima stared at the ceiling. How long could they survive here with nothing to eat but fruit? How did people find meat before fabricators and protein slime? She lifted her arm up and whispered the question to the bracelet.

‹Primitive humans raised animals like cows, chickens, goats, and pigs, which they killed for food.›

"Eww," whispered Sima. "Meat comes from animals? That's *so* sad."

‹Meat has not been harvested from live animals for over two centuries. However, since we are no longer on Earth and lack the necessary technology, when the reserve of protein gel runs out, you would need to hunt if you desired meat.›

She thought about those cute fuzzball things Juan chased the other day. "I don't wanna kill anything."

‹That is your choice. It should be possible to survive on the vegetation you have been eating. I have insufficient data to advise you on the suitability of the local wildlife as a food source. However, it would be best to vary your diet if possible.›

"What did primitive people make clothes out of?"

‹Prior to the invention of textiles, animal hides. Some primitive humans, especially those in warmer climates, did not make clothes. Others living in colder climates treated the skins and fur of animals into clothing. Many also harvested the hair or wool from livestock and wove it into fabric.›

"We don't have any of that. Or any machines to make it into clothes."

‹Primitive people utilized a tool known as 'needle and thread.'›

"How does that work?"

‹You do not have a 'needle and thread' either. However…› The mini screen played a short video showing a woman from several centuries ago sewing. According to the file, the image came from the year 2004. ‹Prior to the End of Nations, humanity utilized vast farms of humans living in poorer regions working together to produce garments.›

Sima watched the woman pushing sections of fabric into a machine that stitched them together. *I'd be happy with just the fabric. I could tie it on somehow. I need more than one thing to wear.* She frowned at herself. *Or I could just pull a Lissa.* She sat there worrying for a while about the fragile child who'd fallen into her life, dreading that she'd screw something up and hurt her. Of course, she worried about the boys too, but Lissa, clearly the most delicate, probably wouldn't make it.

"Are we going to survive?" whispered Sima.

‹In the absence of unforeseen medical complications, your present habits should allow for survival. However, I have insufficient data to determine the long-term effects of a diet consisting solely of that one particular fruit.›

Sima smirked at the 'effect' that diet already had on her. A lack of E-toilets didn't much matter when everything turned into liquid.

Scratching raked at the wall. She rolled her eyes, grumbling to herself about not breaking the metal flange until a low, feline growl rumbled outside. All the hairs on her arms stood on end. Sima froze, tightening her embrace around the kids, hoping the Night Scratch didn't make enough noise to wake them. She lay as still as possible, her gaze moving along the wall in time the squeal of claws on metal. Fortunately, the constant background of raindrops striking the metal roof and water splattering at the floor masked the curious predator.

After a long few minutes, the cat gave up, and Sima closed her eyes.

BY MORNING, the storm had broken, allowing the sun out. Sima awoke to a thick atmosphere heavy with the smell of wet child and plant matter. The day got off to an early start at sweltering, which made the water-filled lifeboat utterly miserable. Steam wafted in the air around the holes, the air so saturated with humidity that it collected on the ceiling and dripped back into the flood.

Sima peeled herself off the floor and got to her feet. The kids stirred at her motion, but made no effort to stand. Austin lay flat on his front, arms splayed to the sides. Lissa curled back up in a ball. Juan half curled on his side, one arm under his head for a pillow.

Leaving them be for now, Sima waded into the waist-deep pool and gripped the lever on the hatch. Unfortunately, the designers had built the lifeboat to prevent explosive decompression by making the door open inward. Foot on the wall for support, she grabbed the handle and pulled, but the weight of all the water against the hatch kept it pinned shut.

"Crap," muttered Sima. "Please tell me we're not trapped in here…"

‹You're not trapped in there.›

"Great." She grinned. "How do I get out?"

‹Insufficient data.›

She stared at her wrist. "But, you just said we're not trapped in here!"

‹You asked me to tell you that.›

"Argh!" yelled Sima.

"What's wrong?" Austin rolled over onto his back and sat up, rubbing his eyes.

She slapped her hands at the surface of the 'pool.' "The water's too heavy. It's keeping the door shut."

He turned his head to stare at her. As realization set in, his dazed 'just woke up' expression shifted to one of panic. "We're trapped?"

"There's gotta be a way to do something." Sima tried again, futilely pulling at the handle, but gave up and waded out of the flood. "After I use the jug."

She slithered over the slick metal floor into the back room and positioned herself over the jug. Her gaze fell on a tangle of two-inch flexible plastic hoses hanging out of a section of smashed wall. A faint memory of a teacher in science class doing something with tanks of water came back to her. Somehow, he'd made water flow uphill from a lower tank to a higher tank. Sima stared eagerly at the hoses while relieving herself. After dumping the jug out a hole in the hull, she ran over and ripped at the wall, dragging a six-foot section of tubing clear. It stank like chemicals she didn't recognize, but contained only a trace of white dust.

"How did that go?" She crawled back to the front room, where all three kids had decided to go swimming.

Sima slid into the water again, pulling the hose under to fill it. The kids watched in curious silence as she capped one end with her hand and tried to stick the hose out through one of the larger holes close to the water's surface. Though, as soon as she took her hand away, the water ran back out.

"Grr." She looked over her shoulder at the kids, sticking the hose under again. "Austin, grab the other end and plug it."

He fished the far end of the tube off the floor. After a moment of failing to get a seal with his hand, he shrugged and held the end of the hose against his belly.

Sima laughed. That time, the water didn't flow back down the tube as fast, so she unspooled several feet of tube out the opening.

"It's draining!" yelled Austin.

"Wow, that's cool!" said Juan. "How'd you do that?"

"Umm." She scratched at her head. "I don't remember how it works. Just something I saw in school."

Pattering drew her attention to the screen over her forearm.

‹You created a siphon.› The bracelet proceeded to explain how a siphon worked, and Sima relayed it to the children. By the time she finished, the water level had gone down more than a foot.

She tried the door, but still couldn't budge it. However, the drain appeared to be working, much to Juan's disappointment. Though, even Lissa had started fanning herself at the awful heat and did not mind the loss of their private swimming pool.

Eventually, with the water only knee-high to Sima, she and Austin working together managed to pull the hatch open enough that the remainder of the water rushed out, forming a foot-deep muddy bog at the lifeboat entrance.

Sima walked to where her clothes dangled from a piece of debris, but hanging all night in a rain-saturated lifeboat had kept all the EGSF-issued undies damp. Considering they intended to go swimming anyway, Sima swallowed her pride and went outside into *much* nicer air with only the bracelet on.

The kids followed her to the river where they drank and had a breakfast of fruit on the bank before jumping in to cool off. While the kids played in the water, Sima experimented with a thin strand of vine and one of the giant, brittle leaves. She fashioned a loincloth out of it, though taking too deep a breath threatened to snap the vine around her waist. Any of the plant material she'd found flexible enough to use as a belt lacked the strength to survive much handling. The tougher plants refused to bend at all, and their leaves had sharp edges.

Sima held up the bracelet. "Maybe we need to go farther off and find some new kind of plant."

‹A possibility. I am unable to detect any significant variations in the local wildlife within my sensor range.›

"What is your sensor range? Like three feet?"

‹That is scanning range. My sensor range is approximately a half mile.›

Sima rubbed the bracelet. "Are you gonna run out of battery?"

‹Unlikely. My microcell has a capacity of about ten years, and I recharge when exposed to sunlight.›

She smiled, but still fidgeted at it. The thin metal band might not have been a restraint, but being unable to remove it still sort of bothered her. After a little more than an hour, she called the kids out of the water.

On a whim, she decided to go check out the lifeboat she'd crashed in. That one didn't have as many holes and might tolerate the rain better. Plus, both stasis pods worked. If she opened the lids all the way, they could sleep on soft beds. Perhaps the bracelet could walk her through fixing the air conditioning so it didn't make the place too cold to survive. Austin didn't seem entirely thrilled at going on a long walk without his briefs on, but he didn't voice any protest. Sima marched on into the jungle, listening to the science teacher voice narrate a documentary about the primitive tribes of Mirage. Lissa and Juan diverted off path every so often to check out flowers, but neither strayed so far she had to call them back. Austin attempted to hang a leaf around his waist, but after his belt broke twice and he cut his finger on the leaf edge, he gave up.

A two-hour trip ended in a pair of disappointments. Less significant, her attempt at plant-based clothing disintegrated after a short while of purposeful walking. Worse, the lifeboat she'd landed in had attracted a group of large, blue-black furred creatures similar in appearance to bears. All had swaths of stubby pink tendrils on the sides of their heads. She counted at least eight of the beasts, all having made a home of the crash trench by the hatch.

Lissa gasped and hid behind her. Juan took a step to check them out more closely, but Sima grabbed his shoulder to pull him back.

"What are they?" whispered Austin, clutching his axe.

"Nothing we are going to mess with." Sima pointed back in the direction they'd come from. "Go slow and don't make noise."

They retreated without raising notice. One of the creatures sniffed at the air, exposing a mouth full of squat, conical teeth and a serpentine black tongue that looked capable of reaching out and catching prey. At the sight of that, Sima grabbed at the kids and pulled them hastily back into the woods.

She led them home, dreading that someday, more animals might be attracted to the lifeboat they lived in. Of course, that one had a much shallower crash trench, not deep enough to offer shelter to animals.

Lissa glided off to the side, chasing every pretty flower or rainbow-colored insect that came into view. The boys largely walked in silence, though Austin had a serious expression, carrying his axe like an EGSF soldier with a rifle.

I feel ridiculous. She shook her head, unable to believe she walked around outdoors carrying an axe and wearing only a bracelet. *This is beyond primitive. This is like people from a thousand years ago. Cassie would be laughing at me.* Sima sighed at the ground, realizing she missed her somewhat-friend. It felt like forever ago since she had a conversation with a person her age or older. Of course, to Cassie, Sima had already been gone more than two years. That girl likely thought Sima had been killed or put in prison.

Juan tripped over something and sprawled flat on the ground. He laughed and scrambled upright. Before Sima could even worry about him, Lissa screamed. She jumped backward, a thin, blue vine wrapped around her right leg, trying to pull her into the underbrush.

Austin and Sima pounced at the same time, both chopping the vine away. The sudden release of tension dumped Lissa to the ground, where she promptly burst into tears and wailed, "Mommy!"

The severed vine lashed at Austin, but he sliced it shorter in midair and backed away.

Sima scooped Lissa up and held her. Fortunately, she'd suffered only a few tiny pinpricks from thorns. Once the shock of it wore off, Lissa went back to smiling. Despite her better mood, the child remained close at her side, no longer interested in exploring.

What am I doing pretending to be a parent? I'm barely educated, too. I can't teach them much. A branch Austin pushed out of his way flapped back at her, scratching leaves across her chest and stomach. *Yeah, right... we're stuck in the jungle. Education won't matter. Not like they need to grow up and learn enough to get ready for good jobs. They didn't send us to another planet; they sent us back to prehistoric times.*

She squeezed Lissa's hand.

If they even get to grow up at all.

Relief washed over her when they reached the lifeboat and found it devoid of monsters. An unusually large number of sky mantas glided overhead, swimming around in the air in pairs or triplets. She figured they either performed some manner of courting ritual or played. Sima couldn't help but see them as smiling, due to the shape of the mouth slit along the underside of their front edge. She stepped inside long enough to get dressed, even if her top and underpants remained damp. Austin, too, hurried to get his briefs on.

Lissa flopped in the grass and resumed her thus-far-futile effort to make some kind of jewelry out of the delicate flowers. While the boys resumed pretend stick fighting, Sima explored the near jungle in search of better vines or leaves from which she could make skirts or something. By early evening, she'd put leaf-skirts on all three kids plus herself. The boys broke theirs in minutes. Sima's burst apart as soon as she sat down.

Damn. Made it too tight around the waist.

Lissa's skirt lasted the longest, mostly because she sat still playing with the grass and wildflowers. When the sun began to set, she got up to pee before bed, and it fell right off.

Sima sighed, and went inside to print out some chicken.

―――――――――

DAYS CAME AND WENT. A different variation of 'mangled bedtime story' happened each night. Sima knew she mixed things up, but the kids didn't notice or care, so she didn't either.

Her feeble hope that they might find more survivors had about died. After more than a full week, having not seen or heard any sign of other people pretty much proved they'd wound up the only humans on the planet.

No longer having any hope that anyone might find them, Sima couldn't summon the energy to care about clothing. Her kids didn't care at all, except for Austin, and even he had started to get blasé. It wasn't as if other people would show up and she'd be mortified. She also worried about rashes—or whatever else might happen—from constantly having sweat-soaked fabric pressed against her skin. *Normal* people wore clean underwear every day. Hell, even as an Outcast living on the street, she had a week's worth of undergarments, and she made use of pay-per-wash places. Having only one set, plus being stranded so far away from humanity that no one would ever see them again, made the whole modesty thing pointless. Apparently, no one would wait to outgrow their government-issued skivvies before going totally native.

All we need now are spears. But I guess we have axes, so that counts.

Daylight hours had lost some of their dread with confidence the 'cat' or 'cats' would only show themselves in the dark. Not once did they ever see a sign of the Night Scratch prowling around while the sun remained out, though the creature did visit every two or three nights as if hoping to find a new hole in the lifeboat it hadn't discovered before.

Sima committed herself to teaching the kids from the data in the bracelet. After a few days, Lissa developed a reading vocabulary of about thirty words, and she'd even managed to successfully make floral bracelets and anklets that didn't fall apart from casual wear. Sima had wandered farther and farther into the jungle in search of different types of leaves, but every attempt she made at crafting garments with local plant life resulted in skirts that disintegrated within minutes or had hazardous edges, uncomfortable (often dangerous) sticky hairs, or sharp points rendering them unwearable. One leaf she tried to collect paralyzed her left hand for three hours simply from touching it.

She considered possibly killing one of those little blue pig things for hide, but thought them too cute, and the bracelet explained that primitive humans had a process for 'tanning' animal skin into leather. It didn't have information about that process, being that no human had actually tanned animal hide for hundreds of years.

As the sun went down on the sixth day after her trip to the original lifeboat, she gathered the kids inside and secured the door as had become routine. In the pale blue glow of the 'portable campfire,' set on 'light only' mode, they sat in a circle munching on chicken slabs and fruit. To save protein gel, Sima only printed two slabs and cut them in half with an axe so everyone got a piece.

In the middle of dinner, the Night Scratch jumped up on the top of the lifeboat, sniffing and clawing at the holes.

Only Lissa reacted with fear. She clung to Sima's side, trembling. Juan ignored the cat entirely.

Austin pulled his axe closer. "Maybe we should move to the cave. This place is full of water too, and there's lots of rooms there."

"There's no door," whispered Lissa. "The Night Scratch can just walk in."

"It's only fulla water when it rains," said Juan. "Where I used to live with my dad leaked, too. And the cave has a door. 'Member I touched the wall and it opened?"

Sima thought back to the body parts littered all over the field by the large crashed lifeboat. *That cat probably had a feast and it thinks there's more here. The Auraks are smart, I wonder if the cat knows lifeboat means people.*

"If the bad kitty goes in the cave after us, we won't be able to get away," said Lissa. "The tunnel out is too slippery."

Austin made an 'oh yeah' face. "Duh. Forgot. We barely got out of there."

"Yeah." Juan nodded. "It was fun sliding, but I don't wanna die."

After another story about a boy made of wood who wanted to become real pulling a magical sword from a rock, they settled down to sleep. Sima stared at the ceiling again, her gaze tracking the weight shift of the cat padding back and forth. Despite death being literally feet away from her, she found herself thinking more about her strange new life where lounging around without clothing had become normal. Compared to being back home with Scathers, Pluggers, Blanks, and a dozen other gangs constantly trying to grab or kill her, living primitive didn't feel so bad anymore.

Come on, karma. I need you now. She closed her eyes, and tried to wish that all the 'positive energy' she banked up not breaking the law would protect her kids.

25

DAY TRIP

The next morning, Sima decided to head to the lake, bringing the portable campfire along. Her bracelet had come up with a design for a spear, using one of the stiffer, rubbery branches as a shaft and some of the long razor leaves as a tip. She planned to go swimming, and, if any of the fish-like creatures in it scanned as edible, she'd try spearing one and cooking it.

Sima carried the briefcase-sized portable campfire in one hand, her axe in the other, striding brazenly through the jungle with only her bracelet on. As embarrassing as it would be for other humans to see her, she'd decided to use her horrible luck against itself. Parading around *asking* for a mortifying moment sounded like a great way to cause a ripple in the universe and find more people. If it meant her kids had a better chance, she'd suffer ridicule.

Even if it happened to be a man who found them, it's not as if he'd do much more than laugh at her scrawny body. She had no illusions of being appealing in *that* way. Barely any shape, not much of a chest, bony hips… Back in the Crash, voices echoed at night. Other Outcasts often talked about who they thought pretty, and girls like her didn't rate. It never bothered her though. Being thin helped her pretend to be younger so she could beg.

Maybe I don't miss Earth. She put thoughts of Outcasts and begging out of her mind and focused on staying alert for danger. The mile-plus walk passed without incident, and they emerged on the shore of the enormous lake.

A trio of Auraks glided swan-like around the far side, scooping their beaks in the water and creating temporary, roaring waterfalls as they lifted into the air. Sima observed them for a while, noting that they appeared to lack the ability to 'suck' up water, and needed to tilt their heads back to pour it down their throats.

The boys dashed straight into the lake. Lissa crept in more cautiously, squealing at the cold.

Sima set the case down on the shore, placed the axe on top of it, and waded in up to her knees. Deciding to get the freeze-shock over with fast, she jumped in headfirst. Upon surfacing, she let out a gasp, shivering, and feeling more awake than she'd been in days.

"Bracelet... can you scan these fish? Are any good for eating?"

‹Out of range.›

"I know..." She rolled her eyes. "But I can't talk when I'm underwater."

The bracelet chirped.

She dove under and swam down to the bottom, gliding past multicolored lumps that varied in size from eggs to small boulders. They could've been rocks, mushrooms, crabs, or some other plant, but she dared not touch any to find out. Whenever a fish-like creature got close enough, she held her arm out so the bracelet could scan it. For as long as she could hold her breath, the largest fish she spotted hadn't been as big as her fist.

Sima went up for air, doubting the lake would be a source of food. Again, she ducked under, paddling out deeper in search of larger fish. Over the course of diving and surfacing several times, she had no luck locating food. The fifth time she submerged, she somewhat got her wish: a shadow moved in the depths quite a ways off... but it looked big enough to eat her whole.

Eep!

Abandoning her quest for seafood, she swam back toward shore before whatever that *giant thing* was noticed her and got hungry. Austin and Juan stood in the shallows, the water a bit past their knees, darting around and splashing each other. Lissa floated on her back, smiling at the sky mantas. Once Sima got to a point where her feet could touch bottom with her head above the surface, she calmed. That enormous sea creature would likely not be able to fit this close to the bank.

‹The aquatic life forms have a gelatinous body structure with cartilage rather than bones. They appear to be filter-feeders subsisting on a diet of microscopic organisms. By my estimation, they would be edible, but I do not think you would enjoy the texture.›

Sima pictured biting into a slime fish and gagged. "Yeah, no thanks."

She sat in the water next to Lissa, whiling away almost an hour helping the girl name various sky mantas. Juan dove under and came back up with a round, bright red disk. After studying it for a moment, he flung it toward Austin and it flew quite a distance before landing on the water.

Austin rushed after it and threw it back to Juan. Sima had seen some Outcast kids play a similar game with wheel covers from gee-vees. She laughed whenever one of the boys took a flying leap trying to catch it and missed.

With her dreams of a fish dinner shattered, Sima resigned herself to planning a lunch of more raspberry-rhubarb fruits. Though, she couldn't quite help but wonder what the sky mantas might taste like, not that she had any possible way to take one down—or the serious desire to do so.

"You missed!" yelled Austin.

Juan laughed.

The spongy disk flew way off out of the lake into the jungle. Austin ran after it, vanishing into the blue leaves. Lissa giggled at him, as did Sima.

A few seconds later, he screamed in terror.

"Austin!" shouted Sima, scrambling to her feet. She started running toward where he'd gone into the foliage, but skidded to a stop at an animal's roar and doubled back to the lakeshore where she'd left the axe.

Austin screamed again, though at least his cry didn't sound in pain. A bestial snarl followed. Sima scooped up the axe and sprinted into the jungle, heading for the sound. Loud rustling up ahead accompanied the boy's continued shouts and the growls of a large animal.

Sima leapt an indigo vine as tall as her thighs, dodged branches, and swerved around trees. A few seconds past the edge of the jungle, she skidded to a stop on her heels, staring at a dark blue furry creature that resembled a cat almost as big as a gee-vee. Its size left her unsure if she faced the Night Scratch or something similar to it. The animal stood on its hind legs, raking claws at the tree Austin had climbed. A narrow tail, longer than its body, swished back and forth behind it, tipped with a pod studded in silver quills.

The boy clung to the trunk, arms and legs wrapped around it almost thirty feet up, the 'Frisbee' abandoned on the ground nearby. Several silvery quills stuck in the wood not far below his feet. That the creature had stopped flinging quills at him gave her hope it couldn't reach that high.

Austin stared at her but didn't say a word. Sima clutched the axe.

Upright on its long hind legs, the creature stretched its slender, sinuous body, raking at the tree in a murderous parody of a scratching post. Sima's head would barely reach its chest. Two pairs of glowing green eyes fixated on Austin as it shredded black claws into the rubbery-spongy 'wood.' The tree didn't look like it would last too much longer before it—and Austin—came down.

She shifted her weight back and forth, squeezing and releasing the axe. "Get away from him!"

The creature emitted a noise part growl, part groan, and dropped down to all fours before turning toward her. Sima leapt to her left, pivoting sideways to put a tree between her and the monster. Sure enough, it flicked its tail up and, with a whipping snap, sent a cloud of pointy darts her way. One landed in her hair, though the rest hit the tree with a rapid fusillade of *thok* sounds.

"Leave him alone," shouted Sima.

She ducked back behind the tree as a second wave of quills came at her. Instinct made her want to duck and curl into a ball, but she resisted. Upright, her body fit behind the trunk. For the first time in her life, she didn't hate being thin.

The critter roared at her, then turned back to rip at Austin's tree some more.

Sima pulled the quill out of her hair, tossed it aside, and stepped into view, brandishing the axe. "Come on. I'm right here on the ground!"

"No!" yelled Austin. "It'll eat you!" He let out a wail of fear as his tree swayed to the side, the trunk fraying into fibrous strands where it the animal had ripped at it.

"What's—" Lissa let off a shrill scream right behind her.

Juan stopped short beside her, gawking.

Sima, both hands on the axe, used her body to push Lissa into Juan. "Go back to the lake. Hide."

The pair ran a short distance away and shimmied up a tree like Austin.

I'm completely crazy. She advanced on the beast, raising the axe. *That thing's claws would tear EGSF armor apart, and I don't even have clothes on.* Austin yelled again, true fear shining clear in his scream as the tree bent even more to the side.

Sima forgot all care for her life and charged.

The large cat-thing pivoted toward her as she ran in shrieking a war cry. Desperation and panic driving her, she swung the axe downward, slashing at its side. Pearlescent blue blood sprayed across her chest. She barely had time to think before an angry paw swipe caught her in the shoulder, swatting her hard to the ground and sending her sliding several meters away.

"Sima!" yelled Austin.

She sat up, head spinning, dimly aware of a burning sensation on her left arm. The creature leaned forward, rear end in the air, tail wiggling.

"Yaaaaaaah!" shouted Austin as he leapt off the tree *at* the beast. He landed on the tail a few inches south of the quill pod and wrapped himself around it.

Burdened by the boy's weight, the flailing appendage couldn't whip fast enough to make quills fly. The creature growled, spinning in place chasing its own tail, swiping at Austin. The length kept the boy out of reach of claws. The faster the quill cat tried to go after him, the faster he moved away from the deadly paw. He wailed in fear, but refused to let go as they whirled around and around.

Sima wobbled to her feet, but before she could charge in, a

deafening screech shattered the air. The intensity of the squawking cry nearly knocked her over and caused the clawed horror to freeze still. Austin yelled as the tail swung around to the other side. Crashing and thundering came from the foliage, growing louder and louder. The great cat backed away, the hair on its shoulders fluffing up. It continued flicking its tail in an unsuccessful effort to throw Austin aside. He clung desperately to the furry noodle as big around as his leg, despite the creature repeatedly slapping him against the ground.

An Aurak charged out from the trees, flapping its wings and shrieking at the quill cat. The much smaller furry creature backpedaled, making a chittering *click-click-click* sound deep in its throat before whirling around and dashing away. Austin let go and tumbled into the undergrowth. Still flapping and screeching, the Aurak thundered off after the cat. A good distance from where Austin fell, the huge bird caught up and ran the cat over, deliberately stepping on it. The feline monster howled as the huge bird picked it up with one foot and threw it, flailing, into the trees. The quill cat bounced and rolled into the underbrush. Furious, the Aurak leaned forward and screeched with enough volume that several leaves disintegrated.

Sima ran to where Austin lay sprawled on his back, staring at the blue canopy overhead.

"You're bleeding," said Austin, calm.

"I... umm..." Sima looked at her left shoulder. Four shallow claw wounds had coated most of that arm in dark red. "Yeah. Are you okay?"

"Forgot to wear a helmet before riding." His belly caved in and expanded with a series of deep breaths. "I think I peed."

"I can't believe you jumped on that thing. What were you thinking?" She grabbed his hand in both of hers and squeezed.

"It was gonna shoot you." He sat up, examining himself. Other than smudges of dirt and a few scrapes here and there, he appeared to have escaped serious injury. "I didn't want it to poison you. They whip their tails to throw darts, but it couldn't throw darts if I held on."

She grimaced in pain while raising her left arm to embrace him. "That was really brave of you... but I don't want *you* getting hurt."

Austin grinned up at her. "Brave? I didn't run at a monster with an axe. You're brave."

Rustling approached from behind. Sima twisted her head around, preparing to run, but the noise came from Lissa and Juan walking around gathering up giant feathers that had fallen from the Aurak's threat display. The kids appeared enthralled by the beautiful blue-violet luster, but Sima had another idea.

Hmm. I wonder if I could make a skirt out of those? The smaller ones would be about down to my shins. They probably won't bend much though.

Fluttering came from the bracelet typing. ‹Wash out your wound and go back to the lifeboat. There is a medical kit there you should use.›

Sima looked down at her chest, still covered in glimmery, pearlescent alien blood. "Washing sounds like a good idea."

"Yeah." Austin stood with a grunt and dusted himself off. "I think we should probably go home, too. Before another one of those things tries to eat me."

"What's the Night Scratch doing outside at the day?" asked Lissa.

Juan shook his head. "That's not the Night Scratch. It's *way* too big."

Trees parted as the Aurak strode into view. The huge bird bowed its head down to human level, emitting a soft coo.

Austin hugged its beak the way a person might hug the hood of a gee-vee. "Thank you!"

It attempted to nuzzle him, but its sheer size lifted him several feet into the air atop its beak. He slid off and landed on his feet, waving his arms for balance while laughing. Sima also brushed a hand at the side of the bird's face.

"Thanks. Wow… he helped us," said Sima.

"They're smart." Lissa set her hands on her hips. "Because Austin helped one of them."

"Or they just hate the monsters with needles," said Juan.

Austin shook his head. "He helped *us*. That monster wasn't attacking a bird. It came running all the way across the lake to help."

"Oh." Juan's eyes widened. "Cool."

For a little while, everyone patted and hugged the Aurak. It eventually appeared satisfied that the quill cat would not return, and headed off in the direction of the lake. Sima led the kids back to the water. She dipped in only long enough to rinse herself clear of alien blood and clean out the claw slices on her shoulder. Looking at the wound made her squeamish, but she had little choice.

Juan retrieved the red, spongy disk they'd been playing with, wearing it like a hat.

"Where did you find that?" asked Sima.

"On the lake bottom. It's the top of a mushroom."

She held her left wrist over to it. "Is it dangerous?"

‹Only if eaten.›

"Okay, you can keep it to play, but do not bite or lick it."

Juan nodded.

After gathering the portable campfire, she walked at a brisk pace back toward the lifeboat. A few minutes into the trip, she spotted a tall bushy plant with broad, lavender leaves. Some reached a size big enough that only two could form a skirt, one in front one in back. Curious, she approached, despite still bleeding from the shoulder.

"Where are you going?" asked Lissa.

"We haven't seen these before." Sima pointed at the plant. "Maybe we can make something to wear out of these leaves."

"It's too hot for clothes," said Lissa.

Austin smirked. "I'd feel dumber wearing a leaf than underpants."

"Which are back at the lifeboat," said Sima. "Eventually, we won't have a choice. You're all going to get too big for them."

He smirked. "Wearing leaves is stupid. They won't keep us warm."

"Wearing pants is stupid!" said Lissa, flailing her arms. "And we don't need warm."

Sima laughed and grasped one of the leaves, giving it a test squeeze. The plant matter tore like tissue paper. "Dammit. Why is everything here so delicate?"

All three kids shrugged.

‹This leaf has a highly fibrous structure that could readily be processed into fabric given the proper equipment. It could become a primary source of cloth with properties similar to cotton.›

"Yeah, well..." Sima shook her head at the little panel above her arm. "We don't have any machines to process it. Do you know a simple way to make cloth? Like tribals did?"

‹I do not have that information in my archives.›

"The colors are pretty." Lissa stood close enough to the plant to pull a leaf into position like a skirt. "I like it." Her fingers tore through it a few seconds later, and the stalk bobbed back into place, leaving her holding a few thread-like filaments. "Bleh."

Sima scratched the back of her head. "Maybe I could make something out of the feathers."

"I got an idea," said Juan.

Everyone looked at him.

"Use wires from the lifeboat for a belt. Metal scraps for a skirt."

Sima squirmed at the mere thought of wearing metal strips. "I don't think that would work."

"Pinchy," said Austin, crossing his legs. "Ouch."

Giving up on the pretty, too-brittle leaves, Sima resumed hurrying back to the lifeboat. The kids followed her inside without detour despite it still being day out. She knelt by the medical kit and looked at the bracelet's display panel.

‹There's a device inside that resembles a silver egg. Hold the narrow end by the injury and squeeze the button.›

Sima opened the box, which contained several devices and canisters in foam. She plucked a silver plastic egg from the packing and looked it over. It had one button at the fat end and a chromatic sheen over the narrow end. With a shrug, she held it near the wound and pushed the button.

Faint white energy appeared at the tip. The claw slashes in her shoulders flared up like a flaming hot shard of metal jammed into her skin. Unprepared for the pain, Sima yelled and dropped the egg. Austin caught it before it could roll too far away.

Sima gritted her teeth. "Oh, crap that hurt."

"It hurt?" asked Lissa.

"Worse than being cut." Sima shivered, then glanced at Austin. "You do it… Please. I'll drop it again."

He nodded and moved to kneel beside her. "Ready?"

"Yeah." Sima closed her eyes and concentrated all her effort on not screaming. Pain ripping across her shoulder almost made her pass out.

"Whoa. The cuts are closing!" said Austin. "This is awesome."

The next thing Sima knew, she lay flat on her back with Lissa's face hovering over her.

"She's not dead," said Lissa.

"Ugh. What happened?" asked Sima.

"You passed out." Austin snapped the fasteners closed on the medical kit.

Sima poked at her shoulder, finding intact skin covered in blood. "Ow. Still tender."

"It's not bleeding anymore." Austin scooted over and hugged her. All the fear he must've had while treed by a quill cat came back at once. He fought hard not to cry, but didn't fully succeed.

She hugged him close, letting him tremble and sniffle until he composed himself.

"That was the coolest thing anyone ever did for me," he whispered. "You could've been killed."

"Yeah, well I'm not ready to die yet." Feeling guilty, she stared at the floor, thinking back to the ledge at the Crash where she stared down at the landfill. Honestly, she hadn't been ready to jump, or she would have. She pushed that grimness out of her mind. "Let me have a look at you."

He sat still and let her examine him. His worst injuries, scrapes on his back from where the creature walloped him into the ground, looked less severe than skinned knees. Still, she took him outside and poured water over the scuffs, rubbing with her hand until she got all the dirt out of the scratches.

Lissa wandered over and sat next to her, seeming listless.

Once Sima could find no more scratches in need of cleaning, she ruffled Austin's hair and hugged him again. Grinning, he trotted off to join Juan in the field near the lifeboat, where they resumed play sword fighting. Though, they appeared to be trying to get more serious about it... as if preparing to have to fend off a quill cat.

The girl's lack of fussing with flowers worried her. She simply sat there, leaning against Sima.

"Are you feeling okay?"

Lissa shrugged one shoulder. "I'm tired."

"Me too." Sima rubbed the girl's back, then put an ear to it. Whispery-wheezy breathing worried her, but at least the scary sounds had quieted. She could only hear the rasping if she pressed her ear close, not out loud on every breath.

"Am I gonna have to have a baby with Juan when I'm big?" asked Lissa.

The awkward question caught Sima so off guard she laughed. "Umm. No. You won't *have* to do anything like that. But if you *want* to, it's okay. However, you are not to do anything like that until you're at least eighteen."

Mercifully, Lissa accepted that answer without further interrogation. Sima was *not* ready to explain where babies came from. Most definitely not to a six-year-old. It probably wouldn't be too much longer before she had the awesome pleasure of having to explain randomly bleeding. Not as though her present circumstances would make it easy to hide that from them. With any luck, the kids would accept a 'girls just do that' and not pry. But if she had to, she'd do more for Lissa than her mother had done for her. Sima had to learn from a total stranger in an alley. The mere anticipation of *that* conversation made her squirm with embarrassment.

The afternoon continued to warm, and within two hours of their return to the lifeboat, Sima felt overdressed in only her skin. She relocated closer to the metal wall, sitting in the shade. It didn't take long for the boys to abandon the field for the shade of the jungle.

They went through their stash of water fast, so Sima left the kids at the lifeboat for a quick run to the river to fill the jug. She returned to find them in good health, Austin standing guard with his axe. She smiled at him, picturing how he must've imagined himself growing up to be an EGSF officer before his dad's injury altered his mind. *Was it losing his father, or being an Outcast that made him hate the cops?*

Sima held the jug for the kids to drink, then set it down in the shade by the hatch.

"Wow, it's hot," said Juan.

"Is it summer now?" Lissa looked up at her, and coughed a little.

‹The current season is roughly equivalent to August on Earth.›

Sima held up her screen so the others could read. "Yeah. It's August."

"How long do we have left 'til we die?" asked Juan. "That monster was really scary."

Lissa clung tight, despite the heat. It surprised Sima not to wince at the squish of a sweaty child pressed at her side. She smiled down at the girl. Lissa grinned back, and a bubble of snot swelled from her nose. Without a second thought, Sima pinched it clear and wiped it on the grass. Both boys made faces at her touching 'someone else's snot.'

"I don't wanna die." Austin patted the axe.

"Umm." Sima forced herself to look away from Lissa's innocent face, unable to bear the truth: that it would be an outright miracle if they survived much longer than a few more weeks.

Between the Night Scratch, the giant cat thing with quills (or maybe that *was* the Night Scratch), lack of food, weather, possible disease or infection, the Pixie exposure shredding Lissa's lungs, or any of a thousand different potential things they hadn't seen yet... the odds of their continued existence felt minuscule. She'd given up scolding the kids for not wearing their pants. What did it matter? What did anything matter? Like why care if a terminally ill person continued drinking booze, they're dead anyway. The best thing she could do is keep them as happy as possible until the inevitable came to pass.

"We just need to be careful." Sima ruffled Juan's hair. "This isn't much different from Earth."

"There's monsters," said Juan.

Sima nodded. "Yes... but there's monsters on Earth, too. Only, back there, they had guns."

Thinking about what the Scathers might've done to her kids, she gathered them close in a protective embrace. The streets would've killed them all anyway, but not before destroying their souls.

Mirage at least had beautiful scenery.

26

THE PROBLEM WITH PLANTS

Distant screaming dragged Sima out of sleep.

She pushed herself upright. Both Juan and Lissa remained close, half-awake in the lifeboat. No sign of Austin. The screaming outside became muffled.

A second later when her brain kicked in and processed what her eyes and ears told her, Sima grabbed her axe and dashed outside. Rustling and muted shouting continued from the left, beyond the corner of the lifeboat. She ran toward the disturbance.

Thirty feet past the edge of the clearing, she skidded to a stop, staring at two feet sticking out of a giant strawberry-shaped plant that had apparently swallowed Austin whole up to his calves. Vine-tentacles sprouted from the base, whipping and thrashing across the ground. Small fist-sized bulges appeared as he punched the giant petals engulfing him.

"Austin!" shouted Sima.

She ran in, disregarding the whipping thorns slapping at her legs, and grabbed the rim of the flower. Rather than swinging the axe, she sliced at the plant. Spiky tendrils wrapped around her legs. She shrieked and chopped at them, severing the vines with ease. Austin struggled in a frenzy, growling while thumping and thudding at the soft walls trapping him.

The high-tech axe sliced the plant with little resistance. Sima hacked at the bottom of where the 'jaw' closed, tearing gaping rents in the tough, fibrous plant. Clear gel, likely some kind of digestive fluid, collected at the bottom of the cup and oozed out of the slashes. Another two good whacks convinced the flower to open and release the boy. The facing three-foot-tall petal lowered to the jungle floor. Austin rolled away from it, floppy and limp. Thin blue vines wrapped around him, coiling around his neck, chest, and thighs. Thousands of tiny bleeding dots covered his body. Before she could take the axe to the thinner vines, they released their grip and snapped back into a snarl of tangles at the center of the flytrap.

Sima grabbed his arm and dragged him away, out of reach of the longest vines sprouting from the base.

"Ow," said Austin.

"Are you okay?"

"Umm. More scared than hurt." He sat up and wiped blood off his legs and stomach.

Sima folded her arms. "What happened? What are you doing outside alone?"

"I had to pee. That flower grabbed me. The blue stuff in the middle like exploded into tentacles and pulled me in."

She frowned. "You peed right on it, didn't you?"

He offered a sheepish grin. "Maybe…"

Sima sighed at the clouds. "What is it with boys?"

"It *does* kinda look like a wall toilet when it's open."

She squatted and wiped her hand at his arm. "You look like you got attacked by a swarm of thumbtacks."

He brushed blood off her shin. "You too. I'm sorry."

"Please don't run off alone again? At least tell me you're going out to water the grass."

"Okay."

Sima asked the bracelet to take a picture of the giant flower, and couldn't stop shaking on the short walk back to the lifeboat. *Great. Even the plants are trying to eat us.* Once they returned, she showed the photo to Juan and Lissa.

"I don't want you two going anywhere near a flower that looks like this. Do you understand?"

"Okay," said Lissa.

Juan nodded

"It's lucky I'm bigger. If I was your size, it would've swallowed me whole and Sima wouldn't have heard me yelling." Austin shivered.

Both smaller kids gasped.

Sima handed out fruits. Juan didn't seem at all interested. Lissa halfheartedly ate one. Sima kept pestering her until she finished a second.

"Come on, man." Austin threw a fruit at Juan. "I'm sick of them too, but we don't have anything else."

Grumbling, Juan begrudgingly stuffed his face.

After eating, Sima pulled her EGSF-issue underwear on and led an expedition into the jungle on the far side of the clearing behind the lifeboat, a section they hadn't yet explored. They eventually happened upon a new plant with sky-blue leaves about twice the size of Sima's hand, and vines thin enough that they might work as belts to hold up a skirt. Her hope died a swift death upon examining the leaves and finding them stony hard with razor edges.

Austin sliced one leaf off with his axe and threw it like a Frisbee at a nearby tree—where it stuck. "Cool!"

"Don't play with those," said Sima a little louder than normal, but not quite yelling. "They're sharp."

He pointed at it. "We could use them as weapons if another quill monster tries to eat us."

"Ninjas!" yelled Juan, running to pull the thrown leaf out of the tree. He jumped back with a yelp, jamming his hand in his mouth.

"See!" Sima rushed over and grabbed his arm. Fortunately, he had only a little cut on the side of his thumb. "These are not toys."

"All the plants here suck," said Austin. "They either want to eat us or hurt us or they're useless."

Juan wiped at his mouth. "The fruits are okay."

"Come on. Don't touch these." Sima tugged Juan back to the group.

They walked deeper into the jungle. Lissa gravitated to bright mushrooms or small flying creatures. Juan kept his attention in the high canopy, and Austin clutched his axe close, ready in case of danger. Sima continued looking for never-before-seen plant types. Eventually, she found a seven-foot-tall bush with waxy leaves. Each leaf ran about twelve inches long, two inches wide with blue edges and white down the middle. This plant felt the closest to anything from Earth she'd discovered so far, neither breaking on contact nor having an edge sharp enough to cut skin.

Figures. Finally, I find a plant I can use for something to wear and none of us care anymore. She glanced at the others roaming around the trees, picking up rocks and such. *Okay. I'm the only one that ever did care that much. Still... when they get older, it's going to be really weird. Maybe they'll get self-conscious.* A sigh slipped out of her nose. *We've all gone crazy. How long before we start worshiping the sun and making offerings to giant rocks?*

She collected some of the usable leaves for practice. It couldn't hurt to teach herself how to make a skirt. A little past noon, she gathered the kids and headed back home.

"Wait," said Austin. "I wanna try something."

Sima glanced at him. "What?"

He pointed up at the trees. The pods with the lime green spheres hung way overhead. "I'm gonna cut one down. So sick of the red ones."

"That's like thirty feet in the air. What if you fall?"

Austin held the axe up to his mouth. "I won't." He clamped the rubberized handle in his teeth and shimmied up the trunk. Sima stood right beneath him, shaking with worry as he got higher and higher. The tree he'd chosen held at least nine of the multi-fruit pods, like some kind of mutant apples—except each 'apple' held twenty or so smaller fruits. As soon as he got within reach of one, he clung to the swaying trunk and used the axe to chop at the stem holding the pod in place.

It soon fell, snapping down through the foliage, and landed with a heavy *thump* barely two feet away from Sima. Three of the lime-colored fruits at the bottom exploded on impact, showering her, Juan, and Lissa with pulp and juice. Both kids licked their arms. Sima couldn't look away from Austin.

He held the axe out. "Gonna drop this so I can climb better."

Sima took a few steps back, pulling the kids with her. Austin let go and the axe stuck into the ground, standing up like an arrow. He scooted down the tree like a human version of a squirrel, jumping off when he got within a few feet of the ground.

"Easy." He grinned. "I know it's still fruit, but it's *different* fruit."

They decided to rest right there and eat the broken ones so as not to waste them. The peachy-lemon mixture punched Sima square in the taste buds, but she couldn't argue that the change of flavor offered a much-needed break.

Once they finished eating, Sima asked Juan to carry the leaves, and dragged the heavy fruit pod along on the way back to the lifeboat. Upon returning home, she salvaged a length of electrical wire from the useless cooling system to use for a waistband. The design she evolved in her head sounded pretty simple: spear the wire through the leaves, making a 'curtain,' then put it around her waist and tie the wire together.

She sat in the grass not far from the lifeboat hatch and got to work. Lissa flopped on her back, chattering away as if talking to the creatures flying overhead. She named any sky manta she believed to be new, and also called out whenever she spotted a cloud animal. Sima played along, finding other cloud animals and even offering a few names for the flying rays while the boys continued 'practicing' how to fight with an axe using the semi-flexible branches.

After a while, she stood with her completed skirt (forty or so leaves strung along on the wire) and wrapped it around her waist. It felt *weird*, like wearing a garment of plastic strips, though as long as she stood perfectly still, it was more modest than the EGSF undies. If she moved at all, the leaves swayed apart like vertical window blinds.

"Ugh. This is more decoration than clothing."

"It's pretty," said Lissa.

Sima tried sitting. The flexible leaves withstood her weight, but it wouldn't take a whole lot of force to rip them off the wire.

Juan let off an anguished, wailing scream.

"I'm sorry!" shouted Austin. "Accident!"

Sima looked up, seeing only one boy off in the tall grass. "What happened?"

Austin turned to face her and gave a sheepish smile. He held up his branch 'sword.' "I hit him in the nuts on accident."

A stick appeared between Austin's legs.

"Look—" shouted Sima.

The stick flew upward, delivering Juan's revenge. Austin crumpled into the grass, moaning.

"…Out," said Sima. She braced for another fistfight, but within a minute or two, the boys wound up laughing like idiots. "I do not understand boys at all."

"They're stupid," whispered Lissa. "Why are they hitting each other?"

"Oh, I think they want to practice in case they have to protect themselves from another monster."

Lissa nodded, then made a pensive face. "Do monsters have nuts?"

Sima fell backward, flat on her back, laughing.

"What?" asked Lissa, peering over at her.

"I guess." She shrugged. "Maybe they do."

Inspired by Sima's 'skirt,' Lissa got up and roamed for a little while, collecting strands of wildflowers and grass. She carried them back over and sat beside Sima, winding them around her waist and braiding them into a decoration.

Daylight began to fade, so the boys hurried over to stay close to the lifeboat in case the Night Scratch emerged early. A distant *bang* went off in the sky. Everyone looked up at a flickering fire trail racing from right to left across a swath of indigo and cyan. It lasted only seconds before disappearing with a flash.

"A shooting star," said Austin.

"Make a wish." Sima smiled and closed her eyes. *I wish my kids will survive here.*

"I want either real clothes or a Wondercube," said Austin.

"Wondercube won't do anything without 'lectric," said Juan.

Lissa rubbed her chest. "I wish for new breaths."

Juan looked up at Sima. "I wish you were my real mom."

Sima covered her mouth, staring at him with tears brewing at the corners of her eyes.

"I know you can't be," said Juan, "'cause I'm like already born and stuff."

"Doesn't gotta be that," said Austin. "A mom's not only who had the baby, it's who's ready to take on a giant quill cat with an axe to protect you."

Sima ruffled his hair, trying not to cry. It took her a moment to figure out where her voice went. "I, umm, can't really do anything about getting a new Wondercube, or giving Lissa new breaths, no matter how much I want to. I'm still trying to find some way to make clothes." She flicked at the leaves in her lap. "This didn't really work."

The kids chuckled.

"But, I guess I can be Mom if you guys want."

"Yeah!" Juan leapt into a hug.

Lissa grinned at her. "Duh. You already are."

"Sure." Austin blushed and glanced off at the jungle. "Mom."

With a playful snarl, Sima flung an arm around him and pulled him into a hug.

A rippling series of bangs filled the distant sky in a brief firework show.

"Wow." Lissa stared. "So pretty."

"What was that?" asked Juan.

"Probably junk from the ship," said Austin.

Sima cringed at the reminder of how lucky they had been to remain alive. "We should go inside. It'll be dark soon."

The kids got up without protest and filed through the hatch into the lifeboat. Sima stood, stared for a long moment at the sky where the flare up happened, and hurried behind the safety of a closed door.

27

SICK PIXIE

An hour into a foraging trip the next afternoon, Austin came running over holding a burned metal scrap. "Hey, I found stuff!"

Sima scratched at her side. Attempting to sleep in the skirt had left a few small cuts all the way around her middle from the broken leaf ends digging into her skin, so she'd abandoned it as a failed project.

"There's a bunch of stuff over there." Austin pointed.

She followed him for a short distance, forcing her way past thick undergrowth to where dozens of metal scraps lay strewn about patches of burned jungle. "Whoa. This couldn't have been the same stuff we saw last night. That was too far away."

"It's definitely from the ship," said Austin. "But it's all junk."

They spent the better part of an hour checking over the debris. Some of the larger pieces, as big as food storage cabinets, offered hope, but contained only mechanical parts. She certainly did not need more junk metal. The lifeboat had plenty of that already.

Giving up on any of the wreckage being useful, she continued roaming into the jungle. Today's journey traveled southeast away from the lifeboat, another direction they had not yet gone. A little over three miles away, she found a swath of plants with long, green fruiting bodies. The small ones stood about three feet tall, seven or eight inches around at the wide end.

"What is this?" she held the bracelet up to one, and the blue laser pyramid appeared.

‹Analysis suggests this is similar to a zucchini or squash. It is edible, but would likely taste better if cooked. However, the plant matter is rich in nutrients. I strongly advise harvesting these for food. In fact, if you locate the means to mash them into paste, you may even be able to feed the resulting liquid into the fabricator to be reconfigured into meat.›

"Awesome!" shouted Sima.

All three kids jumped.

"What?" asked Austin.

She explained their new wonderfood.

"Ugh. Vegetables," said Austin.

"Any food is good food." Juan shook his head. "Even space cucumbers."

"I don't like how they taste," said Austin.

"You haven't even tried it yet." Lissa flailed her arms at him.

"I don't like how starving tastes." Juan frowned.

Sima patted Austin on the shoulder. "Well, you all voted me 'Mom,' and I don't want you getting sick. So, we're going to start eating this plant. Not all the time, but we need to have it. And it might work in the fabricator so we won't run out of chicken."

"Okay." He sighed, and chopped a few free with his axe.

One of the 'space cucumbers' would provide two full meals for everyone, so Sima didn't want to harvest *too* many at once. Lissa struggled to carry one of the huge squash. Sima carried a bundle of five, which almost overloaded her. Juan tried to take two, but couldn't quite manage it. Austin took three, but the effort at the limit of his strength reddened his face.

Everyone focused on their burden, no one wasting breath on conversation as they walked back to the lifeboat. Since Sima couldn't see the bracelet's screen, she asked it to steer her with beeps. Two to turn left, three to turn right, and a single beep if she went the correct way.

Not long after the surroundings became familiar, a soft *thump* happened behind her.

Sima glanced over her shoulder.

Lissa had collapsed face down, and didn't try to get back up.

"No!" She dropped her bundle of vegetables and ran over to the tiny girl. "Lissa!"

When the child didn't react, Sima grabbed her shoulder and rolled her over on her back.

Austin skidded to a halt on his knees nearby and stuck his ear over her mouth. "She's not breathing! Do the CPR stuff!"

"I uhh... never learned that." Sima looked around in a panic.

"I got it." Austin braced a hand at the back of Lissa's neck, pinched her nose, and breathed into her mouth.

Sima checked the girl's pulse at the wrist, calming a little when she detected a heartbeat.

"Ugh." Austin spat to the side. "She tastes like cherry."

Pixie. Sima clenched her hands in anger. If that girl's parents hadn't already been dead, she would've gone straight back to Earth and shown them her axe. "It's the bad chemicals she breathed. Don't inhale it."

He nodded and blew into her mouth a few more times.

After a few horrible seconds of nothing happening, Lissa lapsed into a coughing fit. Sima helped her sit up and held her over sideways while patting her on the back. She threw up a little bile, then hacked out a glob of pink-grey phlegm. Wheezing and choking, Lissa clutched at her throat and convulsed. Sima wrapped her arms around Lissa's middle and gave a few, sharp squeezes until another blob of mucous flew out of her mouth.

Juan and Austin stepped back from it.

Deep breaths whistled in Lissa's chest, making her sound like a broken flute. She gasped a few times, coughed once more, and erupted in sobs. Sima cradled her, rocking her side to side until she calmed.

I shouldn't let her carry anything... or walk three damn miles. I should be carrying her that far.

"I'm sorry for being weak," whispered Lissa, sounding dazed.

"It's not your fault, sweetie." Sima kept rocking her. "That poison you breathed was *not* your fault."

Lissa clung.

"Me an' Juan'll get the food," said Austin. "It's not far from the lifeboat here."

"Okay." Sima wobbled to her feet, carrying Lissa the last few hundred yards to the clearing around the lifeboat.

At the door, she sat in the grass and fed Lissa a few mouthfuls of water. The boys ran back and forth, each taking two of the big green squash per trip. When they dropped the last of them in a heap, they drank the rest of the jug empty. Everyone sat around resting in silence for a few minutes.

Austin stood with the jug. "Be back in a bit."

"Where do you think you're going?" asked Sima.

"To get water."

"Don't go off alone."

He pointed at her. "You need to stay with Lissa. It's okay. I know how to get to the river and I'll come right back." He took three steps before spinning back to smile at her. "And I won't pee on any big red flowers."

She couldn't quite laugh, but nodded.

"Bad people killed Mommy and Daddy," said Lissa in a half-awake whisper.

"I know, sweetie." Sima brushed blonde hair off the girl's face. "Those bad people are very far away. They can never hurt you again."

"Mommy and Daddy were bad too. That's why the bad people hurt them. They wanted glint and Daddy didn't have it. Daddy's stuff made me so sick I couldn't even stand up."

"You're much better now." Sima gave up fighting tears, and wept openly.

Juan sat on her left, leaning against her arm and watching Lissa's face.

"Orange ran away 'cause the shooting." Lissa twitched and coughed. Pink liquid dribbled out of the corner of her mouth. "I tried to find her, but I fell in the street. Other kids brought me to the nice man, but I couldn't beg. He let me stay inna bed, and they gave me food. The cops said they would give me new breaths if I let them send me to space. Did they lie?"

Sima stared down at the girl's frail chest. "No. I think they gave you medicine. You had a lot of bad things inside you and they're gone now."

Lissa's breathing slowed. For a terrifying minute, she seemed to stop moving entirely, but her eyes shifted to meet Sima's. "Am I gonna die? My breaths hurt."

This planet is going to kill all of us. She couldn't bear the truth that Lissa would succumb first. Her brittle condition did not lend itself to the rigors of living in a wilderness. When that EGSF man had carried her onto the ship, she had seemed so happy and hopeful. That made the sight of her now, draped across Sima's lap barely alive, hurt so much more.

"No, sweetie. You're going to be fine."

Lissa reached up a weak hand and touched Sima's cheek. "Thank you for making me feel better. I know I'm not gonna grow up, but I'm happy you're my Mom." She coughed hard again a few times, but settled down to labored breathing.

At another dribble of pink liquid oozing from the girl's mouth, Sima flashed back to standing in the sewer watching the Outcasts from her Crash toss Draz into the flow. 'Floating the dead,' as they called it. Her mind tortured her, replacing the overdosed teen with the body of a tiny girl, dead because of her wretched parents.

Overwhelmed, Sima clutched Lissa tight and sobbed, unable to force the horrible image of watching Lissa drift off in brackish water from her mind. She rocked her side to side, refusing to let go, refusing to let the torrent of filth take this child away from her.

Sloshing water approached. Austin, panting and out of breath, gasped, "What happened?"

"Lissa's sick," said Juan.

"Why's Sima crying?" asked Austin.

"Lissa's sick," said Juan.

"I'm not dead," whispered Lissa. "Yet."

Sima sobbed harder.

28

FLOWER CHILD

G rowling roars rang out in the jungle to the west. The powerful shriek of an Aurak followed, then squawks and snarling.

The boys hurried to move the big green squash inside the lifeboat. Sima, still weepy over an hour later, carried Lissa inside. Austin shut the lifeboat door and pushed down on the lever until he lifted himself off his feet. Sima sat on the floor by the fabricator, balancing Lissa in her lap while printing a full portion of chicken for everyone.

Juan attacked his food like he hadn't eaten in a week. Austin forced himself to take reasonable-sized bites, clearly wanting to eat the whole thing as fast as possible. Lissa whimpered and refused to open her mouth when Sima poked her in the lip with a piece of chicken.

"You need strength," said Sima.

"I'm too tired to chew."

"Well." Sima tapped her on the nose. "You can either chew, or I'll chew it for you and spit it in your mouth like a bird."

Lissa scrunched up her nose. "Eww."

Austin stopped eating and stared at her with a 'you did *not* just say that' expression.

Sima winked at him. "I can't give you new breaths, but if you eat real food, it'll help you get stronger."

"Okay." Lissa sat up and took the chicken slab, nibbling on it.

Another feline roar happened outside, along with Aurak shrieking.

"Is the Night Scratch eating those nice birds?" asked Lissa.

Sima glanced at the wall in the general direction of where the sounds came from. "Maybe *trying* to. That cat isn't big enough to eat them."

‹The Aurak would likely not be the typical prey for that feline predator. It may indicate the animal is desperate for food, or perhaps they are fighting due to territorial aggression.›

"Better it picks on the bird than us…" She smiled at Lissa, tickling her belly.

The girl giggled. "I don't want the nice birds to get hurt."

"I doubt that will happen. The Aurak is gonna throw the Night Scratch into the woods."

"Maybe the cat wanted eggs?" asked Austin.

"Aurak eggs gotta be as big as those." Juan pointed to the stasis pod.

"Yeah." Austin nodded. "Too big for cats to eat."

Everyone laughed.

Sima decided not to sleep in her damp garments and hung them on a jutting bit of metal. Austin got adventurous and crawled into the stasis pod that had initially held the two smaller kids. It couldn't trap him since Sima had pulverized the entire foot-end window panel on the right side.

"Oh, wow," said Austin, his voice echoing. "This is soft. I forgot what a real bed feels like. It's kinda stuffy in here though."

Lissa shivered, refusing to even *look* at the pod. Sima stretched out on the cool, hard metal floor, one child clinging to either side. She debated how to make a sleeping mat out of the soft grass, but didn't finish much of a mental design before dreams took her.

SIMA AWOKE, comforted by the presence of sunlight leaking in from the damaged roof and a breathing child lying on top of her. After waking the others, she picked up one of the squash and went outside. The axe doubled as a kitchen knife, slicing the giant vegetable into hamburger-patty sized discs. Pale whitish-green insides had texture similar to zucchini and a mild flavor reminiscent of string beans. If facial expressions meant anything, none of the kids particularly enjoyed the meal, but they all ate without protest.

After they ate, Sima sat by the door watching the three kids run around and play in grass that reached as tall as Lissa's chin in places. The girl laughed as she raced around chasing fluttering bugs, oblivious to the danger surrounding them. She stopped often to rest, stooped forward and gasping for air, but didn't seem to give in to worry.

After the scare from yesterday, Sima yelled, "Slow down a bit, sweetie. Don't run so much."

"Okay," called Lissa.

It's not fair. She clenched her jaw to stop from sliding into a deep pit of sorrow. Every time Lissa giggled, Sima cringed with guilt for telling the girl she'd be okay. *I can't break her heart. Let her be happy.* She hung her head, listening to the kids play for some time. Lissa got quiet, which made her look up. The girl knelt about ten paces away, playing with the grass. Sima put a hand to her eyes to press back tears.

What did those kids do to deserve this? She gazed up at the rich blue sky, puffy clouds, and throngs of sky mantas. *This planet is so beautiful, but it's a graveyard.*

She jumped at a tickle on her right ankle, expecting a spider. Lissa sat by her foot, braiding an anklet out of grass blades, two blue and one green. The child wore one on each of her ankles as well, as well as a decorative belt of the same strands. She looked like a little forest nymph from *Ancient Legends*, a Wondercube game about elves and magic that she'd played before running away from home. Sima felt like she'd been punched in the chest. She wanted to say, 'Thank you, that's pretty,' but couldn't get words past the lump in her throat. Every time she looked at Lissa, she dreaded losing her. Seeing her so innocently happy, unaware she probably wouldn't live another two months, stabbed Sima in the heart.

Once Lissa finished her weaving, she stood and jogged after Juan and Austin, who ran around mock sword fighting with their branches. Lissa tolerated less than five minutes of darting about before she coughed. She walked back and sat nearby, busying herself making grass bracelets. An intermittent breeze tossed her waist-long hair off her back. Sima stared at the girl's side, watching her chest swell and shrink with each breath. She didn't appear to have gained any weight, but at least she hadn't lost any.

"Orange was funny," said Lissa, while working. "She'd climb on the sofa even when my parents yelled at her. I miss her."

Sima brushed a hand over the girl's hair. "I'm sorry. What's it like to have a cat?"

"She was nice. Bad people visited us a lot to buy the stinky stuff. Whenever a mean one got close to me, Orange would hiss and scratch them."

"She loved you, too."

"You're kinda like Orange, but you have an axe." Lissa smiled up at her for a moment before looking sad. "Are Nix, Asif, and Tamma ghosts now?"

"Who?" asked Sima.

"They were my friends. The nice man took care of them, too. They brought me food when they got done begging. And they came to visit me after the doctor lady made me stay alone in a white room."

Sima took a deep breath. "They were on the ship with us?"

"Yeah." Lissa nodded, then pulled Sima's right arm into her lap before starting on a bracelet for her. "Nix and Tamma got the pod next to mine, but they weren't in our lifeboat."

They're probably drifting through space. Sima bowed her head, hating the Earth Government for what they did to innocent children. But they couldn't possibly have known something would collide with the *Progenitor* before it landed. "The big room we were in split up into little lifeboats. Maybe they landed somewhere else."

A constant *thump, thump, thump* of rubbery branches banging together came from the boys.

"Did they run outta air?" asked Lissa.

"Something broke this lifeboat. If nothing broke theirs, maybe they're okay? Mine didn't break. The lid opened when I hit the button." *But the bracelet told me where to find it.*

"Oh." Lissa looked back at the lifeboat. "I don't want them to be ghosts. They were nice to me, so I'd be sad if they turned into ghosts."

"Me too." Sima squeezed her shoulder.

"The cops found us," said Lissa, continuing to braid grass around

Sima's right wrist. "The nice man who helped the other kids beg ran away, but the cops told us they wanted to help. They promised we'd have families and houses and stuff. And school."

"I don't think they lied." Sima looked out over the meadow, keeping an eye on the boys, who had gone from 'sword fighting' to chasing a glowing, flying butterfly-like bug. "We had an accident."

Lissa patted the completed bracelet. "I don't think they lied either. I *did* get a family."

Sima hugged her. *Don't you dare die. I won't allow it. You don't have permission.*

"They gave us a ride in a big gee-vee, and we got baths and new clothes. But they took the clothes away on the ship." Lissa shrugged. "It's okay. We don't need them."

"We would if the ship was still here. There'd be a city with people."

"Like Earth?" asked Lissa, a hint of worry in her eyes.

"Not exactly. Much smaller and nicer, without all the bad people."

"Oh." Lissa reclined in the grass. "Do the sky mantas ever land?"

Sima shrugged. "I don't know. Wouldn't they have to? They can't fly while sleeping?"

"Maybe they're like flat balloons." Lissa grinned. "They just float."

"Could be."

Lissa resumed coming up with names for the mantas. Perhaps a few, she named more than once. She talked about her friends as if they had survived and might be living like this, camping in the jungle. Sima kept quiet. Even if those kids had made it to the surface in an intact lifeboat, without an adult (or a faking-it-as-much-as-possible sixteen-year-old) they probably wound up Night Scratch food. But, in all their wandering, Sima had only located the one other lifeboat, and it had been smashed to shrapnel. The *Progenitor* carried over eight thousand people. If all the lifeboats had deployed, she should have definitely found at least *one* more. It's not as if they'd scatter themselves deliberately to the far corners of the planet; they'd all more or less come down in the same region. That she hadn't seen any more painted a grim picture of what must have happened in orbit. Perhaps those bits of metal they found yesterday had been the biggest pieces of the ship to survive.

Sima kept one hand on the axe at her left side and held Lissa's hand with the other. Though she reclined in the grass, she remained wary of danger, constantly scanning the trees. Eventually, Lissa found the energy to run again, and zoomed off to join the boys in their effort to catch the small, glowing bugs. The day passed in a blur of laughing children, a trip to the river to fill a water jug, and synthesized food.

As twilight approached, Lissa stumbled and fell, out of breath. While the boys continued racing around, Sima trotted out into the meadow to collect the girl, carrying her back to the lifeboat hatch. Lissa stared at her, both ashamed and scared.

"Your lungs were hurt by the bad stuff you breathed." She pulled hair away from the wheezing child's face. "The doctors did fix you, but you still need time to get better."

Lissa nodded, but didn't try to speak.

Using the bracelet to project a holographic surface she could draw on, Sima continued teaching the girl how to write in GANSEC. The boys made a trip to the river on their own to get more water, and Austin ran the fabricator to produce steaks for everyone.

Sima sniffed the meat and glanced over at him.

"Tired of chicken," he muttered.

"That's fine." Sima took her portion when he handed it over, and tore a bit off with her teeth. *Total cavewoman moment… sitting in the grass eating meat with my bare hands.*

Over the course of their meal, Austin's mood darkened. He kept giving everyone sour looks, but didn't say anything. He even shied away from Juan who'd taken to sitting close to him whenever possible.

"Austin?" asked Sima in as encouraging a tone as she could manage. "Is something bothering you?"

He lifted his head and glared at her, but the surly scowl didn't last long. "Yeah. It's not your fault. It's not anyone here's fault. Sorry if I'm being a turd."

Sima patted his arm. "What's wrong?"

"This. Everything." He wiped a smudge of steak juice off his leg. "I miss home. I miss my friends. I miss having shoes. I miss having clothes." His voice rose until he almost yelled. "I miss real beds and video games and real toilets and real showers and real food. I'm so *totally* bored. Why did they do this to us? Why? It's not fair!" His face scrunched up. For a few seconds, he fought back tears, but lost his composure and cried.

Lissa and Juan blinked at him, though neither said a word.

"Don't look at me!" he yelled, before turning around to put his back to everyone, his face red.

Sima moved to sit beside him with an arm across his shoulders. After a little while of resisting her pulling him close, he caved in and leaned against her. She held him, letting him cry out his frustrations. Lissa got up and wandered into the grass, chasing the glowing bugs at a walking pace.

"Are you tired of it, too?" asked Austin a few minutes later.

"A couple days before the EGSF arrested me, I was carrying a package for a guy. He put something around my neck and told me it was a bomb. Said if I took too long or tried to steal the box, he'd blow my head off."

Austin gasped at her.

"It wasn't really a bomb, but I didn't know that. I was *so* damn scared thinking the EGSF would catch me with an explosive. On the way to deliver the box, I almost got caught by the cops. I ran and tried to hide in an old building, but it was a Scather hangout."

He shivered.

"They threw me in a pit, so there I was, trapped with a bomb around my neck and a pack of Scathers who were gonna kill me whenever they got done partying."

"But it wasn't really a bomb?" asked Austin.

"No. But, again, I didn't know that. Have you ever been so scared that you stopped caring if you lived or died?"

He shook his head. "No."

"In that pit, I knew I was going to die, either to the bomb or the Scathers. So, I figured it didn't really matter *what* I did if I'd wind up dead anyway. I climbed out of the pit and attacked the Scathers, punching and kicking and biting... anything to get away."

"Like you went after that cat."

"Kind of. But different. I wasn't thinking at all with the Scathers. Total desperation launched me out of that pit because I thought I was going to die no matter what happened. I had nothing at all to lose. When that cat chased you up a tree, I could've run away and not gotten hurt… but I *couldn't* do that and leave you there. You know?"

He nodded. "You're awesome. Sorry for being pissy. You really don't mind it here?"

"Going tribal wasn't high on my list, but it beats being dead. And… if I had a choice between going back to my old life dodging gangs and begging on the streets of Earth or continuing to run around the jungle in my underwear… I think I'd stay here."

"Bull." He laughed. "You're trying to make me feel better."

"I really would rather be here than on the street… but I do miss having actual clothes. Not like I *had* real clothes before. My tunic was four years old. I wore scrap fabric for pants. Pulled them off a dead guy."

"Ick."

She stretched out a leg and wiggled her toes. "I had sandals I made from some old boot soles and power cables."

"I had a lot of clothes. Whenever I broke into an apartment where they had a kid my age, I'd always take something… unless it was girl stuff."

She laughed.

"Sometimes I took girl stuff too, but to sell."

"You little thief." She nudged him in the side.

"Yeah." He stuck his tongue out. "So what? They were Citizens."

Lissa crept over and sat on her left, holding one of the glowing butterflies on the back of her hand. "She likes me."

"How do you know it's a girl?" asked Austin.

"It's too pretty to be a boy." Lissa nodded.

He rolled his eyes, then smirked at Sima. "So, you really like it here more than Earth?"

"It's less scary. I'm not constantly worrying about someone attacking me or if I'm gonna even wake up when I go to sleep. Except for the Night Scratch, I really do feel safer here."

Lissa looked up from the butterfly on her hand, blinked once, and said, "But we're all gonna die. There's no doctors."

"Our odds are still better here," deadpanned Sima. "Doctors don't help Outcasts."

"The doctor lady helped me." Lissa tilted her head.

Sima ran a hand over the girl's hair. "Yeah. I guess we got promoted for our last few days on Earth."

Austin grumbled. "I'm tired of being stuck in my underwear."

"You're not stuck in them. You can take them off." Sima raspberried him.

The bracelet buzzed.

Sima turned her left arm over to reveal the holographic screen.

‹Hey. That's my line.›

Austin and Lissa both jumped when Sima burst out laughing.

29

WAYPOINT

For no particular reason, Sima woke in the middle of the night. She stared up at a jagged blue hole overhead, a rip in the metal breaking up the total blackness of the lifeboat. While she had to pee, the urgency didn't feel so bad it explained her sudden wakefulness. The soft breathing of two kids echoed in the silence.

Two kids.

Sima lifted her head and came nose-to-nose with Lissa who'd crawled on top of her, chest to chest. The girl had stopped breathing again, pink liquid dribbling out of her mouth and nose.

"Light!" yelled Sima.

The bracelet displayed its screen, all white, which served as a weak flashlight.

She rolled Lissa onto the floor, braced the back of her neck, and did the same thing Austin had done, pinching her nose and blowing air into the girl's mouth. The flavor of super-artificial cherry exploded into her senses. The older boy stirred with a moan, though Juan remained zonked.

"Come on," rasped Sima after a few breaths. She took another deep one and forced air into the little girl. Again and again, she repeated it until Lissa finally sat up coughing.

The patter of text appearing on the bracelet's screen happened, but

Sima ignored it, too overwhelmed to do anything but cradle Lissa and shake with fear.

Lissa coughed more, and fell into a labored breathing that sounded as if a gallon of phlegm bubbled inside her chest.

"Is she okay?" asked Austin in a bleary half-awake voice.

"I think so," whispered Sima.

She eased Lissa forward and clapped her on the back a couple times. Eventually, the girl hocked up a big lump of slime. After, she collapsed sideways and tried to catch her breath.

Finally, Sima glanced at the screen.

‹She should not sleep on her front. It is more difficult to breathe.›

Sima sniffled. She pulled Lissa closer, resting the girl's head on her thigh while positioning her flat on her back. She sat there in the dark, stroking Lissa's hair in a repetitive, calming motion. Soon, the girl fell asleep again.

Austin rolled onto his side and curled into a ball.

‹You should sleep, Sima. I will monitor Lissa's breathing and zap you awake if she needs assistance due to a respiratory interruption.›

"Okay." Sima lay back, adjusting Lissa to stretch out beside her, using her shoulder as a pillow instead. She closed her eyes, but didn't expect to fall asleep again after that.

Exhaustion, however, had other plans.

SIMA WOKE to Austin poking her in the side of the head with his toe. She looked up at him, covered in a thick layer of sweat and indigo-stained briefs.

"It's hot and crappy in here. Can we go swimming?"

"That sounds like a good idea." Sima sat up and jostled Lissa awake.

The girl yawned, coughed once, and smiled.

After ushering the kids outside, Sima collected the giant phlegm blob with her bare hands (having little other option) and carried it outside. She rinsed her hands off from the drinking water jug, then handed out more 'zucchini steaks' for breakfast.

They spent most of the daylight hours in and around the river since it wound up being another particularly hot day. Lissa's woven jewelry failed to survive the rigors of swimming, but she didn't care. It only gave her an excuse to make more later on. Once again, the kids painted themselves blue with the oil coating the huge ground-running root. Austin found a long rubbery vine that worked as a swing. Cheering and laughing, the boys took turns swinging and diving into the river. Lissa wanted to try it, but Sima didn't think the girl had the arm strength to hold onto it safely, so she triggered a wailing, begging fit by forbidding her from riding the swing.

Sima decided to compromise by having Lissa cling to her back while she swung on the vine and jumped into the water. Eventually, the waning daylight chased them back to the safety of their home. Enough sun remained for dinner to happen outside, and they sat around a circle, knees almost touching, in the grass by the lifeboat door. Much to her surprise, Lissa insisted on having the zucchini-like plant again for dinner—and ate two slices.

Beep beep beep. The bracelet vibrated.

Sima held up her arm. "What?"

A yellow arrow appeared pointing southeast above the text, ‹24.2 Mi.›

"What is it?" asked Austin.

Juan stuck his head in the way. "Compass?"

"No, a waypoint." Sima tapped the bracelet. "To what?"

Lissa leaned up, her nose hovering at the top edge of the screen. Light from letters typing out tinted her face cyan.

‹The signal has transponder codes matching the *Progenitor's* mission.›

The bracelet vibrated in a series of pulses for thirty seconds.

"What did you do?" asked Sima. "What's the pulsing?"

‹Attempting to communicate with remote system.›

"If that's another lifeboat, they're dead." Austin frowned at the floor. "It's been too long."

"Nuh-uh," said Juan. "All the pods can't be broke. Maybe the doors worked."

"If there's more kids, we need to help them," whispered Lissa.

Sima hugged her. "You're right. Bracelet, why did you wait a month to show me this?"

Text disappeared and retyped. ‹Signal began 02M 38S ago.›

"The signal just started?" Sima gazed at the sky. "Maybe the ship is still up there and a new lifeboat landed?'

"Maybe it's smashed or something and wires just made contact," said Austin.

‹Possible. Unknown.›

She looked from one child to the next. Dragging the kids twenty-five miles across the alien jungle seemed like a fabulously bad idea, especially with Lissa weakened. Leaving them here while she went off alone came pretty close on the scale of dumb things to do as well. *If I go off and die, they're not gonna last. If I take them, we might all die.* Sima closed her eyes and breathed for a moment. *New signal. More people might be alive. I have to risk it. Maybe I should ask them?*

"How long would it take me to get there?" asked Sima.

‹Average human walking speed is between three and four miles per hour. Approximately five to seven hours depending on your pace and the terrain.›

"So, an all-day trip." She sighed at the ground.

"I'm going to scout that signal tomorrow. Do you guys wanna stay here or—"

"No!" yelled Lissa.

Juan shook his head.

"Nah." Austin gripped the second axe. "I gotta protect you."

Sima ruffled his hair, earning a smirk. "Okay. We will all go, but everyone has to wear pants."

"I don't wanna," said Lissa, sticking her tongue out.

"We might find other people," said Sima. "You really should wear pants."

"No." Lissa shook her head. "I don't wanna *go*. I wanna stay here. Home."

"There could be other kids in that pod. Maybe your friends, Nix, Tamma, and Asif?"

Lissa's eyes widened. "You remembered their names!"

"I did." Sima smiled.

The girl looked down. "Okay, but I don't wanna wear pants."

Sima laughed.

"I hate pants," muttered Lissa, her attempt to appear 'stern' faltered with a little smile.

The boys snickered.

As the sun set behind the western jungle, they moved inside.

"Everyone sleep," said Sima. "Tomorrow, we're going to take a long walk. Longer than we've ever gone before."

The kids nodded and arranged themselves on the floor.

A few minutes passed in silence before Lissa burst into tears.

Sima sat up. "What's wrong?"

The girl sniveled for a moment before whispering, "I gotta pee, but it's dark out."

Sima pointed at the tunnel through the mangled metal. "Use the bucket."

Lissa stopped crying in an instant. "Oh. Duh." She crawled across the room and slithered under the damaged ceiling.

"Why do little kids cry about everything?" asked Austin.

A distant raspberry came from the 'bathroom.'

Sima chuckled.

Seconds later, Lissa shrieked and yelled, "Sima! Help!"

"She fell in," muttered Austin.

Sima rolled over onto her hands and knees to crawl, but got only halfway across the room before a panicky Lissa scrambled into view with a huge ten-inch-long beetle on her back. The girl's screams echoed painfully loud in the metal chamber. Sima also let out a yell when she noticed the bug dangled by a pair of pincers.

"Mommy!" Lissa headed straight for Sima while scream-crying.

"Austin! Axe!" yelled Sima, bolting to her feet.

In flagrant disregard of her terror at a bug that huge, Sima grabbed it by the pincers, each mandible as long as dinner forks. Lissa howled in pain as Sima pulled the bite open and eased the tips out of the wound. The beetle's legs blurred; whip-like antennae smacked at her arms, but didn't hurt. Scratching and clicking came from the left.

"There's more!" yelled Juan.

A veritable army of beetles swarmed out from the tunnel, following the trail of blood droplets Lissa left on the floor.

With a cry of disgust, Sima tossed the beetle down in front of

Austin, who promptly smashed it with his axe. A wicked *crunch* accompanied a splatter of yellow ooze.

Clicking grew louder as the swarm neared.

Lissa peered at the approaching cluster of bugs and sprinted to her feet, diving without a sound through the missing window into the stasis pod she'd been morbidly terrified of. Juan handed Sima the second axe. She grasped it, but backed away from the approaching bugs, horrified.

"Maybe we should go outside," said Sima.

"The cat!" Austin pointed his axe at the door. "These bugs won't kill us." He ran at the swarm and smashed another beetle.

One sprang at him. He shifted his hips aside like a matador, but the beetle nipped him on the upper left thigh.

"Gah!" He swatted it off before it dug in too much. "Too close!"

Sima gritted her teeth and attacked the swarm. One good hit killed each bug, but they kept leaping into the air. Austin adopted a bizarre fighting stance designed to keep his groin away from flying bugs. A beetle sank its mandibles into Sima's shin, but it came loose when she kicked her leg, sending it flying across the room. The bug hit the wall with a *clank* and landed on its back, legs waving. Before it could tilt itself over, Austin ran over and smashed it.

By the time the last bug burst open at the end of her axe, Sima nursed five bites, Austin three. Juan had caught one with his bare hands and mashed its face into the wall until it died.

Austin swung his weapon at nothing to sling bug guts off it. "I should've put my pants on first. It almost got me in the… umm."

"They wouldn't have helped." Sima flicked bug guts off her axe. "The bug would've ripped a hole and ruined them."

"What *were* those?" yelled Lissa from inside the stasis pod. "Eww!"

"I *really* don't like this planet anymore," said Austin. "Bugs should not be that big!"

‹They are closer to crabs than insects.›

"And I'm closer to not giving a damn what species they are. That was terrifying." Sima shivered. "Liss, come here please. I need to look at your back."

"Are they dead?" whimpered Lissa.

"Yeah."

The girl crawled out of the stasis pod and padded over. "They came through the holes in the wall."

Sima pulled Lissa's hair aside and examined the two puncture wounds. Both appeared shallow, but continued to bleed, so she got the silver egg out of the medical kit. "Okay, sweetie. This is gonna hurt a little."

Lissa trembled.

Sima sat on the floor and pulled the girl across her lap.

"Please don't spank me. I didn't mean to let the bugs in."

"I'm not going to hit you." Sima patted her head. "That bug bit you on the back, and you're bleeding. This medicine stings."

Lissa trembled and squirmed.

As soon as Sima activated the egg, the girl shrieked and tried to wriggle away, but Sima held her down, feeling like a complete monster for doing it. Fortunately, it took only a few seconds to mend each hole, after which, her immobilizing grip became cradling.

Austin took the egg and tended to his bites. The first time, he yelped and dropped the egg. "Wow! That hurts."

"Told you," said Sima.

"Why do they make something hurt?" He gingerly picked the egg up.

"Probably because real doctors have needles that make the pain stop before they use the egg," said Sima, still rocking a whimpering Lissa.

"Oh." Austin gritted his teeth and closed his beetle bites before handing her the egg.

Compared to the claw wound, pain from sealing the mandible punctures barely registered. Sima flinched, but tended to numerous small holes on her legs.

"Now what?" asked Austin. "We can't sleep in here in case more bugs come in. We can't go outside because of the cats."

"I'll cover the holes by the ground when we get back from checking out that signal." Sima gestured at the useless, empty storage cabinets. "Plenty of panels."

Beep.

"What?" Sima held up her arm.

‹Those beetles are edible if cooked. Like lobster.›

She scrunched up her face. "What the hell is lobster? And... Eww."

"Huh?" asked Austin.

"The Omnicomputer said we could eat the bugs we just killed."

"Eww!" shouted Juan, Lissa, and Austin at the same time.

‹Lobster is, or was, a sea-based life form on Earth that had been regarded as an expensive meal for the upper classes. Ironically, when first discovered as a food source, they had been considered 'bugs' and were thought of as trash for the poor to consume. In later ages, they became an expensive delicacy for the wealthy.›

"Well, duh. Only poor people would eat bugs." Sima shuddered.

Austin glanced down at his lack of pockets—or clothing. "I think we count as poor."

Lissa narrowed her eyes. "It bit me. I kinda wanna eat it."

"Eww," said Austin.

Sima's stomach churned. "We don't have a lot of food. I guess we could try it... shouldn't waste them."

Austin gagged.

Despite it being the middle of the night, Sima pulled out the portable campfire from the survival kit and improvised a pan from a sheet of metal Austin pulled off the wall. After cooking for a while, the bug innards didn't smell that bad after all. A few test nibbles (and a lot of mental effort trying to forget the meat came from bugs) allowed everyone to eat.

Lissa snarled and savaged her portion, as if punishing the bug for biting her.

Thump.

The lifeboat shifted as the Night Scratch leapt onto the roof. It sniffed and clawed at the gaps in the ceiling.

Figuring they'd spoil sitting around in the heat, even overnight, Sima tossed the uncooked beetles out one of the holes in the wall, which attracted the large cat. Rather than claws scratching on metal, she listened to teeth crunching bug shells.

Maybe it'll leave us alone if it has easier food.

Lissa, much to Sima's astonishment, crawled back into the stasis pod to sleep, evidently more frightened of a second wave of bugs than the place where she almost suffocated. Juan decided to join her on the soft cushions. Austin wedged one of the storage cabinet doors over the tunnel entrance to the 'bathroom.' Even if the beetles had the strength to get past it, they couldn't do so quietly.

Not that she expected to sleep, Sima stretched out on the floor beside the stasis pod.

Austin sat next to her, resting the axe on the floor at his right. "I really hope there's people in that other pod. Maybe it'll be a big one with stuff in the cabinets."

"Yeah. That would be nice. Watch them have jumpsuits."

"I'll take a jumpsuit. Even if it's pink." He frowned at the blood trails on his legs.

She pulled her hair off her face and tried to get comfortable, patting her stomach, full of… bug. "Those suits would be too hot here without air conditioning."

"Yeah. I guess." He glanced at her. "We really ate bugs, didn't we?"

"We did."

"Go to sleep," whispered Juan. "I can't sleep with you guys talking."

Sima chuckled. "Okay. We have a long walk tomorrow. Bracelet, please wake me at dawn."

The cat once again worried at the walls, picking its claws at any hole it could find and sniffing.

She tried to get comfortable on the metal floor, but no matter how she curled up or arranged herself, sleep stayed out of reach. Though the kids had become numb to the nocturnal scratching, Sima couldn't push aside the worry that they all lived on borrowed time.

30

THE JOURNEY

Beeping dragged Sima out of a strange dream.

She'd been back home in her mother's apartment, only Mom hadn't been there. It had been her with Austin, Juan, and Lissa, living like normal people. She'd cooked the kids breakfast, sent them off to school, and then gone to work—begging.

"I'm up." She yawned and gazed up at one of the holes in the roof. From the color of the light, she guessed dawn. The bracelet confirmed local time at 5:52 a.m. "Stop. Stop. I'm up."

The beeping ceased.

Sima dragged herself to her feet and headed outside to relieve herself. That done, she went back into the lifeboat and plucked her garments off the wall. It felt almost strange to wear them, but as comfortable as she'd gotten in her skin, she retained enough civilization to dread encountering other people with nothing on. Underwear would be embarrassing enough, but she'd deal with it on the off chance additional survivors existed. A larger group meant better odds everyone survived.

"Come on, guys. Get up. Get dressed." She nudged Austin, then banged on the stasis pod window until Juan and Lissa stirred.

While the kids went out to water the grass, she stuck the first aid kit in the backpack, then printed four chicken patties from the fabricator. She peeled some fruits for breakfast and used the rinds as wrappers to protect the chicken before adding them to the bag. Next, she added ten red fruits and the remaining half 'zucchini,' which filled the pack. She didn't want to lug the entire survival kit or fabricator, but if the far-off signal turned out to be a more-intact lifeboat that would be better to live in, she could always come back alone to get them.

Sima slung the backpack over her shoulder and stepped outside. All three kids stood waiting, but only Austin had put his pants on. "Pants, now." She pointed at the door.

Juan shrugged and ran inside. Lissa whined, but eventually capitulated and went into the lifeboat to get dressed.

Breakfast—the fruits she'd pre-peeled—happened on the hoof. Sima walked at the front, arm held out in front of her so she could follow the arrow. In broad daylight, the forest glowed with a palette of color, seeming like they'd leapt into the pages of a storybook. Friendly, inviting, and alive with wonder. Sky mantas glided in lazy circles overhead, cooing like airborne whales. The boys tried to mimic the sounds. Lissa laughed at them. For a little while, the mantas seemed to be talking back.

Thick underbrush slowed their travel after a few hours. A barefoot trek across unfamiliar jungle resulted in frequent pauses to recover from stepping on things that hurt. Sima chopped her way past denser swaths of foliage, creating a path the kids followed. Every two minutes, she glanced back to make sure everyone was okay. Every twenty minutes, she stopped for a five-minute break to let Lissa rest. She couldn't carry the girl *and* the backpack, and as much as she'd rather carry Lissa, the backpack felt like it would be too much for Austin.

A few hours into the trip, she glanced back to check on the kids and noticed Lissa's pants had vanished.

Sima stopped, folded her arms, and tapped her foot. "What happened to your pants?"

Lissa looked down at herself, emitting a fake gasp as if their absence surprised her. "Umm."

"Liss…"

"They fell off, but I didn't wanna go back for them. I'm already too slow."

She sighed at the woods, but spotted a wad of white cloth not too far away. Sima tapped Austin on the shoulder and pointed. He nodded and ran off to get them. Sima crouched eye level with Lissa. "We might find more people there. If we don't, you can forget them again, okay? Just please keep them on in case we find others."

"Why?" whined Lissa.

Sima touched foreheads with her. "It's something that people just don't do, okay? At home, when it's this hot, with your family, it's okay to go tribal. But around people who don't know us, it's not polite."

"Okay." Lissa looked down. "We're not gonna find anyone, are we?"

Austin trotted back and handed Lissa the 'runaway' underpants, which she begrudgingly put back on.

"We don't know that. The signal the bracelet picked up only started yesterday. That means someone might've turned it on. So there *could* be another lifeboat."

Lissa shrugged. "Okay. I think I'll believe everyone's dead."

"What?" Sima blinked, stunned. "Why?"

The girl tilted her head. "If I hope people are there, and they're not, I'll be really sad. But if I think they're all dead and we find someone, then I'll be really happy."

Austin raised both eyebrows. Juan picked his nose.

Wow. This kid's six going on thirty. "All right. Let's keep going. If this turns out to be nothing, I want us to get home before dark."

She carried Lissa for about half an hour before the combined weight of child plus backpack wore her out. After a ten-minute break, she asked the girl to walk, but tried to keep a pace that wouldn't overstress her lungs. As before, she peered back at the kids every two minutes or so.

The eighth or ninth time she checked, Lissa had vanished. Sima's heart almost stopped.

"Lissa!" she yelled.

"I'm here," cried the girl, emerging from some trees ten meters behind Juan. "I'm tired. I hadda sit."

Sima almost fainted from relief. "You scared me. Don't get so far away from—"

In a flash of azure and green, a lion-sized animal with the general shape of a panther burst out of a cluster of foliage the same colors as its fur. It seized Lissa in one smooth motion and zoomed off into the woods with the shrieking child dangling from its mouth, a long pod-tipped tail flowing after it.

"No!" Sima screamed, shrugging the backpack off her shoulders and sprinting after it. "Lissa!"

Austin also shouted, "Lissa!" and chased.

The quill cat bounded with ease deeper into the dense forest. Lissa's intermittent yelps made it possible to follow without being able to see the creature. Sima ran heedless of where her feet landed, ignoring the whips and scratches on her legs and arms from vines and leaves. Burdened by forty some odd pounds of child in its mouth, the cat mistimed a jump and slipped from a boulder covered in glowing purple moss, leaving pale white scratches down the stone. Sima gained ground, catching up to within a few feet of its tail, but the beast darted to the left. She stumbled around a turn, chasing it.

Lissa stopped screaming and went limp in its mouth.

"Lissa!" Sima shrieked. Adrenaline surged in her blood. "Lissa!"

The child reached up and yanked on a handful of whiskers. The cat torqued in the direction of the pull and wiped out, rolling like a log. Lissa popped out of its maw, flopping to a halt a few meters away from the beast, covered in blood.

Sima skidded to a stop next to her, brandishing the axe. Air raced in and out of her throat; her lungs burned with each breath and every muscle in her legs trembled. The cat righted itself and snarled. Sima stared into four glowing green eyes, arranged in two pairs, the upper set slightly wider apart. An indigo feline nose striped with bright green wrinkled with a snarl as it circled. Rich azure fur shimmered with its motion, a mane of longer lime green down along its back. The quill pod at the end of its tail swished side to side.

Damn. This isn't the Night Scratch. That one had a pink nose, and looked a little bigger. How many of these things are there?

"Ow," whined Lissa. "It hurts."

"It's okay, sweetie. I'm here." Sima clenched and released her grip on the axe. *Bad kitty's gonna have to kill me to get you.* "Come on you ugly bastard. Let's dance."

It stared at her for a long few seconds before taking a tentative step as if it intended to nip Lissa's foot and drag her off.

Shrieking war cries, Sima lunged, swinging like a woman possessed. The cat scurried backward each time she attacked, as if trying to lure her from the injured girl. Sima refused to take more than half a step from the spot. It bared its fangs, roared, and rushed in. She traded a superficial gash to its breast for two claw rips down her left thigh. They burned like hell, but didn't cut deep enough to make her leg give out.

"Sima!" yelled Austin, as the boys ran in from the left.

With a startled hiss, the large cat jumped to the side and whipped its tail in the boys' direction. Austin dove to the ground while Juan stood stock still, stunned in fear at the sight of the big cat. The instant the animal's attention shifted to her boys, Sima sprang at it. Rage and desperation drove the axe into the side of its neck, spraying her with hot, pearlescent-blue blood. The creature let off a belabored moan, backpedaled, and collapsed. Sima's wounded leg shuddered and gave out, leaving her on her butt next to Lissa.

Austin charged, emitting a war cry as he raised his weapon.

"Austin, no!" yelled Sima. "Stay back!"

The cat sprang to its feet, roaring with enough force to flutter the boy's hair despite the blood gushing from its neck. He stopped well out of its reach, though he made a show of chopping at the air. A soft *thump* came from behind; the weight of the backpack had pulled Juan over like a plank. Another strangled moan escaped the beast's throat as it struggled to keep its head up. It fell in place, let out a great, raspy huff, and went still.

"Juan!" Sima burst into tears, but got control of herself in a few seconds. "Austin, get Juan."

She spun around, putting a hand on Lissa's cheek. "Lissa, honey, wake up. Open your eyes."

The girl let out a soft moan. Tooth marks across her chest and thighs oozed blood. A fang had punctured her left bicep, but appeared to have missed the bone.

Austin dragged Juan over; the boy stared at the sky, as still as a corpse. A silvery eight-inch quill stuck out of his chest. Sima wanted to scream, but calmed herself when she realized he hadn't stopped breathing.

"Give me the first aid kit." Sima dropped the axe and gathered Lissa in her lap.

Austin rummaged the backpack, tossing fruits out of the way until he found the silver case. Sima set it down and opened it, looking at a myriad of handheld gadgets. Not recognizing any of them other than the egg, she held her arm up.

"Which one do I use? Dammit, tell me!"

‹The egg is the best option.›

Sima grabbed it, crying from fear as well as the pain in her thigh. She pointed the tip at the biggest hole in Lissa's chest and squeezed the button. Orange energy saturated the area, and the wound shrank closed in under a minute, like acid eating flesh in reverse. Sima worked as fast as her shaking hands would allow, sealing all the bleeding tooth marks on the little girl's body, until the machine did nothing when she squeezed it.

That Lissa showed no reaction at all to what had to be agonizing pain terrified her. The shallow claw wounds Sima had suffered on her shoulder days ago hurt like hell.

"Liss?"

The girl appeared to have passed out.

‹Take the third device on the left in the top row. Push the yellow button, then press it against her arm. When it chirps, press it against her thigh or rear end.›

Sima fished the cylinder out from the packing foam. It looked like a giant pressure hypodermic, similar to the ones the doctors used on her before they sent her up here. The side had two buttons, one yellow, one orange. She pushed the yellow one, then pressed the thing to Lissa's shoulder as if giving her a vaccination. Seconds later, it chirped. Sima pressed it down again onto the girl's thigh. The device emitted a hiss, exactly as the injectors had done back on Earth.

"What am I doing to her?"

‹The first touch drew one droplet of blood to analyze for type. The second injected a medium that will help replace some of the blood she lost.›

"Oh."

Sima put that thing back in the case and aimed the egg at her shredded thigh. Clenching her jaw, she pushed the button. Blinding pain swept over her, burning like a flamethrower. She screamed and dropped the device, clutching the oozing wound.

"It hurts a lot," muttered a delirious Lissa before she coughed up blood.

Sima retrieved the egg, gritted her teeth, and activated it again, stifling a howl of agony as her flesh regenerated. When the device ran out of wound to close and the pain stopped, she fell over sideways, clutching her thigh and gasping agonized sobs. Austin knelt nearby, rubbing her back. She grabbed his hand and squeezed. Fear lurked in his eyes, but he put on a brave face.

"You killed a tiger with an axe." He smiled, despite tears rolling down his face. "You're the best mom."

She choked up.

When the pain faded enough for her to move again, Sima crawled over to Juan. The quill stuck in his right breast, close to the armpit. His breaths came in shallow, slow sips, and his eyes remained unfocused. Sima pulled the quill out, threw it to the side, and sucked at the tiny puncture wound.

The bracelet buzzed.

A trickle of blood filled her mouth as well as an alien, sour taste. Her tongue and the inside of her mouth tingled and went numb. She spat, sucked again, spat, sucked again, and spat.

"Brafemet, whaf if thif?"

‹That is a myth. Sucking at an envenomed wound will not help.›

Lissa smiled.

Austin snickered.

The screen blanked and retyped. ‹Unknown request.›

"She wants to know what happened to Juan," said Austin.

Scanning lasers swept over the boy. A moment later, the screen cleared again. ‹Paralytic toxin. Undetermined effect on autonomic respiration. Dosage level relative to subject body mass may cause cessation of breathing. Suggest constant monitoring and CPR if breathing ceases.›

"Umm, nmm." Sima cradled him in her lap. Already, his skin felt cold. She spat a few times to the side and spoke slow, forcing clumsy words around her deadened tongue and lips. "Juan, you hear me? Don't give up. Keep breathing."

The boy didn't react.

31

FINAL STAND

L issa lay sprawled on her back, gasping air in rapid, small sips. Juan may as well have been a clothing store mannequin. Austin knelt beside Sima, clutching his axe while scanning the jungle.

She looked at the two smallest kids, neither one of them in any shape for a long walk. Continuing to their destination or hiking the several miles it would take them to get home both sounded like bad options.

We can't travel like this. Dammit, what was I thinking walking twenty-five miles? We're going to be stuck outside at night. Please be the only cat in the area. The Night Scratch had a pink nose… this is a different one. What's it doing outside in the day?

She tried to remember the one that treed Austin. It had been significantly larger than this cat, so perhaps males and females grew to different sizes, or the one she killed hadn't been full-grown. *Please don't be any more around here.*

Neither Juan nor Lissa could walk. Going home couldn't happen, so she looked around for somewhere that might potentially offer any form of shelter. The trees in this part of the jungle all had dome-like roots between the trunk and the ground, reminding her of the area where her lifeboat landed. About forty meters away, a root cluster as big as their escape pod offered hope of concealment.

"Can you carry Lissa?" Sima looked at Austin.

"Yeah… she's a twig." Austin gathered the fruits into the backpack, added the first aid kit, and shrugged the pack on.

"Don't go," whispered Lissa.

"I'm right here, honey." Sima squeezed her hand. "We're staying together. Just need to move a little ways."

She forced herself to stand despite the burning pain lurking beneath the skin of her thigh, and picked Juan up.

Austin stooped toward Lissa, but hesitated when the pack shifted. He set the backpack down, then scooped Lissa into his arms. "I can't carry the pack *and* Lissa."

"It's okay. I'll run back for it," said Sima. "We're not going far."

The bracelet thrummed with a series of pulsing vibrations, the thin metal heating up.

Even the Omnicomputer is scared… it's trembling. "I know… I know."

The girl squirmed. "I can walk."

"You might be hurt inside," said Sima.

"I want *you* to carry me." Lissa whined.

"I got Juan. I can't"—Sima sighed and stooped—"Okay. Can you hold onto my back?"

Austin didn't let her go, continuing to haul the child forward. "Come on. Don't be a baby. It's not far."

Lissa wailed the whole walk to the base of the tree. The ovoid mass of roots, some as thick as Sima's waist, created an igloo-like hollow beneath a trunk easily seven feet in diameter. Austin ducked and carried Lissa inside before easing her down upon soft dirt. Sima scooted in after and placed Juan next to her. She limped back to the opening, but Austin grabbed her.

"You're leg's hurt. I'll get it."

She pushed him back inside. "No. You're a kid. Stay here where it's safe."

"I'll be back before you even get to the backpack." Austin stared up into her eyes and flashed a roguish smile. "I'm good at running."

Tears streaming down her cheeks, Sima pulled him close and kissed him on top of the head. "Okay. Please be fast."

He nodded, and darted out.

Sima flopped down to sit beside Juan and Lissa, then gazed around at the place she hoped to take shelter. Walls of entwined roots had thousands of gaps, though only two looked large enough for one of the cats to squeeze through. She tugged Juan into her lap. Lissa curled up at her side, thumb in her mouth.

Barely two minutes later, Austin wriggled through the root wall with the backpack. He sighed, shaking his head. "We're going to get stuck out at night."

Sima rubbed her leg. *I'm not walking any long distances for a while. Juan needs constant watching.* "Yeah. We killed the Night Scratch. We'll be fine. Stay quiet. First couple days we were here, we slept outside at night, no problem, right?"

Austin shot her a dubious glance, looked at Lissa, and sat without saying anything.

Rainfall came within an hour, though their shelter proved watertight enough. At the first rumble of thunder and fingers of violet, horizontal lightning overhead, Lissa shrugged off her stupor and erupted with tears. She tried to crawl *into* Sima's side.

"Make it stop!" she wailed.

"It's just a storm." Sima kissed her atop the head. "It can't get us in here."

Lissa twitched with every thunderclap, whimpering at the tame ones and scared mute whenever a louder blast shook the forest. Over the next few hours, Sima kept her hand on Juan's chest, monitoring his breathing. Twice, she got scared enough to lay him on the ground and give mouth-to-mouth.

Rain-scented wind filtered past the lattice of roots, chilling them to the point of shivering. Sima held Juan as close to her body as she could to keep him warm. Lissa crawled into her lap as well, so she cradled them together. Four hours and nine minutes (according to the bracelet's clock) after the quill hit him, the boy moved his eyes toward her.

"Yes!" Sima rubbed his chest, arms, and legs. "Stay warm. Keep breathing. You're going to be okay."

"It's dark," whispered Lissa. "The Night Scratch can get us." An eerie calm settled on her face. "I don't want a cat to eat me. If they come for us, will you please kill me?"

"No!" Sima yelled without intending to. "I... No. We're not going to die. And I'm *not* gonna kill you. I won't even spank you if you're bad."

"Even if I lose my pants after you tell me not to?" asked Lissa with a big grin.

"I'd never hurt you. Any of you." Sima sniffled.

Austin, his face wet with quiet tears, picked his axe up. "There's only one spot they can fit, and they gotta crawl in. I can get 'em in the head."

Juan wheezed and twitched his foot.

"It's dinner time," said Sima. "Eat."

"I'm not hungry." Lissa's teeth chattered. "I'm cold."

"You need to eat. You need strength." Sima handed her one of the chicken slabs. "Eat it."

"Why?" She frowned. "We're not going to live. The cat bit me bad. I'm gonna die."

"Stop." Sima grabbed the slight girl by her shoulder and gave her a firm shake. "Don't give up. Stop talking like that."

"Austin's right. I thought the cops wanted to help us, but they sent us here 'cause we're garbage." Lissa held the chicken to her mouth and nibbled.

"You're *not* garbage." Sima kissed her atop the head, sniffling.

Austin shook his head. "The ship had an accident, right?"

"What kind of idiot sends kids across the galaxy to an untamed planet?" Sima muttered a string of bad words that made the kids gasp.

"Juan's getting better. Let's go to the arrow," said Austin.

"Not now." Lissa whined. "It's still nine miles away, and it's dark. The scratches will get us."

"We need to stay somewhere like this where we can protect ourselves," said Sima. "We'll get moving as soon as the sun comes up."

They huddled together for a while in silence, all staring out into the pitch-black beyond the roots. The rain stopped, though the occasional gust of wind pushed water into the shelter. Lissa's breathing once again wheezed with dangerous volume. Her skin faded even paler than usual.

Snap.

Lissa's hands, with half of her chicken, sank into her lap. She stared out at the dark, mouth agape.

"Finish your dinner." Sima set Juan down beside Austin and picked up her axe. "Keep him warm. Make sure he keeps breathing."

The bracelet vibrated again in three quick pulses. Sima found herself patting it as if to comfort a terrified friend.

More snapping came from the darkness. The sound made her imagine an entire pack of those cats coming to avenge their fallen brother. Sima caressed Lissa's cheek, but the girl kept trembling. She stroked Juan's head, grinning when he smiled. Austin gave her a knowing look, and tolerated another ruffle of his hair. Lissa leaned into her, crying.

"Thanks for trying," whispered Austin.

Sima set Lissa next to Juan. "Stay there. Those cats can only get in at two places, and I'm not going to let them." She dragged herself closer to the large opening, staring into the dark at the rustling of movement. "Come on you furry bastards!" she yelled, raising the axe. "Come and get it. I'll kill you all. You're not gonna touch them. You're not gonna touch my kids!"

32

NOT WITHOUT A FIGHT

S napping and crunching grew louder. Sima's knuckles whitened. There had to be at least ten quill cats out there, but it didn't matter.

Only one of them could fit in the gap at a time, unless they had the strength to rip through the roots anywhere they wanted. A droplet of urine ran down the inside of her thigh as her whole body shook with dread. If she'd finally arrived at the moment her life would end, she would go down fighting. It didn't matter if two or twenty quill cats came out of the shadows, she'd hold that hole in the roots, even if it killed her to keep them away from the kids.

I won't let them hurt my children.

"Come on, bastards! Where are you? Come get it!"

Lissa bawled and struggled to run to her, but Austin held her down.

A cluster of luminous red dots appeared on Sima's chest, flashing off the roots and swarming like fireflies between her breasts.

"Check your target, Winters," said a woman's voice, crackling with static. "It's a kid with a utility axe. We found 'em."

Ten one-inch rectangular lights winked on in a line, mounted to the side of armored helmets. Six men and four women—humans—advanced out of the trees with rifles raised.

"Easy, kid. Put that thing down," said the closest man. "No one's going to hurt you."

"Are you really there?" Sima blinked.

"You still with us, kid?" The woman who first spoke stepped forward. "Been alone for a couple weeks?"

Sima lowered the axe, but kept shaking. "Yeah. Our lifeboats ejected. Are you from the *Progenitor* too?"

The soldiers slung their rifles. Austin released Lissa who limped over to Sima and attempted giggling and sobbing at the same time.

A man with the name 'Winters' stenciled on his pixel-camo armor glanced in the direction of the dead cat before flipping his visor up. He looked older, forties perhaps, with a trace of grey in his moustache. He peered past Sima at the kids.

"Four? Mike, get up here. One of 'em looks hurt. Evie, take Wharton and Cook and give me perimeter security."

One woman and two men hustled off in three different directions.

A man with red crosses on both shoulders approached. Sima crawled forward out of the big gap and struggled to stand, stumbling into Winters' arms. She lost a minute crying with relief. Lissa crawled up behind her, content to remain on all fours—or too weak to get up. Austin dragged Juan out next, stood, and stared at the adults with platter eyes.

Winters looked her over. "How old are you, kid? Hey, Kilgore, let's have some blankets up front pronto. These kids have been in stuck their skivvies for a month."

"Her beacon said she was sixteen," replied the woman.

"My beacon?" Sima sniffled.

One of the men jogged out of sight into the trees. Soon after, he returned with an armload of grey blankets. Sima accepted one and draped it around herself. It felt like forever ago that she'd had fabric covering so much of her body. She whimpered in delight and clutched the blanket closed.

The woman opened her visor, revealing a face the same brown as Juan, a bit lighter than Sima. Her armor bore the name Ruiz. "Your Omni's been transmitting a distress beacon ever since we got our main communications array back online. That's how we found you."

The holo panel flickered into existence above her arm. ‹U R welcome.› After a pause, it added, ‹Still want to take me off?›

Sima hugged her wrist to her chest, crying tears of joy. "No way. Why didn't you tell me you called for help?"

‹I did not have full verification anyone would be there to answer and did not want to create false hope.›

Mike, the medic, took Juan from Austin and set him flat on the ground before plucking a handheld unit from his belt and passing it back and forth over his chest. "What happened to him?"

"The cat shot him with a dart from its tail," said Sima before going into an explanation of the past few hours. At the point she described the animal grabbing Lissa, she broke down and cried.

"You're a brave kid," said Ruiz. "What's this about a criminal record for theft?"

"Probably horsecrap," said Winters. "You know how the EG gets. You're orphans, right? Last minute add-ons."

"Yes, sir." Sima picked Lissa up. "A transport spilled. All I did was pick up food packets in the middle of the street and they grabbed me. I didn't do anything wrong. The investigator said the charges were just a lie to get me on the ship, and they'd be dropped if I went."

"Unbelievable." Winters shook his head.

"W-what happened to the *Progenitor*? Is there anything left?" Sima tugged the blanket tighter around herself and Lissa.

"Soon after we transitioned into orbit, a meteorite struck us while they plotted a course for atmospheric entry. Fortunately, the rock was relatively small and didn't cause too much damage. It hit near the starboard aft, triggering the automatic escape system for two aux pods and four primaries. Our pilots were amazing. *The Progenitor* will never fly again, but they brought it down safe."

"That boat was designed as a one way trip anyway," said Ruiz. "It's the heart of the city we're going to build over the next several generations."

"Aux pods?" Sima decided to sit to stop her leg from burning. Lissa snuggled to her chest.

Ruiz shook her head. "Long-haul ships like the *Progenitor* have more stasis pods than they need for emergencies. The auxiliary ones are pretty tiny, about a quarter the size. The EGSF packed them at the last minute with a bunch of orphans."

Austin, cradled in his blanket, stepped forward. "Nobody knew we were there. We're invisible. No one'll miss us."

The medic gave Juan a few injections from small silver tubes. "He's stable, but I'd like to get him back to the infirmary as soon as we can." He looked at Sima. "Your beacon said the little girl's seriously hurt, but she doesn't look too bad."

"Lissa's lungs are in bad shape. Her parents made Pixie and she breathed the fumes. She also got bit by the cat." Sima explained the bracelet's scan showing she'd had tumors removed, but also how she got tired so fast and randomly stopped breathing sometimes in her sleep. "I got scratched on the leg, too. It burns."

Mike scanned Lissa and continued onto Sima's thigh. "The egg is good for skin regeneration, but you've both got underlying muscle damage. The kid's bleeding internally from a punctured lung, but it's nothing we can't fix up once we get her into surgery." He spent a few minutes fussing at Lissa's back with another wand-like device, then plucked two small capsules from his belt and administered two injections.

"You're safe now." Winters looked them over. "You four are some tough kids. Exactly the kind of settlers we need. Come on... let's get you back to the Nomad."

The medic carried Juan. Despite the hell burning in her thigh, Sima insisted on carrying Lissa with Austin hovering close by her side. They walked, surrounded by soldiers, in the direction of a huge six-wheeled buggy. Each tire had to be nine feet tall, mounted to long flexible struts that suspended the main body high enough off the ground a person could pass under it without stooping.

She stifled a whimper each time she put weight on her left leg.

"Incredible job you did, Sima," said Winters. "Looking after the little ones. I'd say you're lucky, but I'm not so sure it was luck. Glad to have you with us. There's plenty of pairings at the colony. We'll get you set up with a proper family as soon as we can."

She limped two steps to her right to put an arm around Austin and squeezed Lissa close. "I've already got one."

"Yeah. She's our mom," said Austin.

Winters stopped and shook his head at her with a grin. "Fair enough, but you need a parent yourself for a few years yet."

She allowed a soldier to carry Lissa up the Nomad's boarding ladder. Once another man inside pulled the child inside, Sima grasped the ladder and put a foot on the first rung, before smiling at Winters. "I'll think about it."

Sima climbed. Her thigh muscles spasmed near the top, almost making her fall, but the armored man inside caught her. He lifted her off her feet and deposited her in a cushioned seat, which sapped all her energy. Weeks of sleeping on a metal floor made even the basic military padding feel like extravagance. The medic sat in the facing row in front of her and buckled Juan into the seat next to him. The boy managed a feeble wave to Sima. She let her head loll back against the cushion. Austin flopped next to her on the left. Lissa curled up against her right side, wrapping her little body around Sima's arm. Three adoring faces smiled at her.

The cabin jostled as the Nomad backed up, turned around, and got underway.

"See?" She put an arm around Austin and leaned her head against Lissa's. "I told you we'd be okay."

33

FAMILY

Sima opened her eyes to a ceiling of immaculate white with small recessed lights. The unusual sensation of a squishy gel mattress beneath her instead of the hard metal lifeboat floor as well as soft clothing and a blanket made her question reality. For a fleeting instant, she believed herself back in a detention cell having dreamed everything about a dangerous trip to another planet. It had been so real though… Had the EGSF hit her with some virtual reality simulation?

Anger, frustration, and heartbreak crashed together.

She sat up, about to scream, but at the sight of a much larger room than a detention cell, froze and stared. The Omnicomputer remained around her left wrist, and rather than a hot pink detainee jumpsuit, her only clothing consisted of a white garment that couldn't quite decide if it wanted to be a tunic or a short dress, with nothing on under it. Cool air, an unfamiliar feeling, blew on her face from a vent in the ceiling.

A plain grey door stood a short distance past the foot of her bed. Left of it, a rectangular opaque black window blocked any view outside. Behind her, a silver band ran the width of the room, bright light shining out from the gap between it and the featureless wall. A small, square shower stall took up the inner corner on the left, next to a toilet.

Sima blinked, struggling to recall the past few hours. Vague memories of a quill cat trying to take Lissa flashed in her mind before something about soldiers and riding in that nomad vehicle. She remembered going through a large metal gate, driving past small buildings, and a bunch of armored people escorting her into a brightly lit room. People in white rushed Lissa off somewhere, and took Juan from her, too. It bothered her how urgently they'd whisked the tiny girl away, as if something had been *very* wrong with her. She'd tried to go after Lissa, fighting and screaming, but someone had given her an injection that made everything go all blurry and weird. Austin shouting about wanting to go wherever Sima went lingered at the edge of her memory.

"Where am I?"

The screen flickered on below her left wrist. ‹You are in the infirmary of the Progenitor colony. Please do not panic. You are not a prisoner, but you should remain here until someone comes to check on you.›

Unable to resist, Sima ran to the door to make sure she hadn't been locked in. When it opened freely, she exhaled a sigh of relief and pushed it closed again.

"Where are the kids?"

‹I do not have specific information about their location or condition, however, they are also in the infirmary being tended to. For the first time in many years, you are safe. Please allow yourself to relax. Consider a nice warm shower?›

The urge to run to her kids kept her hand on the door, but the infirmary did suggest at least some degree of safety. Sima eyed the stall, an enclosed chamber with three frosted transparent panels, and a lit-up control panel on wall inside. The last time she'd used a *real* shower unit like that had been before she ran away from home. For four years, sneaking into public bathrooms at night to sorta-bathe in the sinks had been her best option.

With a sigh, she wandered over to the shower unit and pulled the dress/tunic thing off, cringing at her lack of underwear. Not so much their absence, but since she didn't remember changing, that meant someone else took them off her. While staring at herself, she realized her left thigh no longer hurt at all. She didn't even have scars from where the quill cat had torn open her leg.

Oh. I guess I had surgery.

For the next twenty or so minutes, she luxuriated in a hot shower, going perhaps a bit crazy with the soap gel. Once the air-dry cycle finished, she stepped out into the freezing room, squeaked, and rushed into the white tunic-dress before crawling under the blankets again.

A knock came from the door soon after.

"Miss Nuvari?" asked a woman. "May I enter?"

"Sure," said Sima.

The door opened, admitting a pale woman with silvery hair and a white jumpsuit. She didn't look *old*, maybe early fifties, but still had a grandmotherly presence about her. "Good morning, dear. I'm Dr. Stinnett. You can call me Evelyn if you like."

"Hi."

Dr. Stinnett approached the bed. "How are you feeling?"

"Fine. Little hungry."

"Good. Good. I've been looking over your scan data, and everything checks out. I'm ready to sign off on your medical discharge."

"Where are my kids?"

"You have children?" The woman's eyebrows shot up. She tapped an Omnicomputer on her wrist, activating a screen about three times the size of Sima's, and scrolled over pages of text and images. "There's nothing in your file that indicates—"

"I haven't had babies. Those kids you guys found me with are *mine.*"

"Oh." Dr. Stinnett nodded. "I understand. Well, normally, we can't discuss medical status with non-relatives..."

"They are my family." Sima stared at her. "I'm their mother."

"You are all still juveniles. However, I do understand the kind of unique arrangement that can form between children put through such a stressful situation." Dr. Stinnett offered a grandmotherly smile. "The boy, Austin, is in good shape. Lissa is still in recovery from major surgery. She did well and we are expecting her to pull through. Juan is recovering. We are keeping him under observation since we are unfamiliar with the toxic agent he was exposed to."

Sima raised her arm. "It's venom. My Omni scanned it."

"We know." Dr. Stinnett clasped her hands in front of herself. "It already provided us with quite a bit of data from your exploration. Come then, I sense you're eager to see them."

"Yes." Sima leapt out of bed.

After sending her back into the room to put on the little paper slippers that had been tucked under the bed, Dr. Stinnett led her out into the hall and past a dozen or more rooms, only about a quarter of which had black windows. The tint level varied, so Sima figured hers had been turned all the way dark for privacy. She gasped at the cold air-conditioning going under her tunic as she hurried along after the doctor around a corner, past a desk, and through a doorway into another hall. Dr. Stinnett stopped once they'd entered a well-furnished office with reddish-brown fake wood walls, matching desk, and a big window that offered a view out over the blue jungle.

A short woman much younger than the doctor with pretty almond-shaped eyes and a wide nose sat at the desk, reading the contents of a holographic display. Two gold rings kept her frizzy hair up in a fountain-like spray.

"Danielle? Are you ready for Miss Nuvari?" asked Dr. Stinnett.

"Oh, of course." The woman looked up with a smile. "Hello, Sima. I'm Danielle Wade, and I'll be helping you get settled in here."

Sima fidgeted, uncomfortable with only a short tunic/dress in such modern surroundings, though it still beat being interviewed while wearing those EGSF undies. Still, the medical smock made her feel like a psych patient from a movie. Then again, she *had* spent weeks running around the jungle without clothes, so maybe they thought she'd gone nuts. *How much of what happened did the Omni tell them?*

"Please, Miss Nuvari. Have a seat." Danielle gestured at one of two chairs facing her desk.

"Welcome to the colony." Dr. Stinnett nodded farewell. "If you'll excuse me then, I've more patients who still need my attention."

Sima glanced back at the grey-haired woman, but didn't say anything before the doctor breezed off down the hall. Mute, she padded across the office and sank into the seat, smoothing her tunic over her thighs.

"I've been looking over your record." Danielle stood and walked to a cabinet on the far end of the room. "Quite impressive for a girl your age."

"I'm not a criminal," muttered Sima. "They made it up."

"Oh, I didn't mean *that* record. Yes, I know most of the older orphans they packed on the ship had falsified charges to justify their illegal incarceration. Don't worry about that. With the exception of those facing serious crimes, we've come to the conclusion that it's almost all hot air." She pulled several plastic wrapped packets out of the cabinet and carried them over. "I'm sure you'll like some actual clothing for a change."

Sima took the bundles.

"There's a bathroom there." Danielle pointed at a door. "I can tell you're a little embarrassed by that smock, so why don't you go change before we start?"

"Okay."

Sima hurried over to the indicated door and slipped past it into a bathroom that didn't match the office, being quite plain and utilitarian. She tore open the plastic, unwrapping a light grey jumpsuit, socks, clean underwear, and a set of plain white sneakers. By the time she finished getting dressed, she felt like she'd traveled through time from prehistoric cavewoman back to modern day. Even if it made her look like a crewmember from a starship, she adored having *real* clothing.

I'm not an Outcast anymore! Or a tribal wild-thing.

Grinning, she stuffed the plastic in an ORC can and carried her wadded up hospital tunic out. If nothing else, it would be good to sleep in. She took a seat once more at the desk and bundled the tunic up in her lap.

"All right, Sima. We just need to go over some quick documentation and get you into the system to add you officially to the colony manifest. Every Citizen has a file, but the kids in your situation weren't properly added."

"Yeah. They threw us on the ship at the last minute. Speaking of kids, I want to see mine."

"You have children?"

"Yes. Three of them. Austin, Lissa, and Juan."

"Oh." Danielle gave a slow nod. "Right. Don't worry; they're fine. You'll all be placed with families."

Sima glared and leaned forward, shouting, "They *are* my family. You're not gonna give them away to someone else. I don't care if I have to declare myself an adult and like get paired off to a husband or whatever. I want my kids back."

"Whoa…" Danielle held her hands up. "Please calm down. Sima, you're sixteen years old. You need to finish school. From the look of your record, you have quite a lot of school to catch up on. Academic work in and of itself will be a full time job for you. Taking care of children is a responsibility you neither need nor are capable of handling at this point in your life."

"Bull," shouted Sima. "What have I been doing for the past month?"

"You performed a remarkable job out there. But that is an extraordinary situation. You don't need to sacrifice your future when there are better options. I'm sure we can work something out regarding a custody situation. Now, it says here that your education transcripts stop at fifth grade."

Sima frowned. "I was in sixth grade, but didn't finish it. Okay, whatever. I'll go to school, but you're not taking my kids away."

"You still need to finish your education. Normally, kids at your age are required to take on a part time OT as well after completing an assessment evaluation. Of course, given the amount of schoolwork you need to catch up on, there's a good chance that will be deferred so as not to cheat you out of your education."

"I don't care what an OT is. Where are my damn kids?"

Danielle forced a smile. "That's an occupational task. Basically, a job. Everyone over the age of fifteen is required to take on some manner of work to keep the colony going."

"I'm not going to do anything until I know what happened to my family."

"Sima, there are 8,292 colonists here, plus about 250 undocumented extras. We are trying to sort the street children to proper families."

"You read my file; you know what I went through to protect them." Tears streaked down her cheeks. "I dealt with carnivorous plants, giant bugs, and a damned *tiger*. I held Lissa's limp body in my arms, thinking she'd died." She shivered and cried harder.

The woman kept quiet.

After a moment, Sima composed herself and shot a stern look across the desk. "I'm not gonna lose them to some damned stupid policy."

Danielle glanced at the monitor, perhaps only to dodge eye contact. "We can try to find an eligible couple who'd be open to the task of taking on four children, but I cannot guarantee that anyone would be willing."

"So? Do some computer stuff and call me an adult. Assign them to me."

"We can't do that. You are still legally a child with an incomplete education and no ability to provide for them."

Sima stood and leaned both hands on the desk, staring the woman in the eye. "I ran at a giant tiger with only an axe… *twice!* If you think I'm going to let a *person* take my children away, you're making a mistake."

"There's no need for violence," said Danielle. "Please, sit down. I promise I will do everything I can to keep you together. My role here is to be on *your* side."

Sima flopped into the chair, arms folded, glaring.

"Here." Danielle handed her an electronic tablet. "Please answer these questions."

Sima kept staring at her.

"The children are all equally adamant about being reunited with you, well, except for Lissa." Danielle sighed.

"What?" yelled Sima, shocked and more than a little heartbroken.

"She hasn't been awake much to be interviewed," said Danielle. "Dr. Bystrova, our psychiatric head, has already advised my group to place the four of you together for their mental health."

"Why didn't you just say that before? *Argh!*" Sima grabbed her hair in frustration.

Danielle offered a weary smile. "I was trying to focus for the time being on *your* future. And what we're *trying* to do and what we will be *able* to do may not be the same thing. I did not want to get your hopes up."

"What is this?" Sima looked down on a list of questions that appeared to be a combination of schoolwork and a personality evaluation.

"It's a general assessment. Something to hand off to our education unit. At some time in the next few weeks, once you've recovered from your ordeal and gotten comfortable in your new home, you will go in for a more comprehensive exam, but this will give them a starting point."

"Can I see my kids when I finish this?"

"I can't say exactly how long that will take, but I'm doing everything I can to hurry things along."

Sima hated being treated like a child. She frowned at the pad, too consumed with worry about the kids to focus on the text. Black letters on white blurred into a mass of grey. "I... can't do this. My head's spinning. All I can think about is wondering what's happening to them."

"They are receiving the best care possible. We have the most advanced medical facility on Mirage."

Sima glanced up at her, unimpressed. "You have the *only* medical facility on Mirage."

"Both statements are true." Danielle got up and walked around to stand beside her. "You've been through a harrowing ordeal, and I don't only mean the past few weeks you've been stranded out there in the jungle. I can't imagine what it must've been like for you to survive on your own back on Earth from such a young age. That same determination kept those children alive here on Mirage. You are a very strong young woman, Sima. But you're still a child. You've forgotten what it's like to let someone take care of you."

"I can't forget what I never knew," muttered Sima.

"You can let your guard down here." Danielle squeezed her shoulder. "You've still got a couple years yet to enjoy not being an adult. Take advantage of it. Trust me. If I could go back to sixteen again knowing what I know now, I would. Don't grow up too fast."

She let out a long sigh, and stared at the first question:

What word most closely matches 'tedious?'

A – exciting

B – colorful

C – boring

D – tasty

"C… just like this test." She tapped the letter and a little black circle appeared around it. "How many questions do I have to do?"

"It's pretty short, only about a hundred."

Sima let her head fall back, slouched in the chair, and sighed at the ceiling. "Ugh!"

"Aha! You *are* a teenage girl."

"Huh?" asked Sima.

"The melodrama gave it away."

Sima sat up straight. "The what?"

"Oh, it's hard to explain, but the school will catch you up." Danielle winked. "Are you hungry? I can get you something to eat while you work."

"Yeah. Starving… as long as it's not fruit."

Danielle chuckled as she stood and walked over to a wall-mounted fabricator. "All right. No fruit."

Sima devoured a turkey sandwich and fries while attacking the test with minimal enthusiasm, though a bit of her pre-twelve-year-old self resurfaced, compelling her to try getting as many questions right as she could despite her contempt for the test. She thought she did all right—except for the weird ones like: *What do you find most appealing: forests, mountains, meadows, or cities?*

34

SOMEONE'S KID

Sima spent the next several hours in a small room attached to Danielle's office, alternating between playing video games and pacing. A few other kids, most younger than her and none of them her family, arrived for meetings with Danielle, but none stayed in that chair anywhere near as long as Sima had. A seemingly endless parade of child voices echoed from the outer room, blurring into meaningless nonsense—until Sima's brain latched onto a familiar word.

"Your thing is wrong. My name is *not* Flora," said a girl. "It's Alina Strauss."

Sima paused the game and ran to the connecting door. A blonde-haired girl of around thirteen sat in the same chair she'd been in two hours ago, wearing a grey jumpsuit and white sneakers. *Wow... Investigator Marr really did save her from Magdalena's.*

Alina noticed the open door and looked over. "Oh, hi."

"Hi," said Sima.

"Do I know you? You look kinda familiar."

Sima walked in. "Can I talk to her?"

Danielle nodded. "You've met?"

"Yeah. Mag's," said Sima.

Alina's face turned bright red. "I thought so. Was it you?"

"Me?"

"Who sent that guy after me?"

Sima grinned. "Yeah, I think so. I asked him to get you out of there. You're too young to, umm…"

Alina grimaced. "I never did that. Magdalena made me so expensive no one wanted me. I think one guy tried, but he, umm… disappeared."

The memory of Magdalena's robotic arms and claws made Sima shiver. "If she wasn't gonna let anyone, uhh, hire you, why'd you sit around in the front room like that?"

"I dunno really. Mag said it would either get me adopted or help her 'clean up.'"

Sima slouched with relief. Perhaps she had misjudged the woman. She still thought her creepy as hell though.

"What are you talking about?" asked Danielle. "Who is Magdalena?"

Alina blushed again. "Just someone who let me crash at their place when I was on the street. She looked out for me."

"Yeah." Sima nodded.

"All right. Well, Miss Nuvari, if you'll excuse us, we're discussing some confidential things."

"Yeah, sure." She held out a fist. "See ya around?"

"Later." Alina fist-bumped her.

Sima wandered back into the side room, closed the door, and flopped on the little sofa again. *How long am I going to have to sit here? Ugh.* She stood again and paced, fretting over the kids, wondering where they were, what they'd gone through since the ride in the nomad, and how long it would take her to see them again. Feeling helpless and frustrated, she curled up on the couch and cried into a pillow.

Hours later, Danielle knocked and pushed the door open. "Come on, hon. I have some good news for you."

Hoping that meant she'd see her family again, Sima sprang to her feet and ran over. "Okay."

Danielle led her down another hallway, across a small room of cubicles, and into another office similar to hers. A fortyish couple occupied the two chairs facing the desk, behind which sat a grey-haired man in a black jumpsuit. The couple stood as she entered, smiling at her. The man had a kindly but somewhat nerdy air about him, and the same shade of olive skin as Sima. He wore a dark orange jumpsuit with 'Akbar' stenciled over his left breast pocket. The woman, the same height or perhaps a bit shorter than Sima, lit up with a huge grin as soon as she made eye contact. Her jumpsuit was pure white and bore the name 'Chen.'

"Hello, Sima," said the man behind the desk. "I'm Mr. Ashcroft. I'd like to introduce you to your new parents, Manoj and Pai Akbar."

Sima walked up to them, offering a guarded smile. She hadn't been around people old enough to be her parents too often, not counting the EGSF officers who arrested her. "Umm, hi."

"Hello." Mr. Akbar smiled. "It is wonderful to meet you."

"Yes, yes," said Mrs. Akbar, before hugging her.

Sima blinked at the sudden affection. In four seconds, this woman had shown more love than her biological mother had in twelve years. Oddly enough, it felt genuine.

"Please, have a seat," said Mr. Ashcroft. "We just need to go over a few particulars and you can take your daughter home."

Sima melted uneasily into the third chair facing the desk. Mrs. Akbar kept smiling at her, which made her feel like a shiny new puppy about to leave the pet store.

"Sima," said Mr. Ashcroft, drawing her stare, "your test results were both good and bad. Based on your answers, you tested about at an eighth grade level. However, given your age, that's going to mean a heavier course load to catch up. We're going to extend a waiver of the OT requirement until you've gotten back where you need to be academically. I also understand you officially stopped attending school back on Earth several months into your sixth grade year?"

"Yeah." Sima looked down at her sneakers. "That's right."

"What happened?" asked Mr. Akbar.

Sima glanced at him. *Wow, he looks actually concerned.* "Umm. Can I tell you later?"

He nodded. "Of course."

"The test showed that you have a high intrinsic intelligence as well as an aptitude toward scientific and technical fields. It is quite impressive that you scored at an eighth grade level despite where you stopped receiving instruction. That helped guide our placement for you with the Akbars. Mr. Akbar is one of the senior electronics engineers from the *Progenitor*, and Mrs. Akbar is with our biomedical division. She is a medical doctor, but has a focus on botanical research for potential medical applications of local flora and fauna."

My parents are nerds. Sima eyed the two smiling people next to her. "I've had enough of the local flora and fauna for a while. What about my kids?"

"Oh, yes." Mr. Akbar nodded rapidly. "I was to understand there are four? A whole family?"

Mrs. Akbar put a hand on Sima's. "We are happy to welcome all of you."

"I apologize for the unusual delay, but it took us awhile to find a matching couple who were also willing to cope with adopting *four* kids." Mr. Ashcroft leaned back, lacing his fingers together. "Since you are too young for guardianship of the other children you were found with, this is the best solution. Also, due to your age, we could not share this information before, but since your parents are now here with you…"

"What?" asked Sima. "Wait? That's it? They're my parents just like that? No hearing or anything? I don't get to say yes or no? And what couldn't you tell me?"

Her prospective parents cringed, both looking worried.

Sima glanced at them. "You're okay taking all four of us?"

They both nodded.

"Okay. I wouldn't have said no, but, it's kinda weird and fast that I don't get the choice."

"Well, you *are* still a minor." Mr. Ashcroft smiled. "However, you would have been able to decline the pairing if you wanted to."

She relaxed a little. "Okay. Well, I mean, I don't know them at all, but they look nice, and, uhh, Mom has already hugged me more often than my birth mom."

"Oh…" Mrs. Akbar leaned over and squeezed her again. "You poor dear."

"Umm. Sorry if I'm a bit weird at first. I'm not sure how to handle having *two* parents who give a crap." Sima fidgeted, glancing again at Ashcroft. "What couldn't you tell me?"

"Regarding your, umm, siblings." Mr. Ashcroft handed an electronic tablet to Mr. Akbar. "If you'll both indicate your acceptance of this document first. Just to make everything proper."

"What is that?" asked Sima.

Mr. Akbar skimmed down document, flicking his finger at the screen. At the bottom, he tapped a button and pressed his thumbprint to the glass. He handed the tablet to Mrs. Akbar, who rushed the document back to the top and read it more cautiously, but still quite fast.

"Once they've both signed it, you are legally their daughter. As well as the other three." As soon as Mrs. Akbar electronically signed it, Mr. Ashcroft cleared his throat. "All right. Now that everything is legal, I can say this. I'm officially talking to your parents here, but…" He kept eye contact with Sima. "The young girl suffered a punctured lung as a result of the animal's fangs. On top of the damage she'd already sustained from toxic chemicals, our medical team decided to clone new lungs and transplant them in. She's going to be stuck in bed for a while, but should be back to normal soon."

Mrs. Akbar tilted her head. "What happened to her lungs? Toxic exposure?"

"Her bio parents made Pixie in the apartment where she lived before," said Sima.

The Akbars winced.

"Austin, the older boy, was given medical clearance within hours. Juan also appears to be in fine shape and we expect he will be cleared for medical release in another day or two. So… that's basically it."

A soft knock at the door preceded Danielle guiding Austin into the room. He looked like an entirely new person in a grey jumpsuit and black sneakers. A hint of blue T-shirt peeked out his open collar.

"Sima!" He ran over and jumped into a hug. "Where's Liss and Juan?"

"In the infirmary. It's okay. We're all going to live together. These are our parents."

Austin twisted to look at them. "Umm, hi."

"If none of you have any further questions, you should show your kids their new home." Mr. Ashcroft smiled.

Sima stood, holding Austin's hand in an almost painful grip. He didn't seem to mind.

Her new father put an arm around her, seeming as proud as if he'd watched her birth.

"My aren't you such a handsome young man," said Mrs. Akbar, patting Austin's cheek before squeezing his shoulders.

Austin glanced at Sima with an expression part way between 'this face is why I had 400 glint' and 'maybe having grown-up parents again *won't* suck.'

Oh this is weird. I have no idea how to be someone's kid. Managing a nervous but hopeful smile, she walked with them out into the hall.

35

NEW BREATHS

Sima stepped through the doorway first and approached the infirmary bed where Lissa lay armpit deep in a pink blanket, wearing one of those dress/tunic hospital garments. Her face had lost the grim pallor, having actual color. Two silver spheres floated nearby, occasionally running scan lasers over her chest.

"Mom," whispered Lissa, smiling.

Too choked up to talk, Sima hurried over to the bed and took her hand.

The parents walked in behind Austin, who also ran to the bed.

"Hey." Austin hopped up to sit on the edge. "We're gonna live together."

Lissa beamed. She leaned to the side, peering at the adults. "Who are they?"

"Our new parents. I'm still just a kid, so they won't let me legally be your mom."

"Oh." Lissa eyed them a moment more, then whispered, "Can I call her grandmom?"

Mom snickered.

"She's not *that* old," said Sima.

Lissa giggled—and didn't lapse into a coughing fit. "The doctors gave me new breaths."

Mom walked over to the console on the wall and looked it over.

Dad followed, muttering, "You shouldn't fiddle with it. She's family now. Pesky ethics."

"I'm not adjusting anything," said Mom. "I'm simply making sure they have the dosages correct."

"How long do I gotta stay here?" Lissa sat up.

Mom sat on the corner of the bed by the pillow. "Another two days at least. You've had a big operation for a little girl. They need to make sure everything is going to stay where they put it."

"Okay." Lissa nodded. "I know it worked. I can breathe. I forgot what it's like."

Everyone sat together talking for a while, the parents mostly telling them how happy they'd be. After taking in four kids, they received an upgrade to their residence quarters. Dad spoke of a park with Earth type trees and plants nearby, as well as a nice fitness center with a pool. Crews *still* worked to reconfigure parts of the enormous *Progenitor* into its city components, a project which they expected to take several more years.

Sima, still holding *her* kids' hands, listened with hopeful curiosity. *It's gonna be weird having people actually care about me.* She looked at Austin to gauge his reaction to the parents. He continued smiling, which she took as a good sign. Her thoughts leapt to the scream he let out when jumping out of a tree to stop that cat from hitting her with quills... and how Lissa didn't want her to walk away and leave her alone. Sima realized that she'd already been with people who cared about her. Unable to talk past her emotions, she sat there as Lissa rambled about all the stuff she wanted to do since she would soon be able to play again without passing out.

"Sima!" shouted a boy.

The parents jumped.

Juan, also in a new grey jumpsuit, dashed into the room away from Danielle, sneakers squeaking on the metal floor. Sima intercepted him before he jumped on top of Lissa, and held him in her lap while perched at the edge of the bed.

"Well..." Danielle brought her hands together with a clap. "That's the whole family then. Can I help with anything else?"

"I think we're all right." Dad ruffled Juan's hair. "Thank you."

"Hi," said Juan to the parents, before clinging to Sima.

"You have my contact information." Danielle nodded at the Akbars. "I'll be your caseworker for the foreseeable future. If you ever need anything, please reach out to me."

Mom and Dad excused themselves and walked over to chat with Danielle out in the hallway.

"You guys..." Sima hugged all three of them at once. "The ship didn't blow up!"

"Uhh, yeah." Austin fake-rolled his eyes. "Kinda obvious now. I'm more shocked that the EGSF *didn't* lie."

Sima snickered. "Yeah, seriously."

"It's nice here," said Juan.

"We're gonna be okay... even if we have to go to school." Sima winked.

Austin shrugged. "School's okay. I'm *so* sick of those fruits."

"No kidding." Sima cringed. *I don't think I'll ever want to eat one again.*

Lissa peered around Sima at the adults in the doorway, then whispered, "I'm not wearing pants."

The eruption of laughter at the bed caused the parents and Danielle to stop talking and stare.

Sima squeezed her newly official siblings. "I don't really know how to be a big sister."

"You didn't know how to 'mom' either, but you did okay." Austin smiled.

"I love all of you," said Juan.

"Yeah." Lissa's hug lacked strength, but she tried. "I love you all too. Almost as much as Orange."

Austin grinned. "Okay. Okay. I love you guys."

"I wanna go home," said Lissa. "It's boring here."

"The doctors need to make sure you're okay." Sima patted her head. "They want you to stay a few more days, but I'll sit with you 'til you can go."

Lissa rested her head on Sima's shoulder. "Thanks for saving me."

"Yeah." Austin grinned. "You're pretty cool."

Juan pointed at Lissa. "What she said."

Sima scooted back and leaned against the wall, one arm around

Lissa, the other around Juan. "So… since we're stuck here for a while. TV or Wondercube?"

"I don't think they have TV here yet," said Austin.

"Wondercube it is." Sima grabbed the controllers from the little stand next to the bed and handed one to Lissa, the other to Austin.

"What's this?" asked Lissa.

"You've never seen a Wondercube before?" Austin gawked.

"No." She shook her head.

Juan blinked. "Me neither."

Austin handed the controller to Juan, then cracked his knuckles. "Let school begin."

Sima laughed.

Playing video games and getting to know their new parents blurred one hour into the next. The weeks they spent barely surviving in the jungle already felt like a strange dream that happened a long time ago.

Best of all, not once over those hours did Sima have the slightest thought about Earth.

---

fin

ACKNOWLEDGMENTS

Thank you for reading Out of Sight!

I would like to thank everyone who helped me make this book a reality, including my beta readers: Dianne Webb, Leslie Whitaker, Brandy Yassa, Louise Feagans, and Daniel Cox (no relation).

Additional thanks to Dianne Webb and Brandy Yassa for proofreading.

Also, thanks go to Tristan Vick (author of the Jegra series) for putting me in touch with the cover artist, Jackson Tjota.

ABOUT THE AUTHOR

Originally from South Amboy NJ, Matthew has been creating science fiction and fantasy worlds for most of his reasoning life. Since 1996, he has developed the "Divergent Fates" world, in which *Division Zero*, *Virtual Immortality*, *The Awakened Series*, *The Harmony Paradox, and the Daughter of Mars series* take place. Along with being an editor at Curiosity Quills press, he has worked in IT and technical support.

Matthew is an avid gamer, a recovered WoW addict, Gamemaster for two custom RPG systems, and a fan of anime, British humour, and intellectual science fiction that questions the nature of reality, life, and what happens after it.

He is also fond of cats.

Visit me online at:

Facebook: https://www.facebook.com/MatthewSCoxAuthor
Amazon: https://www.amazon.com/author/mscox
Pinterest: https://www.pinterest.com/matthewcox10420/
Goodreads: https://www.goodreads.com/author/show/7712730.Matthew_S_Cox
Email: mcox2112@gmail.com

OTHER BOOKS BY MATTHEW S. COX

Divergent Fates Universe Novels

Division Zero series

- Division Zero
- Lex De Mortuis
- Thrall
- Guardian

The Awakened series

- Prophet of the Badlands
- Archon's Queen
- Grey Ronin
- Daughter of Ash
- Zero Rogue
- Angel Descended

Daughter of Mars series

- The Hand of Raziel
- Araphel
- Ghost Black

Virtual Immortality series

- Virtual Immortality
- The Harmony Paradox

Divergent Fates Anthology

(Fiction Novels - Adult)

Alexis Silver series (with J.R. Rain)

- Silver Light
- Deep Silver

Samantha Moon Origins series (with J.R. Rain)

- New Moon Rising
- Moon Mourning

Maddy Wimsey series (with J.R. Rain)

- The Devil's Eye
- The Drifting Gloom

Samantha Moon Case Files series (with J.R. Rain)

- Blood Moon
- Dead Moon

Young Adult Novels

- Caller 107
- The Summer the World Ended
- Nine Candles of Deepest Black
- The Eldritch Heart
- The Forest Beyond the Earth
- Out of Sight

Middle Grade Novels

Tales of Widowswood series

- Emma and the Banderwigh
- Emma and the Silk Thieves

- Emma and the Silverbell Faeries
- Emma and the Elixir of Madness
- Emma and the Weeping Spirit

Standalones

- Citadel: The Concordant Sequence
- The Cursed Codex
- The Menagerie of Jenkins Bailey
- Sophie's Light

www.ingramcontent.com/pod-product-compliance
Lightning Source LLC
Chambersburg PA
CBHW030559180626
46816CB00005B/1602